NO PLACE
TO HIDE

NO PLACE TO HIDE

A Novel

Opa Hysea Wise

Made for Success
PUBLISHING

Made for Success Publishing
P.O. Box 1775 Issaquah, WA 98027
www.MadeForSuccessPublishing.com

Distributed by Made for Success Publishing

First Printing

Library of Congress Cataloging-in-Publication data
Wise, Opa Hysea
    No Place to Hide: A Novel
        p. cm.

LCCN: 2020903448
ISBN: 978-1-64146-477-2 *(Paperback)*
ISBN: 978-1-64146-493-2 *(eBook)*
ISBN: 978-1-64146-517-5 *(Audiobook)*

Printed in the United States of America

For further information contact Made for Success Publishing
+14255266480 or email service@madeforsuccess.net

Chapter 1

Papahanaumoku

—

"OUR LAND HAS BEEN DECIMATED," AKAMU SAID.

"Poisoned beyond repair," Alika replied.

"No—not beyond repair." Akamu turned from his grandson, gazed out toward his backyard and sighed into the depths of his spirit—into the Spirit in all things. Bird of paradise, hibiscus, and plumeria scented the air, yet he took no comfort in their perfume. He considered the makeshift stone wall, built by his own hands several years ago. No more than three feet in height, it ran the length of his property, yet he remembered only the anger he felt as he laid each stone in place. Beyond the wall, a road ran past his property, winding its way toward two of the towns on the island—Waimea and Kekaha.

Akamu recalled the Waimea valley of his youth. A sturdy man who toiled the soil of his ancestors, Akamu lived within a community where everyone worked hard, respected, and relied upon one another to survive. His ancestors were not only hunters but fishermen and farmers. Taro farming was prevalent in the valley then, and the farmers of taro would exchange their crops for fish caught that day. That way of living—of relying on another—seemed to be fading away.

His eyes peered beyond the road to the open-air testing fields of crops, which were sprayed all day, every day by unknown chemicals—chemicals that were beginning to have medical and environmental consequences, particularly for the children living within a few miles of the crops. He thought of the dust and the chemicals from those crop fields that now settled onto his land—the land of his grandfather. He could no longer sit on his porch and enjoy his land, nor would he allow his grandchildren's children to play in front of his home. And, beyond the crops, he envisioned a clear path to the sandy beaches and the breathtaking ancestral waters of the Pacific.

Akamu looked to the sky. The sun was disappearing behind incoming clouds as the day slowly yielded to evening. He tilted his head to the sky, his nose to the air, and inhaled deeply. *It will rain soon*, he thought. *Another storm runoff all da way to ka moana*. He hobbled to the kitchen, pulling out a large envelope from a slat under the floor before returning to his living room.

"But the time to act is now, Alika. Take this. Hide it away from yourself, your friends, and your home. It is of utmost importance. You must see to it that no one finds these documents." He handed his grandson a large manila folder held together by several pieces of twine. "I will contact you soon and tell you where you must take these documents."

"What are they, grandfather?"

"Proof that our keikis' lives are at stake. You must not allow The Company to know of your existence, for if they discover you, they will soon find the documents and destroy you... or anyone who gets in their way, for that matter."

"I understand. Who will I give them to?" Alika asked.

"I cannot tell you now, but soon. Return to the valley on the mainland and keep the documents well hidden in your home until the time comes."

"Papahanaumoku will be pleased, then."

"Perhaps. Go now, out the back way. Let no one see you."

Alika held the thick file in his hand—his thumb and index finger struggling to hold the weight of it. He believed it offered the beginning of freedom for his people from the tyranny of greed by the invasion of a capitalist culture. He shoved the file into his backpack and placed the pack on his shoulders, securing the straps tightly around his waist. Alika moved to the back of his grandfather's house, peeking through the porch window, scanning the area. He gazed upon the land of his ancestors, taking it all in.

Could it be that we can repair our land, or is it too late? He thought of Akamu and his land. A farmer, Akamu owned a small plot of about ten acres. On this land, his father's father taught him the ohana way—the family way of living responsibly and with integrity within the community. He had watched as his father's father provided enough produce for many in the area. As an adult, Akamu followed in his grandfather's footsteps. He grew enough vegetables to feed not only his immediate family but his ohana family—neighbors who lived miles away, many of whom were now sick with various lung diseases. What produce was left, he delivered to a local food bank, using an old pickup truck with a sticky clutch.

Alika smiled at the honorable life his grandfather lived. It was that same ohana honor which drew Alika back to the island. But, tomorrow, he would leave the island under the menace of uncertainty.

With a solemn look upon his face, he turned to say goodbye to his grandfather only to realize Akamu had already retired to bed. Alika pulled the hood of his sweatshirt over his head and placed a bandanna over his mouth, his eyes obscured by sunglasses. His body tense with foreboding, he headed through the porch door toward his car, which sat behind an old, dilapidated barn hidden beneath tangled underbrush.

As soon as Alika was out of sight, Akamu sat up on the edge of his bed and dialed a familiar number on the phone receiver.

"Hello."

"He rides like the wind," Akamu replied.

"Good, good. We are meeting in the next few days. He knows to keep them safe?"

"Yes."

"They are originals?"

"Yes, they are replaced with copies."

"Mahalo."

Chapter 2

I'm So Sorry to Tell You...

———

O ne Year Later...

Smythe laid restless in her bed, noting the date. February 15th. It had been a night of constant tossing and turning. She peered toward the window at the far end of her room. *Where is that light coming from?!* Disgusted with her lack of sleep, Smythe turned her back to the window. She reached for her glasses on the side table before glancing at her alarm clock. She sighed, pulling the sheet over her head and closing her eyes. It was then she remembered the light which streamed through the edges of her curtain came from the porch lamp, which remained on all night.

She thought that perhaps she was uneasy because she had resigned from her position at work the day before. *No,* she sighed, *it had been months in the making.* Still. Whatever the reason for her restlessness, Smythe found herself mentally reviewing pieces of her life. Picking at it, really.

She thought about her name. She could not recall why her parents named her Smythe Windwalker Daniels. It was a name people either mispronounced or made fun of. It was Smythe, like Smith, not Smythe with a long "y" or Smithee. Her father said he named her. He heard the name meant to smite something, or another word for soldier. Her middle name was even more of an issue. Given to her by her mother, Clara, of Navajo lineage, she said Smythe was conceived in the back of an old pickup during a windstorm in the fields of an Illinois farm. Her mother eventually married Smythe's father, Drake, an African American Army officer. Considered late in comparison to the rest of their generation, Clara and Drake didn't marry until their early thirties. Together they raised Smythe and her two sisters, each born a little over a year and a half apart.

Smythe tossed to the other side of the bed. "Perhaps it really is just the uncertainty of my future," she mumbled. After a few more minutes of wandering down memory lane, complete with enough sighing to keep anyone awake, she rose to the stillness of the morning. She fumbled to turn on the lamp on her nightstand and sat up against her headboard. The glow of the lamp bathed her in soft strands of golden light, and there, she quietly sat, wondering what the day ahead would bring. Gazing around her bedroom, Smythe realized she had nowhere to go. Desperate for a cigarette, she quickly dressed and made coffee before heading out her apartment door. As though for the first time, she noticed that her apartment faced north, and it caused her to pause.

She remembered reading that north was the symbol of culmination and fulfillment, infused with clarity of mind.

It's the liminal space that offers us the ability to release the lessons we have learned into our conscious moments. It's supposed to represent wisdom and insight, allowing for a deepening of our contemplative moments.

Smythe stood on the threshold of her front door, scrunching her nose. She wondered what she knew for sure anymore. Everything seemed so new.

She entered her car, pressed her SUV's ignition button, and took note of the time—3:00 a.m. Turning on the heater, she sat, calculating how long she would give herself that morning.

Three hours should be enough. Joao will have to wait.

With a cold front sweeping in from the north the night before, threatening to freeze everything in its path, the morning hours offered a bitter cold, engulfing the valley in frost yet again. She sat back and watched small ice particles melt atop the hood of the car while she waited for it to warm up.

Slowly backing out of her parking stall, she rolled her window down, staring at the darkened windows of her neighbors. *Bed is where I should be.* She smirked, lit a cigarette, and took a sip of coffee before making her way out of the complex.

Just breathe, it'll be ok.

She drove to a small strip mall, a mere two blocks away, positioning her car east to watch the sun rise above the mountain range. Knowing the early morning hour was no place for a woman alone in the middle of a parking lot, she hid along the side of a large department store, away from the street lamps.

After idling her vehicle and smoking a couple cigarettes with a few sips of coffee in between, she turned off her engine. Feeling the morning's cold February air, Smythe gathered her jacket collar around her neck. She sighed and sat in weariness. So much had shifted in her life. Her eyes darted around the parking lot. It was empty, save a car at the far end. She felt the heaviness of the air around her, and she listened. The only sound was the reverent silence an early morning could offer. And here, in the solitude of the morning, Smythe sat waiting.

Her old nemesis began to surface, and it called her crazy. She brushed it aside as old news and dreamt of the many possibilities of a new future. A frown formed across her brow as her mind wandered to the last three weeks. She could feel the weight of grief threatening to take over.

These last few weeks should have been filled with joy.

She stared out the window, taking in a breath. Her inward vision tunneled as she recalled the recent dark days.

Just four weeks before her resignation, Smythe found herself sitting in an emergency room next to her mother, Clara. Smythe's father had become gravely ill. Diagnosed several years ago with a degenerative brain disorder, he barely recognized Smythe and often hallucinated. His gait was slow, shuffled, and stiff, requiring the constant use of a walker. He could no longer swallow food withou violent fits of coughing. As if the physical deterioration wasn't enough, her mother suffered under his obstinate behavior. Refusing to follow directions for even the smallest of tasks, he yelled and berated her. At one point, he threatened her with his cane, causing her mother to call Smythe to come to her rescue.

One day, while sitting in a meeting at work, her mother called to say that her father was unresponsive after attempting to wake him that morning. Clara called the paramedics, and after a brief examination, they rushed him to the hospital. Smythe arrived at the emergency room and found her mother sitting alone in his room where her father's bed should have been. Upon her face lay a trail of dried tears. She began to weep of exhaustion once again as her daughter approached.

"Oh Smythe, he's had a stroke, and they are unsure he will survive it," she blurted out.

Smythe's skin paled, her eyes widened, and she willed her tears to cease their march down her cheeks. She lifted her chin and looked around the room.

"Where is he?"

"They've taken him for tests. They want to see how bad it is."

Smythe moved an empty chair to sit next to her mother. They both winced at the sudden, loud, scraping sound. Holding her mother's hand, Smythe listened as her mother recited yet another chapter of her father's long goodbye. At the end of her story, she weakly asked Smythe to call "the girls."

"I will, but only after we get results about the tests." Her mother nodded in agreement.

When it came to bad news, Smythe was often the unwilling conduit of information to the family. She was the one who called her siblings when her grandmother died, the one who called when their aunt passed away, the one who called when their father had a heart attack, and the one who called with the neurological diagnosis of their father. Now, she was tasked to deliver even more devastating news.

A short time later, her father was wheeled into the room. Placing an oxygen tank behind his bed, the nurse dimmed the lights low. The ER doctor strode into the room a short time later and introduced herself to Smythe before solemnly asking for a meeting outside.

They followed behind the doctor into an adjoining waiting room, which provided sensory relief from the noise of monitoring equipment and chatter in the hallway. Smythe's mother huddled next to her.

"He will not recover, I'm afraid," the doctor quietly stated. "The damage is too extensive." She explained the various tests performed, the reason for the tests, and their results. Smythe pursed her lips together. She felt her mind wander but compelled herself to focus on the information the doctor conveyed.

And then the question.

"What do you want to do?" the doctor asked. Smythe closed her eyes for a moment. When she opened them, she turned to her mother. She watched as tears streamed down her mother's cheeks, her face beginning to become ashen. She took her mother's hand into her own and looked deep into her eyes.

"I can't make the decision, Smythe."

"He would not want this, Mom."

"I know. I just can't say the words. I need you to say them for me," she whispered.

Smythe stood in silence. She imagined her mother and the 50 years of marriage she shared with her husband. Smythe imagined that perhaps by not saying the words, her mother was delaying the decision, if only for another moment. But *someone* had to speak.

To make the most compassionate decision she could on her father's behalf, Smythe looked over to the doctor, her voice steady and strong. "He wouldn't want this existence and would be furious if we kept him alive like this. We need to let him go."

The doctor nodded her head. She went on to explain what they would and would not medically do on his behalf, which would include removing all nutritional supplements.

"We will continue his pain and anxiety medications and monitor his blood oxygen levels but will take away his oxygen."

Smythe nodded and looked toward her mother. Taking her hand, together, they returned to her father's bedside. After a few minutes, she left her mother at her father's bedside and returned to the waiting room to call her sisters.

Her first call was to Nellis, her younger sister. Smythe was particularly fond of her, if only because she, too, had an unusual first name. Smythe found her sister easy to talk to regarding all manner of subjects—and while they did not speak often, a bond had developed between them. Nellis looked up to Smythe, admiring her intelligence and her quiet, "I'm following my own path" attitude. Nellis, who lived in the Chicago area, was also grateful to Smythe for choosing to move close to their parents after being furloughed, and often expressed her relief at Smythe's presence.

"Hello."

Clearing her throat, Smythe stood surprised at the sudden emotion welling up in her voice. "Nellis, hi, it's Smythe. I'm sorry, but I've got some bad news to share."

"What's happened?"

"It's Dad. He's had a massive stroke. Nellis… he won't survive it."

Smythe closed her eyes, willing herself the strength to continue the story.

"We're taking him off of life support. The doctor told us…" Smythe paused, clearing her throat again. "The doctor said it would only be a matter of time…"

"Oh, God, no!" Nellis sobbed. "Please, God, no, please God, no! What happened?"

Smythe, suddenly feeling weary, reached for a chair and sat down. "I don't have all of the details, but Mom tried to wake him up this morning, and he didn't wake. She thought he was just being stubborn. You know Mom. But he wasn't. Based on all of the tests, he would not survive without extraordinary measures."

"But there's hope; there's always hope, Smythe. Don't let him die—please!"

"Nellis. There's very little to no brain activity, and this isn't the way he'd want to live."

"He's our father!"

"Exactly! Which is why the most compassionate thing Mom and I could do for him is to let him pass in peace—not tied to a bunch of machines just to keep him with us."

Smythe listened for a response but could hear only the empty silence of grief. Promising her youngest sister that she would call her with any new changes in their father's status, Smythe hung up the phone.

Father's status, Smythe thought. *Rather cold and formal way to express his death, but how else could I have said it? "I'll call to let you know he died"?*

Smythe took in a breath. She held her phone in the palm of her hand, thumbing through her contact list. *Margaret Kennedy.* She hesitated for a moment, wondering which number to dial. Smythe hadn't spoken to Margaret in years, holding her middle sister personally responsible for Smythe's social trouble in school.

Margaret had been welcomed into the high school hierarchy of girls, dressed in the latest fashion and crazy about boys. But Smythe was different. She wore jeans and button-down shirts with sneakers, preferred girls over boys, literature rather than television, and solitude over company. Smythe's quiet demeanor became fodder for Margaret's clique of girls, and Margaret just stood by and sneered at Smythe, allowing the verbal bullying to take place. Margaret's only response had been to challenge her older sister to defend herself, but Smythe never did.

Smythe clenched her teeth. She tapped Margaret's cell number and immediately stood from the chair.

"Smythe, what's up?" Handing her secretary a file folder, Margaret put the palm of her hand over the mouthpiece and thanked her.

"Sorry about that. What's going on?"

"I'm calling as the bearer of bad news. Dad suffered a massive stroke and will not survive."

"Oh, no!"

Repeatedly making a fist and releasing it, Smythe began to pace. "Mom and I have given the doctors permission to remove all life-sustaining efforts. We're placing him in hospice, where he'll most likely pass away in the next couple of days.

"Oh my God. How's Mom? Can I talk to her?"

"Mom is with Dad right now. I would suggest you try reaching her later this evening. Too much noise and activity here—"

"What hospital are you at?"

"University."

"Good, good." Taking in a breath, Margaret sat back in her chair, swiveled around toward her office window, and stared out at the New York City skyline. Darting her eyes back and forth, she finally spoke. "Let me call Thomas. He may know some neurologists there. Perhaps consult with them."

Leave it to you to want to drag your husband into this.

"Didn't you hear me? His doctors have given him no chance of recovery. The most compassionate thing Mom and I can do is let him go. So, that's what we're doing."

"There's always a chance—I can't just accept this."

"Do you think we can?" Smythe stopped her pacing and took in a breath. "Look, at least he won't continue to suffer. And he has suffered, Margaret. I've already called Nellis; she won't be able to get here to say goodbye in person. If you can spare the time—"

"I can't. I leave for Italy tomorrow. I won't be back until a week from Tuesday. I'll call Mom later to explain. I just can't believe this is happening."

"And yet it has, Margaret. If you want, you can call me, and I can put you on so you can say your goodbyes to him. Or, if Mom is in the room, you can call her."

"Yes, that's a great idea. I'll do my best to clear my schedule and give her a call tonight, then make arrangements to talk to him while she's there."

"Sounds good. Listen, I've got to get back to Mom. I'll let you know when I've scheduled the memorial service."

"Yes, that's good. I'll clear my calendar once I'm back from this trip. If possible, three weeks from now would be great."

"Yeah, sure. Gotta go."

"Ok, bye."

Ass. Your father is dying, and you can't spare a day or two to say goodbye!

Smythe stomped through the waiting room, stopping short of her father's room to compose herself. After a few long breaths, she forced a smile and returned to sit with her mother.

Over the next several hours, all life-sustaining measures were halted. The ER staff made arrangements for a local hospice of Smythe's choosing to take control of his care. Her mother, sick with grief, returned to her home while Smythe remained behind, waiting to accompany her father to hospice.

It would be close to midnight before transportation services arrived for Smythe's father. After a short drive outside the city, the caravan, consisting of the transport vehicle and Smythe in her SUV, arrived at their destination.

The hospice center was a small facility, yet considered one of the best in the valley. Smythe entered the complex and felt comforted to see that it did not have the sterile feeling or appearance of a hospital. As though wrapped in a warm blanket on a cold rainy day, she gazed at a lobby that looked more like a quaint bed and breakfast. The lights were dimmed low. Serene landscape paintings hung on the walls around worn but comfy living room-style furniture. A card table sat off in the far corner of the lobby, with a number of well-used board games and magazines scattered atop it.

She was met by her father's new hospice nurse, Evorah. A plump African American woman in her late 50s with a curly hair weave, she held a tender strength in her movement, a reflective gaze in her eyes, and the gentle spirit of an angel. Her enveloping tenderness allowed Smythe to release any anxiety over concern for her father's care as he journeyed on the last days of his long goodbye.

Evorah, with an accent that belied her southern upbringing, quietly explained to Smythe she and her team would provide "comfort care" for her father. Not completely understanding the term, Smythe gave Evorah a quizzical look.

Evorah stated, "We'll not seek to cure that which cannot be cured. Instead, my team will focus our efforts on easing the physical effects of his dying process." She taught Smythe how they could tell when their unresponsive patient was in pain.

"We'll watch him closely, learn his facial signals. We all have 'em when we're in pain. We look for a slight grimace or restless movement in his body. We watch his blood pressure, too. There'll be no unnecessary discomfort, I assure you."

Smythe nodded.

"It's also not too uncommon that he may feel some level of anxiety. We will administer anxiety medication; no need to suffer that."

There it is, Smythe thought. *The culmination of a life reduced to pain and anxiety medication.*

Evorah offered Smythe a tour of the floor while the hospice team tended to her father. She pointed out where Smythe would be required to sign in and out. With Smythe by her side, she strode through the halls, pointing out the restrooms and nurses' station should Smythe require assistance during her visits.

"And I've saved the best for last," Evorah said, pointing toward the kitchen.

"You'll want to visit our kitchen periodically. We have the most delicious chocolate chip cookies this side of the Ohi'a river. I couldn't bake them any better, if I do say so myself. As you can tell, I've had my fair share over the years, hence my motherly figure," she said with a twinkle in her eye. With her hands on her hips, she shimmied her body effortlessly, flaunting her round figure. Smythe could not help but giggle at the sight of this angel.

Smythe spent a few minutes with her father before she said her goodbyes to Evorah and the nurse's assistant. Evorah nodded and began speaking to her father in a voice that could have soothed a wailing child.

After just two and a half days, Smythe received an early morning call from Evorah. "Smythe, I am sorry to inform you, your father passed away peacefully at 2:05 a.m."

Smythe sat back against the headboard of her bed. Holding her phone, she stared at the keypad. For several minutes, she sat, numb to the news. *It's time,* she told herself. She hesitated before thumbing through her contact list, calling her mother before calling her two siblings.

"I'm sorry, I'm so sorry to have to tell you..." Smythe started, and then listened. She listened as they each poured out their grief-stricken sobs. She bore the brunt of preparing her father's memorial. Perhaps out of spite for her sister, Margaret, Smythe set the memorial service for two weeks after his death and one week before her resignation.

A week after her father's memorial service, Smythe walked away from her corporate position. With no fanfare, she had gathered her belongings at the end of the day and strode away from a life she no longer claimed as her own.

Then, quite unexpectedly, it all fell together.

Chapter 3

More Time

—

Smythe continued to sit in her car. She rolled down her window and lit another cigarette.

So much has happened in the space of a few weeks. Dad dies, and then I decide to turn in my resignation and make a huge career change? What am I thinking?

She took one last drag from her cigarette before she snuffed it out, littering the parking lot with the butt. The black, midnight sky began to turn to gray. With her coffee mug in hand, Smythe became aware of the sound of a man's voice.

"Please, please, don't. I beg you."

The shuffling of labored footsteps came into earshot some distance behind her. She tilted her head to one side as they seemed to draw closer. Her heart began to race, and her breathing shallowed as she turned her attention back to the center. Glancing up at her rearview mirror, two men became visible. One struggled in the hands of the other as they stumbled out from the shadows of darkness into the dull light of a flickering streetlamp.

Smythe peered into her passenger's side mirror. Transfixed by the struggle, she watched as the pair got uncomfortably close to her car. One man stopped to swing the other man around. The taller of the two, a white male in his 50s with salt and pepper hair, stood yelling at the second. He towered over him as he continued to yell out profanities, raising his fist toward the pleading man. The pleading man slowly backed away, his head moving from side to side. He cowered before the tormentor, his outstretched hands facing upward.

Smythe pressed her head as far into the headrest as she could. Sitting perfectly still, she listened as the pleading man spoke.

"I don't have it, and I no longer know who does. It will require time. I just need more time; please, just a little more time."

His tormentor, enraged, moved forward and landed a fist squarely into the man's lower jaw, knocking him back onto his heels. He growled, spitting at the pleading man's feet.

"You've had enough time, you pathetic little man. I told you before Alika, give us the name of the tattletale and the documents—but you didn't heed my warning. I've given you so much time. More than you deserve, but you took advantage."

"All my ohana ever wanted was to live off the land! So many are in agony. Our children have respiratory issues."

"Your people! Your people? Your people are weak! They had an opportunity to make real money, yet they have refused our offer. But, either way, my employer now has their land, and I have you."

Smythe's shoulders tensed. She sensed this man, Alika, was in danger. But what could she do? She was contemplating her options when a gunshot made her jump. The sound, piercing the stillness of the early morning air, reverberated deep within Smythe's body. She sat, frozen in place, and held her breath. She watched as Alika slumped to the pavement and anxiously gulped in air.

Dear God, oh God, oh God, oh God. Hide!

Smythe looked into her rearview mirror one last time before diving toward the passenger seat, quickly bending her torso over her armrest. Her stomach lurched. She pressed her mouth closed, holding the vomit at bay. Her hands began to tremble as she placed her coffee in the cup holder, her face contorting, hoping her movement was not heard. She did not breathe, remaining perfectly, quietly still.

She tilted her head and gazed upward through her sunroof, noticing the night sky giving way to the morning dawn. She began to sweat profusely and squelched the need to scream. She swallowed her acidic bile, screaming silently.

Help me; please help me!

Her internal chatter told her there was no help, and to prepare for the worst. Yet, with just enough hope, she remained motionless over her armrest and did not make a sound.

Oh, God, let it stay dark. Please let it stay dark. Don't let him see me. Please.

Smythe squeezed her eyes tight, the words of the dying stranger playing in a continuous loop— "I just need more time, I just need more time, I just need more time..."

How do I get out of here? How can I call 911 without being heard?

She held her breath and listened. The only sound she could hear was the rhythmic pounding of her heartbeat. It seemed as if time itself were caught in eternal stillness. She felt grossly uncomfortable, her chest aching for air. Her body finally rebelled, releasing her diaphragm to take in a breath. She shivered as she opened her eyes.

Just peek. You can't sit here all morning. Just a quick glance.

She lifted her head just enough to peer into the passenger-side mirror. The only one remaining was Alika, sprawled upon the asphalt, his blood slowly staining the parking lot, barely hidden by the early dawn sky.

She laid her head back down.

Damn it. Where's my phone? Feel for it. Where did you last have it?

She couldn't find it.

Please, do you remember bringing it? Yes, yes. Ok. Don't move. There it is. Ok. Ok, Smythe, it's under you. Please, please, please just lift up a little.

Without a sound, struggling to lift her torso just enough to pull her cellphone out from under her, she raised her head, peering through the side-view mirror, her eyes darting around the parking lot.

Her hands began to shake as she clutched her lifeline.

Damn it! What's my passcode?

She took in abbreviated breaths, her forehead moist with perspiration.

Maybe I should just drive away. Pretend I didn't see anything.

No! I need to call 911!

I can't get into my phone!

Breathe, please just breathe.

In 2, 3, 4. Out 2, 3, 4, 5, 6, 7, 8. In 2, 3, 4. Out 2, 3, 4, 5, 6, 7, 8. In 2, 3, 4. Out 2, 3, 4, 5, 6, 7, 8.

Remember your code. Please. Just remember.

She waited in unbearable darkness. Finally, a bubble surfaced from her memory, and her four-digit passcode emerged. She thumbed the code onto her phone and called 911, whispering her location. While waiting for the police to arrive, she suddenly remembered she could have used her phone's emergency feature. Still bent over her armrest, she tilted her head toward the heavens and quietly whispered, "Ya think you could have helped me out with that little detail a bit sooner?"

Police dispatch kept Smythe calm, requesting she remain on the phone in her car at the scene until police arrived. *Why is this taking so long? He could come back at any moment. Hurry up already! Please help me, please help me!* But then, she heard them. Off in the distance, faintly at first, then increasingly louder, was the sound of sirens.

The wailing became deafening as emergency vehicles drew near, jarring the little emotional stability left within her. Police cars surrounded her vehicle, while fire and rescue vehicles pulled up next to the dead man. The dispatcher disconnected from Smythe as officers began their foot approach toward her car. With her hands raised above her head, she peeked her head up above the bottom of her passenger window, scanning the parking area now full of activity.

"It's me. I-I called police, I-I called police!" she yelled.

After providing officers with identification, she recounted her reason for sitting in the parking lot at such an early morning hour.

"I-I-I came because I couldn't sleep. I-I-I ju-just wanted to pray and smoke cigarettes. G-get direction for the day."

Between her sobs, she described what she saw. She struggled to recall important details as her ego derailed her focus, berating her for sitting in that parking lot at that time of morning—alone! Fear embraced her like an unwanted hug from an uncomfortable acquaintance, yet she remained steadfast to her account of the event. The police held her for what seemed like hours, questioning her over and over again, but each time, she provided the same description of the suspect and what she heard. Satisfied with the information she provided, the police finally released her to return home. With store surveillance cameras corroborating her story, detectives located and arrested the suspect a few days later.

* * *

Day after day, Smythe sat on her sofa, and as she sunk into the cushions, she came to the same conclusion—she had witnessed a murder, and day after day, the terror of it consumed her. Desperate to clean away the memory of the parking lot, she isolated herself in her apartment. She repeatedly mopped her floors, sponged her sideboards, and vacuumed her bedroom. She dusted her coffee and side tables, each and every lamp, every piece of art, and even the doors within her apartment.

This excessive cleaning reminded her of training from childhood. Smythe held memories of her family's constant travel from one Army base to another, rarely staying in one place for more than two consecutive years. Near the end of each assignment, Army protocol required military personnel to inspect an officer's military housing vacated by a family. Using white gloves, inspectors would meticulously seek out dirt and grime. They ran their fingers above and along the sides of door frames, scouring for dirt and dust along the baseboards, and inspected inside cupboards and closets. When dirt was found on the glove, family members were expected to clean it right then and there. Everyone in her family participated when it came time to prepare their home for inspection. As a result, Smythe became a stickler for clean and tidy. In this case, aspiring to an excessively clean, tidy apartment was a refuge from a mind and body desperate to extricate terror.

News of the crime traveled fast. It stunned Smythe's sleepy community, and they were not taking it well. With only the occasional vehicle break-in or DUI incident, residents were shocked at the unthinkable violent crime in their community. They wanted answers. They spoke about it everywhere—grocery stores, bookstores, gas stations. Everyone gossiped, and everyone knew—but no one knew about Smythe or her intimate role in the heinous act of cruelty.

Adhering to the mandate of local police to tell no one what she witnessed (save law enforcement), Smythe began to sense the creation of a new jail cell. Now, rarely going out except to pick up a few groceries, she remained locked behind her apartment door and cleaned. Through a variety of media outlets, Smythe learned the suspect was part of a larger crime ring that had quietly encroached into the valley a few years earlier, immediately catching the attention of the FBI.

If only I hadn't been there at that hour! What was I thinking? How involved will I have to become now? How will this affect my new practice? What will potential clients think? What will my friends think? And my mother!

With the passing of a few weeks, Smythe displayed more resiliency, settling into a routine of writing and studying. Her mentor's teaching also helped to ease her anxiety, and, steadily, she became more relaxed, recognizing she had control over her response. She also chose to no longer follow any of the news reports. She mustered the courage to leave her apartment more often and began to smile again, noticing spring was near. Trees displayed their hibernating buds, the melodic chirping of birds serenaded the passersby, and the sun started to warm the air. Life, she thought, continued to unfold, and she needed to re-engage with it.

Arriving home one morning after an early workout at the gym, Smythe received a phone call from FBI Supervisory Special Agent

Carole Richardson. She introduced herself as the agent in charge of the murder investigation. A ten-year veteran with the FBI, Carole was considered one the best in her field, and an expert in syndicated crime activity. With a dry, matter-of-fact tenor to her voice, she requested Smythe's presence at the local FBI building that day and set up an appointment.

A few hours later, staring blankly at the table in front of her, Smythe found herself seated in a sterile conference room within the FBI building. She tugged at the sleeve of her charcoal blazer and smoothed her matching slacks. She tapped her finger on the table and glanced at the wall clock before returning her gaze to the conference table.

1:50. She's late.

Carole Roberts sat back in her chair. Lost in thought, she peered into the one-way mirror of the conference room, observing Smythe. She narrowed her focus onto Smythe's stubbled head. Carole self-consciously brushed her hand through her own tousled, jet black hair. She reflected on her early years working within the bureau. As an African American female, she learned that in order to fit in, she could not stand out. To fit in, the female normative appearance standard within the FBI had to be met—which included relaxing her hair. She stood, adjusting her black suit jacket and smoothing her slacks with her hands, sighing. Moments later, she walked into the conference room.

She introduced herself to Smythe and remained standing. She told her an information leak had occurred, and an eyewitness could identify the suspect. She paced back and forth as she described her plans to take the necessary precautions to ensure Smythe's safety. Still, Smythe, already disgruntled by the agent's tardiness and curt demeanor, was having none of it.

Maybe it was her childhood experience with police which contributed to Smythe's simmering anger toward Agent Roberts. Sitting in the small conference room, Smythe began to feel the walls close in and around her and immediately felt the memory of her first encounter with local law enforcement.

As a teenager, she had been stopped by a local police cruiser with two officers in her mostly white neighborhood. She was walking along Aimes Avenue. A fairly quiet thoroughfare, Aimes was nestled between a canopy of sycamore trees. Her backpack slung over her right shoulder, Smythe remembered looking down at her feet as she meandered down the sidewalk, her slender frame buffeted by the blustery winds arising in the midday sun.

She checked her watch. Her mother would not be home for another half hour or so. She paused for a moment, felt for change in her pocket and pulled out several quarters, calculating the amount for a phone call.

I'll call her when I get there.

Just then, she felt a slow, heavy movement behind her. She could hear the low hum of an engine and the crunching of a vehicle's tires as they rolled along the asphalt.

Smythe snapped her thumbs and middle fingers together.

Is someone following me?

She clenched her jaw, and her chest began to rise and fall more quickly. *Should I turn around and see who is following me? Or should I continue to walk, pretending not to notice?* She quickened her steps, but, to her growing alarm, the crunching of tires kept pace with her.

After a quarter of a block, she came to a breathless, abrupt halt. With her hands balled into fists, she finally turned around. Her eyes widened. A police car rolled up next to her, coming to a slow stop. She closed her eyes and briefly exhaled a sigh of relief.

A white officer with a chubby, freckled face, and narrow blue eyes rolled down his window and spoke with suspicion.

"What are you doing here, girl?"

Fear immediately caught in her throat, and Smythe found herself unable to respond.

He repeated his question, rephrasing it slightly. "I said—what are you doing in this part of town?"

"I'm going to the library."

"Don't they have a library in your neighborhood?"

"This is my neighborhood," she said defiantly.

With some effort, the red-headed officer removed himself from his car. He seemed to tower over her, even from a few feet away. She frowned at his obese stomach, which hung over his utility belt, a fact all the more accentuated by the placement of his hands on his hips.

As he approached, she took a step backward. He just kept walking, crossing the grassy strip that separated the curb from the sidewalk. He stopped before her and glared. Smythe glanced to her left. The officer's partner, a slender, white man, exited the passenger side of the vehicle and strode onto the sidewalk. Together they flanked her, allowing for no forward or backward movement.

"Prove it!" the portly officer said.

"I live at 111 Cedar Drive. It's about a mile back that way," Smythe said, pointing a shaking finger behind her. "I just got out of school, and I'm heading to the library to study."

"And you study," the second officer said slowly, "at the library?"

"Yes, sir. Every day after school."

"Hmph," sneered the portly officer.

The slender officer asked her to remove her backpack. Smythe dropped her shoulder, allowing the backpack to slide to her hand. She blushed, looking around, hoping no one she knew saw her, yet wishing someone—anyone, would come to her aid. She placed the backpack at her feet, hearing it thump onto the sidewalk and took another step back. The slender officer picked up the pack and unzipped it. Smythe clenched and unclenched her hands, watching as he rummaged through her belongings.

"Do you have any identification?"

"My school ID is in the front zipper."

Smythe could hear the sound of the zipper intensified from the anxiety as he opened the front pouch. He found the ID with her picture printed on the front of it and handed it to his partner, who then examined it, turning it over and over again between his fingers, holding it up to the light of the sun.

It's real, you stupid jerk! Smythe screamed inwardly.

"You'll need to come with us and show us where you live."

"I'm not sure my mom is home yet."

"She better be, for your sake."

Smythe caught her breath. She felt a piercing cold in the pit of her stomach. Tears began to fill her eyes. Willing her tears away, she bit the inside of her cheek. She stared at the stubby finger of the portly officer who pointed it toward his vehicle. She dropped her chin to her chest, and with her shoulders slumped forward, she followed the officers to an uncertain fate, her eyes darting from side to side. The portly officer opened the back of the patrol car, and she reluctantly entered the vehicle.

The seat was low, covered in smooth black vinyl. Her legs were cramped against the back of the front seat. Metal mesh separated the space between the back and the front seat, preventing the occupant from striking at officers. There were no door handles to allow her to open the door from the inside, and the windows were shut. Smythe coughed. The car was stuffy and smelled of stale, rank human body odor. And, while outside the fall air had risen to only 55 degrees, Smythe began to sweat profusely inside the car.

But I didn't do anything!

The portly officer plunked himself into the driver's seat and spoke into his radio. He looked into his rearview mirror.

"What's your address?"

Smythe began to sigh out loud and abruptly caught herself.

"111 Cedar Lane."

After a few moments, the officer drove away from the curb. No one spoke, save the occasional voice of the radio dispatcher. Smythe pressed herself against the back of the seat and leaned her head away from the window, watching through the windshield as the car neared her neighborhood. Once they turned onto her street, she pierced the silence, pointing out her home.

A white colonial, two-story home with black shutters framing the windows sat majestically among other well-cared-for homes. Smythe felt her heart as it beat faster, thinking it would beat right out of her chest. It almost ached. Tears once again filled her eyes.

Please be home, please be home, please be home.

Once parked, the slender police officer strode along the walkway, which separated a neatly manicured front lawn into two halves. The work of her father—daylilies, peonies, and geraniums lined the walkway and front of the house.

The officer eyed the flowers and climbed the three steps to the front door and rang the doorbell. No answer. His brow gathered across his forehead, and he waited. He looked back toward the patrol car. He rang the doorbell again. No response. As he turned to walk away, a heavy-set, light brown-skinned, woman with long brown hair opened the door.

"Are you Mrs. Daniels?"

"Yes, I am. What's the matter, officer?"

"Do you have a daughter by the name of Smythe Daniels?"

Mrs. Daniels raised her hand to her chest and frowned. "Yes, what's happened!?"

"We found your daughter walking on Aimes Avenue."

"Is she alright?!"

"Yes, ma'am, she is. We just needed to verify her residence."

Clara's eyes widened. "No, you didn't! You didn't just—you didn't just pick up my daughter? For what? Walking?"

Her mother snapped her gaze past the officer and eyed the patrol car at her curb. She ran out her door, pushing past the officer, her round figure bouncing down the steps toward the car.

"Let her out! Let her out! She is no criminal! Baby girl! Smythe, are you alright?! Let her out, I say! Please. Right now!"

The portly officer lumbered out of his vehicle and eyed Clara before opening the back door. Smythe slid across the seat. With her eyes lowered to the pavement, she stepped onto the curb. Tears Smythe could no longer contain streamed down her face as she took a step toward her mother. With her arms outstretched, her mother pulled Smythe into an embrace and held her tightly against her body.

"Haven't you ever seen a kid walk to a library?" Clara chastised. She pulled herself back from Smythe. "Didn't you tell 'em where you were going, honey?!"

Smythe simply nodded.

"Ma'am, we're required to stop all suspicious-looking individuals in this neighborhood. We're simply doing our job. We had to *verify* she lived where she said she lived."

Her mother stomped her foot. "She lives here!" she said through clenched teeth.

"Well, this is an upstanding neighborhood with very low crime. We see to it. She was walking alone with a backpack. It's unusual to see that in *this* neighborhood—especially unaccompanied by a parent.

"That's ridiculous!" Clara snapped. Bone-achingly weary of the treatment she and her family routinely received from every corner of society, she reminded herself to hold her tongue. She softened her gaze, a forced slight smile creasing the edges of her mouth. With strained politeness, she continued.

"I thank you for returning my daughter home, officer. However, she was coming from school, like she always does, and heading to the library, like she always does. She is a straight-A student. We live here, and she has done nothing that any other teenager wouldn't do. Nothing."

Clara's eyes filled with the grayness of sorrow, piercing those of her daughter's.

"Smythe, go inside. *Now.*"

"They have my backpack and ID," Smythe whispered.

Her mother slowly, cautiously squared her shoulders, holding back all of the rage and fury which coursed through her frame.

"Please. Re. Turn. Her. Belongings."

The scene reminded Smythe of the writings of James Baldwin in an essay called "A Stranger in the Village." Her mother had a copy upstairs in their family room, next to Smythe's room. Smythe read the writing several times, imagining the scenes in Switzerland and the feelings Mr. Baldwin must have felt. A passage from the essay came to mind. As she watched her mother, she heard the echo of Mr. Baldwin, and a cold shiver traveled the length of the spine.

"The rage of the disesteemed is personally fruitless...the rage generally discounted... There are, no doubt as many ways of coping with the resulting complex tensions as there are black men in the world, but no black man can hope to ever be entirely liberated from this internal warfare-rage... having inevitably accompanied his first realization of the power of white men."

Smythe comprehended the moment, leaned into her mother's tender arms of rage, and felt the rhythm of her heartbeat.

The portly officer regarded Clara and paused before he stooped into the front seat of his car. He reached in, pulled out her backpack, and handed it to her mother. Smythe stepped away as her mother reached for the items.

"Go into the house now, honey. I'll be there in a moment," her mother whispered.

As if pulling her back from a dream, the FBI agent's words finally registered for Smythe.

"Ms. Daniels? Ms. Daniels. Smythe!"

Smythe raised her eyes and caught the gaze of the agent, not letting go.

"You will be testifying against the individual you identified in a police lineup a week ago. Because you will be testifying against someone connected to the crime syndicate, we need to place you into our witness security program until after the trial. We don't want to alarm you, but we feel—"

"No, thank you."

"Ms. Daniels, please. It's in your best interest if we keep you safe until after you testify."

Smythe could feel the heat in her cheeks. She rolled her neck and her shoulders with clenched teeth and narrowed her eyes.

"Until *after* the trial, and then what? You remove all protection from me? What happens to me, then?"

Agent Roberts leaned back against the office window. "It will be a bit of an adjustment for you, Ms. Daniels, but it is in your best interest. We will relocate you to another state until you testify, and then after your testimony, it's up to you. But our witnesses usually choose to permanently relocate."

Smythe's eyes pierced through the matter-of-fact demeanor displayed on the agent's face.

"Wow. Then let's be a little more honest here. Moving me out of the valley really isn't about caring for my *long-term* wellbeing. It's more about the short-term benefits for your agency. It sounds like your objective is to keep me alive long enough to testify against your bad guy.

Raising her right index finger, she swept it downward. "Score one for the FBI; they've cleaned up the valley. But at whose expense? No. No, thank you, Agent Roberts. I'll figure it out myself."

Agent Roberts moved forward. "Ms. Daniels, we cannot stress enough the importance of keeping you safe. You are correct; we want to win this case. This individual has a record a mile long, and his influence is not only here but also—"

Smythe glared at the agent. "I believe I said no. You really can't force me into witness protection, nor can you force me to move or relocate."

At that moment, time seemed to pause. She returned to the memory of the gangly brown teenage girl stopped by police for simply walking alone in her own neighborhood. She felt her stomach chill. Her arms began to tremble. A memory had come to mind—old television footage of African Americans marching peacefully in the street, knocked off their feet by water cannons and beaten by the very same police officers who swore an oath to protect and serve. In the same instant, she found herself thinking about her grandmother's account of the vicious Long Walk to Bosque Redondo. During that time, the indigenous people of North America were forced to move to New Mexico and leave their ancestral lands, a brutal and often fatal journey.

Smythe remembered peering up at her grandmother. Something about the name Bosque Redondo wet the inside of her grandmother's eyes.

"Grandmother, don't cry."

"It is alright," her grandmother said as she held an old photograph in her hands. "I must never forget the sacrifice, and neither should you."

"What was the Long Walk to Bosque Redondo?"

"A brutal 400-mile walk from our ancestral land. The ancestors—they were not prepared for such a journey, were not even told where they were going or how long it would take. They were starved or killed because they could not keep up. Our pregnant women would often go into labor along the trail. Our families were forced to leave them behind, but as they moved forward, they would hear gunshots in the distance behind them."

In a large measure, the memory bolstered Smythe's courage and she stood her ground.

"No. I will not go. I've made huge strides in my life. Significant changes, even. Now you want me to upend my new career, my life... I'm just not going to do it!"

"You can follow me if you'd like, but I'm not going to scurry away and hide in your security program. If you need anything else, call me. In the meantime, I've got things to do."

Smythe rose from her chair. Hands trembling, she clutched her messenger bag and left the conference room. The agent shook her head and followed behind her. Smythe moved quickly through an open row of desks, glancing around the office as she made her escape.

Typical office structure. It could be almost any company I've worked for. Rigid and unmoving. Toe the company line. All the tin soldiers lined in a row. I could have just driven away, pretending as if I saw nothing. But I got involved. I called the police. Against my better judgement, I called the police. I told them what I witnessed, but like my mom always said, no good deed goes unpunished! God, I'm just now pulling it together. Why? Why now!

Smythe glared straight ahead as she approached the double-sided glass doors and exited the office. She glanced to her right and then her left. She approached a bank of elevators at the far end of the hallway, barreling forward once a door opened and nearly knocking a woman over in the process.

Dressed in a trimmed white shirt and matching dark blue jacket and slacks, the stranger's lean musculature typically would have outmatched Smythe's frame. However, the speed with which Smythe entered the elevator left the stranger unprepared for such a swift entry and momentarily unbalanced her. Smythe eyed the stranger and simply regarded her as just another FBI agent. She lowered her head and stepped aside to allow the woman to pass.

The stranger regarded Smythe for a moment and smiled. "Hard day?"

"Yes. That about sums it up. I'm sorry, my mistake," Smythe mumbled.

Letting out a slow breath before pressing the lobby button, she lifted her gaze, catching sight of the woman again. The stranger looked back in Smythe's direction and offered her another smile before striding into the office Smythe just left.

Chapter 4

I Might Regret This, But I'll Do It

—

AGENT CAROLE ROBERTS STOOD NEAR HER DEPARTMENT'S door—fuming. It wasn't just Smythe's lack of cooperation that annoyed her. After all, she was just trying to help the witness. It was Smythe's naivety of her own making that caused this predicament.

She held her breath momentarily as she stared out at her department. In the open space, quiet conversation of colleagues mingled with the sound of telephones ringing, copy machines thumping, and agents standing near fax machines earnestly discussing their cases. The combination of sounds created a cacophony of frenetic energy. Yet, the only sound Carole heard were the last words spoken to her from Smythe: "I'll figure it out myself."

Who does she think she's talking to? It's just crazy she was sitting in a parking lot at that hour of the morning. She had to have known better.

She backed away from the main entrance of the department and opened a file folder containing an investigative summary of Smythe. She thumbed through its contents again, hoping to glean some insight into the defiant behavior Smythe just demonstrated. After a moment, she snapped it shut, the contents offering her little information.

Why so damn obstinate? And foolhardy! She's going to get herself killed!

Her thoughts of damnation were interrupted as the door swung open. She turned her head just in time to watch her old friend enter.

Standing at five-foot-eight inches tall with long auburn hair, olive skin, sculpted eyebrows, and slightly chiseled facial features, Artemis Fione Leone strode into the office and surveyed it. Those on the way to the door smiled and nodded in her direction. With an air of smugness, she returned their smile, her gray-brown eyes softening.

"Artemis! You're early. How are you?"

"Carole. Serious. Why do you do this? For years I've gone by Artie. You know damn well I'm not a fan of my birth name, yet you persist."

"Not my problem. Take it up with your parents."

"Greek mythology—my mother's obsession, remember?"

A smirk flashed across Carole's face. "I remember—paintings and statues everywhere. But I must admit, it gives me such pleasure to call you by your given name. Its meaning rather suits you. Besides, Artemis, it's payback for standing me up last week. Want to explain why?" Carole lifted her hand. "Wait, hold your inevitable comeback. Let me grab my bag."

Artie bit her tongue as she watched her friend walk away. *Trying to gain the upper hand again, are we?*

Artie continued to look about the office. The noise of the department began to quiet. Agents leaned in and whispered to one another, glancing every now and again in Artie's direction. Amused at the thought that they were whispering about her, she stood watching the agents watch her. *God, they look so young.* She looked past them all to the back of the office. From a distance, she could see Carole approaching.

With her purse and file in hand, Carole walked past Artie to the office entrance.

"Where do you want to go for lunch?" Artie asked.

"How about Rodolfo's? It's a block away, and it's off the beaten path so we can hide out from everyone in the office."

"Rodolfo's it is, then."

While strolling to the elevator, Carole resumed their conversation. "Well, what's your excuse?"

"To your point of standing you up, Carole, I was wrapping up an assignment. It took longer than I wanted, and it proved to be a bit unpredictable. I had no opportunity to reach out to you."

"Don't lie to me, Artie. Your very involved mother called—she's worried about you. She told me you dropped Davey off for the summer."

The pair entered the elevator, and Carole pressed the lobby button. Artie stared straight ahead, her hands crossed in front of her and released an audible breath. "No, it wasn't for the summer, Carole. It was for the year. He wanted to spend some time getting to know his father."

"Well, she was worried. You ok?"

"As usual, leave it to my mother to call you. You know, we're adults now. You could have just told her to stay out of my business."

"Umm-hmm, you know that isn't going to happen. It's been a lifetime with our mothers meddling in our lives; it's what they do. Besides, it has its perks. I haven't seen or spoken to you for what now, three months? How else am I going to know what's going on in your life?"

"My life is not that complicated. I work and take care of Davey. That's it."

"Well, the last time I saw you, you had broken up with that new love of yours, and you were pretty much a wreck. I thought she was going to be the one for you."

"I was not a wreck! Davey is my priority, and she wasn't a good fit for him. She checked off a lot of important boxes, except one. You know my rule."

"I know, I know, anyone—"

"Anyone coming into my life must make room for him. That one didn't—end of story."

"So, now Davey is gone?"

"Oh, for God's sake! It's only for the year. He just wanted a male influence in his life. He's seven! It's good for him. I agreed to reach out to his father, and the rest is history."

"So that leaves you free, so to speak. Perhaps meet someone new?"

"What are you? Twelve? No, it doesn't leave me free. I'll pick up a few cases to keep me occupied. My last client used up more of my resources than anticipated, and my bank account is looking a bit thin for my liking."

Carole glanced at her friend, dropped the questioning, and remained quiet for the moment. After exiting the elevator, the pair headed out the lobby doors toward a tiny Italian bistro three blocks south of the FBI building. A crisp wind began to kick up, causing both women to gather their jacket collars tightly around the nape of their necks. With their heads down, they navigated the government districts' uneven sidewalk—the result of the city's utilities expansion project.

Neither one spoke until they arrived at the bistro. Once seated, Artie looked around and smiled. The family-owned restaurant had a quiet, kitschy, old-world vibe with woody décor, simple chairs, muted lighting, and an open kitchen. She opened the menu and scanned the offerings. Carbonara, risotto, osso buco, and of course, lasagne—all dishes she grew up with. She inhaled deeply, taking in the scents of oregano, alloro, and timo.

After ordering their meals, Carole glanced around the bistro.

"So, Artie. Given your bank account, I may have a case for you."

"You don't pay well."

"No, but someone who is keenly interested in this case does."

Artie narrowed her eyes, accepting a folder Carole held before her. She scanned the report while Carole briefed her on the earlier conversation with Smythe. After a few minutes, Artie surmised her own involvement had significant limitations.

"I'd rather protect someone who wants to be protected, Carole."

"Let me finish."

Carole's stomach began to churn, but she pressed into the conversation, methodically describing the case and investigation to her childhood friend and former colleague. Although department policy dictated no FBI agent should knowingly share information about a case without prior consent, she reasoned this case was important, not only to her career, but for the city overall. Drug money, prostitution, human trafficking—it was all on the rise, and so was the violence. Smythe's testimony would be key in striking a blow to the operation.

While Carole also understood the consequences to her otherwise stellar career if her Director discovered she leaked confidential information, she also knew resources were strained. Too much was happening in the city too fast. Local law enforcement could not keep up, and Carole's unit lacked the available personnel to keep Smythe under surveillance and protected 24 hours a day. She also had a hunch that other agencies would not protect Smythe to the extent she would need protecting, and of course, now Smythe had refused relocation. However, with some friendly persuasion, her old friend Artie had the flexibility *and* the resources.

"Sounds intriguing, but it taps even my teams. I've got eight, and two are out on assignment. You're asking for 24-hour protection for months, if not a full year. That's a hefty bill, Carole. Are you sure you can cover it?"

"Your benefactor has the necessary resources. I'm not at liberty to share who it is, but suffice it to say the resources are there."

"I'm not one to take a case without knowing who is behind the purse strings."

"If you trust me, Artie, trust that the benefactor is legitimate. Besides, I think this case is tied to something else. I won't share with you what I know, at least not yet, but I think the ramifications go beyond just the city."

Artie regarded Carole for a moment.

"You said she doesn't want to go into witness protection. Did she say why?"

"From what I gather, her life has changed. I know she recently resigned a corporate position and started her own business, so there is a financial consideration. She's also enrolled in some sort of year-long coaching program tied to her new business. Her father died recently, leaving her mother alone. Beyond that, I don't know. There is something about her, though. Something she may be hiding. I can feel it. All I can say is she seems hell-bent to make life my miserable."

Carole paused, her eyes meeting those of Artie's. "Does that sound a bit familiar?"

"Don't start with me. If it weren't for my hell-bentness, I wouldn't have started my own private security firm, and you wouldn't be talking to me about this case. If you ask me, she sounds like a woman who knows what she wants and is going after it, secrets and all."

"Even if it costs her her life, and me—this case."

Artie eyed Carole with suspicion.

"You up for it?"

Artie looked around the bistro, running her fingers through her hair. She calculated the number of teams it would take to protect Smythe. She would need to get involved and surveil the client to learn the rhythm of her days. Artie reasoned Smythe's recent resignation was a plus, as infiltrating an organization to keep a protective eye on a client was difficult at best.

She tapped her middle finger on the table, weighing the cost. After a minute or so, she nodded, determining the fee would not only cover the expenses of her teams, but her agency's balance sheet would also profit from this unknown benefactor. She pulled out a pocket notebook and wrote down a figure, sliding the scratches over to Carole.

"Yeah. I may regret it, but I'll take her on."

Chapter 5

The Moment That
Changed Everything

—

SMYTHE SAT IN THE NEARLY EMPTY PARKING GARAGE OF THE FBI building. She unclenched her teeth and relaxed her balled fist. Still unnerved by her conversation with the FBI agent, she replayed the agent's words again over and over again. "We don't want to alarm you…"

She slowly shook her head. *Have I fallen asleep? Especially to this? Am I so attached to what my future may bring that I am not living in this moment? Had I not quit my job, I wouldn't be in this current predicament.*

"Not helpful," she muttered aloud.

For Smythe, it now seemed a lifetime ago that she had relocated to the valley. During a particularly nasty economic downturn throughout the country, the government agency Smythe worked for incrementally made cuts to its staff. As the agency's Training and Development Manager, Smythe found herself laid off during the agency's third pass at reducing its spending. Her new unemployment status, coupled with the illness of her father, contributed to her decision to pack her bags and leave the comfort of her golden state and head for the state of sagebrush and silver where her parents lived.

With her mouth turned down and her eyes squinting in concentration, she continued to review the past six years since arriving in the valley. She reminded herself she had felt out of alignment—a more profound sense of belonging to something else.

With an extensive training background, she quickly found work as a corporate trainer in the tech industry. Highly educated, respected in her field of work, and making decent money, people who knew her thought she lived an enviable life. She was an influencer to corporate executives and traveled extensively. Yet, over time, she found she was not as open-hearted, vulnerable, or creative as she once had been. Instead, her generous spirit shriveled as she watched colleagues and managers alike seemingly bathe in greed, pettiness, and fear.

Dissatisfied with her employer, she began to ask herself what she truly wanted in her life. What did it look like? What type of work did she want to engage in that she would find fulfilling?

She held the questions lightly in her heart and eventually found herself applying to a year-long dual speaking and coaching program with one of her long-time mentors, a man considered to be one of America's best success coaches. After she was accepted into the program, she felt the shackles of heartache release, and she formulated a plan. She would combine her mentor's teaching with her background in coaching and training to develop her own company to help others aim higher and obtain the outcomes they sought in any area of their lives.

Smythe lifted her eyes and spoke aloud. "Those questions set everything in motion. Everything. The resignation of my job, my new field of study…"

Since following her soul's calling, she had returned to where she was. More thoughtful, generous, kind-hearted, and loving. Open heartedness had taken a front seat in her life, and she was at peace once again.

Yet, this murder mess… she thought, threatened to askew her homecoming.

Smythe glanced at her watch. It was much too late to visit the baker. His shop would be closed by the time she arrived. Instead, she chose to return home and study, perhaps find some nugget of information to spur her along.

What she found was a return to meditation. After settling onto her dining room chair, she opened her laptop. She watched a video that described the value of consistency in meditation, and thankfully, it offered several guided practices.

That day, and throughout her week, Smythe spent more time in meditation, a process she called *here-now*. She did not spend hours in meditation—*who has time for that,* she mused during her first foray—but found fifteen to thirty minutes was just enough time to ground her. She also discovered that when she peered too far into the future, she triggered anxiety. The process of meditation, however, counteracted those feelings. While the trial was never far from her thoughts, the elegant art of here-now allowed her to regain her sense of equanimity, making room for peace to quietly settle into the fabric of her days.

There were moments where concern threatened to upend her. It had been roughly two weeks since her meeting with the FBI. Since that raucous meeting, Smythe noticed when she was out and about a black SUV seemed to always drive in close proximity to her vehicle. It kept its distance, but it appeared to follow her wherever she went. On one occasion, she made a sudden left-hand turn and believed she lost the vehicle. Within minutes, however, the same SUV was two or three car lengths behind her.

One morning, Smythe sat in the baker's shop, feeling a bit rattled that someone may be following her. She searched her memory and recalled her earlier conversation with the FBI agent. At that moment, she chose to assume the SUV's driver was an agent assigned to protect her. The assumption, in a measured way, provided a certain level of comfort.

At least I'm safe.

The assumption bolstered her to move more freely about her community, and her fear, over time, abated. Funny thing about assumptions, though. Without the necessary confirming data, assumptions are often nothing more than the empty stories we tell ourselves.

* * *

The following morning, a morning like any other, Smythe awoke, made her bed, walked to the gym, and ran eight miles. After showering, she decided to complete a few errands prior to delving into her studies, choosing to complete them at a locals' favorite shopping area on Birch Avenue.

The Avenue, as it was aptly nicknamed, boasted several shops, including organic grocers, kitschy bookstores, outdoor cafes, clothing stores, and home décor outlets, providing the community with an eclectic shopping experience. Today, Smythe found it easy to check off her shopping list and lose herself for a few hours. She walked along a sidewalk in the developing urban district, located on the outskirts of the city's downtown area, which sat nestled among river birch and oak trees. Although not in bloom during the winter months, the abundance of birch trees provides the passerby a leafy green canopy during the warmer months of the summer, and a spectacular show of burnished yellow foliage in the fall. This morning, as she trotted along the winding walkways, she smiled at the emerging wildflowers as they sat basking in the warmth of the morning sun's rays.

Inside her favorite organic grocer, she meandered through the aisles. Unable to choose between two distinctly different bottles of red wine, she sprung for both. She paused to chat with a couple of store employees she had come to befriend. Both offered food recommendations, which were enough to satisfy her palate for an entire week.

After storing her groceries in her car, she ambled toward a sports clothier to find a couple of replacement running tops. Always in search of a deal, she found three tees for the price of two. Satisfied with the purchase, she returned to her car. She checked the time— 11:00 a.m. It was fairly quiet for a weekday, which suited her. She raised her head to the sun. It took the chill from the air and was bright enough to beckon her to throw caution to the wind.

Play hooky for a few more hours...

Yet, in the next breath, she felt a low-level sense of fear develop. Something felt different. She stopped and peered around The Avenue. She watched as sparrows flew overhead, landing a few feet from her car, pecking at the newly planted ferns along the walkway. Billowy clouds drifted overhead, and a couple passed her. *Young love,* she thought as they strode away, giggling while holding hands. Everything seemed perfectly ordinary, yet the feeling persisted. She took in a deep breath and focused on a slow exhalation. Nothing shifted. Unable to shake a growing sense of dread, she nudged herself to return home.

Time to go. You'll have plenty of time this weekend to goof off.

Smythe entered her car, pulled out of her parking space, and drove to the stoplight. She paired her phone to her car's audio system while she sat waiting in the left turn lane and began to listen to a podcast she had started earlier.

This'll do.

Seated in the passenger seat of a black SUV idling behind Smythe, Artie surveyed the area. Dressed in black khakis and a short sleeve black T-shirt covered by a windbreaker, she and one of her team members had walked a distance behind Smythe while she shopped. Yet, now, sitting in her vehicle, her central focus concerned Smythe's vulnerability, unnerved that Smythe took so many risks moving about the city alone.

Artie scanned the area slowly from left to right. Two-story stores flanked either side of the street. A few pedestrians walked the sidewalk, entering and exiting department stores. What few vehicles there were on the road moved easily down The Avenue. Still, her senses were on high alert. Without warning, her intuition was confirmed. A gray SUV accelerated at a high speed, approaching the intersection from the opposite direction. As the red light turned green, she watched in astonishment as Smythe proceeded through the intersection and into harm's way.

"What the hell is she doing, Dennis?!" Artie yelled. "Swing around her! Get between her and that truck!"

This is going to hurt, Artie thought.

The driver of the gray SUV approached the intersection and aimed his vehicle toward Smythe's car. The driver rolled his window down, allowing his passenger an unobstructed view. Raising a gun, she pointed it in Smythe's direction.

Unaware of the danger, Smythe quickly glanced to her right and continued to make her turn. She swept her eyes forward without seeing the present danger and entered the intersection. Then it registered.

Oh shit! I...

She gripped her steering wheel and jerked it hard to the left. With her foot still on the gas pedal, as if in slow motion, she felt herself losing control of her car, feeling it now beginning to balance on only its left wheels. Her shoulders stiffened, and she held her breath, closed her eyes, and braced for impact. The internal sensor control system warned her to brake. When she did not respond, it took over. Her car—now upright—came to an abrupt halt, causing her to slam her head against the top of the steering wheel. She heard the sickening wail of screeching tires and the grinding thump of fender against fender... yet she felt no impact.

Smythe lifted her head and glanced around. She watched as a woman opened the door of a black SUV—an SUV which now sat angled a few feet from her own, its back passenger side pushed in.

How did I not see that vehicle?

"I'm checking on her now!" Artie said. She jumped out of her SUV, both concern and fury etched across her face as she ran to the driver's side of Smythe's car.

Smythe pulled over to the right lane of a cross street, parking her car parallel to a fire hydrant. She unlocked her door and opened it. Attempting to compose herself, she reached across her console for her messenger bag. She became vaguely aware of the sound of running footsteps, and they sounded as if they were approaching her car. Her hands began to tremble, and her body grew cold. Beneath her growing panic, a single thought crept into her consciousness.

"You're safe!"

Smythe turned her body toward the stranger before gently placing her fingertips over her temple. "What? What happened? Where did you come from? Didn't I have the right of way?"

Artie pointed ahead to an SUV that had long sped away from the intersection. "That car attempted to ram you. I cut him off, and they hit the backside of my vehicle instead." She eyed Smythe.

Out and about with a bounty on her head! Is she crazy?

"Are you hurt? What's your name?"

One too many questions. "Smythe. My-my name is Smythe."

"Smythe, are you hurt?"

"No, I don't think so. I have my driver's license as identification."

"I don't need your ID. Remain in your car for a minute."

"What? No, I'm ok," Smythe mumbled. She struggled to maintain focus. Her head began to throb, and she fought nausea that threatened to overwhelm her. *Did this really just happen?*

"Don't tell me no!" Artie retorted. "Stay. In. The. Car!"

"Who are you?" Smythe barked. She winced in pain at the sound and tone of her voice.

"Now the gloves are off," she grumbled. *Don't tell me no? Who does she think she is?*

Without a word, Artie quickly and methodically inspected the exterior of Smythe's car. She glowered from the SUV to the surrounding intersection. She bent low, inspecting the undercarriage of the car. She reached into her jacket pocket, pulled out a small handheld telescopic mirror, and continued her inspection. Reaching her hand under the rear bumper, she found what she was searching for.

She pried the object loose and eyed the small, flat piece of metal that lay in the palm of her hand. Her eyes narrowed and she clenched her jaw, quietly growling. She allowed the object to tumble from her fingertips, crushing it beneath her black boot.

Smythe watched as vehicles moved around the intersection.

Who the hell is she? What is she looking for? Whoever tried to hit me is long gone...

Chapter 6

Return to Your Breath

—

"*Y*OU'RE SAFE!*"

Safe? The agent warned me of an impending threat. "Yet, I'm not safe," Smythe mumbled, shuddering at the thought of the near accident.

Artie quickly approached the driver's side of Smythe's vehicle.

Her eyes narrowed and pierced those of her new client. "You're safe now. We need to get you home and secured."

Smythe's trembling voice betrayed her. "Who-who are you?"

"My name is Artie."

"I think—I think someone tried to kill me!"

"I know!" Artie snapped, her New York accent becoming more pronounced.

"I've been hired to keep you safe, which is no easy feat since you don't seem to understand the gravity of the situation. Running around town without a care in the world! Are you nuts?"

What?!

Moving around to the passenger side, Artie spoke into an unseen com unit.

"Team 1, I'm jumping into the client's car. Move my vehicle and handle the police. Team 2, tuck in behind the client and stay close. We'll meet at the client's residence."

"Wait. What? I don't know you!"

Panicked at the thought of a complete stranger entering her car, Smythe reached to press her automatic door locks. Even so, Artie jumped into the passenger seat much too quickly for Smythe to react.

"Don't worry. Just drive. I'll explain along the way."

"No, wait. I need—"

"Just. Drive. Look, I know you're scared, but ya gotta trust me. I am not here to hurt you, nor am I going to take you to a safe house. Drive home. Just drive home. Now!"

Smythe stared blankly at the stranger. *Ok. She's obviously FBI. She's not going to force me into a safe house. I can go home. Just breathe, Smythe, just breathe.*

"Drive home," Smythe muttered.

"Yeah, just drive home."

Reluctant toward any forward movement, Smythe slowly turned her wheels. She glanced through her rearview mirror, assessing the damage of the stranger's dented vehicle. She wondered what damage had occurred to her own—a new pearl white, mid-sized, all-wheel-drive SUV. It was her baby. Coming directly from the manufacturer's assembly line, with just nine miles on the odometer, she waited two months until the dealer found the vehicle matching her request.

"Is there any damage to my car?"

"No damage, but mine is pretty banged up—thank you for asking."

Embarrassed she hadn't asked out of concern for the stranger's vehicle, Smythe glanced sheepishly toward Artie, gently nodding her head.

"Relax. My team'll take care of it. Keep driving."

"P-please. Who... who are you? You're with the FBI, ri-right?"

Stop it; she's friendly, Smythe reminded herself, as she worked to quell her stutter, which happened when she felt extreme fear.

"My name is Artie. We kinda met in the FBI building a few weeks back. I've been hired to protect you so that you can testify."

Similar to the narrow focus of her everyday life, Smythe missed the grander dance of the world around her. And she missed the Universe's direction. Go, stop, pause. If she would only but pay attention to its melody. But in the here-now moment, a moment where all are called to remain in the present without the internal chatter of one's thoughts, she became too narrowly focused on every word from this stranger, barely avoiding cross-traffic as she drove through a red light.

"Hey! Hey! Pay attention to the road, Smythe."

"I'm sorry. I-I'm more shaken than I thought. I'm not sure I want to go home. I don't know... I don't know you or that I can trust you. I-I want to, but maybe we should go to the FBI?"

Maybe I should pull over and run the hell out of my car.

"You're still too exposed." Artie gritted her teeth, taking in a deep breath before looking over at her new client. She watched as Smythe sat grimacing and squinting her eyes at the sunlight, her hands tightly squeezing the steering wheel.

"Do you have sunglasses in the car?"

"No, I left them at home, I think."

"Ok. Listen and try to relax," Artie gently encouraged her. "You live at 15 South Greenhurst Drive, Unit 552 on the ground floor. You park your car in front of your unit, which faces out to the parking lot. I know this because once you refused WitSec, I was hired to protect you. I get that you want freedom in your life, but right now, that life of freedom may cost you your life.

"I've been tailing you for the last two and a half weeks. You seem somewhat aloof—reclusive even, but when out and about, you're charismatic, funny, and thoughtful. You seem to have a lot of peoples' backs, and a lot of people seem to have yours. And right now, I'm going to need you to have mine."

Smythe heard the compliment but dismissed it. She did that thing she does, always does—she felt sorry for herself. Instead of receiving the kind words, all she felt was shame. Shame because she did not listen to the FBI agent who warned of a threat to her life. And shame because she sat in the parking lot alone at such a dangerous hour.

It was a ghost of a similar feeling she held in high school so many years ago. The African American group of kids at school would not accept her—they considered her skin too light and her hair too straight. For the white kids, her skin was too brown and her hair too curly. Besides, her perfectly round-looking glasses were just too nerdy, her grades too good, her voice too quiet and unsteady. Over time, she developed an intensely flawed belief *she* was something to be ashamed of and that her decision-making skills were just as flawed as she was. Shame.

Smythe blinked away the tears. She settled into her driving and thought about the signals that caused her to make the decisions she had made up until now. *The first step in changing anything is to know and accept that you have chosen it to be what it is. I have to accept what's in this moment.*

God, what's causing all of this mess?

I caused this. I can't blame this on anyone. I cannot even complain about it. I didn't go into witness protection like the agent said. God, Smythe. What were you thinking?!

Smythe took in a breath.

Not helpful. Stop blaming.

Why? Why didn't you listen to the agent? Now, look. A complete stranger is sitting in your car!

Smythe clenched her jaw and continued to drive. She looked out at the rolling hillside and wondered at the beauty of nature. *The trees seem to stand majestically in place, reaching up toward the heavens. Are they without a care?*

A deep knowing floated to the surface of her consciousness.

"Trust."

She caught the gentle thought in her heart and leaned forward as if to listen more clearly. It was hard for her to explain to anyone her understanding of the thought and where it came. So, she didn't try. It was too personal. But in her heart of hearts, she knew it came from her Beloved.

Raised as a Methodist, Smythe's early experience of God—or Beloved, as she'd now grown to know—had only added to her experience with shame. The God she was raised to believe in was a God to be feared. It was a God of judgment and retribution. God, to her, was a Being who hated anything that wasn't white, male, Christian, and heterosexual.

While attending university, her fear of God continued. In order to gather a more rounded understanding of this God she feared so much, she attended a variety of diverse religious gatherings, interviewing leaders and laypeople of many faiths. In the end, she realized many of them knew of God, but few had an experience *with* God. Smythe desperately wanted an experience. And so, quite simply, she started to ask questions of the grumpy God in the sky. Out loud.

Some would call it serendipity, but Smythe knew better. Her Beloved came through and answered her questions. It was hard for her to express how she knew it was the Spirit of God, but she had an inner knowing. At first, she would hear and feel the answer deep within her spirit. Yet, she wanted and needed outside confirmation without any forced effort on her part. So, her Beloved met her where she was. Through a book she by "happenstance" came across, or perhaps a comment someone would offer, she would often hear an internal comment, saying, "Here is the answer to your question." Her questions were constantly answered without her ever revealing aloud to anyone what her initial, private question had been. And it was life-changing.

"Learn to trust."

Yet, the egoic part of herself that loves to blame, complain, and shame her roared its voice and highjacked her thinking.

Think, Smythe. Think.

A frown formed around the corners of her mouth.

What did you think would happen? We're you just going to pretend everything was normal—that everything was going to be ok?! Whether you like it or not, you are a part of this murder mess now. Stop denying your responsibility!

Her internal flogging in full force, Smythe tightened her grip on the steering wheel and stared straight ahead.

Artie, on the other hand, made no further attempt to talk with her new client. Instead, she held a clipped conversation with a team member following behind them. To ease her internal angst, Smythe chose to return home using a two-lane back road. It was still a bit early in the year, and the hard cold that swept into the area was slowly beginning to release its grip upon the valley. Although the leaves had yet to bloom on the elm and birch trees that lined her route, Smythe began to understand that in their apparent slumber and stress, they were nonetheless preparing for new growth.

New growth, she sighed. *It has an annoying way of occurring under stress.*

"Once home take positions around her building. We won't know if the client's address is known until we get to the unit." The ominous tone of Artie's words drew Smythe to her present task—driving home.

The two-lane back road expanded into a bustling thoroughfare the closer Smythe advanced toward her home. She flipped her right turn signal on and glanced into her rearview mirror to ensure the trailing SUV would follow her. Winding her way through her neighborhood, a mixture of relief and trepidation washed over her as she neared her complex. The updated Spanish revival buildings sat unassumingly at the far end of a row of upscale homes. For Artie, the location of the complex was a plus. Unless someone knew the area well, it was quite possible to miss the complex entirely.

Smythe slowly drove onto a newly paved two-lane road leading to the property grounds. While flora and palm trees welcomed residents and visitors alike, signs also politely warned the driver their speed should not exceed a leisurely 10 mph. The caravan approached the leasing office, which sat at the end of the road with two remote-controlled gates located on either side of the building—the only drivable access points into and out of the complex.

Surrounded by lush green belts and walking paths, eight two-story buildings comprised the small community. Awash in light gray stucco, accented with dark brown trim and Spanish roofing tiles, each unit offered the latest in apartment design, giving residents a sense they entered into a standalone home. Built with nine-foot ceilings and custom finishes, including stainless steel appliances and quartz countertops, each unit seemed to whisper "welcome home" to its resident.

Artie spoke quietly into her com unit and began choreographing the movement of cars as Smythe used her remote to open one of the gates. She opened her window, motioning to her team to move forward while instructing Smythe to wait before proceeding to her unit. Team 2 slowly drove past her, adhering to the 10-mph sign. Artie scanned the parking areas as the caravan approached her building.

"Grab this spot on the end," Artie said.

Smythe spotted the open parking space near the corner of her building and headed for it, her tires slipping a bit as she rolled over the newly painted parking lines.

"Keep your car idling for a minute," Artie said.

Smythe parked her vehicle and followed Artie's instructions, watching the occupants of Team 2's car with rapt interest. They pulled into Smythe's assigned parking spot and kept their engine idling. Artie's second in charge, Dennis, exited the vehicle, scanning the rooftops in front of him before quickly striding to Smythe's apartment. His long legs covered the ground in just a few steps. The scene all but took Smythe's breath away.

They have been watching me.

She noted Dennis drew his weapon, the barrel of the gun pointing to the ground as he approached her apartment. Fear churned her stomach, and for a moment, she felt she would vomit. She could not help but think a lethal weapon was now drawn on her behalf. Every part of her begged to flee—her hands repeatedly releasing and contracting as she gripped her steering wheel.

Smythe glanced at her protector. A cold, empty feeling in the pit of her stomach threatened to drown her in panic. She wondered if this woman would also draw a weapon. She frantically searched her memory for a lifeline, and in searching, she found her breath. She simply inhaled deeply, willing herself to focus on the life that breath now offered her.

"I'll need the keys to your unit," Artie said, breaking into Smythe's thoughts.

"They're in my green bag on the floor," Smythe gulped.

Artie reached behind her, handing Smythe's messenger bag to her. She watched as Smythe's trembling hands rummaged through it. Smythe's skin further paled, and tiny beads of sweat formed around her forehead. Artie's eyes softened, and she extended her hand, lightly touching the top of Smythe's forearm to offer reassurance.

"Hey, Smythe. It's going to be ok. It's why I'm here. Just breathe and follow my instructions."

Smythe nodded, handing over her keys. As she glanced up, she was startled to find a second member from Team 2 had arrived. He stood with his back to her door, providing a protective shield, sweeping his head from left to right and searching for any additional threat.

With keys in hand, Artie exited the vehicle and headed toward the apartment. As she stepped onto the patio, she unknowingly answered Smythe's silent question. She drew her weapon from a holster hidden beneath her windbreaker in the small of her back. At the front door, she nodded to Dennis. Her eyes scanned the door frame before placing the key into the lock, slowly turning the handle to open the door.

She stood standing on the threshold and listened. No sound. She cautiously stepped inside, her eyes scanning the living room. A dark brown, vinyl faux hardwood covered the main living space, giving the unit a cohesive feel. The living room was framed by a large picture window nearly filling all of the front wall space. She noted Smythe furnished the room with a flair for the eclectic. With furniture ranging from mid-century modern to farmhouse, Smythe added a touch of traditional and boho pieces to add interest. She glanced at the collection of indigenous paintings and handcrafted pottery, nodding her head. A former FBI profiler, her interest in what her client surrounded herself with offered Artie additional information to her client's psycho-social makeup.

Knees bent, her hands pointing the weapon down her line of sight, Artie moved forward from the living room through a large archway into the dining room. A small, circular cherrywood dining table with matching fire engine red chairs sat in the middle of the space. A cherrywood cabinet stood against the far wall. The top shelf served as a bar with wine and whiskey glasses gathered on one side of the shelf, a variety of red wines and whiskey bottles placed on the opposite side. The remainder of the shelves Smythe used as a library, full of fiction and non-fiction works by some of her favorite authors.

Artie motioned to Dennis. With his weapon drawn down his sightline, he moved toward a closed closet on the opposite wall in the dining room. He checked the door frame for wiring, finding none. The closet was deep and served as the internal structure to a set of stairs for an upstairs unit. Very little was contained within it except for cleaning supplies, a small file cabinet, and several suitcases of varying sizes.

A breakfast bar divided the dining room from the galley kitchen. A well-used nook to the right of the breakfast bar held a countertop printer, pencil box stuffed with pens and pencils, an empty stationary holder, a variety of glue sticks, erasers, scissors, and a calculator.

The kitchen ended at the far side of the apartment. Dennis moved through the kitchen and opened the door to a compact laundry room, complete with a full-size washer and dryer with shelving above both.

While Dennis searched the kitchen, Artie continued into a small hallway. To her left was Smythe's bedroom. She peered in. At the center of the room sat a craftsman style sleigh bed. She bent low, checking the space underneath it. With her back against the wall, Artie swung open the door to a walk-in closet. Three hanging shoe caddies holding mostly running shoes of various colors and styles hung among her clothing. She noticed a large eighteenth-century steamer trunk sat opposite the bed, with a row of books displayed across the top. Two smaller, mismatched steamer trunks served as side tables. The room offered a small sitting area at the far end. Unlike the rest of the apartment, very little wall art was present in this room, save a sizeable multi-colored piece of canvas pop art, which hung above her bed.

Dennis checked the adjoining bathroom before meeting Artie in the hallway. She spoke into her com unit, confirming the safety of the unit to team members holding vigilance outside the apartment. Artie holstered her weapon. She returned to the dining room cabinet and scanned the library of books. Paulo Coehlo, Oriah Mountain Dreamer, and Jack Canfield were all heavily represented in the library with a number of additional works on topics including race, politics, spirituality, and psychology. Artie squinted her eyes, surveying the living room.

"Peaceful," Artie mumbled under her breath.

Satisfied with no present danger in the apartment, Artie left with Dennis following behind her. She stood outside the unit and surveyed the rooflines of the surrounding buildings before returning to Smythe's car. She motioned for Smythe to exit.

Eyes wide with fear, Smythe opened her car door and pointed to the trunk space. "I have packages in the car I need to grab. Some of them are perishable."

"I'll move your car and retrieve your packages for you, Ms. Daniels. Go inside now," Dennis replied.

Perspiration began to dampen Smythe's T-shirt. She hesitated momentarily before removing herself from her car. With Artie at her side, she swiftly crossed the sidewalk to her apartment. She could feel her shoulders relax and let out a slow sigh as she opened her door. As her foot stepped across the threshold, Smythe remembered the meaning of the word north again. North—the liminal space that offers us the ability to release the lessons we have learned from the past into our conscious moments of the present. The representation of wisdom; insight which allows for a deepening of our contemplative moments.

What have I learned? she thought as she slipped onto her sofa. She looked around, grinning at the sight of her humble abode.

She continued to scan her living room, becoming increasingly aware she was both mentally and physically exhausted. She closed her eyes and concentrated on breathing deeply from her diaphragm. With each exhalation, she silently spoke the word "relax."

Artie stood in front of the picture window with her back to Smythe and surveyed the all but empty parking lot. She opened the front door for Dennis, who arrived carrying Smythe's packages. He placed them on the countertop in the kitchen and turned toward Artie. After confirming her security team's assignments, Artie closed and locked the door behind him. She butted a security bar Smythe had purchased at the local hardware store shortly after the murder and secured it against the door. She then coded a verbal message to her team.

Artie turned toward her client. As though listening to a melody, Smythe's head was tilted to the side, and her eyes were closed. Artie watched the slow rise and fall of her client's torso and quietly remarked, "You're safe, Smythe. You're home, just as I promised you."

Smythe opened her eyes. She stared down at her hands resting upon her lap.

"How could I have allowed this to happen?"

"You can still go into witness—"

"No. I'm sorry, I've made my decision. I won't, but thank you for the offer," she retorted, stroking her hand along the top of her stubbly shaved head, her eyes piercing Artie's.

"Look, I'm on a really tight budget. I'm living off of my savings. I can't allocate the kind of money necessary for whatever this is."

"You won't have to allocate anything to me. It's been handled. And whatever *this* is, it's for your protection. You just need to stay alive."

Always one to hear the unspoken word and notice things unseen, Artie paused momentarily. Her intuition whispered that something much deeper than the attempted murder was at play in her new client.

"Whatever you are going through, Smythe, know that I have your back. You're not alone."

"Alone. That pretty much sums it up. I've come to know my neighbors' routine if that helps. On either side of me, they leave for work every morning between 7:00 and 7:30. They won't be home until after 5:30 this evening. I just thought you sh-should know."

Artie smiled and nodded her head.

Not exactly the life confession I was hoping for, but she's talking.

"I'm sure it must feel weird," Artie replied.

Before Smythe could respond, a loud bang filled the air. Smythe dropped to her knees and crouched low, her shaking arms covering her head. Artie took a defensive stance in front of Smythe and drew her weapon from its holster. The sound repeated. Artie's shoulders relaxed, and she slowly pointed her weapon to the floor.

"Team 2?"

"Team 2," came the response. "A passing moving truck backfired. Team 3 has arrived and is checking it out."

Artie acknowledged the information and turned toward Smythe. "Smythe, it's ok. We're all just a little jumpy. It was a moving truck. My team's gone to check it out."

Smythe slowly rose from the floor and entered her dining room. She paused as if a thought caught her attention. Darkness enveloped her internal sight. And slowly, she began to pace in circles.

Unaware of Artie's presence, Smythe continued to pace. *Help me, help me, help me,* she pleaded silently. Artie watched with curiosity as Smythe aimlessly walked around her dining room. She could see a vacancy in Smythe's eyes and quietly approached her. She reached out her hand to touch to Smythe's elbow. Smythe recoiled at the touch— lost in a memory she attempted to suppress.

"Don't scare me like that! Always—always tell me when you are approaching!"

Smythe lowered her head and grimaced. A headache had returned with a roar, and her ears were beginning to ring.

Return to your breath. Just breathe.

Alarmed at Smythe's reaction, Artie took a step closer to her client. "Hey. Hey. It's alright, Smythe. Look at me. C'mon, look at me." Artie gently said.

Smythe glanced up and into Artie's direction.

"I give you my word. You are safe. No bad guys."

"O-ok. I-I'm fine." Smythe was anything but fine. Cold beads of sweat began to form around her temples. Flashes of darkness continued to flood her consciousness as she struggled to suppress the panicked energy of an old acquaintance.

"Why don't you come into the living room and sit down. Catch your breath."

Smythe nodded her head slightly. She took Artie's advice and walked to the sofa, taking a seat on the far end of it. Artie followed behind her and crouched to the side of Smythe, resting her hand upon the armrest.

"Do you have a headache?"

"Yes, a bit."

"How about nausea or dizziness?"

"Initially, yes, but not as much. Just a headache. And my ears are ringing."

Smythe opened her mouth wide several times in an attempt to stop the ringing. Artie asked a few more questions before concluding her client probably had developed a concussion.

"So, I have a suggestion. Just for today, let's restrict your movements. Rest for a bit."

As Artie moved onto the sofa next to her, Smythe detected an aromatic scent of lavender. She smiled slightly, recalling the lavender fields of her youth while living in Europe. She remembered the calming effect the fragrance had upon her. Inhaling deeply, she allowed the scent to infuse her soul, providing reassurance to an otherwise chaotic day.

Chapter 7

Choose Wisely

—

"ARTIE? WILL I BE ABLE TO MOVE ABOUT MY NORMAL ROUTINE? I mean, I'm feeling the need to visit an old friend at a baker's shop that I go to most mornings. Well, except for the morning of the murder."

"You mean, Joao's?"

"Yes, you know it?"

"Yeah, I know it. Remember, I've been watching you for a bit."

"Oh." Feeling a bit embarrassed, she asked, "Did you get a pastry?"

"Yes, and coffee. He's a funny little guy, that baker."

"You mean his first question?"

"Yeah. When I placed my order, he offered me a second pastry and said, 'Choose wisely.' Kinda weird, right?"

Smythe understood. She had become very familiar with her quirky friend. Upon arrival at the baker's shop, each customer was asked a simple question. "What may I offer you?" After the first selection is made, he then asks his customers what their second selection will be and cautions, "Choose wisely." Regulars like Smythe understand the invitation. The customer pays for their initial selection of a pastry. He then offers the customer another at his expense.

Most new customers refuse his offer. If they do make an additional selection, it is typically a duplicate of their first or something they are familiar with. So hurried to get to the next task of the day, or perhaps too unimaginative, many of his customers miss the opportunity to interact with this wise man. The invitation, she discovered, is to choose something outside of one's habit.

"The baker always greets new customers with that phrase. So much of the time, we want predictability," Smythe shared. "So, we often purchase what we know; we stay in the same old lane. The baker calls it the Camazozt Principle, from the book *A Wrinkle in Time.*"

"The what?"

"The Camazozt Principle. It's where everybody in this neighborhood on a different planet did the same thing in perfect unison. No questions were asked, and no choices were offered. The characters almost seemed fearful of deviating from the expected norm. Joao loved that book. He said he watched the movie three times."

Smythe smiled as she remembered her friend recalling scenes from the movie.

"The baker offers choices that we know and are comfortable with," Smythe continued, "as well as the risk of choosing something different—something outside of our normal habit. Since you've been to his shop, you know he has a standard list of pastries to choose from, but he also creates selections that have never been made before, and may not be made again. I know because I've often selected pastries of the day that were so mouth-wateringly delicious that when I went to order one the following day, I discovered they weren't there anymore! It's not uncommon those special pastries are not repeated for weeks, if not months. Unfortunately for those who will not choose something different, the opportunity is lost. For those of us who do choose, well, you get the idea. Did you choose a second pastry?"

Listening intently to her new client, Artie smiled. "I did. It was so unusual. The texture was so light and fluffy; it seemed to melt in my mouth. I gotta say, I savored every bite. And like you said, it wasn't available the next day, which was a real bummer."

Smythe frowned. "Did you visit the bakery before following me?"

"To be honest—no, I hadn't. So, thank you for stopping by. It's a delightful, if not quirky hangout for me."

"My favorites are his malasadas," Artie continued. "I must confess, I've ordered them each time I've entered the bakery while checking in on you. The last time I had one was at Leonard's Bakery on Oahu a few years ago."

Smythe grinned sheepishly. "I didn't really notice you. I think I'm glad I didn't—notice you, that is. Probably would have freaked me out a bit."

"Good! I'm glad to know I was stealthy enough. You weren't supposed to notice."

Smythe blushed and changed the subject. "His malasadas are my favorite, too. I haven't tried them on Oahu, although I hear they are amazing. I'm hoping to go back one day. Forget the ocean or the hotel room—I swear I'll head straight for the shop from the airport!"

"You'll find they're similar but ever so slightly different. Each delicious in their own way."

"Can I go see him?"

"You mean the baker? Right now? Yeah, no."

Artie frowned and looked at her watch. "It would be closed by the time we got there. You can go tomorrow, if you must. But honestly, you're looking a little pale. I'd really prefer you rest. If you're hungry, let's order in instead. If you are up to it, maybe watch a movie? Do you have Netflix?"

"Yes, I do."

"Ok, then. Why don't you go get comfortable? Take a pain reliever if you have to, but don't take anything other than acetaminophen. I'll have my team deliver something to eat. Any preferences?"

"I'm kind of picky. I'm not a fan of beef, pork, chicken, or broccoli. With that said, I do love Asian food."

"So do I. It's settled, then, vegetarian Asian food it is. Go get comfortable."

"This may sound weird, but are you or your someone from your team going to be staying here? I mean, in the apartment, overnight. Or will you be outside? I'm not quite sure how this all works."

"Yeah. I'm hanging here during the evening and night hours."

Artie caught the slight frown that furrowed Smythe's brow.

"I'm sorry, I've created what's called a double layer of protection for you. It's going to require protection both in your unit and outside of it. Especially now, after an attempt was made on your life."

She paused for a moment.

"I've arranged for an air mattress to be delivered. I'll put it up every night and take it down every morning. I'm already having sheets and towels delivered so that I don't inconvenience you too much."

"Oh, hmm, ok. No, it's-it's ok. I was just wondering. I do have extra sheets and towels, and I wash them every week. I use environmentally safe detergent and it's really good on the skin—that is, if you have allergies to harsh chemicals. You don't need to buy them."

Artie smiled warmly at the offer. "It's ok; it's covered. Go do what you do. I'll handle everything else."

Artie's gaze followed Smythe as she moved into the kitchen. She regarded her client for a moment. She had a hunch. She hoped this first evening would be an opportunity to get to know Smythe. The more she knew her, the easier it would be to gain her trust and cooperation. She would soon discover her instincts would prove accurate.

Smythe put away her groceries before retreating into her bathroom. She followed Artie's advice and removed a couple of pain relievers from their bottle and turned on the faucet sink. Holding the pills in her hand, she stared at herself in the mirror, tracing her index finger around her reflection. She shook her head, popped the pills in her mouth, followed by a palmful of water before taking a long hot shower.

Smythe stood, savoring the stream of water as it cascaded over the top of her head, finding its path down the length of her body. Soaking in the healing properties of the steamy shower, she pondered her circumstances. She considered her options, finally making the only decision that felt reasonable. Few choices would keep her alive and free, except the one who now sat in her living room and outside her front door. The deciding factor was the word—*free*. Remembering the airline instruction, "Feel free to roam about the cabin," Smythe smiled. In some ways, she felt a sense of relief with a security agency now attached to her.

Refreshed after her shower, Smythe changed into a T-shirt and sweatpants. She appeared from the bathroom and cleared her dining room table, which served as a makeshift desk. A short time later, Team 1 delivered food, clothes, toiletries, sheets, a single blowup mattress bed, several clips for Artie's weapon, and a duffle bag. Artie rummaged through the duffle bag before placing it in the dining room closet along with her other belongings.

Artie observed her client closely as they shared a companionable, early dinner. She made several attempts to convince Smythe to get bed rest, but in the end, acquiesced to Smythe's objections. They settled into the living room and continued to exchange small talk before choosing two comedy movies to while away the afternoon and evening.

With each passing hour, Smythe's body became heavier.

"I think you're right. I need to go to bed. I'm finding I'm more bushed than I thought."

"Good choice," Artie replied.

Smythe slowly rose from the sofa and walked into her bathroom and opened the pantry door. When she returned, she held a blanket and pillow for Artie. Artie accepted the items and watched as her client retreated to her bedroom. Satisfied that Smythe was tucked away for the evening, she checked in with her night crew before spending a couple of hours developing security plans for the following day. A visit to the baker was at the top of her list.

"An unnecessary risk," Artie mumbled. "She just doesn't comprehend it yet."

* * *

The next morning, Smythe arose well before dawn. While her headache subsided overnight, another ache had settled into her soul. She felt engulfed by its energy and desperate to see the baker. She hoped his simple presence would ease the gnawing sense of dread she felt. If she were completely honest with herself, while a security detail brought a certain level of comfort to her, they also frightened her. Their weapons and companionship served as a constant reminder of the murder she witnessed and the recent attack on her own life.

She showered, dressed, and attempted to spend a few minutes reading in her room. Unable to concentrate on one of her new books, she gave up and snapped it shut.

In the living room, Artie sat up and listened as Smythe rustled around in the bathroom and then her bedroom. She rose quickly, showered, and dressed, preparing for Smythe's appearance. She disassembled her blowup mattress and glanced around the living room. For a moment, she thought of allowing Smythe her space. Yet, she dismissed the thought as nothing more than wanting the convenience and comfort of her own home rather than the discomfort of a blowup mattress each night. She placed the disassembled mattress in the dining room closet, pulled out her laptop, and reviewed her notes from the previous day.

Smythe continued to sit in her armchair. *Why so restless? You're safe.*

She glanced at her alarm clock.

God, it's only 3:00 a.m. Much too early to leave.

Smythe sighed. She rose from her chair, walking quietly toward her steamer trunk. There she picked up her tablet and opened it. She searched through her files until she found a meditation led by her mentor. Returning to her chair, she slowly closed her eyes and deepened her breathing.

Feeling calmer after twenty minutes, Smythe opened her eyes and steeled herself.

It's going to be ok. Just greet her. And try not to be so geeky or mean.

Smythe exited her bedroom and walked into the dining room, finding Artie sitting on the sofa, hunched over her laptop.

"Hi. How did you sleep?" Smythe asked, forcing a half-smile.

"Fine. How about you?"

"Nothing that a tenth of a muscle relaxer couldn't fix." She watched as Artie rose from the sofa and pulled out the duffle bag from the closet.

"I'd like to go to the baker's shop."

Artie frowned. "I know." She turned to look at Smythe.

"We'll go, but before we do, I need to outfit you a bit." Artie lifted up a black bulletproof vest and reinforced mesh sports cap from her bag and handed them to Smythe.

"Put the vest on under your sweatshirt. I need you to wear both the vest and hat when you're out in public. It'll deflect any flying debris."

"You mean bullets."

"I mean bullets."

Smythe accepted the vest and cap. *Dear God. This can't be happening.*

"It should be easy enough to figure out, but ask for help if you can't. One arm in and then the other."

"I think I can manage, thank you."

Smythe lowered her head with the cap and vest in her hands and returned to her bedroom. She laid the vest upon her bed, her fingers lightly touching the nylon. It felt stiff beneath her touch. She took off her sweatshirt and found a T-shirt in her closet and put it on. She lifted the vest from her bed. Placing one arm through the opening and then the other, it felt heavier and more confining than it looked. She fastened the vest tightly to her torso. She slipped her sweatshirt on over and returned to the living room, stopping before Artie. Artie smiled, asked permission to lift the sweatshirt and inspected the fit of the vest. She gave an approving nod, taking the cap and placing it on Smythe's head.

"There. You're good. Let's go."

"Just so you know, I'm not a fan of baseball caps."

"Neither am I, but it's necessary."

With Smythe behind her, Artie exited the apartment. Team 2 positioned themselves at the front door and directed Smythe to their vehicle. Smythe, however, had other plans. She made a beeline for her own SUV and climbed into the driver's seat. Artie paused for a moment, her eyes harpooning a glare into the back of Smythe's head.

Driving! What next?! Might as well wear a sign. Here I am!

Artie looked at her team. "Did you inspect her vehicle?"

"We did. It's all clear."

Artie sighed. "Alright, then." She pursed her lips. Her tactical training required she place her client in the back of her team's' vehicle, yet she also reasoned she needed Smythe's trust.

Another give.

She shook her head and strode around to the passenger side of Smythe's vehicle and got in.

"Is there a problem?" Smythe asked.

"It's foolhardy for you to drive and for me to allow you to drive. But then again, I can often be a fool. For now, I'll let it slide. You'll drive, but only between both of my vehicles. No wobbling. First sign of trouble, you better follow my instructions to the letter. Understood?"

"Yup."

"When you are out, turn off your cellphone and disengage Siri."

Smythe pulled her phone from her messenger bag and turned her guidance system off before shutting down the phone completely.

Sandwiched between her two security SUVs, Smythe made her way through the sleepy enclave and wondered at the entirety of it all.

Just a short time ago, my life had such a different trajectory. Yet now, on a day like any other, I've got armed security on two sides of me. How did this get to be so out of control?

Smythe continued along the route Artie mapped out. She looked toward the heavens and quietly mouthed, "Help me." As always, the Universe responded—perhaps in ways she did not understand, or want. But responded.

Chapter 8

Litter or Treasure?

—

N ESTLED BETWEEN SMYTHE'S SUBURBAN VILLAGE AND THE LARGER city, the baker's shop sat along a sparsely traveled road. A collection of family-owned dry cleaners that specialized in difficult alterations, sure to impress even the most finicky of clients; a small used book store that prided itself as "a store full of welcome," and a large grocery store sat on either side of the baker's shop.

Her first visit to the baker's shop occurred several months ago. A co-worker recommended the bakery to her, raving about the fluffy deliciousness of his signature pastry—malasadas. Excited to try someplace new, she plugged the address into her phone and headed for her treat. Her mouth watered as she thought about the pastries she would order. A maple bar would be high on her list. And yes, she thought, she would try a malasada, too. She parked directly in front of the shop, yet when she pulled on the front door, she found it locked.

Confused, she stood staring blankly into the shop's window. She checked the sign. Open at 5:00 a.m. She then checked her watch—4:00 a.m. A bit embarrassed by her mistake, she turned to walk away, but the tinkle of a bell caused her to pause. She turned toward the sound, and the gentle voice of a man called out to her.

"Hello. You wish to order?"

Smythe smiled widely. "Yes, I would. I very much would like to order."

"Welcome, welcome my friend, please come in."

Smythe described the baker to her friends as an older, petite, Portuguese man with more salt than pepper in his dark brown hair and the kindest dark eyes that allowed one to drink in divinity. He stood no more than five feet eight inches tall and walked with a slight limp, which, over time, became more pronounced.

From the first day, and almost every day thereafter, the baker moved to the rhythm of Smythe's arrival. With a broad smile and a starlit gaze, he engaged her in warm conversation while he prepared his shop to open. The smell of pastries wafted through the shop as he busied himself, placing pastries onto cooling racks, setting chairs in place, starting coffee, and heating water for tea. Before ordering food and coffee, Smythe would empty her messenger bag onto the furthest booth away from the door. It looked more like an office desk with her iPad, assortment of books, journals, and pencils neatly placed on the table. She would sit quietly for an hour or so, observing the flow of patrons in and out of the shop, before heading to work.

After the murder, she often sat for half the day, longing for the comforting presence of her friend. This morning would be no different, except now, Artie was at her side.

In order for Smythe to move about the city, Artie developed a three-car caravan of security personnel whenever she traveled. Each member had a law enforcement background, and each vehicle held a two-person, plain-clothes-wearing, armed security team.

As the caravan approached the shop, Artie directed Smythe to park her vehicle in an alley beside the collection of storefronts. The alley was wide enough for other vehicles to pass, but, more importantly, hid their bakery visit from the general public. Artie quickly exited the car, her weapon drawn in front of her as she scanned the area. The only light offering any measure of sight was a flickering lamppost, providing only the dimmest of illumination. She squinted her eyes, slowly turning her head, searching the empty alley for any sign of threat. Prepared for any contingency, Artie stationed one team vehicle in front of Smythe's car, a second team vehicle near the front of the shop, and a third team vehicle sat in a small area directly behind the bakery. After surveilling the area, Artie opened Smythe's door, ushering her toward the front door of the bakery.

The baker watched as Smythe's car passed by his shop and now stood waiting at the door. He smiled widely at the sight of Smythe as the pair approached and unlocked it. "You have brought a friend, I see. Welcome, please come in."

The overhead pendant lights offered a warm and inviting atmosphere to the shop, rebuffing the chill of the early morning air. Smythe smiled as she entered. *It is good to be in the presence of my friend at a time like this,* she thought. Clearing her throat, she replied, "Hi, Joao. Yes, I did. I hope you don't mind. This is Artie."

"I do not mind. She has been here many times. She seems to come in right at the time the shop opens."

He directed his starlit gaze toward Artie, "It is good to see you again. What may I offer you?"

Artie nodded toward the baker and eyed the partially filled display cases. Her stomach lurched a bit as she thought about biting into a pastry so early in the morning.

"I'll wait on the pastries. Too early. I do need a large coffee, though, if it's ready."

"One coffee coming up."

While the baker tended to her coffee, Artie swept the shop with her eyes. The shop was small, holding only four slate-gray booths anchored along the wall opposite three display cases. Less than half a dozen smaller tables sat in the middle of the shop. The white tile, speckled with gray inlaid flecks, held a brightness that glimmered against the white walls. The baker celebrated his heritage by adorning the walls with colorful images of Portugal. Picturesque paintings of simple, white façade homes and cobbled streets, along with lush, mountainous countrysides hung on the walls. As an avid football fan, or soccer as the sport is called in the west, several smaller images of the country's national football team were well represented.

Artie reached into her pocket and pulled out a small, silver money clip holding several twenty-dollar bills. The baker smiled, waving off her attempt at payment as he handed Artie her coffee.

"You will want pastries later. Remind me and pay then."

Artie's stern face softened, and she politely thanked him for his offer. She chose a seat at a table near the middle of the shop. It was from there, she surmised, she had a clear vantage point of everyone entering and exiting the shop.

"For you, Smythe, what may I offer?"

Smythe smiled at her friend.

"An ear?"

She moved to her usual booth and took a seat that offered her a full view of the bakery. The baker gingerly followed behind her, sitting in the opposite banquette. He studied Smythe's furrowed forehead, glimpsing the sorrow that darkened her eyes behind her glasses.

"Why so troubled, my friend?"

Smythe glanced in Artie's direction. She remembered the FBI agent's warning to tell no one what she witnessed, yet she needed to tell someone. She took in a breath.

"They tried to kill me!" She finally blurted out. With tears streaming down her face, she poured out her story.

"I'm afraid, Joao, I am so afraid. I thought—I thought, I was strong, but inside I'm quaking."

"Hooray for you, my friend!"

Confused and somewhat incensed, Smythe retorted, "What?! Didn't you hear me? They. Tried. To. Kill. Me! How is this a celebration?"

The baker sat very still. He gazed deeply into Smythe's dark brown eyes and smiled.

"My friend, you are here, so they did not succeed. This is cause to celebrate. The Universe took care of you."

Smythe flashed to the day she felt called to resign her position. After arriving home one morning, feigning illness, she struggled to figure out what she wanted out of life. After a time, she felt a question surface from the bottom of her heart that caused her spirit to stand at attention, an expanse blossoming within her. Yet, the mere presence of the question also surfaced a rolling tension. She listened again, asking for clarity. For it seemed here, in the midst of her misery, in the form of a question, was her answer.

Feeling as though pinned against a wall, she paced back and forth in front of her stove. *You're not ready,* she thought. *How will you survive? What will people think? What will your mother think? This is ludicrous!* Yet, the question remained.

She thought about her Beloved, whose presence now overwhelmed her. She knew her Beloved had her best interest at heart, yet the question terrified her. Her response required a level of trust she was unsure she could willingly offer. No longer satisfied with the approval of others, she knew it was time to follow her soul's calling.

The question then became, quite simply, "Will you trust me?" Smythe knew it required a response. Her head bowed low, she peered out her living room window. She mouthed a fearful "Yes," knowing full well she was about to resign from her position.

"How did the Universe take care of me? I'm wracked with fear. My mind keeps replaying yesterday's events. I'm unable to write, and I have armed security now in my house 24/7. This isn't what I had in mind when I said 'yes' so many weeks ago to the Universe! I had other plans. I was going to write, read, learn, create. I'm taking 12 months to pull it all together, living off my savings. I thought I was doing what my Beloved wanted me to do. I took a leap of faith. Finally, I took a fucking leap of faith. And for what?! This? Why did this happen, Joao? How could this happen? I thought I was finally following my heart's calling, and now this."

Artie, who sat only a few tables from Smythe, could hear every word her client spoke. The level of vulnerability Smythe expressed was a far cry from what she displayed just a short time ago. This was raw and unfiltered. More importantly, she thought it offered new insight into her client's psyche. Staring coldly out the front window, Artie's shoulders began to stiffen. She took in a deep breath and held it for several seconds before releasing it.

"All paths are littered. You must first see, my friend, what the litter is and then turn it into treasure."

"Well, I would call witnessing a murder and then having my own life threatened as litter!"

"It takes great courage to get up in the face of adversity. Great courage. Even more so when your physical life is in danger. Yet, here you are. You have faced the darkness and overcome." The baker paused for a moment, searching Smythe's eyes. "Did you not ask for this?"

"What? Ask for this?!" Smythe narrowed her eyes. "Why would I ask for this? Who would ask for this? No one in their right mind would ask for this!"

"Did you not say you heard a calling deep within you. Something that kept tapping you on your shoulder?"

"Yes, but—"

"So, the journey has begun!"

Smythe sat, stunned, her mouth agape.

"My daughter, you are so attached to the 'how' things should be to get the thing or experience you desire. You live in the busyness of getting on with your life, but you have forgotten to live in the present be-ing of your life.

"What do you mean, Joao?"

"You seek to become something and to live from that place. You do not understand that you are *already* something. There is nothing to become but who you really are. You must simply be present in each moment that comes your way. That, my, friend is be-ing. In the be-ing of your life, you will follow the path set before you. But you made a decision and believed that was it—that all would be well, didn't you?" Not waiting for her reply, he continued.

"It is good to have a vision of what you desire. But you must also let go of *how* it happens by remaining in the moment of be-ing. Now, there are always, how you say... circumstances along the way, and you must always respond. That is a form of be-ing. This killing, it is litter, yes? Tell me, what is the treasure?"

"I don't know, Joao."

"Yes, you do. What is the treasure?"

This was *not* what Smythe was expecting or hoping for. She wanted a hug from her friend, comforting words, even. Instead, she was experiencing tough truths. She thought again of her mentor Philip Caulfeld. In the first chapter of his book, he discussed taking full responsibility in every area of life by managing the reaction to the events as they occurred. It was a difficult chapter for her to navigate, yet, in the end, she recognized that she had not been taking control of her responses. She had been allowing life to happen to her—making excuses, blaming, complaining, and avoiding every bad decision she made. The good that occurred, she attributed to nothing more than luck or her Beloved's intervention. She had fallen asleep within her life, and this form of sleepwalking slowly developed insidiously over the course of her life.

"So, you're saying I am responsible for this mess?"

"Did I?"

"How could I be? I didn't ask to see the murder. I didn't ask to get involved."

"Yet you did, and here you are."

"So, if I got cancer, I would be responsible for that, too?"

"You smoke, no?"

"Yes, but—yes."

"I know the Universe, yet, I do not know *how* the Universe works. But, all things in our path may hold a treasure. What is your treasure?"

With her head bowed low, Smythe sat and reasoned with herself. She remembered all of the times she read about or watched someone engage in a heroic event. Someone who had overcome their challenges. Someone who, against all odds, stayed the course and attained their goal. She remembered the conflict as part of the hero's journey. The hero ventured out into the unknown to obtain what they sought. They faced unexpected conflict, but ultimately triumphed over adversity. Her face softened as she recalled wishing for that same kind of courage and steadfastness. She wanted to overcome all odds and become a success story in her own life.

"Courage. I wanted courage, but it doesn't feel like courage. It feels like fear."

The baker beamed with delight.

"When we see people who face great struggle, we only see the action. We imagine they stood strong with this thing called courage. We imagine the person felt nothing but a conviction to do that which they were doing. Yet, my friend, we do not see the inward struggle. We do not see their fear. Think on this. I must, for a moment, tend to my creations before my other guests begin their arrival."

Artie sat, smiling to herself. She understood only now the importance of this human in Smythe's life.

Smythe began to reflect upon her responses to events great and small along her own journey.

It's been fear. So much fear. My life, ruled by it. So afraid of taking a risk, afraid of failing. What had Philip said? "Fear is nothing more than fantasized events appearing real." I could have struck out on my own so long ago, followed a different path. But I allowed myself to be ruled by fear cloaked as practicality. It just kept me stuck, never really moving toward what I truly wanted.

Eventually, she began to understand that when her mind focused on fear, it placed her in an emotional cage. She reviewed some pivotal past decisions and noticed when focused on the "what if's," she attempted to outthink and control every situation in which she found herself. She often reacted out of fear. Fear, she comprehended, lived only in her thoughts and was based on past events and experience. She had listened only to the bellow of her ego in the recent past, the constant "I," instead of her heart—the songstress of the "I AM."

In the end, she knew fear often caused her a paralysis—one that stunted the life she was capable of creating, building such a thick brick wall around her soul, she could no longer clearly hear her songstress. Brick by brick, so afraid of making the slightest mistake, she eventually sheltered herself from what she truly wanted—a life of possibility.

Instead of thinking about what could go right, and moving in that direction, I've allowed myself to be ruled by what could go wrong.

As she continued to examine her past choices, she remembered one of her book treasures, *Conversations with God and Uncommon Dialogue* by Neal Donald Walsch. "Through God," he had written, "the way to reduce the pain you associate with earthly experiences and events, both yours and those of others, is to change the way you behold them…" He went on, in part, "You cannot change the outer event, so you must change the inner experience."

Muttering to herself, she remembered a quote, "Our actions are based on only two things, love or fear." Both have a different energy signature.

As a sponge sitting in warm soapy water, gently used to scrub away the dirt from a well-used plate, Smythe sat soaking in all of her previous readings. She understood that fear was simply an emotion of the past. A signpost of previous experiences. She only had to pay attention and make considerations about the choices set before her now. Here, in this moment, she could choose to change her internal responses to her here-now present moment, or choose the old pattern of fear.

Easily brought to tears, Smythe's eyes began to water.

No more ostrich hiding, even though my emotions are barking a different story. I can break my soul's heart yet again, or I can continue to take the next step.

Her concentration was broken by the sound of Artie's voice. She stood standing at the counter, asking the baker for three malasadas and a new creation he just placed in one of the display cases. Artie turned toward Smythe and asked if she wanted anything.

"I think three malasadas and a coffee, if you don't mind."

Artie smiled and nodded to the baker to add the additional items. Smythe rummaged through her messenger bag and found her wallet, sliding out of her seat to join Artie at the counter. She took the box from the baker, laid her cash on the counter, and returned to her table. Artie picked up a newspaper next to the cash register before walking quietly back to Smythe's booth and handing over her coffee. Smythe separated the pastries and placed them on two plates, handing one to Artie. With a simple nod, Artie turned toward her own table.

"Aren't you going to join me?" Smythe asked.

"Nah. You and the baker have yet to finish your conversation," Artie responded tenderly.

Artie offered Smythe a smile and returned her own table. She opened the newspaper, scanning for information on the upcoming trial and Smythe's role in it. She stopped to bite into the baker's new creation and savored the sweet, delicate texture of the pastry.

God, this is good.

The baker returned to Smythe's booth and slid into his seat. Smythe looked down at her coffee.

"I look back and think of how, just a few years ago, I was swept up in a reduction in force event."

The baker tilted his head in confusion.

"A layoff is the simplest explanation. My position was eliminated. At any rate—I would have never guessed that some years later, I would be sitting here, starting my own business, defining the thing I do for a living. It's as if I am rediscovering the seeds of my life. Yet, in the midst of it all, I'm forced to deal with a murder trial with me as its star witness. All I ever wanted to do when this all began was to follow my Beloved's direction. In essence, I wanted to offer others some measure of hope and assistance in the midst of their own circumstances. It seems a bit ridiculous now."

The baker appeared to look past Smythe to the hallway that led to his kitchen. When he finally spoke, the air seemed to still, and a palpable peace settled into the very fabric of the shop. He spoke so softly that he appeared to only mouth his words.

"When the sun only begins to rise, a wind often arises with it. If it has been windy through the night, the force of the wind often becomes stronger as the light of the morning sun begins to break through the darkness of nighttime. Yet nothing can stop the sun from rising—not even the force of the wind. It is similar for all things. When we emerge from our slumber and set out on our journey, many things occur along the way. They are neither good nor bad. They just are. We must overcome that which we perceive as struggle and keep going."

He paused for a moment to allow Smythe to think. With a glint in his eye, he continued, "Just as we are to reach that which we have been moving toward, the forces of life become even stronger, but they exist only to teach us that which we have learned—and perhaps to test us. Just perhaps. I do not know of the testing part, but I do know that courage and fear are two sides of the same coin. Both sides light our way. Face the fear of your past and move through it. Remember, you are in the process of be-ing and undoing."

"I thought I knew what I wanted, but with the chaos around me, I find myself unsure."

"Allow the mystery of the unknown to guide you, my daughter. Think on these things."

Chapter 9

The Choice Is Yours

—

T HE TINKLING OF A SMALL BELL SOUNDED AS A NEW CUSTOMER entered the shop. The baker slowly rose from the table, turning to greet the customer as she walked through the door.

"Ahhh, hello, my friend—and welcome. What shall I offer you? Choose wisely."

Smythe glanced in Artie's direction. Artie had not removed her gaze from the stranger.

Choose wisely.

A woman in her early thirties, dressed in trimmed black blouse, blazer, and slacks, sporting a thick, black overcoat warm enough to push out the early morning cold, strode toward the display counter. She stood before it and offered the baker a courteous smile and whispered, "Mahalo."

Smythe watched Artie, perplexed by her change in posture. Her eyes danced between watching Artie and watching the stranger. Smythe saw the woman as nothing more than a customer looking forward to a pasty before heading off to work or whatever awaited her for the day.

Yet, Artie sensed danger. She sat more erect in her chair, and her fists and jaw began to tighten. Forcing her breathing to slow, she could hear every sound in the shop, and something felt... off.

She narrowed her eyes as the stranger moved slowly from one display case to the next. The woman held no purse or pocketbook, and the overcoat was a bit too heavy for this time of year.

"Give me a moment to decide, brah," the stranger politely said.

Artie did not wait to determine whether what she was sensing emanated from this customer or something else in the area. With the stranger's back to Artie, she tapped into her com unit, signaling her team. She placed her hand underneath her jacket to the small of her back and unsnapped her weapon's holster. She rose slowly from her chair, gesturing to Smythe as she moved toward her.

Team 1 and a member of Team 2 entered the bakery moments later. Dressed in casual business attire, they appeared to be nothing more than additional customers. One team member stood behind the woman and the other two walked to the side of a display case, appearing to peruse the pastries, severing any direct threat or sight to Smythe or Artie. The woman continued to look at the display of pastries. She glanced at the agents out of the corner of her eye, offering them a polite smile. She moved with deliberate ease and placed her order.

Smythe hastily gathered her items into her messenger bag while continuing to watch both Artie and this new customer. As she began to slide from her seat, Artie reached out the palm of her hand to Smythe. Smythe took her hand, slightly taken aback by the pressure Artie applied. She looked into Artie's eyes, who glanced toward a hallway at the back of the shop. Smythe understood the request, and without a word, headed down the brightly lit corridor. She noticed a sign to the women's restroom and turned to enter. Artie, however, had other plans. She placed her hands on both of Smythe's arms and redirected her down the narrow hallway.

"There should be a door down here leading out to the back alley," Artie whispered.

"You don't know?!" Smythe whispered back.

Artie did not respond. They rounded the corner, and Artie spotted the exit sign.

"C'mon, over here."

"Wait! My car is still here!"

"I know, let's first get you into our vehicle."

They exited out the back door and found Team 3's vehicle idling at the back entrance. Artie quickly ushered Smythe into the backseat of the SUV and followed behind her.

"What happened, boss?" asked one of her agents.

"Something felt off."

She asked Smythe for her car keys. Using her com set, she spoke to Team 2. Team 3 drove from the alley and turned on to a street that led away from the baker's shop. As they slowed their vehicle, Artie rolled down her window.

A member of Team 2 walked quickly down the sidewalk toward the baker's shop. He stopped momentarily to catch the keys Artie tossed out the window.

"Team 1 is checking in on the baker, and Team 2 will secure your vehicle. We'll regroup at your place."

"Artie, no! I know that customer. I've seen her here before."

"When did you first notice her? Before or after the murder?"

Smythe slapped her fist on the seat's arm rest before crossing her arms in front of her chest. *Barely an hour with the baker. What the hell! It's not like I'll go scurrying away to my apartment!*

"I don't know, maybe after. I mean, the woman would come in and grab a coffee and talk with the baker. I assumed he knew her. Sometimes she would sit, other times—I don't know. I mean, she smiled at me. She seemed nice enough. I thought she was a regular. She just seemed harmless, Artie!"

"Perhaps, but my gut's not usually wrong. Something changed when she entered the shop."

Smythe had so much more to say, but bit her tongue, knowing that her words would be biting and caustic. She remained quiet and simply stared out the backseat window.

"I'm not sorry, Smythe."

Silence filled Team 3's SUV for the duration of the drive. Smythe was worried. The baker was her friend and confidant. She reasoned that any injury to him would be her fault, and Artie and her teams were the only ones who could protect him. Right her apparent wrong—to visit him. Once safely inside of her apartment, with an air of command, Smythe snapped.

"I need you to find out if Joao is ok!"

Artie stood in the middle of the living room, her New York fighter rage rearing its head. While she understood the need Smythe felt to remain in the presence of her friend, she also had a job to do, and nothing would prevent her from ensuring Smythe's safety. She did her best not to verbally pummel Smythe, responding coolly to her. "He's alright. I received confirmation. As I said, I have a separate team with him right now."

Smythe took in a long breath. She moved in front of her picture window and exhaled, simultaneously realizing knots were beginning to form around her shoulders from the stress. She rolled her neck from side to side and drew in another long breath before releasing it. She bit the inside of her cheek and stared expressionless at a nearly empty parking lot, lost within her thoughts.

"Please move away from the window, Smythe."

Reluctant to heed the warning, Smythe held her tongue and complied. With her head bent, she concentrated on each footstep she took into her dining room. She turned to face Artie, her arms crossed against her chest, and glared.

"I don't have much going for me at the moment, Artie. To get out of my head, I usually stay at the baker's shop and write. It's a great place to people watch and talk with Joao. I'm not convinced that woman was a hired assassin. But if she was, what really concerns me is Joao. When we left his shop, he was all alone. If she was there for me, to harm me, she could have easily turned on him. And—and I never got to say goodbye. My momma didn't raise an animal!"

Artie softened her tone. "Smythe, Team 1 arrived before we even left."

Smythe slowly shook her head from side to side.

The ache within Smythe's voice was noticeable. "I don't know what to do. I can't imagine not going back to the shop. But at the same time, I don't want to place his life in danger. I'm not even sure if I should visit my mom."

"We got this, Smythe. I have a team stationed inside his shop. But this is the thing. All of the people that you care about are at risk. All of them."

Artie walked into the dining room and stood before Smythe. "You refused WitSec, so we're working with a less than an optimal plan, at least where your safety is concerned. I would love to keep you confined to your apartment until—"

"Don't you dare!"

"See what I mean? It is a less than optimal situation, but I'm working on making it doable. I've got enough teams to cover you and some of the most important people in your life, but it would be helpful if you limit that number in your sphere for now."

Smythe fell silent for a moment.

"So, I guess, in a way, I *am* in witness security; only I'm confined to my apartment most of the time."

"You were already confined, Smythe. Listen, not a whole lot has changed for you. Two weeks ago, even a week ago, you were visiting the baker. He wasn't harmed then. Nor was he harmed today. You've visited your mother since the murder, and she's not been harmed."

"But—" Smythe started.

"No, let me finish!" Artie caught the anger rising within her voice. She released her shoulders and changed her posture, standing with her feet only slightly apart and unfurrowed her brow. "Their lives are no more in danger if you went into WitSec or not. What I am more concerned about is your movement. They want you, Smythe, not Joao. They want you, not your mom. But they may try to use them to get to you, which is why I have teams covering them. Your benefactor has allowed me to use all of my available personnel to keep you safe and to keep tabs on your mother, as well as the baker. You're my only long-term case right now. Just keep your circle small. The less people in your life right now, the better."

Smythe finally understood and nodded. She took a seat at her dining room table. So much of her wanted to bask in the waters of self-pity and woe. Who wouldn't? After all, like so many people, she was conditioned to think the worst, referring to past events to confirm present circumstances. The problem with such emotional conditioning is she unknowingly continued to train her body to live in the past.

Smythe stared out her window for a few moments. She knew she had a choice: she could wallow in self-doubt or stay on task. Remaining on task by studying seemed the better of the two. She forced herself to smile at the blue sky and white billowy clouds as they drifted by until she began to actually feel grateful for the peace the clouds gently demonstrated. Eventually, she nudged her thoughts toward the mountain of studying she set out to accomplish for the day. Artie watched the change in Smythe's demeanor. *Let her be for now,* she thought. *This is a lot for her to handle.* She moved into the kitchen to grab a bottle of water from the refrigerator.

Artie turned around to face Smythe, unsure of what to say next, but Smythe excused herself and entered her bedroom to change. When she returned, she carried three books in her arms. She looked around her space—Artie had left the apartment. *It's better this way,* she thought. *I don't owe her an apology. Just forget about it and get to work.* She placed her books onto her dining room table alongside a notebook and her tablet and settled in to begin her work.

After a couple of hours, Smythe leaned back from her chair. She recalled an Albert Einstein quote which said, "Everything in life is vibration." She thought about her last video module. Her mentor spoke about vibration. Ever the one to think deeply about new concepts, she began to weave a construct.

Our thoughts, our emotions, our very words are vibrations as well. The energy of our thoughts, emotions, and words manifest into reality. They become a creative force.

I've buried my father, resigned my position, started a new business, took on a year-long education program, and witnessed a murder. What the hell kind of energy is that?! What stories am I telling myself? What am I creating, even right now?

Everything I'm reading says that we can shift our vibration, lifting ourselves out of a state of mind through intentionality and positive action.

It was then that her Beloved spoke. A tingle flowed from the base of her neck, and a single thought emerged.

"You have the ability to transform hate into understanding, fear into the purest form of love, and sorrow to the highest mountain peaks of joy."

She stopped to jot down that last thought. She read it, then read it again, lightly touching the paper.

"Thank you," she muttered. "But it begs the question, *how?*" She returned to her dining table and continued to study.

Chapter 10

How Did We Get Here?

—

T HE MORNING GRAY SKY GAVE WAY TO A SUNLIT SPRING AFTERNOON, filling the air with a hope of sorts. Smythe stood up. She shook her legs and bent over, stretching out her hamstrings and calves before walking into her bedroom. She sat on her recliner, comfortably erect, feeling the support of the chair. She breathed in deeply and slowly, releasing her breath, and gently closed her eyes.

Similar to a news crawl at the bottom of a television screen, her thoughts began to scroll through her mind, demanding her attention— demanding her agreement. Yet, she chose to simply observe them momentarily before focusing her attention on her breath. After a few minutes, for just the briefest of moments, she glimpsed her life in its totality. She remembered a meditation her mentor recorded.

Without judgement, she whispered, "I am not my thoughts. I have thoughts, but I am not my thoughts."

She continued to breathe, silently repeating her mantra. After a time, she became aware her thoughts quieted to a whisper. Much like the way the clouds from her window continued along their path, without placing her attention upon them, her thoughts moved into her conscious awareness and then floated away.

She slowly opened her eyes and began to scan her surrounding area. A small polished burnished sage pebble sat on the arm of her chair. She picked it up and held it gently in the palm of her hand. It was a stone of gratitude, given to her by a medicine woman several years ago. It served as a reminder to return to the creative Universe to offer gratitude for all that is. To remember the earth, the wind, the lakes, and the forests; to honor all living beings, to remember the abundance of life itself. Recalling the significance of the stone, she spoke quietly for all that she was grateful for.

"I am immensely grateful no harm came to me. And grateful for my protector and her team. Thank you for a home of safety; for the abundance of life in and around me. For the food I eat and the clean water I drink, I offer appreciation. And most of all—I am grateful for this moment. For in this moment, I am grateful for you, my Beloved, for I know you hear me."

Silence deepened around her. She repeated her gratitude quietly, discovering additional reasons to appreciate all that is. With each offering, she allowed her words to synchronize with expanded feelings of gratitude. And with each new offering, a smile shone brightly upon her face, and the exuberance of love embraced her.

"The journey really has begun," she quietly mouthed.

It seemed for just a moment Smythe experienced a deeper truth. In the midst of chaos and uncertainty, the power to change her vibration and her responses to any situation were always available. The sheer act of gratitude has the cleansing power to raise her energy, and reconnect her to what is present in the here-now moment. She need only to connect this gratitude to additional higher vibration emotions and linger in the present. In so doing, she would come to understand time as not a linear entity, but vertical, stacked upon itself with the power of choice. For the briefest of deepening moments of consciousness, Smythe glimpsed the here-now moment, which contained all time in the present and in which all that she would ever need was available to her. From the present moment, she would know all was well, even in what appeared to be chaos.

Not yet fully able to grasp the elegant art of emotional elevation, but glimpsing the truth of it all, peace enveloped Smythe. She sat for several minutes before returning to her dining room to resume her studies. She watched as Artie paced back and forth along the sidewalk. Artie's presence reminded her of the abrupt departure from the baker's shop. She frowned and swept the thought away with intention, returning to the task at hand. She replayed specific portions of her videos, opened her manual, and reviewed corresponding sections.

Hours later, saturated from all that she learned, she stood up again and began to pace. She couldn't help but think about her circumstances once again. She thought about the people who made an attempt on her life. She glanced at her library of books as she replayed the moments leading up to the murder. Cold shivers danced along her spine as she remembered the terror she heard in the man's voice. "Why did he have to die?" she questioned aloud. She scanned the book titles, looking for something that would answer her question. None popped out at her.

She stared at her image reflected in the glass of the cabinet and wondered about the effect of the crime ring's tactics upon community members in her tiny enclave. She imagined the intimidation used against them and the resources taken from others.

She looked deeply into the eyes reflected back to her. *How did we get here? How did that poor guy get there? What was it they offered to this man that we as a community could not give?*

In the present moment, Smythe was unaware of her role in the divine intervention of circumstances she was now uniquely a part of. If she had, she would rest in the grand design of her soul's reason for participating in a seemingly violent reality. She could have rested in her role to offer a community a certain measure of justice and let go of the how. But like so many with a myopic view of the world, she missed what her soul was up to.

She turned toward her front window and stared out toward the sidewalk. She could hear faint bits of Artie's conversation as she stood outside. Her mind was spinning with thoughts of the fragile fabric of trust within her community and the role she and Artie were playing within it.

Could there be a positive outcome, or are we destined for more bloodshed?

My Beloved, I recognize my own issues with trust. Yet, I understand trust is an essential element in the overall health of any community member, not to mention the community as a whole. To trust not only each other and ourselves, but to trust You as well. Yet here we are. Our trust has been so easily eroded by the echoing cacophony of divisiveness. I guess what I'm saying is that I'm not sure I know how to trust or to build trust. You've asked me to, but it is such a struggle.

She recalled French sociologist Emile Durkheim using the term "collective consciousness." She could recite the definition, "The set of shared beliefs, ideas, and attitudes which operate as a unifying force within a society." Intrigued by the term, Smythe studied it as it related to her work in diversity education.

She imagined not only her energy, but the energy of the community, wondering how the disease of distrust grew so terminal. And she, too, wondered if there was a cure.

* * *

Artie stood outside the apartment and paced. While Smythe aspired to live within the spiritual realm, knitting a tapestry of unity, Artie moved solely within the physical plane. She held no interest in anything other than what she could see, touch, or hear. Even when her intuition was at work, she simply attributed the intuition to prior experience and her ability to read her environment. In her present circumstance, she gave no thought to the "why" of the crime ring and the community's role in its rise. Implacable to treachery and deceit, she held only the perspective the group was a menace to her client, seeking to gain power, and she was determined to drive the group from Smythe's life.

Artie thought about her unconventional way of protecting Smythe. Her training taught her to work by the book, making the necessary adjustments for only the most important activities in a client's day, restricting all other superfluous movements. Her former clients understood her edict and had been fearful enough to make the necessary changes in their lives, but Smythe was different. She was "headstrong," as Artie had nicknamed Smythe to her team.

The nickname was not used as a putdown, but instead as a way to understand the overarching behavior of her client—the client who would not cooperate and get herself killed if she was not granted the necessary freedom to move about her life. Her earlier insistence to drive to the baker's shop was Smythe's most recent example for the nickname. But, long before that, Artie and her teams had been tailing Smythe, dismayed at the number of risks she took tooling around town without a care in the world. The dilemma was a risk Artie was uncomfortable with. Yet, she had a reputation for looking at all angles and calculating the best chance for the desired outcome. And, with each passing moment she spent in Smythe's presence, the more focused she became.

She continued to pace outside Smythe's apartment and called Carole to fill her in on what she believed was a veiled threat to Smythe's life. With that news, Carole became angry and second-guessed herself. Replaying her previous conversation with Smythe, Carole's initial judgement to place her in Witness Protection was the best overall choice, but Smythe refused. Now Carole wondered if placing Smythe under WitSec's protective custody was the necessary option, whether she wanted to relocate or not.

While Carole trusted her friend, the unexpected threat concerned her. Was Artie using enough of her resources set to keep Smythe from harm? Perhaps moving her out of state, with Artie and her team, was a better option instead of WitSec. Her mind raced. She thought about the career changes her friend had made. FBI special agent to defense attorney and now, CEO of her own private protection agency. Artie certainly had the experience to handle this assignment.

They discussed their initial assumptions when they first met to discuss Smythe's protection. Both women believed Smythe was nothing more than an annoyance to the crime ring. They theorized those closest to the case, which included the judge, the lead District Attorney, and members of the jury would be likely targets through either bribery or threat. At the time, they had no reason to believe the crime ring knew who Smythe was; therefore, any attempt against her life would have to occur at trial.

However, recent circumstances now shifted their belief. Most troubling for Artie was the fact that the crime ring apparently knew identity of Smythe as the anonymous witness. Since her identity had not been revealed publicly, Artie continued to question Carole, particularly how the crime ring determined it was Smythe who had identified the suspect and what they believed she had witnessed.

"After all, it's quite possible Smythe could've simply found the victim lying on the concrete," Artie said.

"It doesn't matter how they found out. Given your report, they obviously know! Trust me, Artie, I've been working this case hard. From my end, we're investigating several members of the ring and their affiliates. They may even be involved in several homicides on the island of Oahu. If you recall, just as you left the bureau, this ring was becoming more ruthless and widespread. Remember the Chris case at your firm?"

"How could I forget? I was barely out the door when it hit the fan."

"Well, after Chris was acquitted, we started an investigation. One of the partners at your firm was intimately involved in some shady dealings during court proceedings, and it had far-reaching consequences outside just this city."

"What?!"

"I can't go into specifics over the phone. Suffice to say, you got out just in time."

"Who else was investigated?"

"What I can tell you is that you were cleared. You weren't the attorney on record. But some did call your timing into question."

"You know why I left. What little I knew of the case, I still knew the guy was guilty. Yet the firm still took on the case and got the guy off. He had ties to some local chem company. That acquittal cost the witness her life. I just couldn't—"

"I know, I know. That's one of the reasons I chose you for this assignment. You're stellar, Artie. You can't be bought, and you can't be intimidated. Look—I'm only bringing up the Chris case because you were left completely in the dark about what was happening two floors above you. Right now, with this case, I just need you to look at all angles. All of them. Question everything and everyone. Your sole job is to stay ahead of the ring, keep me informed, and keep Smythe alive."

"I get that, but information goes both ways. What you know, I need to know."

"I'll do my best. I've got a bit of a hunch, but I'm working on the evidence."

Although she held little hope of persuading the District Attorney for an earlier trial date, Carole agreed to at least try. She was suspicious of holding ongoing conversations about Smythe over the phone and opted to meet with Artie in person. She set up several in-person meetings over the next several weeks before abruptly ending the call.

Artie stood, clenching her jaw and holding her hands in tight fists. She was suspicious of the FBI and considered that there was a leak within the FBI that perhaps Carole was unaware of. *How else could the syndicate know of Smythe's existence?* The reference to the Chris case also troubled her. She unconsciously cupped the bottom of her throat. She had held a suspicion about the witness' safety and voiced her concern to her agency's law partners. They discounted it, steadfastly stating their client was innocent; therefore, the witness was safe from harm by their client. Grief began to swell within her.

I should have reached out to Carole. Told her what I suspected. And now the witness...

Artie cleared her throat and motioned to Dennis, who sat in an SUV outside Smythe's apartment. Together, they reviewed team logistics for Smythe's protection. She also wanted an update. While the trial would be months away, Artie placed her number two in charge of interviewing potential new team members who would be assigned as needed during the course of the trial.

"I like four of them—I'm running background on them now. I should receive the reports back in about three weeks, and I've just received a new batch of apps. I'll keep you posted."

"Excellent. We're going to need four additional teams of two. Keep on it; we may not have a whole lot of time. Get them on my calendar when you've decided they're worth the trouble to interview."

"You ok, boss?"

"Yeah. I'm good. Old wounds. I'm going to take one of the team vehicles. I'll be back in about an hour or so. Hang out with Smythe until my return."

Artie left the complex and chose a route that skirted the city limits, eventually taking her to an isolated dirt road. The road rambled around the side of a hill through a smattering of oak trees. She continued to bounce along the rocky road, deep into the hills, until the road abruptly ended. She peered up at the steep slope, which rose before her as she parked her car. The rolling hills around her showed signs of recent use. She exited and stood beside her vehicle, hands on her hips, her eyes following a line of the undulating terrain. Gashes scarred the gravel beneath her feet and lances of sunlight speared clumps of dirt unearthed by recent travel through the area.

Off roaders.

She remembered the journey she made to this area after hearing the news that the witness against her law firm's client had been brutally murdered. She walked forward up the rising slope and retraced her steps along a sparsely wooded path. She could hear the soles of her boots scrunch the mixture of fallen leaves and gravel beneath her feet. After several minutes, she pushed her hand through a thickening of oak tree branches and arrived at a clearing. Twenty or so feet in front of her, the clearing gave way to a steep jagged drop-off. The hush of silence surrounded her. She breathed deeply and surveyed the vista of rolling hills below. A freeway off in the far distance was light with traffic in both directions. She rested her gaze on the drop-off. It was there where the victim's body was found. She looked up to the oak trees. The spot offered her a bit of shade. She bent low, grasping at the dirt in front of a small wooden cross with carved initials, standing no more than a foot high among a patch of dandelions at the base of a tree. She sat down next to the cross, picking at the dandelions. She spoke no words, but sat in quiet peace, staring out onto the vista.

She remained at the memorial for close to an hour before she stood up, brushing off the back of her pants. The dandelion bunch she picked laid before the cross. Turning to leave, she paused briefly, her words caught in her throat.

"I'm sorry," she whispered, returning somberly to her vehicle.

Chapter 11

Until You Needed Me

—

Later in the day, Artie relieved Dennis, who sat on Smythe's sofa reviewing electronic applications of potential new team members. She glanced toward Smythe and assumed she was still seated in the same position since the last time she checked in on her. She casually strode into the kitchen, grabbed a glass of water, and set the glass on the table in front of Smythe.

"It's been several hours, and you haven't moved from that seat. If you don't mind me saying, you need to stay hydrated."

Smythe picked up the glass and drank from it until she had drained it. She realized she was thirstier than she thought, but too engrossed in her learning to stop and do something about it.

"Thank you. I do tend toward dehydration, but I have shifted."

Staring at the empty glass, Artie moved past Smythe and sat on the sofa.

"So, I'm curious, what have you learned today? I mean, your lessons."

"Well, to begin with, I learned a pretty cool activity to help people begin to gain clarity. I then learned some language to use for a seminar that I am planning to offer when I get back from my first conference."

Conference?! Seminar?! Artie made a mental note. "When is the conference?"

"In a couple of months. I'll give you the calendar of trainings."

"And the seminar?"

"I haven't scheduled it yet. Once I do, I'll let you know. There will probably be several of them. It's required for my coaching and training certification, and they will prepare me for the conference."

"Ok. That would be helpful. So, how has the learning helped you?"

"What do you mean?" Smythe said, annoyed.

"No offense, Smythe. I read your file. From where I'm sitting, you jumped off a ledge to pursue a dream. That takes a fair amount of courage. I know a lot of people wouldn't have done what you did. I also know that even when you decided to jump, there still wasn't a lot of clarity. People like you and me; we just know we need to jump. As we're jumping, we figure things out. I'm wondering what you have learned that you can implement in your own life as it is right now."

Smythe smiled and nodded. *Settle down, Smythe. She's just making conversation.* "Sounds like you've had some experience with jumping."

"I do. I was an FBI agent before becoming a criminal defense attorney in a large law firm. It was busy and very profitable. Only thing was, I wasn't happy. My office was often defending some pretty bad people. I must admit that on at least one occasion, my firm's clients did some horrendous things." Artie paused, her eyes examining the geometric pattern of the front door.

Smythe gazed at Artie. "I'm sorry. That had to have been difficult. I do find it interesting that you've been on two sides of the law, though. Law enforcement and defense attorney. Sounds like you were at a bit of a crossroads back in the day."

"Back in the day? I'm only seven years older than you!" Artie said with a smile, continuing to gaze at the front door.

"I was at a crossroads, though. My firm cost someone their life. It was a dark time for me then. A really dark time. Finally, I had enough. So, I took a step back, used some vacation time, and when

I returned, I up and quit. I had to really figure out what I valued and what it was that lit a fire under me; what made me burn inside."

"How did you do that?"

"By first determining what I didn't want. I didn't want the bureaucracy of the FBI or the District Attorney's office, but I also didn't want to get the bad guys off either. From there, I thought about what I wanted. What I discovered was that I am passionate about fighting for the underdog—the people caught in the middle of both worlds. I realized then that I have a keen sense of justice and fairness."

"What do you mean?"

"Let's just say, there are a lot of people who find themselves in difficult circumstances. They just need a little help to do the right thing for their lives. That's where I decided to come in. So, I quit and opened up this agency. I knew just enough information to be dangerous, but I had crazy passion. With a lot of work and a fair amount of courage, I slowly built the business to what it is today. Many of my clients like you cooperate in FBI investigations."

"A personal security agency?"

"Yes. It's the best of both worlds. I don't have bureaucracy nipping at my heels, running my decisions about cases by anyone, and I don't have to defend bad guys."

"Hmmm. I had never even heard of you until you showed up beside my car."

Artie turned toward Smythe. "You didn't need me until you needed me, and you wouldn't have known about my agency anyway. I don't advertise. I like to say my job is to make a mess of things behind the scenes and then put it all back together again seamlessly in favor of my client."

"You mean like having your car hit instead of mine?"

"Well, kinda. And even at that, I've sat with what happened and analyzed it. Could I have done things differently? If so, what? I'm always fine-tuning. I have to. People's lives are at stake. But, back to my original question. Has the learning helped you?"

"I have more questions, if you don't mind."

"Such as?"

"How do you get clients? I didn't seek you out, yet I'm your client. How?"

"Referrals. All of my clients are referred to me, even you. You have a benefactor whose name even I don't know. That person, for whatever reason, has a vested interest in keeping you alive." Artie eyed Smythe. Although Carole would not reveal the name or the relationship the benefactor potentially had to Smythe, Artie wanted to figure it out. Now was as good a time as any to ask Smythe if she knew.

"So, you don't know who it is? I thought it was the FBI," Smythe said.

"No, it's not the FBI. They do want to keep you alive, but they're not footing the bill for your round-the-clock protection. I honestly don't know who it is, but my referral says the person is legitimate. Do you know who the benefactor could be?"

Smythe's eyes widened. "Why would I? I don't know anyone with *that* kind of money. And I haven't told anyone about what I saw. Except for Joao, and I just told him."

"Yeah, I know. I was there."

"No one knows you are protecting me except for the FBI." Smythe remained quiet for a moment. "Artie, should I be worried? About who it is, I mean."

"Nah. Worry is my job. Besides, whoever it is has got to be on our side. At any rate, you were asking me about how I get clients."

"Yes. So, if all of your clients are referrals, that must make it difficult to get clients."

"Actually, it doesn't. With the work that I do, there is usually no shortage. Former clients, friends, or families of former clients—they all refer people to me. Some cases I take, some I do not. I just have to be patient. The right work always comes along. Even when hiring new agents. There is never a shortage of applicants." Artie smirked as she thought about those who had applied for a position in her agency. Current and former law enforcement, ex-military personnel. Everyone wanted to work with her.

"So, am I the right work?"

"Yes, you are."

Smythe sat perfectly still, pondering Artie's response.

"Why am I the right—"

"You ready to answer my question?"

Smythe scrunched her nose. "Sure. The year-long training program I'm now getting into, which may seem otherworldly, I'm actually convinced will allow me to continue training and coaching but at a much deeper level than I have at any other time in my career. Of course, there will be opportunities to weave this knowledge into some of my prior courses and offer them to organizations, which really excites me. Yet, honestly, when I strip away that side of my business, the thing that ignites my fire is writing. I have a constant novel in my head at all times. I'm always creating a storyline, especially as I'm learning new concepts."

"I'd love to read some of your work sometime."

"Perhaps. But it all has to get written. So, I spend about two-thirds of my day working on the business side of things and devote one third to writing."

"Makes for some long days, I'm sure."

"Usually, about 16-17 hours."

"I'll let you get back to it then."

Smythe smiled. It was nice to get to know a more personal side of her protector. She continued to work until early evening, and by the time she completed her day, she was mentally exhausted. She found herself beginning to nurse a slight headache and realized she was ravenous. She sighed as she walked toward her bedroom. It was very much like Smythe to go for several hours—sometimes a full twelve hours—before she would wrestle herself into the kitchen to make a bite to eat.

Not good, she thought. *You're increasing your mileage and need fuel.*

While Smythe changed clothes, Artie sprung for pizza for her team and had them deliver a box to the apartment. Once Artie and Smythe finished dinner, they watched whatever was on one of the few channels Smythe paid for on television. As the evening turned to night, Smythe excused herself for bed.

"I'd like to get a five-mile run in before I head to the baker's shop tomorrow. It's been a few days, and I really feel the need to run."

"Outside?! I don't think so."

"No. The gym here at the complex."

"Ok. When are you getting up?"

"Probably 2:00 a.m."

"Ooof! Is this a habit?! Because if it is, 9 p.m. is a bit late to be going to bed."

"Yes. Lately, it's been a normal wake up time. At least if I want to run before seeing the baker, which I do. I'm sorry to have kept you up. Thank you again for dinner. It was very thoughtful of you."

Chapter 12

Restless

—

SMYTHE WOKE WELL BEFORE HER ALARM SOUNDED. SHE LAY IN BED, tossing from one side to the other, siphoning energy from her here-now moment by reviewing her to-do list. For her, the workload seemed daunting. Not only did she have to learn the course material, but she had to integrate it into her own life. She turned to lay on her back. She did not want to get up, but she could feel her shoulders tighten. Unable to coax herself back to sleep, she tumbled out of bed in a huff. She opened her chest of drawers and pulled out running attire. She dressed quickly, trying to move past the stress that came with no sleeping, and strode into the kitchen.

Artie was just beginning to stir. She peered up at the oval wall clock hanging against the wall over the kitchen pantry door. It read 1:00 a.m. "Oof," she quietly said to herself as she leaned her elbow on the air mattress.

Had I known she was this much of an early bird...

She sat up and stretched long, her palms extending up toward the ceiling, before making her way to the bathroom to change.

Meanwhile, Smythe puttered around the kitchen. She pulled her French press from the cupboard and set down two mugs. Once the coffee was ready, she poured herself a cup, inhaling its mesmerizingly nutty notes. She took a sip, feeling the body of it against her tongue as it slid down her throat. The first sip was always the best, in Smythe's opinion. She looked down at Artie's air mattress and continued to sip on her coffee as she prepared to leave, gathering her phone, earbuds, and a couple of towels.

Artie returned to the kitchen, bypassing the mug Smythe left for her and pulled out a small thermos from the cupboard. Preoccupied with her previous conversation with Carole, she slowly added cream to her coffee, taking several sips before deflating her bed and storing it in the back of the dining room closet.

The clubhouse was barely a two-minute walk from Smythe's apartment. Still, unwilling to take any chances, Artie chose two teams to escort them both to the gym. They moved quickly along the mildew-stained walkway, providing a cocoon of protection around the pair. Smythe gazed beyond her team as they passed a small grassy park that sat between two buildings. Droplets of rain from the night before covered two well-worn park benches. She remembered sitting during the warmer months of the year, watching dogs bound along the grass, playing fetch with their owners. One of her favorite four-legged creatures, Lucas—a caramel-colored, four-month-old Labradoodle—would bounce up to her and stand in front of her, waiting for a response. Lucas' human would give Smythe a handful of the dog's favorite treats to offer him, which he gladly accepted. After a while, Smythe purchased the same treats and would wait patiently for Lucas to arrive with his human. Smythe smiled at her memory. It was love at first (and every) sight between them.

The group continued along the sidewalk until they reached the clubhouse. The gym, spacious in its design, rivaled any paid membership facility, offering contemporary cardio, weight, and resistance equipment. The walls, painted in vibrant aqua, matched the geometric pattern on the floor. As if to motivate the member toward a fruitful workout, upbeat music played softly throughout the space.

Standing at the entrance, Smythe noted the gym once again sat empty, devoid of additional residents. She explained to Artie it was the reason she enjoyed the early hour—the emptiness allowed her the freedom to move about the gym unimpeded or gawked at by other residents. Artie nodded.

Smythe climbed onto her favorite treadmill, put on her headphones, and clicked on one of her playlists. The music mostly consisted of classical artists, with a few rhythm and blues artists thrown in for diversity. She kept a comfortable cadence to the tempo of her music, speeding through five miles. Artie, however, chose an upper body, free weight routine followed by several sets of squats. They completed their workout in well under an hour and returned to Smythe's apartment.

"Why don't you shower first? I need to spend some time in meditation," Smythe said.

"Do you meditate every day?"

"I try. I am not as consistent as I'd like to be. Truth be told, I tend to lean into it more when I am troubled. One day I'll learn."

"Learn?"

"To be more consistent. Perhaps, if I were more consistent, some of the old ways of thinking wouldn't be as bothersome."

"Care to explain?"

"There's the thought that meditation allows us to quiet our ego and allow for our gifts to be more perfectly honed. I have found that the art of it enables me to stop searching and to simply be. At least, that is what I am practicing. Spending some quiet time with some choice music, I feel more connected to the Source of all things. If I don't search for anything, including revelation, that is when insight occurs—at least for me, anyway. I've heard that the more consistent we become in meditating, the more beneficial it becomes.

"Sounds lovely. I'll head into the bathroom, then. I'll be out in about ten."

Smythe smiled. She walked to her bedroom, shut her door, and placed a towel upon her chair before seating herself. A Navajo flute, which sounded like a prayer, played softly in the background. She thought about the enchanting melody of the instrument. Her grandmother would say the flute had something to say, not only about the traditions of her people, but about oneself. Smythe slowed her breathing and listened to its dulcet sound. Still disturbed by yesterday's events, she could only wrestle herself through ten minutes of meditation. She furrowed her brow as her mind concerned itself with the inconvenience of a security detail. Replaying her recent conversations with Artie, she noticed her jaw beginning to tense and recognized she disdained the idea of anyone getting to close to her.

Stop it! You're getting too vulnerable with this woman. She doesn't need to know that much about you.

Her eyes snapped open. She remembered her conversation with her Beloved about trust, and she could only smirk at herself. *Ok, so I'm learning to trust. It's only been a day.*

She listened for any sound that indicated Artie had exited the bathroom. She rose from her chair, walked to her door, and opened it slowly. Artie stood dressed at the counter in the kitchen, her hair wrapped in a towel, pouring herself another cup of coffee.

Smythe strode out of her bedroom. "My turn?" she asked, pointing toward the bathroom. Artie nodded and walked toward the living room.

Both were ready to travel in short order, and the caravan arrived at the baker's shop well before Smythe's usual 4:00 a.m. arrival time. After she ordered her coffee, Smythe smiled at her friend as he continued to prepare his shop to open. He had just placed a batch of malasadas on a cooling rack and fiddled with the placement of some of his other pastries.

"Joao, how is it that you arrive to work at 1:30 in the morning every day? Well, except for Sundays. Normally I'm just beginning to stir from my sleep."

Standing behind his counter, the baker offered her the wide smile Smythe had come to appreciate.

"Why do you think it is work, my friend?"

"Because I see how people enter the bakery. It's 5:00 in the morning when you open. Most people seem cranky and show some level of disrespect to you in their tone as they place their orders, especially as the morning revs up into high gear. Puts a bit of a damper on the whole experience of coming to a bakery shop, if you ask me. It feels like it's just another task on their to-do list. There's a certain lack of civility."

"You cannot go by body language alone, my daughter."

Waving towards the variety of pastries placed in perfect formation in the display cases, the baker continued.

"Every morning, I create these. You are only partially correct in your observation of my guests. It is true—every morning, people start coming into my shop. I can see the stress on their body, the grumpy, how you say—*harried* expression on their faces. Then they come closer to my counter like you did earlier, and it all goes away. They become mesmerized by the treats before them and a slight smile—one that you do not see, Smythe—lights up their faces. My creation did that!"

His exuberance was contagious.

"My creation made a frown into a smile! No, my daughter, this is not work, this is joy—for it is this work that I do which allows me to keep pace with the soul of our earth so that I may move with the infinite of all that is."

As an afterthought, he added, "Perhaps the work that others do should not be the work that they *continue* to do. Especially if it does not bring them joy. I think joy should be the work we all do, for it draws out our gifts for all to partake."

The baker proudly swept his arms around his shop. "Every dream we dream, for, umm… good purpose—the reason we are getting up in the morning, that which sings to our heart—is from our ALL. It may feel like work at times, but it is also for the good of us all."

"What do you mean by ALL? Do you mean God or the Divine?"

"Yes. The Universe contains ALL there is. When I say ALL, I connect everything there ever was, is, and will be as ALL. You say Beloved, yes?"

"Yes."

The baker beamed a wide smile at Smythe. "That is good. So, my daughter, what are your plans for good today?"

"I don't quite know yet. I haven't been able to get quiet enough to determine that."

"Well, whatever you do, make sure you do good for ALL. I offer you this prayer—may the work that you do today be the music of the everlasting song of love. I hope its melody will be a tender hope as reverent as the flute of your Navajo people."

"You remembered," Smythe replied, smiling at the thought.

"Yes, of course. I remember everything."

After spending a couple of hours in the shop, Smythe returned to study. Several hours later, as tension mounted within her, she decided to run a single errand. However, once she was out and about and feeling less claustrophobic, Smythe made up several errands she forgot in order to escape the walls of her apartment. She went to her favorite bookstore, a small market, and a clothing store. Artie did her best to accommodate her client, but as time went on, she grew increasingly tense at the last-minute requests. She looked at her watch and the growing amount of traffic, her anxiety rising by the second.

"Smythe, I get that you may have forgotten that you need to run an errand here or pick up something at the market, but you really need to plan what you want to do each day so that I can plan for your safety. The later it gets, the more people are out and about. You are stretching my teams thin and placing yourself at needless risk."

Smythe could feel her face redden, but to avoid an argument, she bit the inside of her cheek and refrained from speaking. As far as she was concerned, it wasn't her fault that she was cooped up behind closed doors. What did Artie expect? That she would never go out? She simply nodded and asked to complete one last errand. Once she finally returned home, she spent the rest of the day studying and writing.

Every hour, like clockwork, Smythe would take a break in attempt to get out of her head. She would stand up, leave her dining room, and retreat to her bedroom. By evening, Smythe began to relax. She thought about all she had accomplished and learned that day. She silently congratulated herself, something her mentor had taught her to do. She looked around her space and smirked. She rather liked the idea of completing the workday with spoken, uplifting remarks. She wondered how often people actually congratulate themselves. But then, she immediately knew the answer.

Her mentor had spoken about the need to develop the practice of positive affirmation. Most people congratulate themselves on their more significant accomplishments of life, but he suggested people acknowledge the smaller successes as well. The daily acknowledgement was the most important affirmation a person could offer themselves because it allows the person to positively stroke the subconscious mind, allowing it to pursue further accomplishments. Over time, it also allows the person to re-program negative beliefs.

Smythe stood before her bathroom mirror, looking herself in the eye. She could feel the tension building in her shoulders again. It was more than just the trial that disturbed her, and she wondered how long it would take to re-program her own thinking. It would be a question she would silently hold before her Beloved until it was answered.

Artie chose to cook that evening, preparing a simple meal of angel hair pasta and salad. Grateful for the meal, Smythe smiled and hummed the entire time during dinner. Artie could only laugh at Smythe's delight.

"I didn't know you liked pasta."

"In small doses, it tends to inflame me. But this was really, really good."

"Mmm, good to know."

"What else do you cook?"

"Soup. I'm pretty good at soup—osso buco specifically, which is braised veal with vegetables."

"Oh, do you ever make it without veal?"

"Haven't ever tried to. You don't eat veal?" Artie asked, a bit disappointed.

"No, I don't. I'm pretty much a vegetarian. I feel better without meat. I'm not judging, mind you. There's enough of that going around. It's just that even as a child, I wasn't that crazy about eating meat.

But I wasn't really given a choice. 'You better eat everything on that plate before you leave the dinner table, young lady,' was the edict in our house."

"Mine too. My mother wanted us to learn how to cook, so when we married, we could feed ourselves and our husbands. So, I spent a lot of time learning to cook."

Smythe smiled.

"Do you cook?" Artie asked.

"I do, but I'm usually too busy to think about food—as you could tell when you got back. I apologize. I sometimes forget to offer to make you a meal."

"I didn't notice. Don't worry about it; you're not my housewife. I had a hankering for some homemade pasta. I noticed you had pasta and all the fixings for a salad. So, wha-la—we had a meal."

After cleaning the kitchen, Smythe joined Artie in the living room. She was unsure how to start the conversations she wanted to have with Artie. If she were truthful with herself, she was a bit afraid. Afraid that the information she would ask for might trigger anxiety. Yet, she also wanted to face her fears. Taking a seat on the sofa, she turned toward Artie.

"Tell me about them?"

"Tell you about who?"

"About the people that want to hurt me. Tell me about them."

Artie narrowed her eyes.

"Why?"

"Please, just tell me."

Searching her memory, Artie questioned just how much she wanted to share.

"I think first you need to understand what a syndicate is; particularly, a crime syndicate."

"I already know. A syndicate, by definition, can be formed to promote, coordinate, and engage in a specific business to pursue a common or shared interest. A company or a group of companies and corporations could, in the broadest sense of the term, be considered a syndicate."

Artie blinked at her in astonishment. *Does she have an eidetic memory?*

"I looked it up, but I'm not referring to that. I'm interested in the people who want to hurt or kill me—the way they killed the guy in the parking lot."

Artie let out a slow sigh. "Smythe, what we're dealing with is a bunch of local yokels organized by local leaders bent on crime. It is always a for-profit venture, and there are always winners and losers. In this case, the city is expanding at an exponential rate. This group simply wants a piece of the expansion. They may be part of a larger whole, operating under a number of businesses, to control as many aspects of the community as possible."

"But why? I get that they want to control the community, but I am talking about the cultural traditions of the community. I understand the rings of hierarchy. It forms social and cultural traditions. How are they doing it here? How did our collective consciousness allow it into power?"

"Heady questions, Smythe. I don't have all of the answers. What I can tell you is that as long as people abdicate independent thought, there will always be a crime syndicate."

"Say more."

Artie smiled to herself. "Well, in order for a group to take power, there have to be willing citizens—people who don't want to think. Ever notice the first thing a lot of people do when they get home is turn on the television? Even us. We watch the news and think the brief 45-second segment is the totality of the story. There is no contemplation of the untold story. A lot of people can also tell you what show comes on what day and what time. Their excuse for sitting in front of a television all evening—night after night, week after week, year after year—is that they've had a hard day at work, and they don't want to think."

"I get that. That's why our smart devices have become so popular."

"In part, yes. That lack of thinking also spills out into other areas. For example, the people we elect to lead us. We don't take the time the read ballot initiatives or understand exactly where a candidate stands on the issues most important to us. We support a government—hell, we even follow religious theologies so that we don't have to think. Instead, we want those leaders to think for us. Feed us what we need to know, but not too much. We listen to sound bites without asking important questions. We rely on newscasters to tell us their version of the truth. There's very little independent thought from us, the citizens of the community, asking the deeper questions. So, when I talk about lack of thought, it's much deeper. From all of us, it requires contemplation and willingness to understand the bigger picture and the effect on each of us, and the community as a whole, rather than just a sound bite."

"I see that. We want it easy. We want *everything* to be easy."

"It would seem so. We want someone else to tell us what to do, but then we get disillusioned or disgusted because we followed all of the rules and didn't get what we wanted. We're left wondering what the hell happened. Where was the return on our rule-following? Where do I go now? Where do I sit? What do I eat? What should I believe? Just tell me what to do. Is it any wonder that when our independent thought is abdicated, a gap forms? In fact, several gaps form.

"Commerce, Smythe, is big, big business. This local crime ring saw a gap, and they stepped in. They offer something. Usually, some form of protection to a community member in exchange for their souls, i.e., a piece of the business or straight out dollars. Soon, community members recognize they are playing with the devil, and they want out. The problem is the devil plays for keeps. There is no out."

"It just saddens me. Is there any hope that the crime ring will just leave? I'm sorry, I know I sound naive."

"It is naive to believe they will just leave. They have to be driven out. That's where the FBI comes in. They have an entire division dedicated to rooting them out, but it's a long process. And usually, when they convict one member, there are others in the wings ready to take over. So, the idea is to take down the big guns in hopes the ring will dissolve through power struggles."

"So, what you're saying is that really, my testimony won't do a whole lot."

"It will, Smythe. It has to." Artie paused, believing that perhaps she had said too much. This was not what would ease her client's mind.

"Having said all of that, let's do some of our own abdicating. This kind of talk will only add to your restlessness."

"You noticed."

"I'm trained to notice everything."

Artie grabbed the remote and browsed through Netflix until she found a documentary on climate change.

"This might allow your brain to chew on something else. Interested?"

"Absolutely."

After the documentary, Smythe decided to retire to bed. It had been a long day, and there were longer days to come. Resting her head and shoulders against her headboard she thought about her conversation with Artie.

She's right. I am restless.

She closed her eyes, feeling the rhythm of her breath and deepened into meditation. Slowly, she became aware of a mud-stained window. She recognized the window as herself, which had been muddied by the life she had long ago created. Taking some effort to clean, Smythe watched as she wiped away the caked grime and smiled.

Smythe settled into her bed and reached for one of several books she was reading. Interestingly enough, she began to read about individual responsibility. Through her reading, she understood individual responsibility was not what the distortion of her country told it had become—a dog-eat-dog philosophy. Nor was it an "every person for themselves" mentality, but instead, individual responsibility had always been, and will forever be, the highest expression of oneself—the expression of love.

She suddenly understood the collective "we" were not created so a select few survive and prosper, but that everyone could and should grow, survive, and thrive together. The goal for the human race, she surmised, was that people would not turn their backs on the needy, never say no to the hungry, and share abundance so not one is homeless. But, in order to live into the highest form of responsibility, no one could abdicate individual responsibility. Smythe's eyes began to close. She slid more fully into her bed, feeling the gentleness of her Beloved envelop her as she drifted peacefully off to sleep.

Chapter 13

The Divine Dance

—

T HE NEXT MORNING, SITTING HUDDLED ACROSS FROM THE BAKER, Smythe broached a topic with him. Her lifelong desire to deepen her understanding of the human experience, particularly as it related to her Beloved, interested Smythe, and she enjoyed his perspective.

"Joao, how do you hear God? I mean, do you even hear God, or whatever you call God?"

"Oh yes, I hear the whispers of the mystery."

"How?"

"Many ways. The Universe communicates in many, many ways. Thoughts, feelings, experiences, and words. For me, lately, it is a feeling. I feel a certain way about something I am doing or saying; a tingle like electricity I feel at the base of my neck."

"Interesting."

"I also have a knowing, like a thought. They are like pictures in my mind. Often, feelings come with the images to complete more of what the Universe wishes to communicate to me."

"I have heard God in similar ways as you've described. How do you think experience plays into all of this?"

The baker tilted his head to one side.

"Tell me, daughter, why so many questions?"

"I keep thinking I made a mistake, that I wasn't really hearing or feeling the Universe. That all of this jumping into the great unknown was just some made-up crap that I just got myself into. Nothing seems to be working out the way I wanted it to. I had this clear path in mind, and it is anything but clear. Forgive me, for I am simply attempting to more deeply understand."

"The Universe has not ever given us the complete guidebook to our journey, my daughter. There is only an overview. You can choose to walk away at any time, but that would only delay your journey and grieve your spirit. You must have faith—'tenha fe' in my language.

"It is hard to have tenha—"

"Tenha fe. Only if you make it so. Do not seek to know the how. Seek only to be in the now."

Smythe rolled her eyes. *That could have been a meme.* The baker caught her look.

"In so doing, you will follow the next step that opens to all the Universe desires to do through you."

"How then? I thought I was."

"My daughter, you had in your words an inspired thought. The Universe whispered to you, yes?"

"Yes."

"Good, good. We must now believe that we can do the thing we are inspired to do. This is where you are now. You must choose to believe or not to believe. Believe, my daughter."

She smiled. "Can I come back to that?"

"Ok."

"You've used the word communicate versus speak. Are they different?"

"Mmm, yes and no. Yes, often words do not convey the entire meaning of the Universe. So, for me, images happen in my mind, and sometimes feelings, too. It is more complete for my little soul to understand."

"So, they're like visions?"

"Yes, in a way. Although the word 'vision' has had a variety of meanings and understandings. But yes, I get a picture in my mind, and I know what is being communicated. Often, I find it is so that I prepare for something or offer someone a word of encouragement or knowledge."

The "shadow of a thought" unexpectedly returned to Smythe's consciousness. Her breathing became shallow, and a frown furrowed her brow.

The baker beheld the change in his friend.

"What troubles you, daughter? Something has shifted your energy."

"An old story."

"I love stories. Tell me."

"You wouldn't like this one. At any rate, it's not important. Do you ever get warnings?"

"Yes, of course. When I go to the market, I may have a feeling to not go a certain way that I would prefer to go, like a path that I am more comfortable going. You know we all have our sulcus—mmm, how you say... ruts. Forgive me. I move often between languages. I sense danger, or I see cars hitting each other. I have learned to heed the feeling or sight. I simply think for a moment and go a different way, and I am grateful for the direction."

"I think, sometimes, I have a knowing to say go one direction, but my experience tells me to do something else. I'm not sure which to follow."

"Often, we must take a step in order to know. The Universe will always let us know if we are on the right path."

"Explain."

"Joy, my daughter. There is joy on the right path."

"That's funny. My mentor does this activity; he calls it feedback. We're to take a step into action and then pause and listen to the feedback, then take another step and listen to the feedback again."

"That it is good advice. Does he speak of joy?"

"Yes. He says he doesn't do anything unless it brings him joy. He just follows the next inspirational thought and listens to the feedback."

"Good, good. That is correct."

"But doing it that way seems to take so long. Act, wait. Act, wait. I must admit that I tend to want to rush things."

"And it is in the rushing where you often miss the stillness of the Universe speaking. Your journey is like a dance. The Universe leads, and you must simply follow."

Smythe smiled. "I like to lead."

The baker laughed out loud. "Oh, my daughter, do you not understand. The Universe dwells within you. You are leading as the Universe leads through you."

"But it often feels like I am dancing in the dark."

"You want control, but the dance requires you relinquish it. It is similar to hiking at night. I used to do that quite a bit in my home country, especially when the moon was bright in the sky."

The baker paused for a moment, fondly recalling the days of his youth as he hiked through the mountains of Pico Ruivo, a rugged, volcanic green island with high cliffs. Its sister, Pico da Torres, is the second-highest peak of Madeira.

"But I digress. Imagine you hiked at night. It is not advisable, no, but perhaps there were unforeseen circumstances, and to get to safety, you must go forward in the dark. Yet, your headlamp only allows you to see so far. You must slow your pace and go only as far as you can see, no further. You must go at a pace that allows you to see all that is around you. Otherwise, you will fall off a cliff. That would be bad feedback."

"Advisable then to slow down and follow the light in front of me."

"Yes. Follow the whispers of the mystery. Those whispers dwell within you."

The baker eyed his friend. He studied her change in demeanor. He closed his eyes and sensed the ache within her soul and shuddered.

"Smythe, do not allow your old story to darken your spirit. Release it."

Smythe bowed her head, pursed her lips, and nodded. "I have. It just comes and goes."

"Then it has not been released. Look up, Smythe."

Smythe raised her head and met his eyes. The kindest eyes which allowed one to drink in divinity were now glassy.

"Then it has not been released. I sense your trouble—there is fear, and that fear you feel lives within your heart. Go to the core of it and see what it has to say."

"I know what it says," snapped Smythe. She took a breath and willed herself to shove the memory aside.

"Daughter, we can only be free by unhinging the chains we have placed around ourselves. Your freedom is not the thing connected to attaining a goal, but that which lives within your spirit. Release the chain that binds you."

Smythe smiled at him. "Thank you for the conversation. It has helped, but I have to go now."

"My pleasure, daughter."

The baker watched as his friend left the shop. A tear trickled down the baker's cheek as the door closed behind her. The only sound in the shop was the echo of the tiny bell which hung over the door.

With no one left in his shop, the baker spoke aloud. "What shall we do for her? I feel her ache. It lives within her and has grown cancerous, threatening her progression. She is needed."

The Universe remained unmoved as the silence spoke. "While she edges near the abyss of despair and may soon plunge into its waters, she will not drown. She need only use the gifts given to her to find her way out."

Chapter 14

Let Go of the How

—

THE WEEKS ROLLED BY, AND SMYTHE BEGAN MORE TO FEEL JOY AS she put into practice the baker's advice. She read, meditated, studied, wrote, developed lesson plans based on her mentor's teaching, and followed leads for new clientele. Yet, the mundane had begun to settle into an uncomfortable place within her. She had grown accustomed to her unwelcome guest, but found herself in what she thought was a monotonous routine. She limited the time she spent with the baker from several hours per day to a little over an hour and remained in her apartment as much as possible. At the end of the day, she showered and settled into the evening, but every evening also held the same routine. She would read and drift off to sleep in a chair in her living room before cajoling herself out of slumber a few hours later. Padding off to bed, she would sleep for a few more hours before starting a new day.

One early morning, as she and Artie made their way to the baker's shop, Smythe asked if she could have just a bit more privacy with him than what Artie typically provided to her. To her delight, Artie agreed. The baker smiled widely and, with his usual greeting, welcomed them in. Once Artie determined the shop was safe, she positioned herself in Team 2's vehicle directly outside the shop with Team 1 posted in the alley.

"What may I offer you?"

"This morning," she replied, "I'd like some advice."

He moved gingerly behind one of his display cases and listened intently as she began to speak. He did not lower his gaze nor look in another direction, his gaze piercing deeply into Smythe's eyes as though reading her very essence. His energy of love and acceptance encompassed Smythe—so much so, it nearly brought her to her knees.

"Ev-Every night is the same," Smythe began. "After I shower, I plop myself into a horizontal position on my couch or a chair and watch TV with Artie while perusing my emails. Sometimes I read if Artie is still on her tablet, but really, I'm numbing myself out until I am peaceful enough to fall asleep. Slumber comes as it usually does, and then the morning comes as it usually does, and I repeat the day and evening—again and again and again.

"I've thought about this behavior, and it occurs to me that I'm in this perpetual cycle of numbing myself. Or, perhaps, I've unconsciously developed a rutted routine. At least that's what I'm sensing. I'm attempting to understand where it's coming from, but I don't have answers yet. I enjoy studying and working on my business. But what I know is that I feel this void. I've often wondered if I'm doing numbing, and I know others do it—why? Why are we numbing? Hell, Artie and I had a discussion about it. She said that we abdicate thought to numb to fill a void. I just can't stand it, numbing out that is—especially night after night."

They both remained silent for a while, allowing the sweet aroma of the air to again still around them.

Finally, the baker spoke. "You will never be enough until you believe you are enough. Now, what may I offer you?" he said, his tongs pointing toward a pastry she had yet to try.

What the hell was that?!

Dumbfounded, she simply made her selection. Once seated, she decided to eat the newfound pastry the baker's tongs had pointed toward earlier. Her usual selection of malasadas would have to wait. She lifted the delicate pastry to her mouth, taking in the aroma of coriander and cinnamon before taking a bite.

What IS this?! she thought, fighting not to spit it out. The pastry was bitter and dry, and she struggled to swallow it. *How and why would he sell this? Did he forget the sugar or honey?*

The baker remained behind his display case and nonchalantly observed her while arranging and rearranging his pastries. Choosing not to offend him, she continued to eat the pastry.

The last bite cannot come soon enough.

The baker watched until she ate the final bite. His eyes narrowed slightly, and he quietly sighed.

"In life," he began, "people often force themselves down the same path every day, even if it disagrees with them. They rarely deviate from it. You are a writer, and for a long time, you forced yourself to remain in the business world. Day after day, you struggled to swallow the bitterness of your job. You could have simply put it down so long ago, but you did not believe you were enough to do what your heart wanted you to do. But you finally listened to it. Yet, you are again unhappy. You will never be enough until you believe you are enough."

"But I know that I am enough, I just don't know how to create the life I want," Smythe said, somewhat surprised at the whining disposition she felt within her.

"The Universe always guides us; you only have to ask. Then, watch and wait for the response and trust the change you wish to make will happen. I will tell you a secret that you will need to hear countless times: the how of the Universe is not in the predictable. Let go of the how, Smythe, and stay in the now."

The baker brought her a glass of water to wash away the bitter taste of the pastry. He smiled and excused himself for a moment to tend to his creations that sat on cooling racks in the kitchen.

Smythe sat perfectly still for a moment.

Let go of the how. Control. I still want control.

The baker returned and began to add additional pastries to his display case.

"It's control again."

"More than that."

"More than control?"

"Yes. Control is ultimately what you want."

"I don't understand. What is more than control?"

"The predictable, for in the predictable lies control. Let go of the predictable. That is what you have noticed, yes?"

"Yes. It's been a lifetime of it."

"Yes, for us all. Yet, the joy is discovering the Universe does not live in the predictable. You may shift now. Keep going, my daughter, and do not give up."

"I will, but I can't guarantee I won't swear like a sailor along the way."

The baker howled in laughter. "My friend, you have made my day."

Smythe smiled. She wrapped up her original choice of pastry and ordered an additional two dozen malasadas and a coffee. Once the baker completed her order, she bid him a good day and left the shop to see Artie standing right outside the door.

Surprised by her delight in seeing Artie, Smythe smiled and handed Artie a coffee. She bent down and placed a bag on the concrete before reaching in and pulling out a small pastry box.

"Here, this box is for you. I'll drive so you can eat."

Picking up the bag that held a second, larger box, she added, "This box is for the other teams."

She walked over to Team 2's vehicle and handed the driver the box. She returned to her vehicle, entered in on the driver's side, and started her engine.

Opening the box, Artie grinned. "You do care."

Smythe turned to Artie as she fastened her seatbelt.

"I'm sorry, I just needed to talk to Joao alone. It wasn't about you. It's just I've had this nagging thing inside of me."

Artie held her first malasada between her fingers, her eyes fixated on the Portuguese sugar-dusted doughnut.

"No explanation needed, I'm just happy you thought of me."

Smythe headed home, but true to form, rather than remaining on the most direct route, Smythe chose a scenic route to return to her apartment, veering from the caravan. It caused her to lose the lead car instead of remaining sandwiched between the trailing vehicle. The lead car would eventually adjust to the route, and, once again, sandwich her between the other team's vehicle. This behavior was an annoyance that caused Artie to insist she turn around, take the more direct route, and allow her team to do their job—on more than one occasion.

"It's too dangerous, Smythe. This area is too crazy remote. It's beautiful, yes, with its rolling hills, but it's a needless risk," Artie had said. Today was no different.

"Smythe! C'mon. Turn it around or pull over and we'll switch drivers. Those are your only two options. Remember, driving is a privilege that I offer. I can easily revoke it!"

"You're eating. I've got this."

"No, you don't got this. I've got this. Turn around!"

Smythe continued to drive and watched the passing grassy hillside beside the two-lane road. The road began to gently curve from left to right, lulling her into peace. She noticed the ride was smooth and smiled. It seemed the road had recently been re-paved. *This stretch doesn't allow me to safely pull over. Therefore, Artie's demand will have to wait*, she reasoned.

She continued to drive, longing for the smell of the ocean, remembering the ocean breezes of a few short years ago. She would find a quiet place to park along the side of the road and pull over, often scooting in between an encampment of RV's. At the beach, she would walk along the ocean's edge, allowing the water to lap against her ankles, leaving a sandy residue of a thousand lifetimes across her feet. She remembered the coolness of the air as it tingled the hair along her forearms, the scent of salt and sand infusing her spirit.

Her eyes gazed around the rolling hills.

But I'm here. God, am I the only one who always seems so restless? Am I the only one who longs for the vision of my heart to manifest right now?

Smythe thought about her conversations with the baker.

The now versus the how.

She began to understand her restlessness was of her own making. She was wishing for a different future; a future away from where she currently resided.

I could potentially end all of this in the next breath. I could just move. But I am choosing not to, so what's the answer?

Smythe took in a slow breath and gazed at the beauty around her. She willed herself to begin to appreciate the green hills of the valley. The tiny grasses shooting up from their slumber, the grayness of the sky offering a modicum of cool air. She grinned. It was the only place that was important, and up until now, she was choosing to discount it.

She thought of the city. City folks longed for the countryside, country folk longed for the experience of the city, valley folk longed for the ocean, and ocean folk longed for the valley. They all chose restlessness instead of contentment.

This being in the moment of "what is" sucks!

Smythe continued to drive, and like a feather drifting upon the path of a gentle breeze, her Beloved spoke.

"It is the why."

Smythe, in an instant, remembered a vision she had one morning shortly after moving to the valley. It was a vision she dismissed, believing it to be the result of her longing to move away from the valley. She remembered feeling stressed and grumpy about the traffic in the valley before experiencing the vision. For her, it was disconcerting to feel a sense of peace while at home, only to drive and experience the aggressive energy coming at her from all sides as she navigated morning or evening traffic. She recalled holding ill will toward those who tailgated her, willing her to go above the speed limit.

In her vision, she sat on the back deck of a farmhouse between a smattering of Monterey Cypress trees and the ocean. Walking into the house, she strode to the front window and peered out. About a quarter mile away, she could see a two-lane road. Four small, quaint shops lined a portion of the street, catering to the occasional tourist who would wander by. As she passed through the living room to return to the deck, she smiled at the eclectic furniture—a mixture of farmhouse and mid-century pieces. She sensed it was her own home. She returned to the deck and sat upon a patio chair with a cup of coffee warming her hands. She noticed her tablet sitting at the table and recognized it as a piece of a novel she was editing. The image was so strong and real that Smythe could smell the mixture of pine needles and ocean air, even hearing the occasional car pass by. She also noticed she could hear the sound of the ocean as it lapped onto the shoreline. Then, the vision abruptly ended.

Here, now, it occurred to her that this energy of the vision she felt caused her to take the back roads often. It was her "why." She had grown weary of the demonstrative doing, instead of just being, and she longed to remove herself from the drivenness the city residents were demonstrating.

It also occurred to her that her soul's need was to set in motion an unconscious action to manifest a way to permanently move to this place she held within her heart—a place where this driven energy did not live.

The whisper of her Beloved responded, "It is the *why* that is important."

As she felt the feeling which accompanied her why, she felt at peace. It was as if her spirit aligned more fully to this vision of a different environment, and her act of driving along the remote road, here and now, was only practice for what her vision had shown her. Somehow, she knew it was vital in manifesting all that she longed for.

But when?

In that moment, she also experienced an additional truth. It is the heart, the seat of our soul's desire, that will offer us our why. She knew she had to feel this place fully and wait for inspired thought or action to manifest what she longed for. She also knew she could not rush the timing.

"Patience," came the reply of her Beloved. "Your freedom lives unbound, regardless of your circumstances."

Chapter 15

Returning to Darkness

—

ARTIE SPOKE AGAIN, "SMYTHE! PULL OVER. THIS ROAD IS TOO dangerous!"

"Fine, you drive! I need to think, anyway."

God! I just need to breathe! Why can't she understand that!

Incensed at Artie's demand to pull over, Smythe scanned her surroundings. The road had become straight and allowed her to safely pull to the side. Thankfully it was quiet, without a car in sight. In fact, she had not driven the road at that time of the morning. Her eyes lit up at the sight of the lush green hills flanking either side of the road. Pine trees had released a smattering of their cones, and debris dotted the hillside.

Team 2 pulled in behind Smythe's car while Team 1 idled their vehicle in front of her. Disgruntled at the length of time it took Smythe to pull over, Artie exited the car and peered up and down the road before trading places with Smythe. Artie wanted to speak, but decided now was not the time to chastise her client. Instead, she allowed an uncomfortable silence to sit between them.

Artie began to pull away from the curb, but suddenly sensed danger and stopped. Something was coming—she could hear it. She squinted her eyes as an SUV approaching from the opposite side of the road blended into the gray skies, its position only given away by the glimmer of its silver bumper. Unencumbered by traffic, it barreled down the remote road, picking up speed the closer they neared Smythe's vehicle. Artie honed in on the driver's side window. It was down, and the muzzle of a handgun was pointed in her direction.

"Gun! Smythe, get down!"

Artie hit the gas pedal and moved forward. In a perfectly orchestrated movement, Team 1 veered backward toward Smythe's vehicle and swerved their car between Artie and the gunman. Dennis drew his weapon, squinted his brown eyes, and focused on the driver's window, waiting until the last possible moment before squeezing the trigger. He fired past his driver into the window of the oncoming SUV. The SUV lost control, momentarily moving along the gravel curb, but regained control and sped past Smythe and Artie without firing a shot.

Smythe crouched her head low between her knees. As if in a dream state, she experienced a moment of déjà vu, reliving the morning she witnessed the murder in sickening detail. She felt the sound of the gun in the deepest parts of her soul—the noise jarring her chest. She began to tremble uncontrollably, squelching the need to scream.

Team 2 peeled away from the caravan and drove off in pursuit. Team 4, tasked to serve as a trailing backup vehicle, was one minute behind Smythe's caravan. As the gunman passed them, Team 4 picked up the pursuit, allowing Team 2 to rejoin the convoy.

"Keep your head down, Smythe. Don't look up."

Smythe remained perfectly still, save the jostling of her vehicle, as Artie navigated the roads. Though the morning sun had only just begun to break through the clouds, Smythe was engulfed in complete darkness. Her only thoughts were the repeating images of the parking lot. Over and over again, Smythe's memory emanated the sound and violence of the gunshot and the image of the dead man crumpling onto the pavement. Smythe squeezed her eyes shut, covering her ears in an attempt to force the sound and images from her mind. She began to feel sick as Artie made no niceties when navigating turns.

Artie continued to remind Smythe to keep her head down and used her com link to keep in contact with her teams. She drove for roughly 30 minutes in the opposite direction of Smythe's apartment before taking an exit, turning into a gravel road lined by eucalyptus trees. She barked an order for Team 2 to remain hidden just off the road as she continued to follow the well-hidden path.

She found a pull-off along the abandoned roadside sitting across from a burgeoning marigold meadow and parked, quickly jumping out to check the underside of the SUV. When she did not find what she was looking for, she ordered her teams to check their vehicles with meticulous detail. She grabbed Smythe's messenger bag and rifled through it, finally locating her cellphone. It was off. Meanwhile, Dennis checked all of his team's electronic devices to ensure they too had been turned off and made a mental note to have each vehicle re-inspected.

"For now, she's safe. Team 2, remain where you are," Dennis commanded, using the com link.

He spoke with an irritated Artie to confirm safety protocols were in place while they waited for Team 4 to check in. Satisfied that the present danger had passed, Artie strode to Smythe's SUV and opened the passenger side door to find Smythe still crumpled into a human ball.

"Hey, baby. It's ok."

Smythe had yet to lift her head from her knees, her body convulsing in uncontrollable spasms.

"Where-where are we?" she asked weakly.

"Safe. C'mon, let's get you some fresh air."

"I don't seem to be able to. I'm having trouble sitting up, Artie. I'm—"

"You're ok, baby. Give me your right hand," Artie gently whispered.

Smythe, engulfed in darkness, hesitated to unfurl her arms. Yet, slowly, she pulled her right arm out from under her torso. She inched it toward Artie's voice, searching for Artie's presence. Artie lightly wrapped her hand around Smythe's trembling, outstretched arm.

"Do you feel this? It's me supporting you," Artie whispered. Smythe nodded slightly, attempting to remain present, begging quietly for the panic to subside.

Artie tenderly held Smythe's hand in the palm of her own. She allowed her thumb to softly trace the veins on the back of Smythe's hand, offering just enough pressure to enable Smythe to concentrate on the human touch.

"I've been with you from the beginning, and I am here now. We're ok. Can you sit up for me?"

"Yes."

Commanding all of the courage she did not know she possessed, Smythe painstakingly sat up. With her eyes still closed, she gently lifted her head. She shivered as she felt the cold air sweep across her forehead.

Now seated upright, Artie noticed Smythe was sweating profusely, her forehead glistening under the breaking gray skies.

"Baby, slowly open your eyes. You don't need to relive the murder. Just open your eyes."

"I'm having trouble, Artie."

"I know. Turn your head toward my voice."

Smythe complied.

"Good, now slowly open your eyes. It will be me you see."

From her darkness, Smythe gradually opened her eyes and beheld the tender expression of Artie's gaze. She shifted her bottom to allow her legs to swing out the door. Drained of physical strength, she leaned into Artie's arms, a tear trickling down her cheek.

Artie held her until she could feel Smythe's shoulders begin to relax.

"What you've experienced was a flashback. You're not alone in this. A lot of people who have witnessed violence like you have tend to have them. It's perfectly normal, just breathe."

Smythe nodded her head. "Ok, I understand. It-it really sucks, though."

She took in a jagged breath, inhaling the lavender scent of her protector. After a few minutes, she began to look beyond Artie. She sat back from her embrace, disoriented, for she assumed she was in front of her apartment.

"Where-where are we? I-I don't recognize this place."

"It's a place I visit to center myself. I have a few. I enjoy this one because it's not as barren as some of my other spots, and it's off the beaten path. You have to know where you're going to find it. It's a safe place for me, and now you."

Smythe began to peek around, the chirping of birds filling her ears. Through an opening in a cluster of trees, she could see portions of the lower valley and its urban sprawl. Around Artie's ankles, marigolds and other wildflowers danced in the light breeze. She could hear the whispers of Team 1 as they maintained a vigilant eye. Her body still, Artie's eyes were soft as she reached in and held Smythe's hands to steady her.

"How long are we going to stay here?" *There is so much of this place I want to experience. This is Artie's safe place? I would have never guessed.*

"Until I hear back from Team 4. I have water in our team's car if you'd like some."

"I-I'm good. I still have the rest of my coffee."

"Work on that slowly. You still haven't gained your color back yet." She tenderly brushed the back of her hand against Smythe's cheek. "Now, I want to help you become more grounded. Take your hands and rub them together like this." Artie demonstrated by rubbing her own hands together and watched as Smythe mimicked her, facing the palm of her hands together and slowly rubbing them against each other.

"Good. Now wiggle your toes." Smythe blushed a bit, feeling a bit foolish, but did as Artie asked. After a few moments, Smythe stopped. She looked sheepishly into Artie's eyes.

"Artie, my stubbornness did this. I'll follow your instructions. I'm sorry. I could've gotten you—"

"Stop," Artie began, her voice gentle and low. "What's done is done, and we're all alright. Trust me. You're not the first client to buck my directions, and you won't be the last. Just know this is the real deal, Smythe. Someone wants you dead, and it's my job to make sure that doesn't happen."

"I know that now. I guess I just thought the last time was a fluke."

"Well, I would've wished that were the case for you, but it's not. Just rest a bit. There are some malasadas left in the box. I can snack on the other team's."

"How did they find us?"

"I don't know. They came from an entirely different direction, but I'll find out. Just rest for now."

Artie took a step back and allowed Smythe to exit her car. Smythe opened the backseat car door to retrieve a malasada from the box. As she took a bite and savored the sweetness of the pastry, she thought about how amazing the malasadas at Leonard's Bakery on the island of Oahu must be. She peered around the grove, taking it all in. The eucalyptus trees across the road reminded her of Hawaii, and her thoughts wandered to the island of Oahu.

She recalled her first visit was as a teenager, accompanied by her parents, siblings, and grandmother on a family vacation. At the time, she stomped around angrily and then pouted at the thought of going with them. She had hoped to tend to her highly introverted self by spending some alone time in the house. Her mother, however, was insistent she join them, reminding her daughter she was much too young to remain at home alone. Her only other option would have been to send Smythe to stay with her aunt and her two sons. That option was enough to encourage Smythe to make the trip.

On her arrival to the island, Smythe wondered why she was so resistant to coming. The air was humid, but a gentle breeze cooled the temperature down, and the air was infused with the smell of sweet pineapple and hibiscus. Set amongst sandy beaches and blue sky with a diverse culture in language, art, music, and dance, the island and its residents enchanted Smythe. The people were friendly, laughing often, and willing to share their culture with anyone interested in hearing the history of the island. Helpful and gentle in all ways, Smythe could not help but fall in love with the people and knew she wanted to call this island home one day.

Her second visit occurred several years later when she entered the island's full marathon. Her one and only time entering a race of any length, she jumped at the opportunity to return to the island she had fallen in love with and scraped enough money together to buy a round-trip airline ticket and hotel accommodations. After the race, once she recovered from the stiffening ache of her endeavor, Smythe toured the island. Locating a couple of secluded beaches off the beaten tourist path, she met and befriended several locals who lived in the area.

Over the course of her remaining week, she held deep, soulful conversations with them. They "told story" about the island and the colonization of it, and Smythe was fascinated. She learned current Hawaiian people make up less than 20% of the population and, similar to the indigenous people of the United States mainland, Hawaiians suffered the horrors of first contact—massive depopulation, landlessness, Christianization, and economic as well as political marginalization.

"When da U.S. military invaded our land, they overthrew our Queen. Our fate was sealed then, and the Empire was built. They banned our language, and it was replaced by English. Our land and water rights are no more, given to da corporations," her friend Kona had recounted. As a mixed-race woman, Smythe understood the deep pain and grief of marginalization in their own land and the desire to reclaim it. She also remembered leaving with a heavy heart, concerned for the future of her beloved friends and their land.

Her third trip had been with her partner at the time, who attended a business conference. While her partner spent days in meetings, Smythe found her way back to her secluded beaches to find many of the same locals still living there. For her, it was a heartfelt homecoming, a moment in time which she held as sacred. It offered her a connection to people very different from herself, yet wholly accepting of who she was.

She looked down at the malasada she held in her hand and glanced in Artie's direction. She was genuinely grateful her protector had been to Oahu and that she loved malasadas. Her eyes scanned the grove again. It looked as if it could have been plucked from the island and set secretly into this valley. She began to feel connected to the grove and made a mental note to ask Artie for directions to this piece of paradise—after the trial had ended. She needed to feel safe enough to return alone.

Dennis approached Artie with news.

"Hey boss. Team 4 tracked the SUV to a warehouse on the edge of the city. The perps were no longer in the car, but there was a trail of blood leading away from it."

"Where are they now?"

"Don't know. Heavy foot traffic in the area. Our team is not going to find them. I called off the pursuit."

Artie sighed at the news and looked over toward Smythe. On the one hand, she was grateful her client was not injured. But she also wondered what would have happened had Smythe not taken her annoying route. Would the occupants have tracked Smythe to her apartment? More importantly, how was it that the occupants in the SUV, coming from an entirely different direction, tracked Smythe? Artie immediately thought of Carole. She knew relaying the information to her would cause yet another conversation about moving Smythe to a safe house out of state. But, for the present moment, she needed information on the owner of the SUV.

"I need the license plate number, Dennis."

After receiving the plate number, she reached out to Carole through a secured link and relayed the events. None too happy with the current threat, Carole said she would run the plate and send a team to the area and requested a meeting with Artie later in the day.

Artie approached Smythe. "Smythe. We can travel now. Bad guys are gone."

Smythe meekly nodded. Artie leaned in toward Smythe and tilted her head. "What's wrong?"

"Nothing really. Just a bit of a bruised ego. I knew better than to take the route. How many times had you previously told me not to veer from the planned route. But I didn't listen, did I? Seems like a recent pattern in my life—not listening and following instructions."

"Stop beating yourself up. It doesn't do you or me any good. Awareness is key Smythe and it looks like you just figured out an old behavioral pattern that isn't serving you. If I can be so bold—look at the reason for the behavior. From where I'm standing you don't yet trust me—which I don't understand," Artie said with a smile. "I'm really quite trustworthy."

"Now, let me have your keys. One of my team members will drive your vehicle back to your apartment."

* * *

Carole sat back in her chair after returning to her office from an impromptu department meeting. She could feel the heat rising in her cheeks as Artie provided the details of her latest encounter with the syndicate. Carole confided she was having difficulty moving the case forward, feeling some unexpected hesitancy from the District Attorney's office, but would pressure them again.

"I'm beginning to wonder, Artie, if moving Smythe out of the valley is now a viable option. This makes at least two attempts."

"They'll find her, Carole, whether she's here or in Witsec somewhere in the middle of nowhere. I ensured my team vehicles are clean as well as Smythe's, and our devices have been swept, but something still doesn't feel right. All I know is that moving Smythe will not stop them from locating her. Remember the Jennison case?" Artie said, defending her stance to keep Smythe where she was for the moment.

"Yep, I do. Your instincts were right then. All I can say is that I'm glad you were a sharpshooter; otherwise, he wouldn't be alive today."

"To your consternation as well. But eventually, you trusted me, right?

"I did."

"Then trust my instincts now, Carole. Don't force her out of the valley."

Carole hesitated. She knew her friend had good intentions, and there was no doubt that Artie's experience would go unmatched to anyone in the FBI. Yet, this case was much more complicated than even Carole could have imagined, and her director was beginning to pressure her. Carole stared out her office window to the empty conference room where she first met Smythe, recalling Smythe's behavior. As far as she was concerned, Carole had only two options. Reluctantly place Smythe into federal custody, or leave her with Artie.

"For now, I'll agree. But I may have to remove her at a later time, Artie. You've got to figure out how they have been able to track her."

"I understand. Let me worry about that angle."

"Listen, I'm going to change the subject just slightly on you, Artie. I've been doing some digging. Can we meet in an hour?"

"Yes, I'll leave now. Normal place?"

"Yes. See you in a bit."

An hour later, Carole and Artie sat at the back of Rodolfo's restaurant. With only a smattering of patrons, the waitstaff paid little attention to the women as they prepared for an event later that evening.

"This syndicate came into the valley from Hawaii. Specifically, Kauai," Carole said.

"What?"

"Yeah, my sources tell me the murder of the vic had nothing to do with the extortion of money. This was a planned hit. What I now know is that there are some missing and potentially incriminating documents from a global company located on the island of Kauai. Evidently, those documents point to the intentional spraying of toxic chemicals on agricultural land. Not only are they poisoning parts of the island, but there are potentially harmful effects on humans who consume this food—meaning us."

"What kind of chemicals?"

"Chemicals that have been sanctioned by the FDA in limited use only, while some of the other chemicals have not been sanctioned at all. And here's the thing—there is some evidence those chemicals that have been sanctioned are overutilized."

"The vic was in possession of those documents?"

"He was, or at least he knew who had them. The documents were to be delivered to an environmental group here that has the legal muscle to halt the spraying. From what I've pieced together thus far, the island has an interesting history of global agriculture."

Artie stopped picking at her salad. "How so?"

"Well, to begin with, the establishment of sugar plantations. Sugar plantations pulled the Hawaiian islands, specifically Kauai, into a capital agricultural production industry, leaving a legacy of issues related to consolidated land ownership and control over water rights. During the late 1980s, those large sugar plantations eventually shut down. With the Hawaiian economy dependent on tourism by then, conversations were started about making Kauai the center for biotechnology research to diversify and take over some of the agricultural economy. It seems these companies began creating test fields for genetically engineered crops, experimenting with seeds and pesticides on every food type within these fields."

"What has any of this got to do with Smythe or the vic who was killed?" Artie asked.

"Hear me out, Artie. Because of the climate on Kauai, multiple formulations could be tested in the same fields all year long. Those bioengineered crops, i.e., genetically modified crops, have been created by chem companies."

"Wait, you're telling me that chem companies are the ones that created GMO crops?"

"Exactly. It took me some time to wrap my head around that, too. GMOs, which are a product of the deliberate engineering of an organism's characteristics by the manipulation of its DNA, are the new food source in the United States."

Artie sat dumbfounded and shook her head. She glanced down at her salad once more before pushing it to the side.

Carole took out a piece of paper and began to draw.

"Let me see if I can explain it differently. Let's say you have a tomato. Tomatoes don't do well in harsh climates, and are notorious for having issues with pests, right? If you were a chem company, you might figure out a way to make the tomato impervious to harsh climates and pests through the use of chemicals. So, you have your bioengineers figure it out. They take the genes of, say, a specific fish, and transfer it into the genes of a tomato. Now they have a tomato that can withstand a cold climate. They've boosted the yield, subsequently boosting the bottom line.

"The chem companies, from what my sources tell me, are experimenting with genetically modified seeds, exceeding the allowable limit of pesticides many times over—pesticides which, by the way, are banned in Europe because of the potential danger to both the environment and human health."

"Wait, you just jumped from fish DNA to pesticides. Pesticides in what? The tomato?"

"That's what we're finding out, or at least it would seem so. If you create seed that repels insects, you have genetically altered the seed to create their own insecticide."

"Insecticide in a tomato? So, your vic had evidence of this?"

"The evidence is out there already, Artie. As I said, this is no extortion case. This is about the potentially harmful effects of chemicals used in our food."

"So chem companies create crops with their own insecticide within them, which then means you can't wash the chemical compound out of the tomato because it is a part of the tomato," Artie said aloud, attempting to digest the information. She sat staring at the diagram in front of her and then at her salad, jabbing a wedge of tomato with her fork to examine it. She twirled the fork around, looking at all sides of the fruit. She thought about the number of people she knew who now had cancer—healthy people who ate well and exercised. *Where did it get them?*

"But not all tomatoes are bad, right?"

"No. Not all tomatoes are bad. You eat organic, right?

Artie nodded. "Mostly."

"Then stick with it."

Carole reached her hand out and crumpled the diagram in front of Artie.

"So, then it's not a local yokel group. They're connected to something much larger on the island of Kauai, which means they are probably well funded."

"Yes, and our own government may be turning a blind eye to it all. Artie, you have got to keep Smythe alive in order for her to testify. We've got to give a clear signal for the watchdog group to come forward with the information. I don't know who has it, but when we searched the vic's home, we found nothing. His home had been tossed."

Artie nodded her head.

"When I know more, if I can share, I will."

Instead of returning to check on her client, Artie headed to her office. She felt stunned by the information Carole shared with her, and she needed to time to digest it. She paced in circles, her mind bursting with theories surrounding who the chemical companies were in bed with. Government officials? If so, were they island or Washington officials, or both?

She began to research GMO seed and quickly found which chemical companies were currently on the island. While she did not have FBI clearance to begin looking into their financials, Carole did. She could only hope Carole was investigating that angle. She thought about past FBI cases with Carole. Artie had always been the better agent, meticulous in all of her investigations and possessing an uncanny sense to read her environment. Carole, on the other hand, could be careless in her investigations, missing the less obvious angles—and sometimes, the obvious ones.

The expansiveness of the case caused Artie to revisit her security plans, again wondering who was tracking her client and what resources were available to them. She felt an urgency to identify any weak spots in her security plans, knowing a well-funded crime ring would be difficult to stop.

Chapter 16

What Do You Want From Me?

—

T HE NEXT MORNING, SMYTHE AWAKENED WITH A START. A LOUD BANG seemed to come from right outside her window. She held her breath; anxious someone attempted to force their way into her apartment. She listened for any sound of Artie in the next room, but heard nothing. No quiet footsteps, no click from a weapon. The apartment was at rest. Well, apart from the annoying click of her ceiling fan. She figured she should fix the part making that god-awful noise—or at least contact the maintenance department.

I wonder if Artie would even allow them in.

She rolled over to her side and glanced at the time displayed on her bedside clock. Occupied by the tic-tic-tic of her fan, a quiet thought began to surface and wreak havoc in her consciousness.

Something is off. Why in the world do I want a cigarette at this time of morning?

Smythe turned onto her back. The baker's words created a quiet onslaught within her soul. "You will never be enough until you know you are enough."

Two-thirty in the morning or not, she could take it no longer.

I need to breathe. I need to feel the cold air against my face. And I want a cigarette!

She rose silently, tiptoeing from her bed to close her bedroom door and twisting the knob on her bedside lamp. She let out a quiet sigh. Opening her closet door, she pulled a T-shirt, sweatshirt, and sweatpants from the dresser. She stared at her vest and cap for a time before placing them on the bed. She quietly dressed, putting the vest on under her sweatshirt and the cap on her head before tiptoeing out her bedroom door. Trying her best not to make a sound, she walked to the kitchen counter where her car keys and wallet lay. As she felt around for them in the dark, Artie shifted on the air mattress.

"Where are you going at this ungodly hour, Smythe?"

"I want a cigarette. I need to talk to my Beloved, and I need to do this alone, Artie."

"Smythe—"

"Please, Artie. I need a cigarette and some coffee. I need just to breathe again."

Artie could hear the angst in the tone in her client's voice.

"You can be alone in your car Smythe, but my team and I will surround you. That's the compromise."

"No, you don't understand," Smythe whispered. "I need to be alone. I don't want to endanger you or your teams any longer. It's really early. I also don't want the distraction of someone else, much less an entire *team* watching my every move."

"We're not watching you, Smythe. We're watching your surroundings." Artie yawned. "And you are not endangering our lives. It's our job to protect you by any means necessary. We all understand the danger of what we do."

Smythe turned on the light in the kitchen. To her surprise, Artie was sitting upright on her mattress. "Artie, I really need to clear my head. I think I need to drive to the mountains—watch the sunrise from there."

A slight tinge of annoyance began to surface within Smythe. *Is it too much to ask to simply watch a sunrise at the spur of the moment without such a production? God, how I miss doing whatever I wanted, whenever I wanted to!*

Artie looked at Smythe, her eyes masking the confusion and anger rising within her heart. Finally, she pierced the silence. "I can be ready in about five minutes. I'll alert my teams," she groaned, starting to stand up. "Actually, make it 15 minutes. I need to make coffee for them."

Artie alerted her teams and started a pot of coffee. "Don't forget your vest and hat, Smythe."

Still fuming, Smythe pointed to her head.

"Well done," Artie mumbled. "And the vest?"

Smythe grit her teeth and lifted the bottom of her sweatshirt.

Once the coffee was made and distributed and her bed dismantled, Artie nodded to Smythe, who was now sitting on the sofa.

"Ready?" Smythe asked.

"After you."

"Please, let me drive. It's a lot to ask, I know. If you see something, I'll stop. I just really need to be alone."

"At least you've said please," Artie smirked. "Smythe. This is a *huge* risk." Artie watched her client for a moment. "Do you want to talk about what's going on?"

"I can't pinpoint it. I'm restless, scared, angry—just a bit of a mess. I need to get out of the city for a minute."

There it is again, Artie thought. She could hear grief in Smythe's voice. Something deeply troubled her client—something beyond the attempted murder. She pursed her lips. "I'll allow it, but I will have one of my team vehicles in front of you and another behind you. We'll take back roads to the mountain. There should be little traffic, if any. We'll drive at your pace, but at the slightest sniff of trouble, I'll need you to stop, duck your head, and wait for one us to get to you. Understand?"

"Ok. I understand. Thank you."

"This is a risk, Smythe."

"I know. I get it."

Artie nodded. She outfitted Smythe with a tracking device and a com unit. Satisfied both were functioning properly, she escorted Smythe to her SUV before entering the Team 1's vehicle.

"Boss, are you sure about this?" Dennis asked.

"No. No, I'm not. Do you have a tailing team ready?

"Yes. Today it's Team 5. They'll hang back about a mile."

"Smythe, we're all set. Let's go."

The caravan headed out through a winding road that led to the mountain range an hour away. Smythe drove in silence with her windows down, feeling the embrace of cold air as it swept across her face. She inhaled the smell of concrete and smiled. It reminded her of adventure. Her shoulders began to relax, her hands lightly holding the steering wheel as she began to hum. Surprised by her reaction, she realized she was outdoors, heading into nature. While she was never really fond of the great outdoors other than the ocean, the mere distance from the valley offered her a sense of freedom.

She continued to drive, her playlist playing softly in the background. She turned up the volume. The artist, Israel and the New Breed, quietly pierced her heart with the lyrics of "Take the Limits Off". In many ways, it felt as if it were a theme song to her journey sung by her Beloved.

Ahead of her, the darkened sky held the splendor of the approaching mountain range. As traces of the mountain came into view, the lyrics ended. Smythe lifted her gaze, and a small aching tear traced down her cheek, dropping from her chin onto her sweatshirt.

The caravan arrived at the base of the mountain and paused long enough to receive direction from Smythe on the location of her destination. Without a car in sight either before or behind them, she proceeded up a two-lane highway, navigating the road carved into the side of the mountain. As she drove, she could begin to feel the rhythm of the road's curvature. It held a melodic cadence, offering the traveler an opportunity to dance to the majesty of its unique song. Smythe took the hand of the mountain, allowing herself to dance to its gentle rhythm, arriving at her destination—a turnout that offered a spectacular view of the valley below. And they arrived just in time to witness the morning sun hinting at its upcoming arrival.

Smythe turned off her car and lit a cigarette. She found herself in reverent joy at the shimmering valley below, beholding the red and orange glint of the sun beginning to peer over the mountain ridge on the other side of the valley. She could see the bluish lights of the city twinkling below, even making out some of the major roads that cut the valley into quadrants.

Perfectly imperfect. We try so hard to march in a straight line. Geez, what a mess we've made. When will it stop? When will I stop?

She continued to watch the color of the sky change to brilliant shades of burnt orange, golden hues of yellow, and hints of cerulean blue breaking through the gray light sky.

I cannot be anything more than what I am. But what am I? Am I just deluding myself? I've stepped out onto this ledge because I believed that I have something to offer, but I'm beginning to wonder— again. Yet, here I sit, doing the exact things I've learned through my modules, and nothing has manifested in my life. Very few clients, no love in my life, the book is more daunting now than ever, and I'm still living in this fucking valley! And oh, let's not forget the reason I have a security detail LIVING IN MY HOUSE!

Smythe looked up to the heavens.

"I have done everything—everything YOU have asked of me! And for what? I'm standing on this ledge, savings slowly dwindling, and everything I'm trying to manifest just sits there like a big fat blob! What do you want from me?!"

The sound of her voice echoed off the rock face of the mountain, and she sat motionless for some time, her anger pulsating through her temples. She glanced around before lighting another cigarette.

Artie sat in the passenger seat of Team 1's vehicle. She squinted her eyes in the direction of Smythe, recognizing the angst. Although Artie had saved an enormous sum of money with several thousand more sitting in investments, she had plowed through nearly half of it in the first few months of her new business venture. She understood the frustration of being open for business and having no one knock on her door while watching her bank account dwindle to overwhelmingly uncomfortable levels. She understood the fear and the courage it took to keep plugging along in the face of unrelenting doubt. She also recognized the need to give yourself permission to pause for a moment and find your bearings. before doing the next thing that must be done—even in the face of bracing fear.

"C'mon Smythe, you got this," she quietly encouraged.

Smythe faintly became aware of a word within her. "Patience." She wanted to retort but held her tongue. She felt the presence of a deep abiding peace that emanated from an interior door of silence. It was a peace that beckoned her before her Beloved.

Through this door, she dragged out her thoughts and feelings and gently laid them before her Beloved. Closing her eyes, she slowly began to disengage from them and settled into meditation. Here, in this space, she felt a deep sense of belonging. It was where her creativity, her strength, and her compassion for herself and others lived. This space provided an expansion of her being in the here-now.

She inhaled a deep, slow breath, counting silently to the number four before releasing her breath to the count of eight. She repeated this several times, focusing on her breath to fully hear and feel her present moment—to feel the nature that surrounded her, breathing in peace and relaxation.

Over time, she became aware of her higher self observing the compulsive, anxiety-ridden thoughts of her ego. She held a deep sense she was existing beyond the rattling noise of the voice which echoed through the chambers of her soul. For a time, with deep compassion, she chose to listen to what it had to say, holding space for that voice and all of its concerns.

Her ego told her she was in pain. It was frightened; it did not want to go down the path she was leading anymore. That voice did not want to be patient, feeling it had been patient long enough and that it was high time she put things into motion. It also told her it was too late to be trying this experiment of a new self, and that she would fail. That voice held cynicism with its every thought.

She took in additional slow breaths and released them. As she observed her thoughts, she realized her ego's voice was starkly different from her Beloved. There was an incompatibility of what her thoughts and accompanying feelings said to the quietness of her being-ness. She quickly became aware of a tension within her body.

She relaxed her shoulders, redirecting her focus to the energy she felt emanating within her hands rather than the onslaught of her ego, which, when given an inch, took a mile. Slowly, as she focused on the energy, her thought attacker faded into a whisper. She focused on her arms until, finally, she became aware that her whole body was alive with energy—her own electromagnetic field. Her ego had taken a silent backseat and the more conscious interdependence she felt with her Beloved began to emerge. Her Beloved whispered, "You are more than you imagine, and you have more to offer if you only would believe and release."

In her connection with her Beloved, she was reminded she consciously made a choice to draw closer to love and expansion rather than hopelessness and despair. For her, this was a path she had willingly chosen so many months ago.

Smythe began to feel the discomfort creep through her body, and it was then she realized she was living in her discomfort zone. She remembered the school of thought that said we as humans will always find a way to remain comfortable. She understood that life. She also understood many others were living that life—a life lulled to sleep. Lulled asleep to the calling of their heart which all have been created for. She reasoned that this type of sleep kept people caged. Over time, and with constant lulling, it was possible to simply become accustomed to the cage. Yet, there is a time where someone is awakened—if it were only perceived as such.

Her Beloved reminded her of the deep core restlessness, and she realized the angst she felt was the alarm bell to awaken her to the life that lay before her. Her willingness to open the door and jump from the cage of comfort allowed her to learn where her creativity, compassion, and awe and wonder lived. She knew they lived—and would always live—outside her comfort zone.

Smythe finally understood she had to willingly be uncomfortable. She had to become uncomfortable facing her cultural programming, digging out the stories she was telling herself, facing her limiting beliefs, and then re-examine the lure of the story of the world and its various trappings.

As she rested in her Beloved, she realized that even her smoking was a type of energy to regain a sense of comfort. It was self-sabotage that threatened to delay, if not derail her sense of full expansion. It held and soothed hopelessness and despair, offering only a toxic temporary reprieve. Although it lit the way as a pointer to something that was off emotionally, she began to recognize she could no longer allow the energy of the tobacco to maintain its grip over her. In that moment of inspiration, she decided to begin a prescription given to her months ago that offered hope to reduce her desire to smoke. Smythe reasoned it would give her a fighting chance to quit.

The dawn continued to break into spectacular strands of orange, red, and golden hues. Smythe opened her eyes and watched the sky display its brilliance. As she continued to watch the majesty of the moment, she was struck by a completely different thought—a deep thought she had not allowed herself to ponder for years. A thought which came from her heart. She listened with interest and heard her heart say to her, *I want a relationship outside friends and family.*

An unsettling tension began to creep into her body. She remembered thinking after an amicable separation from her long-time partner several years ago that she was not "good" in relationships; that she didn't have what it took to sustain a "forever" love of another. She stuffed any desire for romantic connection into the deepest recesses of her heart long ago.

Yet, here, in this moment, she heard her heart. Frustrated she had not reached out toward intimacy; to at least try again. She did not pretend to understand love; in fact, she thought of herself as a bit of a novice. Yet, for Smythe, there existed a deep longing to love another, to grow into a relationship, to have a real sense of belonging, and perhaps even to marry. It was this last thought of marriage that woke her up like a cold bucket of ice thrown over her head, drawing her quickly to the surface, away from the singing of her heart. Just as quickly as the thoughts had come, she discounted her heart and lit another cigarette.

Smythe continued to watch the colorful remnants of the rising sun. It had been a spectacular showcase, yet she sensed it was now time to go. She slowly turned her head toward the car that held Artie and Team 1. She snuffed out her cigarette and opened her car door. As she exited, a member of Team 1 quickly headed toward her. She walked slowly toward Artie's vehicle, and then stopped. She scanned her emotions and began to feel light-headed. Her hands were beginning to perspire, and her breathing shallow. She wondered what it was that she was afraid of.

I can't have the same sense of danger that Artie has.

She took in a breath and stepped to the passenger side of the vehicle. Artie opened the car door.

"Are you ready to leave?"

"Yeah, I think so."

"Ok, we'll caravan down. Once we're down in the valley, is there anywhere you want to go?" Suddenly hungry, Artie was mildly hopeful for a swing by the baker's shop. Smythe tensed her jaw and put her hands underneath the bottom of her sweatshirt.

Why the hell am I so nervous?!

"Well," Smythe finally said, "I was wondering if you might consider driving back down in my car? I'm sure everyone is hungry. We could make a plan for breakfast before I need to get to the day's work."

Smiling brightly at Smythe, Artie replied, "Grabbing food is the first sensible thing you've said to me this morning." She began to put one foot on the dirt pavement and then hesitated. "But I have a different request."

"Let me guess, malasadas to eat and take home?" Smythe said, laughing.

It's good to see her laughing, Artie thought.

"Well, yeah, there's that, but in all seriousness, I need you in the backseat of this vehicle. I really dislike like you driving, especially after the last incident."

There it is, Artie said to herself. *Today will be Smythe's final driving experience until after the trial.* She observed Smythe and braced herself for the objection. The last thing Artie wanted was an argument that she was determined to win, even if it meant hurting Smythe's feelings.

Looking down at the dirt and shuffling her foot around the gravel, Smythe glanced up at Artie.

"I can live with that. I knew it was coming, and I'm grateful you allowed me to drive this morning."

Artie nodded and mouthed, "Ok." She got out of her teams' SUV and opened the back door for Smythe. Smythe gave her car keys to Artie, who then handed them to a member of Team 1.

"Retrieve her bag," Artie said to the agent. She closed Smythe's door and moved around the vehicle and joined her in the backseat. Dennis took the driver's seat while his team member would be the bait centered between Teams 1 and 2.

Along their return journey to the valley, Artie and Smythe remained quiet, allowing a peaceful silence to sit contently between them. Finally, Artie poked the silence.

"I expected that you would have given me more grief about driving."

"I had time to think about it. My insistence on driving has been foolish. Yet, here's the thing. I need a lot of Beloved time, Artie. Before you and your team came along, I spent a significant amount of time alone so that I could be as centered as possible every day. I've been used to just taking off and finding my way to a place and spending time in meditation and prayer. The thought of losing that seemed unacceptable to me, and, honestly, I didn't want to change that part of my routine. I wanted—no, I *needed* some modicum of freedom. For that, I'm not sorry. Yet, I am sorry for not communicating to you what I've needed. You've really done a great job trying to protect me. I've been unreasonably bullheaded and have made your job difficult."

"Smythe, you can still have as much time as you need. You just need to tell me. Tell me what you need, and let me work up a plan. If what you want to do is too risky, I'll let you know, and we can find a workable alternative—*together*."

Smythe nodded and peered at Artie with a side-eye. She wasn't used to expressing her needs or wants, much less having someone want to accommodate them as much as possible. Artie sat back and simply nodded in response.

That evening, Smythe noticed her ego berating her for not accomplishing more of the tasks she set out to do for the day. Sighing, she excused herself from Artie's presence, wandering into the bathroom and closing the door. She looked into the mirror, deep into her own eyes, and the tears began to fall.

"Would you berate your best friend like this had she not completed her task list?" Smythe said out loud to herself.

No, of course not.

"Then why won't you treat yourself with the same compassion and love that you would offer to Susan?"

For the first time, she recognized her first best friend had always been, and always would be, herself. Her epiphany opened a door of love and acceptance, settling lightly into her body. She apologized to her friend and offered, "You did a great job today. Y'all had a great breakfast! You accomplished what you needed to do. And with the knowledge skills and abilities available to you in the moments of the day, you did the best job that you could. I am proud of you, of who you are, and I love you."

It Was a Set-Up

—

THE NEXT MORNING, SMYTHE'S BELOVED BECKONED AGAIN. SHE WAS about to retreat to her room, but a thought occurred to her. She walked out of her apartment and asked her detail to allow her to walk among the paths within the complex and keep a distance from her. They agreed, having already secured the complex.

Smythe began a slow, deliberate walk along the paths. As she walked, she glanced around and noticed a breeze wafting through the leaves of birch trees scattered throughout. She stopped and stood, watching the leaves dance upon the current of the wind.

"Where does the wind come from?" her Beloved asked.

"I don't know. It just is," Smythe replied.

"Ask the trees."

She looked to the trees. "Do you know where the wind comes from?"

The tree branches did not move, yet the leaves seemed to answer. Smythe watched intensely, and she noticed they simply danced. If they could speak, she would have bet they would say, "We only know that there is a flow and that we are pleased to dance upon it."

Her Beloved spoke, "All life is connected to itself and to Me. Life must only dance to the flow. Understanding that all things given from Me offer to all both balance and harmony."

Smythe scrunched her nose.

"Your vision is a vision I have planted within you. You must only dance to the rhythm of the flow of life in the present moment, and leave the rest to me."

"How? Everyone seems to have this notion to do, do, do?"

"Notice the palms above the buildings compared to the trees hemmed in by the buildings. The current of the wind freely flows when above all things. Rise above what you see and come and see through my eyes."

"Yet, I am not as tall as the trees. Beloved, I am like the trees below which barely move—the ones that are hemmed in."

"You only believe that to be. Place your thoughts to my thoughts, above the circumstances which hem you in. Rise your mind to my mind. Meditate upon the trees. Notice they move in the direction of the current." Smythe watched the palms overhead and noticed the leaves of the birch. They, too, moved along the direction of the wind.

She remembered the baker's words. "Your freedom is not the thing connected to attaining a goal—but that which lives within your spirit. Release the chain that binds you."

Later that morning, Artie left for an off-site meeting, and Smythe found herself alone. She took the time to view a webinar suggested by her mentor through an email. Unfortunately, after the webinar, she found herself becoming increasingly annoyed.

"Damn it, damn it, damn it! This feels like a marketing ploy," she said to her Beloved. "Tell me, was the initial investment for my training just another marketing ploy, too? One that bilks unsuspecting idiots like me out of money? I don't have time for this, nor do I have the capital! I quit my job and started this business venture and the book on a wing and prayer. Was this you, or was it my torrid imagination? A kind of self-sabotage? I took all of my money out of my savings. I am doing everything I thought YOU wanted me to do! Was I wrong? Answer me!" She screamed so loudly that her throat began to burn.

The words she had heard a thousand times before came quietly, gently into her consciousness once again.

"Trust. Just trust."

Smythe was in no mood to listen.

"To hell with it!! I don't want it. I don't want what YOU want!"
She glanced at her kitchen wall clock. 1:30. She texted Artie.
"I have errands to run—all in one place."

Geez, even my text is snappy.

She paced, waiting for a reply. Within a few minutes, her
security detail knocked on the door, ready to escort her. As she sat
in the back of their SUV, her Beloved reminded her no dream could
be achieved unless she could make it a reality. Her Beloved also
reminded her of what her mentor once said.

"You're not given a dream unless you have the capacity to do
it. You might have to go back to school, or interview someone to find
out how they got started, but it can be achieved."

Whatever.

"Are you so willing to give up now? There is always a time of
preparation. You have only just begun. Trust in my knowing, and do
not give up," her Beloved said.

I'm not in a space where I want to hear this right now. With tears
beginning to fill her eyes, she continued her conversation with Beloved.

"You know what bothers me the most? It's that his company
endorsed this other guy. It feels like he was just offering a marketing
thing for his next great adventure. Truly, that cuts like a knife. I
mean, he does this amazing work. Why does everything have to be
at such a high cost? Maybe that's the way it works. I get it. He needs
to earn money, but it leaves such a bad taste in my mouth."

Once parked, the security team escorted Smythe into the store.
Smythe flashed her membership card to an employee at the entrance
and pointed at her security detail, indicating they were with her. She
stomped through a maze of aisles before arriving at the pharmacy
department. While standing in line, Smythe allowed herself to get
quiet enough to listen to her Beloved.

"Regardless of how you perceive him, your dream to do the work
I've called you to do is uniquely suited for you, and that's all I will
ask of you. What you have discovered is that this new program is not
a good fit for you. Consider it a 'no' from me for now."

Smythe crossed her arms in front of her and stared down at the floor. Although enormously frustrated, she was also able to call herself out, admitting she was "storytelling" and exhibiting her old go-to behaviors—anger, blaming, and complaining. A bit embarrassed with herself, she examined the trio. She had to admit, instead of responding in ways that would positively feed her subconscious, she was reacting with survival emotions, which would only keep her stuck in her current situation with little forward movement.

Damn it.

The line to pick up prescriptions inched forward. Smythe admitted she had hoped some nagging questions about book publication would have been answered during the prerecorded webinar. Unfortunately, the information did not go into the level of detail she hoped for.

I just don't want to call his team. And who knows, they may not know either.

"That is not entirely accurate, Smythe. You, dear one, are afraid," her Beloved said, responding to her thoughts.

"Of what?"

"Think."

Smythe pondered her current mood. Before long, she began to identify her response as nothing more than unresolved doubt. She shook her head and nibbled the insides of her lower lip.

Deep inside, I doubt the dream... and my ability to make it come true.

"Next in line," came the call. She stepped up to the cash register.

Once she paid for her prescriptions, she asked her team if she might wander through a couple of food aisles. Artie had been picking up a lot of the food tab for both of them, and the least she could do was pick up some groceries for the next few weeks.

And beer, she likes beer. Maybe some wine too—oh, and whiskey. Her team agreed and surrounded her as she moved through the aisles.

Once she paid for her groceries and settled into the SUV, she allowed her mind to again ponder the unresolved sense of doubt.

It was then, in the briefest of moments, that something shifted. As though examining herself as a character in a film, she sensed she had grabbed onto her dream as if she were pulling a baby from a kidnapper. She pressed her dream tightly to her chest.

It's my dream. The thought caught her by surprise. *No, it's our dream. Perhaps* your *dream; your thought for me.*

Regardless of whose dream it was, she felt somehow attached to it. In the briefest of moments, the vision ceased to be something "out there," but instead was a tangible reality awaiting her arrival.

You're not given a dream unless you have the capacity to do it. You might have to go back to school, or interview someone to find out how they got started, but it can be achieved.

Smythe was reminded of Hildegard of Bingen. She had described herself as a feather on the breath of God. Smythe sighed as she seemed to sense she had been set up by her Beloved.

Stupid ego, lower vibration. Always wants to do things on your terms. 'Be of service,' you said, but on whose terms? My Beloved's or yours?

She could only smile at herself and settled easily into the return trip home.

Smythe put away her groceries and continued to ponder what it meant to truly be of service. As she thought about her many virtual mentors, she wondered how they came to understand service. She knew that many of them felt they had been called—they claimed they had an internal sense of knowing. They chose to focus on what their hearts wanted from them and followed it. For Smythe, it was a troubling query that would continue to surface. She knew that each time it did, a greater sense of clarity and knowing would emerge. At least, that was her intention.

Artie arrived at the apartment about an hour later and offered to order food. Smythe explained she had gone shopping and offered to prepare a meal. Artie accepted the invitation, and together, they created a meal that, by all standards, they were both impressed with— pumpkin risotto, a kale salad, and organic red wine. Laughing with one another, they wondered why they hadn't done this more often.

Chapter 18

A Fish out of Water

—

O VER THE NEXT FEW WEEKS, SMYTHE PREPARED FOR THE FIRST ten-day conference. She re-read the dress code as she contemplated what to wear. Business casual. It was then she noticed a low-level anxiety surfacing within her body. She understood the anxiety well.

Hello, old friend.

She remembered she was often teased by her classmates about almost every aspect of her appearance. Her hair, although wavy, had a little too much frizz to it. Her clothing not cool enough. Her skin tone was either too dark or too light. She felt completely out of step with current conversations about boys, fashion, or all the other topics girls her age would discuss amongst themselves.

As an adult, she quickly came into her own and dealt with her feelings of inadequacy over her appearance. Proudly sporting a shaved head, she draped her body in tailored, gender nonconforming attire which suited her quirky—if not awkward—personality.

While Smythe prepared for her conference, Artie created a detailed travel plan which, to Smythe's delight, included arriving by vehicle caravan.

"Can you say road trip?!"

"Cool your jets, Smythe. You won't be driving."

"I'm ok with that. Just tell me which vehicle I'm in, and I'm good."

"I thought you said you weren't keen on traveling as a kid."

"I grew up. I realized I hated traveling the world—settling in a different part of the country every couple of years. Plopped into a new school in the middle of a school year. It was tough."

Artie nodded her head. "Well, this girl here has to *plan* for your road trip."

"Is it complicated?"

"Only if you consider the route which has to be created, as well a secondary route, infiltrating the hotel staff, staking out the floor you will be on, and generally keeping you safe while you're in class… nah, it's a breeze."

"Smart aleck. I only ask because I've noticed you've been meeting with Dennis a lot lately and you've been away from the apartment more than usual. I didn't know if it was because of something you weren't telling me, or simply because you were planning for this trip."

Artie thought about her conversation with Carole and the chemical company. That information was something she was unwilling to share with Smythe. Smythe, she thought, only needed to know enough to remain vigilant during the conference and refrain from taking any spur-of-the-moment trips out of the hotel.

"I'm not gonna lie, Smythe, these conferences are really risky. There are just too many unknowns. So, while there hasn't been a direct threat on your life in a while, there are a number of details that I need to address in order to keep you safe. I would prefer that you don't attend the conference, but, given that you've spent months preparing for it and your certification depends on your participation, I'm making do. Safety is key."

"I appreciate the effort, Artie. I'll listen and follow your direction."

"I'm not worried about that. Oh, and by the way, about your room. We'll be sharing one, so I changed your reservation from a king bed to two queens. Same price."

"Without asking?"

"Security privilege." Artie smiled.

"Next thing I know, you'll be borrowing my clothes without asking," Smythe said in a feigned mumble.

"Now that you mention it, I've had my eye on that burgundy sweatshirt you just bought a few weeks back."

"Get back to work, you!" Smythe balled up a piece of scratch paper and threw it at Artie as she left the apartment.

* * *

The early morning offered very little traffic, allowing the caravan to move easily through the highways and outlying cities to her destination. Smythe sat in the backseat of one of the SUVs and watched as they traveled through the barren landscape. It was the intricacy of it all that Smythe seemed to notice for the first time. The complexity of the desert scenery offered a glimpse of its grandeur, simply because of its apparent lack of diverse terrain. The architecture, she noted, blended in rather than announcing its presence. The lack of precipitation throughout the year left the land arid, allowing mostly cacti and Joshua trees to flourish. Not a fan of cactus, she frowned, diverting her attention to a novel she recently started.

The longer the caravan traveled, the more the landscape began to change. Hints of green grass covered the Transverse and Peninsular ranges. Soft chaparral and woodlands replaced cacti and sagebrush. Palm trees replaced Joshua trees, and traffic became denser.

As commuter traffic began to fill the highway, Artie surprised Smythe with a brief trip to the ocean's edge about an hour from the hotel. Smythe sat mesmerized as her vehicle drove along the highway next to the Pacific Ocean. She rolled down her window to smell the ocean air, her heart beating in ecstasy at the sight of the water. She watched as her driver slowed, taking a side road which led to a parking lot adjacent to a boarded-up restaurant overlooking the ocean. Once they came to a halt, Smythe shot out from the car like a cannon, kicking off her sandals as she ran through the sand to the ocean's edge.

"Smythe, hold up. Wait!" Dennis yelled.

Dennis and his team member bolted toward Smythe. They immediately surrounded her and surveyed the surroundings. Expressionless, they moved around her, scanning the parking lot. Not a single car was present, and the beach was all but deserted. But then again, that was the reason Artie chose the location. It was still a bit early for tourist season, and, compared to other locations, this area did not offer a wide beach most were accustomed to, nor bathroom facilities that other, more popular beaches offered. The only restaurant for miles sat vacant, closed for repairs—the result of a fire in the kitchen.

Artie casually walked alongside Smythe and stood next to her with a grin lifting the edges of her gray-brown eyes. "You want to explain yourself, Lucy? That little stunt could have ended badly."

"I'm so sorry. I could help it, but then again, I didn't want to. I've so missed the ocean. Just look at it! Isn't it glorious?" Smythe's smile continued to grow as she scanned the vastness of the ocean, watching as waves lapped upon the shoreline. She looked up. The sun provided a clear blue sky, and the air felt crisp against her skin. Full of jubilation, she unexpectedly wrapped her arms around Artie's neck and hugged her, causing Artie to blush.

Additional members from the caravan approached and casually formed a U shape around Smythe. With that wide grin still spread across her face, she surveyed their appearance.

"I've never seen the guys in shorts and such casual attire. I must admit, Artie, I rather like it. They're not so stiff-looking."

Artie smirked. She knew her team was well prepared. Like Smythe, they wore body armor, but with one dangerous difference. Hidden beneath their windbreakers were their weapons—ready to be drawn on her behalf should the need arise.

"All part of the façade, Smythe. We're just a group of tourists enjoying a quick minute on the beach. You've got five minutes. I suggest you take in as much ocean air as you can."

Smythe nodded and breathed deeply. She could smell the stench of drying seaweed, and the briny scent of plankton. *Salt air,* she thought. *I've missed your smell.* She bent low and scooped up sand in both of her hands and gently rubbed them together, raising the remnants of the sand up to her nose.

"You really love the ocean, don't you?" Artie asked.

"I do. It reminds me of Hawaii and my friends who live there," Smythe said with a tinge of longing.

Smythe shook the bit of sand from her hands and pressed her feet into the sand. It was cool to the touch. She walked forward and allowed the gentle waves of the water to lap upon her feet as she stood, soaking in every sensation of her treasured ocean.

Artie left Smythe alone for a time, observing her body movements. Smythe's shoulders had relaxed, her stance casual and her head tilted in reverence to the sky. She smiled to herself. If she could be sure that no one was tracking the caravan, she would have given Smythe more time—perhaps a good part of the day. But she could not be sure, and she had a job to do. The quick stop needed to be just that—a quick stop. Artie moved toward Smythe and touched her elbow, indicating it was time to go.

Smythe took in a big gulp of sea air before turning toward the caravan. She watched as her feet left an imprint of her visit as she ambled along the sand. Artie strode to the back of the SUV, opened the trunk, pulled out a small towel, and handed it to Smythe.

"Here, you can clean your hands and feet with this."

Smythe smiled and accepted the towel, wiping off her feet. She turned around and took one last look at the ocean before entering the car. As they pulled away and continued along their route, she peered out her window and watched as the ocean disappeared behind the homes.

She side-eyed Artie, who sat next to her.

"You didn't have to stop."

"I know, but it was necessary. For your well-being."

"Thank you."

An hour later, Smythe and her teams arrived at the hotel. It was a typical conference center hotel; the grounds were spacious, offering a large fitness center, spa, several restaurants, and business amenities for conference guests. As they checked in, casually surrounded by Smythe's security detail, she recognized just how contained her world had become. So much so that once she arrived at her room, she found it difficult to return to the lobby and engage with her new group. Her initial instinct was to hole up in her room, telling herself Artie would want more control over her surroundings. She walked out onto the balcony overlooking the lush grounds of a pool and outdoor restaurant and began reasoning with herself.

Besides, the views from the balcony... Just wow. I bet evenings are glorious.

"Away from the balcony, Smythe," Artie said.

Smythe rolled her eyes and walked inside.

"You have free rein to meet up with your new friends. I have their profiles, so I know who belongs and who doesn't. Just remain within the hotel. Breakfast, lunch, and dinners in."

Smythe pondered her last few months and observed that her only real ongoing human contact had been with her security detail and her mother. It did little to prepare her for real-world engagement, and she had to muster up enough courage to interact with her cohort. That left Smythe with a choice: be ruled by fear, or reach out in love and engagement.

On the second day, she coaxed herself out of her room and into the lobby for a pre-conference cocktail hour. Out of her element, she found herself trying to adjust to the open-hearted humans she met. This group had a way of accepting one another. Hesitant at first to engage them in conversation, she mostly remained quiet, offering only her first name, where she was from, and her line of work. Yet, over the course of a few hours, she began to relax. It dawned on her that no one in her group attempted to outshine one another. She took in long, deep breaths, as though sitting beside a fire on a cold winter's day, drinking a hot cup of cocoa, smiling, and laughing easily.

With a cohort of 48 attendees and 20 staff assistants, she came to know people from Ghana, Brazil, Canada, Czechoslovakia, Philippines, Mexico, Hong Kong, and Iceland, just to name a few. She was invited to several dinners where participants whiled away the evening getting to know one another. They reviewed what they learned and the activities their mentor had demonstrated, which supported the learning content. She participated in heart-centered conversations and discovered these inquisitive, sincere, tender-hearted souls were working hard to face their fears and move out into the unknown world they had been called to serve.

This type of interaction had been a first for Smythe, and as her new friends shared their stories, she reveled in their vulnerability. They were so open about sharing their experiences. She reminded herself of an earlier conversation with her Beloved about the dreams she had for her life. Now, sitting amongst her new group of friends, she could almost feel her Beloved smile and hear the words of encouragement. "Everyone feels fear. Yet, notice, while each of you have felt the fear, you have moved through it. Movement is key. Slow, steady forward movement."

Smythe later remarked to Artie she felt an affinity for them. "They all have a gift to offer a world which seems to be tearing itself apart. It's as though we're part of a really close-knit family, even though we've only just met." For Smythe, it was both exhilarating and overwhelming, yet each evening, her heart felt full.

* * *

One evening, near the close of the conference, Smythe sat upon her bed, deep in thought.

"You ok?" Artie asked.

"Yeah. I'm great, actually. I was just thinking that I didn't have to have 'that' conversation with a single person in my cohort."

"What do you mean?"

"I've been derided about my looks most of my life; particularly, my hair. Finally, about fifteen years ago, at the age of 22, I had enough and just cut it off completely. But the behavior of others only intensified.

"People would often stare or give me weird looks when I was out running errands—you know, like the ones you get so annoyed about," Smythe teased. "At first, I didn't understand. But some audacious soul would come up and say something like, 'Why would you do that? I wouldn't have the courage to do that.' It's rare that someone would boldly come up to me and compliment my hairstyle."

"So, with this group, you thought you might have to defend yourself?" asked Artie.

"Yes, actually I thought I would. I've had to have *that* conversation. Politely, of course. Well... sometimes politely, depending on how much energy I wanted to put into the conversation! I realize now, that out of the sixty-plus people I met, I expected I would have had to have that conversation with at least *one* person. However, it has yet to materialize. It's funny; I caught myself storytelling."

"Storytelling?"

"Otherwise called narrative bias. It's a tendency to make sense of the world through the stories we tell ourselves, especially when it comes to the unpredictable. As humans, we tend to like predictability. So, our brains create a story to connect different pieces of information together. The problem is, we often leave out the other important facts that don't fit the story we are telling ourselves. We assign meaning where none should be made.

"In my case, based on past experience, I made and created a story in my head by replaying past experiences and consciously created a story in my head. A story of how I've been treated and expected to be treated—thus, storytelling. I was so wrong in this case."

"Storytelling can be exhausting," Artie mused.

"I would agree there. It's wasted energy, yet it begs the question: When does one use their past experience to inform or ready oneself for present dealings?"

"For me, it requires that I remain present and watch body language as well as listening to the verbal words spoken. I only use the past as passive information," Artie said.

"Makes sense. I think I've had enough negative experiences around my hair that I've come to expect the reaction. It's really a breath of fresh air. With this group, I don't need to relive those past experiences.

"I get it, Smythe. You're a woman of color with an unusual hairstyle. I get the shield. And I'm sure it's been difficult. I know our country's behavior for anything out of the ordinary, regardless of what it touts. Just... I don't know. I'm not sure how to respond."

"I know there's a wall that I put up, Artie. It's just that I feel the 'ism' every single day. The otherness. I'm just learning balance and hoping I have finally found my tribe; somewhere I can just be and be supported."

Artie nodded her head as an ache filled her heart. *Another aspect to her,* she thought.

If Smythe could describe what she felt from her group during her week at the conference, it was that she simply felt loved. She was enfolded into a group that headed toward something more expansive and, to be honest, rather frightening. In any case, the interactions allowed her perspective to shift. She didn't need to explain herself. She just *was,* and her enough was enough.

One evening as both she and Artie were preparing for bed, she explained further. "What's weird is that I don't need to fight to just *be.* My mentor's assistants have a way of simply making space for whatever shows up in the room and to welcome it. I'm so glad I've been able to experience this. And your team? Can I just say, they've been great."

Artie smiled at the compliment.

Artie and her teams made themselves clearly visible to Smythe at all times and offered her both a sense of safety and a bit of humor throughout the week. Dressed in casual attire and split into pairs of no more than two, her detail acted their parts. They were Smythe's protectors, but they appeared to be nothing more than either patrons of the hotel or hotel employees.

Smythe was rather amused by their behavior as they kept a protective field around her that only she could see. On more than one occasion, Smythe burst out in laughter and had to recover as she watched her security detail mingle with members of her cohort group during breaks. She remembered an occasion where a pair of Artie's team members were disguised as hotel guests. She watched as they interjected themselves into her conversations with her cohorts. They asked questions of her, pretending to get to know her, and asked her classmates questions about the conference. Serious in their explanation, her new friends politely described the reason they were there and some of the learning that had taken place. Dennis, Artie's second in command, made silly faces to Smythe, which only she picked up on. Smythe considered their behavior lighthearted, which was an aspect of the team that she hadn't seen before. Through their playfulness in conversations, they lost a little bit of their robotic, devoid of emotion demeanor and seemed more... human.

Yet, as amusing as their behavior seemed to Smythe, from Artie's perspective, they were simply doing their job. Profiling each of the conference attendees, the teams were scanning for potential threats to Smythe's safety, questioning conference-goers on particular aspects of their learning, looking for any signs that a person did not belong.

Now, sitting in the back of her team's SUV, returning to the valley, Smythe could not help but chuckle and smile brightly. Her heart was lightened, and while watching the rich green give way to the dusty brown landscape, she continued to fondly reflect upon her week. She felt a new sense of accomplishment and drive to meet her upcoming goals, yet she also recognized a nagging uneasiness which began to make its way into her body the closer they approached the valley.

Still, for the first time, she discovered that instead of dreading whatever it was which attempted to erode a renewed sense of becoming, she began to actively search for the source and meaning behind it. Whatever it was, she knew it would offer her the insight she needed to dance her way forward along the breeze of life's flow. Courage to meet the unknown was taking root in her psyche.

Chapter 19

Digno

—

SEVERAL WEEKS LATER, AFTER RETURNING HOME FROM THE conference, Smythe awoke from a dream. The words, "Made in his image and made in his imagination to be authentically and uniquely ourselves," played over and over again in her mind. She knew she had either read or heard those words in the recent past.

She lay in her bed and listened to the silence of the night, replaying images of the people in her life who had given her concern; people who had spoken ill of her. In turn, she confessed to herself that she had done the same. She remembered the words, "God spoke over each and every single person. When we devalue someone, we are devaluing what God spoke over. If we devalue their dreams, their creativity, or their unique way of expressing themselves for the higher good of all, we have spit into the face of God. You are celebrated in the eyes of God."

It was Maya Angelou who spoke it, I think. Celebrated in the eyes of God. I am celebrated, as is everyone else. But how am I the expression of the character of God—the thought of God? I. Celebrated in the eyes of God?

Smythe rose from her bed and dressed quickly and silently, hoping not to disturb Artie. She grabbed her jacket, turned off her bedroom light, opened her door and tiptoed out into the hallway, making her way to the dining room. She stood at the foot of Artie's air mattress and wondered if she should wake her up. It was then she remembered her promise not to drive.

She tiptoed into the kitchen and turned on a low-beam oven light. Artie sat up and asked her instinctively, "Where are you wanting to go, Smythe?"

"To talk with the baker."

"Ok, give me a second."

Artie reached her arms to the ceiling and stretched. She rose from her makeshift bed and grabbed a pair of dark blue khakis and a matching sweatshirt. Quickly dressing, she called her teams before escorting Smythe into the waiting vehicle of Team 1.

The baker unlocked his door and ushered them in with his usual greeting.

"Welcome, please come in. Choose wisely."

He was in the process of completing his final preparations before opening his shop, placing the last of his pastries into their display cases and removing his chairs from the top of the tables, setting them into place.

Artie checked the restrooms and took a peek into the baker's kitchen. Once she was satisfied the shop was empty, she asked Smythe to call her when she was ready to leave. Before locking the door behind her, the baker offered her a cup of coffee to go, which she gladly accepted. As Artie turned to leave, he called after her, "I will take good care of her."

"She is not hungry right now," Smythe replied.

The baker nodded and smiled. "I enjoy her presence when she is here, my friend."

Smythe did not reply, feeling grateful for Artie's absence. She had begun to enjoy Artie's company, yet there were some conversations with the baker she did not feel Artie needed to be privy to. This, she felt, was one of them. The baker brought Smythe a cup of coffee before returning to the back of his display cases, fiddling with the placement of each pastry.

"I keep dealing with feelings of unworthiness," Smythe said to the baker, a bit annoyed with herself. It had barely been a month since the conference. Her mentor had spoken about unworthiness, stating unworthiness was a limiting belief and a form of self-sabotage, yet here the feelings were, in all of their glory. She thought about all she wanted to be, do, and have, and noticed thoughts of inadequacy pop into mind, causing her to question herself.

Why hadn't the information taken hold? What am I missing?

The baker removed his disposable gloves and threw them into a nearby trashcan. Walking over to Smythe's table, he asked, "What is this unworthiness that you speak of? Americans have such an unusual way of speaking. What do you mean?"

"Um, not feeling deserving of something. Not good enough. Does that make sense?" Smythe asked, knowing that she really didn't understand the word herself—only the feeling.

"That is ridiculous!" the baker exclaimed. "We are all… how you say… what is the opposite word called unworthiness?"

"Worthy."

"Worthy! Yes, worthy. My language it is digno. From the word worth, yes?"

"Yes."

"Yes, it is just the opposite of what you said. That word unworthy should be erased from you. Everybody has merecimento and is digno; everybody has worth and is worthy."

"I mean," Smythe began, feeling a bit unsure of herself, "people say, 'Well, you failed at this, you did this, you did that, you don't deserve what you hope for. Who do you think you are?' Or worse yet, you get the look of, 'Nah, you're nothing important.'"

"Do people say that to you?"

"I'm sure they have. Often, even if someone hasn't actually said it directly to me, I can feel what is unspoken. Unfortunately, I am a bit sensitive to the energy of others."

"Who cares what they think. You are already be-ing. Be-ing to the higher good of all. Your things from your past have no place in your present. Do you believe things from your past make you unworthy?"

"Yes, at times," Smythe admitted.

The baker began a lengthy explanation of the word worthy, and Smythe pondered the word as he spoke. When she thought of the term worth, it was usually when she was determining whether a thing is worth the money that she was being asked to pay. For example, diamonds have worth, a car, a pair of pants; there is an inherent worth based on the quality of the thing, the material used in its production, and the time to create it.

The idea of worth as it relates to a human does seem a bit shocking. Makes sense why Joao is so animated. How is it that we place value on a person? And even more so, how is it that we place such low value on ourselves by the mere inference of a word's usage? Perhaps we might place value on the services that an individual might offer us. There is a value equivalent to someone's services or something under consideration, but to say that a person—their inherent personhood as a thing—unworthy seems far-fetched.

Smythe, preoccupied by her own thoughts, became acutely aware that the baker had stopped speaking and was staring at her.

"Sorry. I was pondering what you were saying. It does seem a bit ludicrous now that you mention it."

"You—and everyone coming awake—cannot move into your highest calling in that way of thinking; this *unworthiness*," he said with disdain. "You must change your perspective."

"I know how I might do that, but how do *you* change your perspective?"

"Many, many ways. Meditate, say prayers, listen to the wind. It changes my mind for the better when I think of a problem I cannot solve and feel badly about it. When people say things of me that are not true, I remember the Universe has a different understanding of my being. I do not listen to what others say. Instead, I listen to who the Universe says I am, and I live into that. Sometimes it just makes me come back to what is here and now. And then I know my problem, whatever it is, will have an answer soon."

Smythe remained silent for a moment. So many thoughts surfaced. She thought of her audacious dreams, and how she had so often said to herself, "Who do you think you are!" The only thing she could hear was the nagging past list of failure and mediocre effort she had put into most of her work. She wondered if now the feelings of unworthiness resulted in that mediocre effort, creating a kind of self-fulling prophecy.

"You take this course on your calling, no?"

"Yes. I am taking a year-long course, but it's not really about a calling, although it has useful information. In many ways, it's about becoming awake. The idea is to have people live more abundantly into every area of their lives."

"Yes, yes, and what does it say about this thing you call unworthy? Such a coo-coo word, unworthy. Only worthy exists," the baker chuckled.

"It says that we are all worthy, but that we don't *know* we are worthy.".

"Coo-coo this conversation. We are worthy. You, me; everybody worthy. We do bad things, we must pay for that. There is always a karmic debt. Yet, we are worthy. Of love, of friendship, of our calling. We are worthy. You must remember *who* you are, Smythe," the baker implored.

"Then why this nagging persistence?"

"Why do you nag yourself?"

"Well, that's not what—"

"It is *you* who give this word dominion over you. The cross you bear is empty, precious one, but its power remains, and it is now alive in you. It is, how you say, a journey of forever which has set upon you. It is a power that you did not ask for but was given because you are *you*—all of you. Yet you are afraid, no?" the baker asked, somewhat accusingly.

"What do you mean, Joao?"

"What were the whispers of your childhood?" he whispered loudly.

Amidst the whirling of an overhead fan to waft the aroma of pastries, a quiet thought began to emerge within Smythe. She attempted to push it away, believing it was a young child's blasphemous notion.

The baker sensed she would not answer, but determined, he continued.

"A long time ago, a young carpenter boy believed he was the son of God. He walked amongst his people, doing many miraculous things: healing the sick, raising the dead. Miraculous things, no?"

The baker sighed. "But he was put to death. Why?"

"Because he claimed to be the son of God, as you said."

"No. That is incorrect. He was put to death because his own people feared him. Because he said if he could do such miracles, so could they. He showed them the way, the way of love. Yet they feared their own power—this power manifested in human form, in *ordinary* form."

The baker asked again, "What were the whispers of your childhood?"

"You're going to think I am crazy coo-coo."

The baker remained perfectly still, waiting for her to respond. Time seemed to stand still, and she felt pinned against a wall, seemingly unable to utter her memory out loud.

"Joao, I—"

"If you do not speak it, you will deny that which has captured your heart."

For a brief moment, Smythe closed her eyes.

"I remember thinking that I was Jesus, or kind of like him incarnate. That I had this specific power, only I didn't know what it was. But I sensed I had the same power as Jesus. I shoved it deep down inside, never to think of it again. But at times, it surfaces." Tears began to fill her eyes.

"What does it surface with you, my daughter?"

"What?"

"What did you then long for?"

"I dunno. By the time I remembered it, I was working. Climbing the corporate ladder."

"What brings you great joy, my daughter—that which is effortless?" the baker pressed.

"Writing. I can get lost in writing. I could write all day. Mostly I write lesson scripts for courses that I teach. And even at that, I can get lost all day writing out a script and planning the course. I can visualize it in my head, so I capture it on paper."

"What is the feeling that drives you to write?"

"Compassion. There are so many people in pain."

In a sudden moment of clarity, the baker understood. He stood up from the booth and walked to the back of his kitchen. When he returned to Smythe, he held a small seed in his hand.

"We all have a seed of God/Universe/Source/All—you choose the name—within each of us. I choose God, Universe, or All—they are the same to me," he began.

"That seed of God has the power of God and it lives within us, and that, my daughter, makes us worthy. You have been given a gift, placed in you at birth to do miraculous things for others. You denied it for so many long and arduous years, and you suffered. Yet, the gift in you remains. And no one is ever too young or too old to expand their gift. You must know that this path is your path. As with all paths, it will challenge you, including your own worthiness.

"It is not an uncommon thing to doubt your worth. But you must discount the opposite meaning, and simply replace it with worth. For you are of more worth than the heavens above. The thing you thought as a young child was our Universe letting you know who you are in a way that was hoped you would understand. You simply became afraid of the power you knew was in you."

Tears rolled down Smythe's face. It was a far cry from his "hooray that her life was in danger" reaction several months ago. She mulled over that day—the day when she told him that she was afraid, and she uncovered she was learning and leaning into courage. She thought of their bracing conversation where he said she would never be enough until she knew she was enough. And now this. To confide in him her young "blasphemous thoughts" in the light of what he just uttered made perfect, clarifying sense.

She wondered if her Beloved was attempting, back then, in those initial conversations, to awaken her. That, much like Jesus, she was a seed of her Beloved. She wondered if perhaps the seed in her had grown restless as she walked in her own rebellious energy. She wondered if the seed—still wishing to express itself through her—had created opportunities to express the gift within her. The gift of writing, in any form which would offer connection.

She smiled and thought of Artie, who, on several occasions, would bring her water because so much time had passed as she sat fixated before her computer screen. In addition to all of her other business tasks, she would write for up to seven hours a day, nuancing her current novel, developing articles, or crafting lesson plans for future teaching or speaking engagements.

The baker broke into her thoughts and asked, "Can you look up on your phone the meaning of worthy?"

She pulled her phone out of her messenger bag, found her Google app, and typed in "meaning of the word worthy." As she did so, he took one of her notebooks sitting on the table and picked up her pencil.

"From the dictionary online," she began. "Worthy as an adjective: 'having qualities that merit some form of recognition.' Here's another meaning: 'deserving effort, attention or respect.'"

He wrote down the definitions she offered and then wrote again. When he finished, he placed the notebook into her messenger bag.

The baker looked down at their shared table.

"The seed of God which lives in everyone, whether they know it or not, merits recognition. For in a specified way, we express the creative expression of our All. You, my daughter, express the creative expression of our All, the very essence of God. And not just in what you do, but in who you are. All of the parts of you."

The baker rose from his table and glanced at the clock on the far wall. It was well past 5:00 a.m., and it was time to open his shop for business. He walked gingerly to the door, unlocked it, and placed an open sign in the window before stepping behind the counter, awaiting guests to begin their arrival.

Artie was the first to walk in. She placed her order with the baker and eyed Smythe, who sat at her usual table in the back of the shop. Deep in thought, Smythe did not notice Artie's attempt at gaining her attention. To Artie, Smythe appeared mesmerized, as if in an awakened meditation.

Smythe sat pondering the term unworthiness, and, as if a bubble surfaced from the depths of muddy water, the word *privilege* emerged. Unworthiness. Privilege.

What the hell?! No, don't brush it aside. Welcome them in. They are there for a reason. Stay with it.

She allowed herself to relax, and almost immediately, a beautiful memory surfaced—one she held in the innermost sacred spaces of her heart. It was a memory of her visit out of the country with her partner several years ago.

She remembered she had been struck by the appreciativeness of the hotelier, a friendly fellow who smiled warmly at their initial arrival. He had welcomed them in with a joyful greeting, almost as though they were treasured family members whose arrival he had been anticipating. After they were settled into their room, Smythe and her partner returned to ask him where they could go for a drink and a bite to eat. He recommended his favorite tavern and offered them directions, stating it was only a two- or three-minute walk away. Smythe remembered feeling the genuineness of this man and had made a mental note to engage him in a much deeper conversation before she left the country.

The couple followed the hotelier's instructions, strolling down a snowy, quaint side street. They were teasing each other along the way when, abruptly, Smythe stopped. It had occurred to her that very few brown-skinned individuals were present, but she also noticed she did not seem to hold a sense of fear. She compared it to the ever-present sense of danger she felt in the States.

It's lacking here.

Nearing the entrance of the pub, she reflexively did the thing she normally did to deflect unwelcome behavior she had come to experience—she tensed her body. So accustomed to having stares and glares darted her way at her mere entrance into a bar or restaurant, she often lowered her head, momentarily steeling herself, as if to remind herself that she had the right to enter.

As she opened the door and walked in, what few people did look up glanced at her and offered her a gracious, welcoming smile. In addition, they nodded in her direction before returning to whatever held their interest before her arrival. She approached the crowded bar and was surprised by the immediate, friendly greeting by the barkeeper and was able to place her order right away.

How is this possible?

At dinner that evening, she and her partner discussed their collective interactions with the locals at length. Her partner, who was of Irish descent, had intimately witnessed the ongoing racism that Smythe lived under every day in the States. On more than one occasion, her partner had become enraged at the insidiousness of racially biased behavior extended toward Smythe—behavior Smythe had no longer noticed, or at least appeared to un-notice. Her partner had secretly cried out in anguish, recognizing how habituated Smythe had become to the behavior to those around her and questioned the implications of that shield in their relationship.

Throughout the week, the couple felt a sense of relief and belonging and relished the freedom where race appeared to play no role in their experience. During one particular encounter, an elderly couple invited them to tour the inlets in and around the coastal waters. Smythe and her partner were thrilled to accept the offer and were treated to a small, private yacht tour. When Smythe broached the subject of racism with her host, his response was one she found of interest.

"We did not have slavery of your people in this country. We did have our own stain of slavery, yes, but it was not of your people."

"I'm of mixed heritage. African American and Navajo."

"It doesn't matter," he politely said. He looked directly into Smythe's eyes. "We don't see color the way your country sees it. All are welcomed. Besides, we're a very friendly country."

"Indeed, you are. It just feels so freeing to be here. I really appreciate the tour, but more importantly, this conversation. I forget that not every nation in the world has the same stain toward people of color.

"Well, that is not entirely true. There are countries which are not welcoming of people of color. But, in my country, it seems to be less the case. I remember, as an adult, watching the treatment of African Americans in the States. The water hoses, the dogs..." her guide broke off his speech, his tears caught in his throat.

"Ahem," he said, clearing his throat. "I remember the brutality," he choked out. He remained quiet for the rest of the tour, save the occasional explanation of a land or sea mark.

If it weren't so damn cold here, I might just see about immigrating.

While his explanation seemed too good to be true, she simply held the curiosity in her heart and chose to enjoy the moments of freedom along her inlet tour. Even though she got a little seasick as the boat slowly skipped along the water, she reveled in the liberty as her host continued to point out landmarks along the way.

Allowing another thought to form, Smythe slowly looked up from her table at the baker's shop and then down at her hands, which lightly touched her coffee cup. It occurred to her that she participated in the constructs of unworthiness and privilege as both a victim as well as one who perpetuated oppression. Her exploration was not an indictment, but she believed it held a key.

She thought of all the ways she had been privileged: a two-parent family, raised in middle-to upper-middle-class neighborhoods, college education which opened doors to better jobs than those without college degrees, and no psychological or physical limitations. She examined at length how she had benefited from her privilege and how that privilege had sustained to the oppression of others—of other marginalized people. She also reviewed the ways she had been oppressed.

She thought about the intersectionality of her mixed-race heritage, her sexual orientation, and her gender.

Yet celebrated in the eyes of God.

She smiled at the wonder of all that she was.

The gentle spirit of her Beloved settled in and around her and turned her focus toward all of the ways she had felt unworthy. The haunting lyrics of the song "Ballad of Birmingham" came to mind, and she struggled to hold in her tears, recalling the ache of the story told from a mother's perspective.

She remembered her own youth and the years living in an upper-middle-class neighborhood of Chicago. She ached at the remembrance—the constant harassment by police officers she endured for simply walking from school to the local library to study. Their disbelief that a child of color could possibly live in such an affluent location and therefore had to be up to no good was sobering. The messages they sent were clear. She was not good enough and unworthy to be, do, and have what she wanted out of her life—no matter how hard she would try.

Her Beloved whispered to her. "Your birthright. You are my unique creation."

Smythe shook her head.

The programming from my birth, not only by my parents, but by my own country. So much need to maintain power. Such fear, yet all people unknowingly are celebrated in the eyes of God. What do you choose? The lies, or your truth?

She shook her head again. In light of her conversation with the baker, as though noticing for the first time the muck that still clung to her mirror, she suddenly had the urge to return home and take a shower.

She glanced up to find Artie standing a couple of feet from her. Smythe smiled warmly, and her heart sang as Artie approached her table.

"Hey there, I didn't see you come in."

"Yeah, that's me—stealth. You complete what you needed to do?"

Smythe gazed at Artie for a moment.

"Yeah, I did. Been thinking a lot about privilege, worthiness, intersectionality, and Spirit."

"Is there anything that you don't think about?"

"There probably is," Smythe said with a smile.

"Want to talk more about them?"

"Yes, but no. I need to sit with it for a bit."

"Ok then. If you're ready to leave—"

"Let's go."

Chapter 20

I Think I Died

—

SMYTHE CONTINUED TO MORE DEEPLY WORK THROUGH OLD WOUNDS that surfaced during the conference. She dove into old emotional blocks and limiting beliefs and examined them as she would an old pair of running shoes; reflecting on the influence they played in all of her decisions, her thought patterns and accompanying behaviors. Given this ongoing work, professionally, she continued to press forward and expand her business.

Over a few months, by invitation only, she held several half-day workshops working with community members who wanted to shift into more abundant ways of living. On one particular evening, Artie and her team watched as Smythe worked with community members as they began the process of releasing some of their own limiting beliefs. Artie listened intently as Smythe worked with several people who stood to ask questions, only to pour out their sorrow before the audience. As Artie observed Smythe, it seemed to her as if Smythe were reading the very essence of her audience members. Smythe asked the right questions, made connections between their limiting beliefs and their current behavior, and made suggestions for each person who chose vulnerability that night.

"That was impressive," Artie said, sitting in the back of the SUV with Smythe.

"Thanks. It's all based on the material I've studied. My mentor asked that we immerse ourselves in it and trust it, and I have."

"It seems beyond that, though. I watched your gaze—you were transfixed on each person, especially that last woman. There seemed to be so many issues that distressed her. I honestly had a hard time figuring out which one of the issues most concerned her. You seemed to be listening to her on a level I don't understand, and somehow figured it out. Yet, there was something else in the way you understood her."

"You give me too much credit. Her issues were all connected, so I simply chose the first one. As she continued to speak, it was clear that every example she offered was tied to the first issue."

"Yeah, I get that, but how did you figure it out?"

"One of the keys my mentor taught us during the conference was that a lot of issues are based on a limiting belief. As she and everyone else spoke, I do what I always do. I pray. I simply asked that I would get out of the way, and that the Universe help me understand and then speak to me, and I in turn to her. So, as she spoke, I could hear my Beloved. It is the sound of a gentle whisper in my ear, and I often get a tingle down my spine.

"But, still, it all requires that I just stand there with an open heart, without judgement. If I did that, I just knew the Universe would reveal the right questions to ask in order to assist her in shifting her perspective. Or I'd remembered a passage in the material I studied or the supplemental reading I've done to support my mentor's material and had a knowing it fit in. The idea is to offer a different perspective to any given situation and allow each person to mine their thoughts and dig up and confront their own limiting beliefs."

"Well, I'm all the better for witnessing what took place. I think she will be, too."

"I hope so. I remember a quote I once read. Something to the effect that God cannot be held to the earthly traditions of man and uses ordinary people to do extraordinary things. If I can help someone else, it's what makes all of this worth it."

Smythe was beginning to flourish, and she felt like she was in her element. The more workshops she offered, the more confident she became. Yet, with her constant external companions always surrounding her, she began to sense areas of emotional constriction within her spirit.

Her biggest constriction was the constriction of her heart. It was taking up a considerable amount of her time as of late, reminding her daily of love. It told her while she had agape love for friends and family, she still needed romantic love and a willing belonging to another. It was there that her heart told her she would grow and, one morning while studying, she had enough.

There is an uneasiness I have about Artie. What am I not facing?

She began to recollect all of the books she had come across on the construct of attraction and love. Those books had all but scared her away from the idea of relationships, and her ego pattern confirmed the fear through its own brand of torture that roared into her consciousness.

You're simply not good in relationships. People disappoint you. Besides, she'll want you to change. You'll change and won't be your authentic self. Just be single; it's easier.

Yet, her heart continued to sing… and it was singing of Artie. To her consternation, she found herself inextricably, soulfully attracted to her. Hoping to side with her ego and tuck the growing feelings for Artie safely away, Smythe decided she needed to write out her thoughts in her journal.

There is a tendency when we find ourselves romantically attracted to another to begin to visualize the ideal relationship with that other. We place our needs, wants, and desires onto them. If we are not careful, it becomes an expectation that the other could never completely fulfill. I wonder if it is possible to simply be attracted and be mindful of what I am needing. If I need to be protected and safe, can I create that protection and safety within myself, without seeking to have her fulfill that? If I need her to demonstrate a deep sense of love for me, can I provide that deep sense of love in myself rather than searching for it from her? If I need strength, do I not possess that within myself? If I need vulnerability, am I not capable of demonstrating that to myself? Whatever I seek in another is the pointer to offer that to myself. Am I willing to express my needs to her?

Smythe continued to write, and as she did, she continued to dissect her thoughts. She was hoping not to inch toward love, but instead to put away any tangible movement toward it.

So, what is the glimmer? What in Artie am I attracted to? Certainly, her strength of character. Yes, her tenderness and insightfulness as well. I must admit, I am embarrassed at my weak—

Smythe abruptly stopped her line of thought.

There it is.

"Weakness," she murmured.

She caught herself thinking she was learning to become more vulnerable in front of Artie. Struck by her slip of the thought, she immediately recognized her subconscious gave her insight into her own limiting belief.

Do you really see your display of vulnerability as weakness?

She leaned back in her chair and closed her eyes, listening intently to her ego. It told her it had been bruised, battered, and taken advantage of. It told her that it was afraid to be vulnerable for fear of being hurt again.

Her heart, however, also spoke. It told her that it desperately wanted to love again. And it said that it wanted to try with Artie.

Smythe opened her eyes, allowing herself to drift her gaze into the living room. Sitting on the sofa, bent over her own laptop, was the person of her affection. Sensing Smythe had quieted her thoughts for a moment, Artie looked toward her.

"Hey, you want to grab something to eat? We've been at this for a while. It's now 2:00. I need a break. How about you?"

Smythe gazed deeply into Artie's eyes, still transfixed in thought.

"Hellooo, Artie to Smythe?"

"It hit me just now, like a ton of bricks. Years ago, I think I died."

"What?!" Artie exclaimed, her mouth agape.

"Yeah, I did." Smythe frowned and wondered why that thought burped from her mouth.

"Well, aren't you full of surprise and adventure," Artie said as she walked to the dining room table. She took a seat across from Smythe and waited in rapt silence for a more robust explanation of the event.

"I had gone in for routine surgery. Unfortunately, I had a thyroid condition, and for some reason, during the procedure, my lungs started to fill with liquid. According to the anesthesiologist, I was drowning. What I remember was, at some point, I was looking down on my body, which was inverted—my head was pointed toward the floor, and my legs were higher than my heart."

Smythe demonstrated by holding her hand in front of her and pointing her fingers toward the floor at an angle, indicating her fingertips as her head and the top of her hand as her body.

"Everyone in the surgery room worked quietly but quickly. I could sense their feelings. There was a sense of surprise and panic, as if there was nothing in my chart which would indicate this should have happened.

"The next thing I remember, I was no longer in the operating room. I didn't seem to have a body, but I was conscious that at one time, I did have a body. It was completely dark, just blackness. I couldn't see, but I was aware of a presence that was just out of reach of my sight. It—it terrified me. I remember being there, wondering if I was in a Christian version of hell."

Artie involuntarily pooched her lips out and bit them.

"Don't give me that look. I had been attending an evangelical church at the time, so there was that influence."

Artie nodded in understanding. "Hey, I'm Catholic. I get it."

"Today, I now wonder if I were on the outskirts of the quantum field. Everything I've read indicates the quantum field, if it could be described, is complete and utter blackness, void of anything physical.

"Sorry, I digress. So, I was just there, and all I could think about was that I had taken my life for granted. I thought of things I still wanted to do, but because I thought I had all the time in the world, I just kept putting off my dreams."

"We all do that at some point."

"Yeah, well, that's all I kept thinking about. I took it all for granted. I took it all for granted. Slowly, a dim light began to rise out of nowhere, but not toward me. It was illuminating the figure just outside of my line of sight, and I remember having an impression that it was Jesus.

"He was dressed in all white. I couldn't make him out completely, but his voice was one of deep love. If love had a voice, his voice was it. I could tell he was looking at me. I didn't hear his voice audibly, but I knew his voice.

"He said, 'I have always loved you and will never leave you, but you must fight, Smythe. You have given up, and in giving up, the stepping stones you've used to climb have cut into you as you have fallen.'

"He said that my life was one of perfection. That I was the expression of the character of God in all that I am. I recalled at that moment, that, in the last few years, I had given up. I don't remember why—but I let something in me die. I remember, as though seeing through His eyes when He was speaking, that in giving up, I had fallen. When I fell, there were sharp edges cutting into me.

"He said, 'Fight, Smythe. Fight for your life. Begin to climb and do not stop until you reach the top.' I remember beginning to climb. There were sharp hand- and footholds, and whenever I slipped, those holds would cut into me. I remember wondering what I had become, and then, in a flash, I was in post-op throwing up. People around me were telling me it was alright, and some were even clapping. I heard someone say, 'Thank God!'

"For a few months after that, I was angry. I was more angry at God than myself. I never spoke to anyone about it. At times, I thought it was a figment of my imagination, but over time, I began to read about similar after-death experiences. I became even more enraged, partly because everybody I read about was describing pie in the sky experiences. They met loved ones. They were given a choice to return to their lives. Blah, blah, blah. That wasn't me, though. It's taken a few years, Artie, and a lot of physical, financial, and psychological sweat and tears to finally more fervently fight for my life. Yet, there are still areas where I have not been as brave as I've needed to be."

"How so?"

"Well—" Smythe started, cut off by the sound of Artie's cellphone ringing.

"Hold that thought," Artie said, removing her com set earbud and reaching to answer her phone.

Smythe rose from her dining room chair and headed into her bedroom. She was having second thoughts about talking to Artie about her feelings for her. She changed out of her flannel shirt as she had now become too warm to wear it and put on a T-shirt. When she headed back into the dining room, Artie was still on the phone. She seemed irritated with whomever she was speaking with.

"Look, I don't care. You earn great money. I have not asked you for a dime in caring for him. He's your son, too, so pick up the tab! Goodbye!"

Smythe walked into the kitchen, opened her refrigerator, and grabbed a couple of beers. She walked over to Artie and handed her one.

"I know you're still on the clock, but I thought just this one time."

Artie gave a half-hearted smile to Smythe and took the bottle from her.

"Sorry about that. It was my son's father."

"What's going on, if you don't mind me asking?"

"Nah, I don't mind." Artie let out a slow breath.

"They're heading to Maui next month for a couple of weeks, and for some reason, Davey's father believes I should foot half the bill. I gave him written permission to take Davey, but that doesn't include paying for the trip. He's been angling for money ever since Davey arrived."

"Wow. Isn't that a bit presumptuous of him? Sorry, I know little of custody."

"Right!? It is. It just tells me that either he isn't making as many business deals, or that caring for Davey is costing him more than he had anticipated."

"Didn't you say he's a millionaire?"

"A cheap one at that. He's extremely frugal with money, which I can appreciate, but he decided he wanted Davey in his life. In fact, over the years, he's all but begged to have more time with him. Obviously, he didn't factor in a financial responsibility that comes with more time. At any rate, enough of my drama. Where were we?" Artie said, feeling the need to change the subject.

"Talking about you," Smythe said with a grin.

"Nah, I don't think so," Artie teased.

"Yes, I'm sure of it. You asked me if I wanted to grab a bite to eat. I said a few things, you received a phone call, and we are now discussing you."

Smythe began to rise from her chair, but Artie reached out for her hand and motioned for her to remain seated. Smythe reluctantly re-seated herself. She placed her remaining hand over Artie's and stared at them.

"Look," Smythe started. "We are always discussing what's in my head. Rarely do we discuss you. I like you, Artie, and I'd really like to stop being so selfish and hear what's going on with you."

"You like me?!" Artie said, feigning disbelief. "You like me? Me, the one that keeps you cooped up— your words—like a prisoner? Now you dig your jailer?"

"Well, you're kind of growing on me. But you keep that up, and I'll think twice about it."

Smythe removed her hands and looked across at Artie. Artie was searching Smythe's eyes when a knock at the door interrupted them.

Artie quickly rose from the dining chair and motioned Smythe into the back portion of her apartment. Artie took a defensive position to the side of the door, drawing her weapon and pointing it toward the door. As she held her position, she realized she had removed her ear com bud from her ear when she answered the call from her son's father and had yet to put it back in, essentially removing herself from communication with her team.

"Who is it?" she demanded.

To her relief, it was a member of Team 1 reporting in. He had attempted to reach Artie by the com link, and her lack of response put into motion a tactical response from the team. She opened the door.

"Sorry, guys. We're good. Thanks for the check." The team member nodded and returned to his post.

"Smythe, it's all clear."

Smythe sauntered out of her bedroom. "Well, it's a good thing. I just cleaned yesterday. Last thing I need is blood and guts all over the place."

"Want to grab something to eat?" Artie asked.

"Annnd, we're right back to where we started. Yes. Yes, I do. I'm thinking pizza."

"And I'm thinking Greek."

"Um, no. Beer and Greek, they don't go together. Well, at least for my taste buds. Beer and pizza do."

"I just can't with you," Artie said, shaking her head and smiling in Smythe's direction. She opened the apartment door and raised her hand, signaling to a member of Team 1 to be prepared to travel in five minutes.

Chapter 21

Find the Good

—

CONCEALING HER WEAPON, ARTIE GRABBED HER JACKET AND PUT IT on. Smythe smiled widely, her face giving away her elation to get out of the house for a few hours. She moved swiftly to the sofa to sit down to put on a pair of shoes. As she rose, Artie extended a hand to help her to her feet. In true Smythe fashion, she hesitated for a moment, old patterns of behavior attempting to kick in, but instead, she took Artie's hand and allowed Artie to assist her.

"See? I told you you were growing on me. Normally I would have just stood up on my own," she said, smiling.

"That's progress right there, I tell ya."

"Just so you know, there will be more beer."

They left the apartment, climbed into the back seat of Team 1's vehicle, and headed to a local pizzeria called The Joint. Located several miles from Smythe's apartment, Artie had chosen the spot as a regular local hangout for Smythe to visit, mostly because it was owned by a friend and retired police officer. It helped that local law enforcement was known to frequent the pizzeria, therefore she felt assured there would be an abundance of officers and weapons should the need arise.

The Joint sat among a row of elm trees, a constant companion to the developing valley. Weaved between the densely planted trees, a credit union, dry cleaners, and a movie theater bordered both sides of the restaurant. Foot traffic was a constant, especially after work and weekends. The Joint bustled with patrons most evenings, with local bands playing in the background while the wait staff, gregarious in their mannerisms, welcomed all. But now, at 2:00 p.m. on a weekday, the restaurant was quiet.

Artie and Smythe took a seat at the furthest corner booth and spent a few hours enjoying each other's company. They laughed and teased one another throughout their meal, trading bits of their life stories. Smythe, who mostly asked questions of Artie, was struck by how open-hearted Artie was, especially about her life. To her, it felt refreshing. Refreshing because she believed it was important to give Artie a break from her own ongoing internal drama.

Way too much time spent picking into my life.

"The least you could do is offer me the courtesy of knowing who's behind the protector that always dresses in blue or black clothing."

"Do I disappoint?"

"No, not at all, Smythe said as she blushed. "I mean, you look great in those colors. I can make assumptions about why you only wear them, but I would rather hear it from you."

"Well, when not on duty, I wear any color *but* black or blue. The thing is people don't pay attention to these colors. They're just drab enough not to draw attention. Besides, black especially conceals my weapon."

"Mmm—there's that. Do you wear yellow?"

"Can't stand the color. So, no."

"Me either. Bleh."

"You have a yellowish, golden-hued pot above your kitchen cupboard."

"Yes, but it's the only one, and it has a golden *hue*—just as you stated."

"I wanted to smash it," Artie said with a smirk.

"Don't you dare! Sheesh." Pausing for just a moment, she finally added, "I think someone gave it to me. I can't be sure, but I know I didn't purchase it."

Artie eyed her with curiosity. Smythe was finally emerging. From a highly introverted, rightfully frightened woman to what she did not yet know. She thought about the first few months with Smythe. Smythe was someone who had shown signs of anxiety and depression, and seemed emotionally unavailable. But now, Smythe was different. Perhaps she was growing into a more confident person, or maybe she was beginning to show that side of her. Time would tell. Regardless, she was delighted to witness the positive change.

"So, moving away from smashing my belongings, tell me more about your son. Does he know what you do for a living?"

"No, he does not," Artie said, shaking her head. "And I rather like it that way. He knows that I work with law enforcement, but beyond that, he doesn't know much. He's only seven, and it seems a bit too early to fill him in on the details—but that day is coming. Even his father doesn't know what I do. I find it… advantageous. You know, to minimize my particular role in society."

"And not publicizing that to anyone minimizes the risk of exposure. Makes sense."

"Your profile didn't indicate you had children—did you? I mean, ever have a kid?" Artie asked.

"Hey, we're not talking about me right now, remember? But, to answer your question, no, I don't have kids."

"How come?"

"You're just not going to give up, are you?" Smythe laughed.

"To answer your *final* question, while I like kids, I didn't want to go through the whole birthing process. Besides, I wasn't in relationships with anyone who wanted children in their lives. I never discounted getting involved with someone who had them or wanted to have them, but it just hadn't played out."

"So, you have a—" Artie began.

"No more questions, missy! My turn. What made you decide to leave New York?"

Artie chuckled and looked down at her plate before she answered, her eyes softening as she began.

"It was really about college. My best friend and I were accepted to several of the same universities, and in the end, we just sat down together and weighed the pros and cons of each. With our scholarships in hand, we chose the university that got us as far away from our parents as we possibly could."

While Artie laughed at her memory, Smythe sat dumbfounded.

"Wait, you get several scholarships, and your deciding factor was how far away you could live from your parents? Why not the prestige of the university?"

"You have to understand; I come from an Italian family. Very close-knit, and while I do love them, I needed some breathing room. Besides, it was getting to a point where they were beginning to hint that I should find a guy while at university. I hadn't come out to them yet, or to myself, for that matter." Artie paused, her eyes distant as she recalled the memory.

Sensing a deeper story, Smythe gently asked, "Tell me more about coming out."

Artie lifted her gaze and searched Smythe's eyes. Out of all of her friends and girlfriends, none had shown an interest so directly. With a tinge of seriousness, she furrowed her brow and voiced her recollection.

"I recognized that I was attracted to girls in high school, but I was so busy with my studies that I never really paid attention to my attraction. I had male friends and one that I hung out with quite a bit, but it was really only to study. We both were driven to go to college, so he was easy to be with. When I arrived at college, that same drive to get good grades and move toward my goal of becoming an FBI agent was all I saw. I had a trajectory.

"During my senior year, I got involved with a female classmate. We were in a lot of the same classes, and we just clicked. Over time, I found my feelings for her getting stronger, and one day, just before spring break started, she asked me if I wanted to spend some time with her up at her parents' cabin. I agreed, and the rest was history. We came back, finished out our last semester as girlfriends, graduated, and ended up going our separate ways. I went on to obtain my J.D., and she went off to Europe to travel."

"Just like that, plop, you ended your relationship?"

"Actually, she did. She wanted to travel Europe, like a lot of kids do. I didn't. There was a world to save, and I didn't want to waste time traipsing through the countryside of Europe. At least right away."

"And you, Smythe? What's your coming out story?"

"Not so fast. What happened after that?"

Artie grinned.

"I obtained my J.D. While getting my advanced degree, I decided to take up a language. Arabic. I was already rather fluent in Spanish and thought it might come in handy in my line of work. And, yes, before you say anything, it *is* profiling. But I knew what the FBI was angling for with new recruits, and I wanted to make myself marketable—and it worked. I jumped through the hoops of the FBI academy and became a field agent for several years, specializing in behavioral profiling. And, of course, I'm a sharpshooter, one of only a few at the time. But that's all you're getting from me for now. What about you? What's your coming out story?

"Is that in my file?"

"Actually, it is."

"Wow. I didn't disclose that."

"Don't worry about it. Only those that have to know, know," Artie replied, nodding her head in reassurance.

"Understand, I'm not closeted. I'm just always fascinated by the assumptions people make."

"Well, I've been living with you, in a way, for several months."

"It hasn't been living with me *in a way*. You are living with me. I should charge you rent!"

"For a blowup mattress as a bed? I don't think so," Artie teased. "So, in all seriousness, give it up. What's your story?"

Let her in Smythe. She seems genuinely interested. Just take a step, she said to herself. She twisted a napkin on her lap. *Why am I so reticent about talking about me?*

Smythe sighed and murmured, "Good grief, Charlie Brown."

Artie sat patiently waiting.

Taking in a breath, Smythe finally leaped into recounting that part of her life.

"It's really not so dramatic, Artie. I just always knew I was different. I didn't have the same interest in boys that my sisters did. As I got older, I realized that I was attracted to girls. Once I learned the term of my attraction, I pretty much kept it to myself until I was out on my own. Had a couple of girlfriends, but my love went off to Europe as well." Smythe stopped and shook her head. "What is it with lesbians and Europe, anyway?" No longer twisting her napkin, she chuckled to herself, recounting the number of friends who took off on an adventure to Europe after college.

"I then had a longer relationship that lasted for several years before we ended it. Since her, I haven't been in a real significant relationship. Haven't really wanted to."

"Haven't found the right one yet?"

"Something like that."

"What about your son? How did—?"

"One-night stand," Artie interrupted.

The ringing of a bell caught Artie's attention, and she looked up. A man approached, dressed in an apron and covered in dried tomato sauce. He strolled over with his arms outstretched. Artie stood up and warmly greeted him, but refused to hug, opting instead to hold out her hand for him to shake.

"Ah, come on, Artie. We're old friends."

Grinning widely, Artie pointed at herself. "Not with paste all over you, Leo. These clothes just came back from the dry cleaners."

Artie took a moment and introduced Smythe to Leo, the owner of The Joint, and the two exchanged pleasantries. He turned his attention toward Artie after a few moments and eyed her, giving an approving nod as he darted his eyes toward Smythe. Artie squinted, her eyes piercing a warning to Leo. The message was clear—relent! After a few minutes of catching up, he left only to return a few moments later, ripping up Artie's check in front of her.

"We're family," he said as he shrugged his shoulders. Scanning his restaurant, he searched for members of her team. He could never tell the difference between regular patrons and her team, that is, until they rose from a separate booth and walked out behind Artie.

"Your team around?"

Artie looked at him without responding.

"Yeah, I know. I get it. Can't blame a guy for asking, now can ya? How many ya got now?"

"Enough to take you on," Artie bantered.

"Ha! Well, listen, buddy, I'm baking two large pies for 'em. Tell 'em hi for me, will ya?"

Artie smiled and said she would. The sun was still bright in the sky, and while Smythe enjoyed her outing, she still had several hours of writing to accomplish. After the pies were delivered, they returned to the apartment where Smythe spent the remainder of her day tapping on her tablet, nuancing an upcoming class she would give as part of homework her mentor gave her class in preparation for the next conference. By mid-evening, she reluctantly retired to bed.

You were a bit of chicken today, she mused. *But it was nonetheless a really good day.*

* * *

For Smythe, a couple of productive weeks flew by. Her writing progressed at a steady pace, and she had several leads for corporate training. One afternoon, however, Smythe's tablet was not operating efficiently, and it surfaced an old, unwanted friend.

Smythe sat with her phone in her hand. It was the 4th call she made to her tablet's support team. While sitting on yet another interminable hold, she thought she would assess her checking account. To her chagrin, she discovered a rather large accounting error had occurred and quickly began to spiral.

I thought it was gone, this thing called doubt... but it's crept back in.

She felt a sickening ache in the pit of her stomach, and it threatened panic.

What am I pretending not to know?!

Smythe sobbed. She sobbed so hard, had her neighbors been home, they might have knocked on the door to see what was going on. *What if I can't fix it? What if the bank doesn't believe me? I have too many action items to complete in the coming months, which will require those funds. Hurry up already, I've got to call the bank!*

Unfortunately for Smythe, her technical issues were only just mounting. What had begun as a simple software application problem had created a much larger issue. She was told that it would be best to reset her hardware to factory settings, but in the middle of working with the service representative to complete the reset procedure, her Wi-Fi connection went down. Unable to proceed until her Wi-Fi connection was re-established, Smythe called her cable provider.

"Hi, I am working from home today, and my Wi-Fi connection went down."

"Let's take a look at your account, Ms. Daniels. Please hold."

The silence on the other end of the phone only heightened Smythe's mounting anxiety. Her only focus was to resolve the connection issue so that she could continue studying after calling her bank. Her mentor's next conference was in less than two months, and there was so much homework for her to complete. She took in a breath, feeling her heart pounding through her temples. She balled her hand into a fist repeatedly as she allowed fear to occupy her thoughts and emotions.

Why is this taking so long?!

"Ms. Daniels, hi," the representative said, breaking into Smythe's thoughts. "I'm not showing any issues on our end. I have remotely rebooted your system. Can you check to see if it is up and running?"

Smythe did as she was instructed, but to no avail. Her Wi-Fi connection was still down.

"Well, we will have to schedule a technician's visit to your address. The representative checked for availability, but the earliest date available is two days away."

What the hell am I supposed to do without Wi-Fi?!

"Um, how early?" Smythe asked, curtailing the fury she felt coursing through her body.

"We have a 9:00 a.m. appointment."

"And you're sure you don't have an earlier date available?"

"No, ma'am. And please be aware that if the technician finds that the outage is something you caused, we will charge you for the visit."

"Wha—fine! But I didn't cause this," Smythe said though gritted teeth. She caught her tone and softened it a bit. "If a cancellation occurs, please consider reaching out to me. I'll take the canceled appointment, no matter what time. I've just got so much to do."

Smythe disconnected from the call, and her thoughts began to race again. She had a mountain of writing to complete: a course to write, edits on her book, and an article to complete, all due in the next few days.

"And because of the murder mess, Artie won't let me spend days out in public to utilize free Wi-Fi!" she bemoaned. "How can I save my own part of the world?!"

She sat motionless, staring at her tablet. Of course, it was Wi-Fi capable only. She then called the bank and spoke to a service rep. After verifying her identity, she explained what she discovered.

"Listen, I've been with your bank for years, and this has never happened, but I found an error in the amount of $1,500.00. I only just noticed the mistake."

"When did it occur?" the representative asked.

"It occurred two months ago. Why I didn't catch it before, I just don't know. I apologize, but I never authorized that money to come out of my account."

The agent was friendly enough and seemed professionally concerned, asking her to pinpoint the date of the transaction, the name of the merchant, and the amount deducted.

"Ms. Daniels, thank you for holding. I see the amount of $1,500 was deducted from your account. It seems to be a merchant you've frequented before."

"But I've never spent that kind of money there. If you look at my history, you will see that I've only ever spent $150, and that was for a new pair of running shoes. In fact, I purchased the shoes right around the time $1,500 was deducted from my account. Is it possible that $1500 should be $150? I would never spend $1500 at that merchant. And if I had, I would have used a credit card. I just don't have the finances to give away that much money all at once."

"I understand, Ms. Daniels. What I will do is open a case number and send it out for investigation. It will take up to ten business days to reply, perhaps longer, since the issue has gone undetected for this long." The agent gave a reference number before politely disconnecting.

Smythe sat dumbfounded, beginning to fear the worst as she began to sob. As she whimpered, she caught herself and wondered, *Why the tears?* Yes, both issues were concerning, but it didn't warrant the degree of emotion she was displaying. She scanned her emotions. She definitely felt fear. It was then that she reminded herself of the acronym of fear: fantasized events appearing real.

Find the good in all of this, Smythe.

At first, her ego refused. It wanted to sit in self-pity and accusation.

I swear you are so stupid! What possessed you to forget to check your account? If you can't manage your own bank account, what makes you think you can manage your own business? And the Wi-Fi. If you hadn't said yes to the article, you wouldn't be in this predicament. Now, look. You're behind the eight ball.

She then heard the F.E.A.R. *What will happen if the bank doesn't rectify the error? We won't have enough. And if you caused the Wi-Fi issue, that's going to be even more money out of your pocket.*

After listening to her ego's toxic charge, Smythe took in a breath and made a conscious choice to quiet her thoughts by doubling down on her ego. She focused her attention on finding the good until, finally, her egoic part dimmed its berating attempts at accusation. She focused on her breath and listened to the silence.

After several long minutes, she began to appreciate that her Wi-Fi was inoperable. Almost at once, she noticed how quiet her apartment had become. It was the first time she hadn't heard the low volume buzz of electronics, and it was almost eerie. She continued to listen to the deafening sound of silence and thought about her response.

Like so many, I have given a part of my life to these devices. But now, just for a minute, maybe two days, I can breathe a bit. Let it go. I wanted more time to read; to meditate. Isn't this an opportunity? I no longer have the latest episode of my favorite TV show to occupy an evening, nor the collective angst of Facebook posts in my head. I can read the three books I have started. Just shift, Smythe... please.

She turned her to attention to her finances. *Out of my control, for now,* she thought as she took in a breath and closed her eyes. The issue was concerning, and she would have to make adjustments, but for the moment—in the here-now moment—she understood there was little she could do.

Artie arrived at the apartment a short time later and noticed the quiet almost immediately. Concerned that it was more than just a Wi-Fi issue, she contacted her teams to look into the outage. Satisfied that the outage wasn't the start of something sinister, Artie relaxed, spending the rest of the evening reading one of the books she had picked up at their local bookstore.

The following day, Smythe could hear the familiar buzz of electronics start up once again. She quickly tested the Wi-Fi connection on her tablet. "Yes!!! It's up. Oh, thank God." But then, just as swiftly as her elation came, it went. She sighed heavily.

Oddly enough, she had come to appreciate the deafening sound of silence.

Chapter 22

Blind Commitment

—

W ITH THE MORNING CAME AN EXISTENTIAL CRISIS FOR SMYTHE. SHE had been working long hours, writing and preparing for a conference she was invited to speak at near the end of the month. It would be a big deal, for it was the first time she would deliver her material to several hundred community members. Her tears flowed yet again as she felt everything that came along with fear.

Where is this coming from? I've given similar talks to much smaller crowds. Damn it!

She wanted out of her head and found herself seeking refuge at the baker's shop. As she recanted the past day to him, he listened intently with a solemnness she had not before experienced. After finishing her story, he sat with her for several minutes before finally speaking.

"Fear and doubt are painful," the baker began. "They rob us of our ability to live the life that is before us. They take all hope, all creativity, all love from us. They bond together and consume us, leaving no room for our ability to care for ourselves and others. This fear and doubt will attempt to push you off your path, dear daughter."

Slowly shaking his head as if remembering a thought, he continued.

"Both fear and doubt, they also leave us blind. They lean toward hatred and, how you say, cropping of deceit and violence. Mmmm... Instead of unity, we sow discord; instead of compassion, we sow judgement. And this is the truth my daughter; for all of these things which fear and doubt create, they are only behaviors of what we feel within ourselves. I am sure many of your faith leaders and experts have more eloquently come to this conclusion."

"Blindness. Perhaps I am walking in blindness," Smythe replied, deep in thought.

"It is the inability to see, no?"

"Well, yes."

"Whether clearly or not at all, we often cannot see that which is before us or around us. Yet everyone who has this physical inability to see still moves forward. One step at a time, maybe, perhaps with a cane, an animal, or another human being, they move through their day."

The baker paused for a moment, thinking through the list of his regular customers. He then continued.

"I have a guest who comes in every day, just like you, but promptly at 2:30 p.m. He cannot see, so he has no idea what my creations look like. Yet he still manages to choose correctly for himself and is always appreciative of the selections he has made. He can identify the ingredients in each of them through smell, and we often discuss them. When he sits down to eat them, he runs his fingers lightly over them, observing the texture. His expectation is that he chose correctly.

"You have spoken about a blind commitment. For me, it seems a blind commitment requires us to see with our other senses. Take forward that one first step, and then another, knowing that the path is true."

"Has he ever made a bad choice for himself?"

Smiling with a glimmer of enthusiasm contained within his slender frame, the baker stated, "There are never bad choices, for each choice offers a lesson. So, no, he has never made a bad choice. He eats my creation enthusiastically and always thanks me for the experience."

"Are we still talking about blind commitment, or are we talking about your pastries?"

"Of course."

"But what about those who make a blind commitment to hatred and violence?

"There will always be those who have given into fear and doubt. To love, to be compassionate requires a different kind of blind commitment. It is agape. To love requires that you choose perhaps an unrewarded path. It is an unspoken agreement."

"Too few make that agreement."

"Yes."

"It is the hardest kind of commitment to make."

"Yes, and the best kind," he said.

"So, how do you believe this relates to fear and doubt?"

"Always will there be both as long as you choose to live from the past. What is your blind commitment, daughter?"

"It's that I made a commitment to this journey cloaked in starting a new business, and then to writing without really thinking it through."

"You did think it through. Again, predictability and control, my daughter. You want to see the end from the beginning, but you cannot. Continue to commit. In the end, you shall see how far you have come and turn to help others who wade in the mud of fear and doubt which lives only in the past."

The baker rose from the table and stated, "I have another customer coming through the door. I must attend to them. Stay for a while. I have missed your presence."

Chapter 23

Aversion to Love

—

Aʟᴏⁿ FTER HER ENCOUNTER WITH THE BAKER, Sᴍʏᴛʜᴇ BEGAN TO WORK more directly through some of her fear and doubt. She used several techniques to abate the duo, but her favorite was the mirror work. Her mentor taught her to look deeply into her own eyes in front of a mirror and recite love and acceptance of who she is. At first, it seemed perfunctory, her ego naysaying her every word of love, but she continued.

Without conscious awareness, over time, her fear diminished. While her doubts persisted, she simply made a daily choice to say, "We will see," whenever she doubted herself. It was a challenge to the doubt. Instead of giving in to it, she consciously decided to allow the doubt to hover and move into consistent action, allowing her Beloved the space to do what she could not.

Yet, one morning, something seemed to be very much off. She was getting more than enough sleep—from a paltry four hours, she had stretched her horizontal position to seven. She was spending more time in meditation, and more time reading. Yet she felt intensely restless. It was 6:00 a.m., and her hands began to tremble, her breathing halting.

In her here-now moment, she made the mistake of looking too critically at her past. Through a skewed lens, she saw only the constant state of emotional upheaval. She failed to see the budding relationship between herself and Artie. She failed to notice how much she learned from her mentor and then taught to others. She failed to see that the seminars she gave were changing the lives of participants. She did not see her own progress in the beautiful life she was creating, and she forgot that everything her soul was up to was part of the process of creation to more fully step into who she had chosen to be.

To get out of her head, she abruptly pushed back her dining chair from the table and stood up. In the living room, Artie sat upon the sofa and watched as Smythe opened the storage closet in her dining room. Near the front of it, she pulled out a small, empty suitcase and carried it into her bedroom.

Artie listened to Smythe's movements with rapt attention. She could hear Smythe rustle around in her bedroom closet, the sound of clothes being pulled off of hangers and dresser drawers opening and closing. Artie quietly arose from the sofa and walked to the doorway of Smythe's bedroom. She found the suitcase sitting on her bed with shoes already placed into it, along with underwear, T-shirts, and socks.

"Where are you wanting to go?" she asked.

Standing in front of her bed, with clothes strewn about, Smythe did not look in the direction of Artie's voice.

"I'm through for now. I need a change of scenery. Perhaps to the beach," Smythe said.

"Really? Can you afford to take that much time off, with so much on your plate?"

Smythe turned and glared at Artie before continuing her packing frenzy.

"Talk to me, baby, what's going on?"

"I just want to escape for a little bit, Artie. A change of perspective will do wonders. The conference organizers ran into some financial difficulty, and they've postponed it until early next year. So, I'm free to roam about the country, so to speak."

"Is that what this is about?"

"No. Actually, I'm a bit relieved. I just figured I can now skedaddle!"

"It takes a good bit of preparation to ensure your safety, Smythe. Let's talk about it and plan it out."

"No! No planning, just going! I need to escape from myself, and I'm not going to hang around for one more minute. Not a single one! I have to think about rebuilding my future—a future that, for some reason, I can't see. A future that I seem to be fucking up, even now! Baaad energy, ya know. Gotta change it. I know I promised you I would abide by your wishes, but this, now... I just can't."

"Smythe—"

"Stop it. I'm leaving. I'm leaving," Smythe said, holding back tears.

Artie walked toward Smythe and held out her hand.

"Don't! Don't feel sorry for me, don't do another fucking thing for me, Artie. Just please leave me be." Smythe grit her teeth, willing the tears to stop their flow.

"Baby, I won't let you leave. I've got to make plans with my team. Just tell me where you want to go."

Smythe walked past Artie into the bathroom. She grabbed an assortment of toiletries and returned to her bedroom, summarily dumping them onto the bed. As she turned to head back into the bathroom, Artie stood in the doorway.

Mustering as much patience as she could find, Artie asked again, "What is driving this, Smythe? Talk to me."

Smythe stared at the space where Artie stood. She knew she would lose a physical confrontation, and she did not have it within her. Instead, through halting sentences, she finally conveyed her grief.

"I think I'm losing my *mind*, Artie. No amount of workouts, no amount of journaling, no amount of *anything* releases the tension. I'm trapped in this apartment, and my future seems to be slipping away from me. I just feel a bit lost right now, and I need to run away for a while. I'm sorry. I'm not brave, or courageous, or anything. I'm just tired. Please, just let me go. Please. I'm just so tired."

"You're the bravest woman I know."

"I don't need you to lie to me, not on top of how I already feel. Please don't lie. I see it in myself. I disappoint myself every single day."

"And every single day, you get up, and you move forward. That's pretty damn brave. Do you know how many people just give up? The world is full of them. Your trainings are fantastic, and your writing is incredible. You seem to have written a mountain's worth.

"I get it. There's a lot going on. You had a death in your family earlier this year; one that I'm not sure you've completely dealt with. You've started your own business and, right after that, you witnessed a murder. And not just any murder. Because of that, you've got a bounty on your head. You're living off of your savings; you've invested a lot of money in learning this year, and the amount of traveling just for that... I know it has got to be straining your budget. And then you've got me living under your roof and my team surrounding you and moving where ever you move. It's a lot, Smythe."

Smythe took a step back from Artie, touching the top of her sleigh bed.

"I just can't do it a second longer. It's not you. I appreciate everything you and your teams are doing. It's 100% me. I just need a breather for a minute, and I need to get out of this city. So, before I talk myself out of being irrational, which I know this is, I need to do the most rational thing I can think of—pack a bag and get lost for a few days. Please, Artie, just let me go."

"I can't, and I won't, Smythe. I've got a vested interest in you."

Taking in a deep breath, her fingers splayed across the wooden frame of her bed, Smythe risked her next words.

"I'm also distracted and disrupted by you, Artie. Up until we met in the intersection, my life was one big quiet mess that I was just trying to sort out. I am nothing more than a simple woman of meditation, prayer, hope, and just a sprinkle of practicality. Everything I've ever done has turned into success, and I have only put in a modicum of hard work into it.

"A few months ago, before I met you, I started on this crazy journey. I didn't know what I was doing, and, at times, it feels like I still don't. The only thing I knew was that the work I was about to engage in was going to be massive—at least for me, anyway. In so many respects, it has felt like some sort of faith walk, and you know me. I am in no way religious! Not. In. The. Least. Yet, I seem to have this crazy connection to God.

"So here I am, out on a limb, working to get my bearings and calm my fears and the branch breaks. It breaks! My father dies, and then, right after that, I witness a murder.

"And the murderer. This guy is part of some sort of syndicated crime ring. Some big shot. And now, as an eyewitness, my life is threatened. I didn't ask for this, and for so long, I fought against it.

"Then you came waltzing in to save the day, and I didn't want saving. I wanted to pretend you weren't there—that, at any moment, this would be all over, and I could go back to my quiet life. But you're still here. You're a constant reminder of the danger I'm in.

"And I like you, more than I should, and that's a problem! Artie, I'm not at my best, and I'm not moving easily through the physical world right now because I feel disconnected from it. I'm just not at my best!"

Artie took a step toward Smythe. "Baby, you don't have to be at your best—"

"It's a scary place for me, and I hate being afraid! Yet, this same scary place is the place where I feel compelled to show up and have the courage to heal my corner of it. So, my retreat is the spiritual realm. There I can connect to something larger than myself. Find safety and sanctuary—because I am afraid Artie. I'm afraid of my own shadow right now. In so many ways, I'm just stumbling around in the dark.

"I'm sorry—vested interest or not, I've got to go. If it will take you more time than I have right now, I can hold off, but I need weekend trips away, beginning now."

"Listen—"

"No, please—"

"Do you trust me, Smythe?"

"Trust you? Yes... I guess."

"Then, if you trust me, hear me out."

Artie's eyes narrowed, and her pulse raced. With a speed in her speech Smythe had never before heard, she listened intently to Artie.

"My eyes are trained to see things in the physical world that most people don't see. Most people don't see the day-to-day changes that take place. Those changes are often subtle, and most people just don't do subtle. Why? Because they have become habituated to their environment. Even though they are living in the present, that doesn't seem to hold their attention. So, they look to their past and dissect the hell out of it. Or, they look to a future they could only *hope* will happen. They don't see the present. But I've spent years to see things simply as they are. I've trained myself to see them. Why? Because my life depends on it, and if I'm hired to protect someone, like you, then their life depends on it as well."

"But—"

"But you, Smythe, you see into the psychological and spiritual world. You behave and work in ways that I haven't seen many people do. You have an insight that makes me wonder where in the hell it came from! It's pretty impressive. I've watched you change the lives of people in dramatic fashion. I've watched how you've offered insight to a casual person in the grocery store that I know has the potential to shift their lives for the better. I've been there, as well as my teams, as you've delivered trainings. It's downright shocking, Smythe. The material you've learned and weaved into stories to help people shift. It's incredible.

"If only you would relax into your own present and the gifts that you have. But you're so busy trying to build and protect your future from danger—real or imagined—that you aren't concentrating on the things of your God in the present that pertain specifically to you. Focus on the problem in front of you! The past no longer exists, and your future is a choice. Logic and emotion will not fully serve you here.

"Do you not know you're shouldering a burden that isn't yours? Danger, real or imagined—that's my job! *My* job! Do spiritual, Smythe. Do magical. I need it; the world needs it. Just do the next thing you're inspired to do! Let me do the physical. Leave the logic out of it. You've tried. Reduce your past emotion.

"So much has happened in the last few months. But it seems to me that you are living *from* the past, instead of now.

"You said you see a 'God who cannot be held to the earthly traditions of man.' You quoted that to me. You want to know what I see? I see your God who uses an ordinary person like you for the extraordinary."

"And I've risked my very life because of what I know and see, Artie! I've invested my entire future!" Smythe blurted out.

"No, you haven't. For there are endless choices in the present to obtain the outcome of your future. It's always going to be risky, baby. In my world, life is just one big risk. But it's worth it. Damn it! It's worth it. Baby, you've gotta do life anyway. In the present moment. Don't run. I've got all of the courage for the things you do not see in the physical world. But I don't get the spiritual world. It scares me. You gotta have the courage in the spiritual world in the present for both of us. Can you do that?"

"Yes, but—"

"But what?!"

"No, Artie. You interrupted me, now I'm interrupting you!"

Pushing past her, Smythe walked into the kitchen with Artie following behind. Smythe poured herself another cup of coffee and turned to face Artie.

"You've had a few years to figure out your path. I'm just now redirecting mine, and I'm clunking around in it and I'm feeling awkward, especially with you in the picture. You're beautiful, smart, funny—you're pretty much a badass. You command attention. Even I was intimidated by your presence when we first met, and that's saying something! I may look like I'm navigating things all right, but the truth is… the truth is I'm not. I'm just doing the next thing I think I am supposed to do, and guess what? I've grown weary. I need to stop and catch my breath and just be. And you know what else? I really need someone in the midst of all of this who will ground me, because, a lot of the time, I feel like I'm *losing* my mind. I find myself searching—"

Artie stepped toward Smythe with a haste that caught Smythe off guard. She pulled Smythe into her arms and held her tightly. Both hearts beating rapidly, Artie wrapped Smythe in her strength, and Smythe held Artie gently in tenderness. For some time, they stood silently in their embrace. As Artie began to slowly release Smythe from her arms, Smythe felt the release and allowed her lips to caress Artie's neck with a gentle kiss. Artie gently reached out to caress Smythe's cheek. Yet, in an instant, fear backed Smythe away from her.

"I've got to get a run in and go by and visit my mom. There's no time for this. As I said, I've become distracted by you."

* * *

Smythe turned and walked into her bedroom and closed the door. She was visibly shaken and breathless. Her vision tunneled as she walked toward her armchair at the far end of her room. In an effort to ease her turbulent thoughts, she reached out toward the chair as she approached it, her hands firmly grasping the canted arms and seated herself. She examined the cherrywood finish of the narrowed spindles which held the arms in place. She touched the arms as though for the first time, allowing her fingertips to run along the uneven finish of the wood.

The chair was her first real piece of furniture. It was a near-century-old Stickley chair—a high-end piece of furniture characterized by solid construction and clean lines. Smythe found it in a local antique shop several years ago and became instantly intrigued by it. To her, it felt like an old friend. She expressed to her partner at the time that her only reservation was the color of the fabric, an odd hunter green. She feared it wouldn't blend in with the couple's décor. As she and her partner discussed the chair, they determined that the color was needed to offset the monochromatic whiteness of the living room furniture decorated by her partner well before they became a couple.

Smythe had listened intently to her partner's argument in favor of the purchase, but in the end, she had decided against it. She considered the chair too high a price to pay and settled for the sheer joy of discovering it, hoping to return to purchase a similar piece one day. Her partner, however, made a decision to later return to the shop and purchase the chair for Smythe as an early birthday present some seven days away.

That was then; this is now.

What was I thinking, I'm not ready for love. I'm just not "couple material."

Smythe trembled at the thought of falling in love again, especially with Artie. She had not allowed herself to even contemplate love since the breakup of her previous relationship. She held herself responsible for its demise, watching as they grew apart and seemingly helpless to course correct the relationship. In the end, she walked away, moving out of the small apartment the couple rented, taking only her clothes and the Stickley chair with her.

She wrestled herself out of the notion of a future love and doggedly maintained her single status, even though her friends attempted to set her up with people they knew. She convinced herself of the many reasons why she shouldn't date again: not good at relationships, relationships were too much trouble, and relationships restricted her ability to be free. In essence, she built a fortress of fear and lies around her ability to love, and she believed them.

A couple of years played out, and, with the help of a few friends, she concluded that perhaps she could at least entertain the possibility of another love in her life. Yet, each time she attempted, she found herself unfulfilled and once again retreated into a world where she held little hope for romantic love. Over the years, she built a sheltered life that allowed little time for friends, much less love.

And now, the distraction of Artie. *How stupid could you be, Smythe! She's your bodyguard. She's getting paid to babysit you.*

Why would she be interested in you? You're a fucking mess, and she's observed it for months. Forget about it. Just pretend it didn't happen.

While Smythe sat in her room, Artie slowly dressed into her workout attire and notified her teams of their destination. A few minutes later, Smythe emerged from her bedroom dressed for the gym, barely glancing in Artie's direction, who now stood waiting for her in the kitchen.

"I'm ready if you are," Smythe said, grabbing a water bottle from the kitchen bar top.

"In a minute. Smythe—"

"It's ok, Artie. I'm sorry. Let's just forget about what I said, and I'll stand down from leaving for now."

"I was going to say you have your T-shirt on inside out."

Smythe stopped dead in her tracks. She could feel the heat of embarrassment fill every pore in her face.

"Damn, I do that so often! I usually catch it before I walk out," she said.

She attempted to quickly take her T-shirt off, but the water bottle she held in her hand prevented its removal. Walking over to Smythe, Artie offered to assist her. She took the water bottle Smythe had been clutching, allowing Smythe to easily remove the T-shirt and turn it right side out before placing it back on.

"Smythe—"

"Please don't, Artie. I'm feeling embarrassed enough."

Artie, determined to have her say, placed a hand on Smythe's shoulder and squeezed it. "I'd like to tell you that I feel—"

Yet Smythe would have none of it. She felt too exposed, fearing her feelings for Artie were nothing more than a childish crush that Artie would rebuff. She walked away and opened the door.

Artie bit her bottom lip and stared after her. Frustrated Smythe had closed the door to any further conversation, she sped past her, stopping Smythe from exiting the doorway first.

"Never walk out this door, unless, I, or someone from my team is in front of you!" she snapped.

Smythe nodded. She sensed she hurt Artie, yet moving toward the direction of love terrified her. She left for the gym in awkward silence.

After their workout, a quick shower, and change of clothes, Smythe and Artie drove in an uncomfortable silence to her mother's home, deep in the valley. Smythe stopped a block away, allowing Artie to rendezvous with the car in charge of surveilling her mother's home.

After a day with her mother, Smythe returned home and spent a few hours reading. She could feel the words unspoken between herself and Artie. Feeling a need to bring closure to their conversation earlier that morning, she sat beside Artie on the couch.

"I'm sorry for my outburst this morning. It was uncalled for. I won't happen again."

"Smythe, I get it, I really do. You don't need to apologize, and you certainly shouldn't promise to never display your real emotions in front of me. It's the first time you've let me into your world and what you're really thinking."

Artie paused, weighing her words carefully. Finally, she added, "Especially... especially about me."

"Artie, I'm afraid of my feelings for you. I'm sorry, I just can't have this part of the conversation right now."

Smythe rose slowly from the sofa and walked to her bedroom, where she prepared to spend the rest of the evening.

"Smythe, what are you running away from?"

"From me."

Chapter 24

Lean In

—

T HE FOLLOWING DAY, ARTIE MET WITH CAROLE AT THE TINY BISTRO where they initially met to discuss the "Smythe assignment." This bistro's location allowed for ongoing weekly meetings between Carole and Artie, providing both with an opportunity to clarify information not expressed, even in the most encrypted of emails. They initially caught up on each other's families, but sensing something stirring in her friend, Carol waited for Artie to complete her security report. Finally, she decided to gently press Artie.

"You seem unusually quiet today, Artie. Anything you want to share, or that I should know about?"

Artie averted her eyes, contemplating just how much she wanted to say.

"I've been with Smythe for what? A little over six months? I must confess, I'm beginning to lose my objectivity. I may have to hand her over to Dennis and take a back seat."

Carole raised her head slightly in Artie's direction.

"It can happen, Artie. It's a long assignment, but, nonetheless, you can't just hand the details of Smythe's security over to Dennis. Once you accepted the assignment and I briefed your benefactor, that person specifically requested that you be heavily involved in the day-to-day interactions with Smythe. You accepted that requirement."

"Carole—"

"No, Artie. You indicated that since Davey was out of the picture for the coming year, you could take on this kind of assignment. The benefactor was satisfied that their request had been granted. And you are being handsomely paid."

"However—"

"Let me finish, please. Dennis is a good guy. He's sharp, and it helps that he has been with you since the inception of your company. I trust his level of expertise completely. However, if this had been any other case, I might well have gone to bat on your behalf; but your benefactor will want him only as your number two."

Artie shifted in the booth, glancing past Carole into the almost empty bistro. Vacant of any activity from the window she gazed through, Artie's eyes dulled to the world around her.

Carole watched her friend's demeanor. She reminded herself of the recent change in Artie's behavior—the ever-present sharp edges in Artie's countenance softening over the last several weeks and now, in front of her, she could see how much her friend had compromised her objectivity. After a few moments, Carole spoke again.

"Your benefactor has done the necessary homework on you, Artemis. You're it."

Artie ran her fingers through the sides of her hair. It was a tell that Carole had become familiar with. Artie was uncomfortable, and on more than one occasion, Carole had used it to her advantage.

"You really like her, don't you?"

Artie sighed. "Yeah, I do. There's something about her. She's intelligent, kind, compassionate, stubborn as a mule, and she likes kids." Artie said, half smiling.

"All the more reason to keep her alive, then."

"That's cold, Carole, even for you," Artie shot back, her gray-brown eyes glaring at her friend.

Artie shook her head and stared into her coffee cup before taking a sip. She was conflicted, something she had never experienced in her professional career. Her own ethical standards prevented her from becoming emotionally involved with her clients, friendly or otherwise. They were the job. Period. That standard had never been an issue—that is, until Smythe. Yet, from the moment she officially met her in the middle of the intersection, her heart had begun to sing. While she did not understand the rise in emotion at the time, she maintained her laser focus on the protection of her new client and simply shoved whatever feelings she had for Smythe aside.

But now, months of living with Smythe had worn her defenses, and she was beginning to question some of her security decisions around her protection. She needed her *friend* Carole to help her navigate her increasing feelings toward Smythe—not Carole, the mutual colleague concerned about the same case.

"Look, I don't know Smythe the way you do, but I've seen that stubborn side of her. Her stubbornness is the reason you're protecting her now. She should have gone into WitSec. However, with that said, I've discovered that life has a funny way of bringing things together for the benefit of all, in some of the most outlandish ways. The trick is to keep our hands off of the how and just do the next thing we're supposed to do."

"You're beginning to sound like Smythe."

"Well then, pay attention. I don't know about you and Smythe, but perhaps the gods have planned this all out. Let's face it—you don't get out much anymore, and from your pattern of life assessment of Smythe, she doesn't, either. Maybe this was the only way for the two of you to meet."

Artie shot Carole a look.

"Don't give me that look. All I can tell you is that if your feelings for her are hindering your objectivity, you are going to have double down on your efforts. Lean on Dennis to be a second and third pair of eyes around your protocols."

"I'm already doing that."

"I figured as much. So, does she know?"

"I don't know, but—well, I don't know. Right now, I've got to keep her alive. As you said, I've got to get her to trial."

Carole paused, choosing her next words carefully. "Might not hurt to lean into her a little bit. You might actually get more cooperation from her."

Artie raised an eyebrow.

"Listen, love, I've known there's been something between the two of you, or at least with you. You've been more, mmm, *protective* in your speech about her rather than your usual clipped descriptions. I've read your reports. I'm not sure she fully grasps the significance of the case. And the amount of traveling she wants to engage in over the next few months makes me really nervous. Leaning in a bit might get us the necessary cooperation."

"To your last comment, the answer is no. Next, I've added the necessary security detail for the trips. I've also taken away all but one day of her driving privileges. Beyond that, it has to be business as usual, or she'll bail, Carole. She was really close yesterday."

"I know you've taken the necessary precautions. I'm just saying that if she has similar feelings for you, she might be more willing to be more security cooperative out of loyalty to you."

"You obviously don't know Smythe."

Carole reached her hand out and placed it over Artie's.

"No, I don't, but I'm hoping to. Just keep the ranks closed in around her as much as possible and get her to trial."

Artie nodded.

"I need to change the subject. I have additional information to share."

"Sure."

"My sources in Kauai have been doing some snooping. PAC money has been given to several local government officials to turn a blind eye to what the chem company is doing. We're looking into corruption from local government officials. I'm not sure any of this is connected, but we've also learned the local syndicate on the island is connected to the one here. We don't have all of the pieces, yet it seems likely through some backdoor dealing that the chem company has hired some muscle to keep their dirty dealings a secret."

"What?!"

"Yeah, and we also have evidence the vic was part of a local valley group here, which was hired to look into the company. He obtained the missing documents from his grandfather on the island of Kauai."

"Where did the grandfather obtain them?"

"From a company employee. The employee has a daughter who has become very ill with the illegal spraying of those GMO crops."

"Jesus. Are the employee and the grandfather safe?"

"Right now, yes. I can't say much more than that."

"Understood. So, what exactly would this vic and his group have been able to do? They're up against giants."

"There is a lack of political courage. Ultimately, this local environment group is fighting for a political system that works for the people, and not big business."

Artie rolled her eyes.

"I know, I know, Artie. But it has to start somewhere."

"So, my client got caught up in the middle of a political mess. Politicians, chem companies, and the syndicate are all cozied up, and in walks Smythe?"

Carole remained quiet.

"Keep her alive, Artie. Take no unnecessary risks. Trial may come toward the end of the year. I'll keep you posted."

Artie nodded. The two finished their meal and set up a tentative meeting before going their separate ways.

* * *

Artie climbed into sat in the back seat of her team's SUV, stunned at the news Carole shared.

Nothing is by coincidence, she thought.

"Where to, boss?"

"To the client."

The late summer sun seemed at its brightest, and temperatures were climbing. Yet, for Artie, her internal season felt like winter—darkness prevailed in the early morning and late afternoon.

She reflected on the notion of the word "darkness" and all of the misconceptions around it. She held a curiosity both for the physical and emotional darkness. She maintained that it was in this place—where it was difficult to see, much less navigate—where real growth took place. Darkness, she believed, required we become very quiet and lean into our senses. Firmly planted into the physical realm, she had come to befriend the dark, recognizing the rich texture of complexity contained within it.

Artie turned her thoughts toward her recent conversation with Smythe. Artie's understanding of the human condition and her keen sensitivity to energy rarely steered her wrong. After initially surveilling Smythe, Artie used her behavioral profiling skills. She determined Smythe's recurring pattern of normalcy—how she interacted with others and reacted to any given situation. That pattern assisted Artie in creating a psychological profile of her client. She felt Smythe was stable, if not just a bit eccentric at times, highly intelligent, learned in a variety of subjects, holding a wide variety of interests given the sheer number of books she read per week—especially in the arts and psychology—and highly introverted, needing calm and minimally stimulating environments.

Yet, beyond that, Smythe was hiding something, of this Artie was sure; something she kept well hidden in her darkness. Given yesterday's meltdown, her intuition told her there was a deep undercurrent of pain Smythe had yet to express to her, perhaps even to herself. It was that deep undercurrent that concerned Artie, as she believed it would prove deadly under stressful conditions.

"What are you hiding?" Artie questioned aloud.

"What's that, boss?" her team member asked.

"Nothing, just thinking aloud."

What do I know about you? What are you hiding, baby?

"Boss, we're being tailed," her driver said.

Artie looked up.

"Alpha tango, now."

She pulled her weapon from its holster and braced herself for the bumpy ride that was about to ensue. She leaned forward and peered into her driver's side-view mirror, taking note of a gray SUV sitting two car lengths behind her vehicle.

"I'm really beginning to tire of this," she sighed.

In the left lane, her driver executed the maneuver Artie requested. The series of movements would allow them to drop back to an open right lane, abruptly reducing their speed and force the tailing vehicle to pass them. A quick maneuver would allow Artie's vehicle to tail the SUV that had been following them. It was a well-executed move that often drew the attention of everyone around them, but Artie was in no mood to play nice. She simply wanted to lose the vehicle.

Artie's driver found what he was looking for in the maze of city traffic. Without warning, he abruptly pulled over to the right lane. With no time to tuck in behind Artie, the gray SUV drove past them. Now the SUV was in front and to the left of her vehicle which allowed her driver to trail their nemesis.

"Well done," Artie said, as she sat back against the seat.

Artie's driver copied the license plate to discover the identity of the owner, but Artie shook her head in resignation, confident his endeavor would not provide them the information they wanted.

"More than likely, it will be registered to a shell company, but run it anyway," Artie said.

Another event to give Carole an ulcer over.

The suspect drove along a route which eventually led them out of the city and away from Smythe's location. After tailing the vehicle for a few miles, Artie instructed her driver to conduct another driving maneuver, which allowed them to lose the vehicle in the maze of traffic well before leaving the city limits.

"Boss?" the passenger team member started. "Is it possible they don't have a bead on our client's location?"

"Unlikely, but it *is* curious. They seemed to have made themselves known. That wasn't sloppy surveillance work on their part. Did you notice them while I was with FBI?"

"No, not at all."

Artie made a call to Dennis, who reported Smythe was safe within her unit. She described what happened and asked that he dispatch a team to conduct a perimeter sweep of the complex as well as an interior sweep of Smythe's apartment.

"I'll be there shortly."

Sensing danger for her friend, Artie called Carole and offered a security detail, but Carole refused.

"I'm good. Use your resources for Smythe and yourself. And I agree. It wasn't sloppy tailing."

"Carole..."

"No, Artie. I mean it. Your resources aren't infinite. Thanks for the offer, but I'm ok."

Chapter 25

The Renovations

—

A SHORT TIME LATER, ARTIE'S TEAM ARRIVED AT THE GATE OF Smythe's complex.

"Drop me off in front of the rental office. There are some construction issues I need to check on. Then sweep the streets around the complex."

As her team left, Artie entered the office. Knowing full well the complex offered only one- and two-bedroom units, she introduced herself as a prospective tenant looking for either size apartment. The office manager was a young female recently hired by the management company to oversee the sweeping changes that had just begun to impact residents. She was all too pleased to entertain Artie's questions, spending the better part of an hour with her. Polite in her demeanor, Artie asked for a tour of both apartment sizes, preferring to physically see the location of each available unit.

"I would be happy to give you a tour. We're spending quite a bit of money to renovate each unit," the manager began. "As you are probably aware, there have been several new complexes that have sprung up in the area, and we feel we are positioned in an ideal location to do some cosmetic upgrades that will yield not only a benefit to our tenants, but to our owners as well."

"So, these units are differently renovated? I ask because I have a friend who has lived in this complex for a couple of years, and her unit appears to be upgraded."

"Oh, yes, some of them have been, but even those will be further renovated once a tenant moves out. The units you speak of were renovated before the new owners purchased the complex. We also have a lot of tenants who have been here for seven years or more, and their units were never upgraded. As they are vacated, we will be putting in new flooring, as well as updated cabinetry and hardware in the kitchen and bathrooms. We're also redesigning the kitchen slightly, taking out the breakfast bar between the kitchen and the dining room. We believe it offers a more modern feel."

Artie smiled and nodded her head.

"I would be happy to show you our recently renovated units. However, those units that are vacant and still under construction are unavailable for viewing," the manager said.

"Can you point out those that are empty and currently unavailable as well? At least so I can see where on the grounds they're located. I'm kind of picky about location. For me, it's all about how the daylight dances within the unit. A unit that receives midday sun is not preferable, given the summer heat here in the valley," Artie pressed.

"I understand. Sure, we can do that for you."

The property manager escorted Artie along the property grounds, pointing out the location of apartments under construction. She opened several renovated units, allowing Artie to get a feel for each apartment.

"How does the light feel in here?" the manager asked as Artie gazed around a unit. Artie's response was always the same: "It feels stuffy and hot. Let's see the next unit."

Standing in front of a two-bedroom unit, Artie asked, "So how many units are there in the complex?"

"Well, what I can tell you is that we have five one-bedrooms and about a dozen two-bedroom units available now. And this is the last of the two-bedrooms that have been renovated." The manager placed her key into the front door and opened it, allowing Artie to enter first.

In a unit adjacent to a small parking lot positioned directly across from Smythe's building, the manager followed behind Artie into a newly renovated two-bedroom apartment. Artie gazed around. The layout appeared exactly like the last eleven units she had toured. The hallway extended further out to allow for a second smaller bedroom. All of the units were bathed in white quartz countertops. New, wider pearl white shutters replaced the easily bent white blinds that were still in Smythe's unit.

Artie slowly walked around, opening a closet in the dining room. She walked into the kitchen, allowing her fingertips to roll lightly over the surface of the countertop. She opened the door to the laundry room to find a new, more efficient washer and dryer ready for use. But Artie was stalling. She was calculating the number of units currently vacant, but what she really needed was the number of new tenants who started occupancy over the last three months.

"So, this is the last building where we currently have empty units immediately available," the manager pressed, a bit frustrated at what she considered was a nit-picky prospective tenant. She watched as Artie opened yet another kitchen cabinet, walked into each bathroom, and finally stood in place in the living room, staring directly ahead to Smythe's unit.

"So, how many new tenants have come into the complex? I'm looking for stability when it comes to my neighbors."

"Well, we've had a bit of turnover, but nothing unexpected," the manager said wryly.

"I would imagine that your rent for the units has increased for new tenants," Artie replied a bit offhandedly.

"Well, yes, they have. The valley has seen an increase in population as well as business. So, in today's market, prices have risen."

"Yeah, I know. I've lived in the valley for the past ten years. I've noticed the increase in traffic over the past six months or so."

"Yes. That would be the downside of growth."

"Supply and demand," Artie said.

Artie thought about the population in the city—twenty minutes from where she now stood. There had been a time where she could have driven from one end of the valley to the other end in under forty minutes. There was open land and blue sky. But over the past six to eight months, the population of the valley had exploded. Open land had been developed to accommodate new businesses and home developments. The blue sky had taken on a brownish haze. Traffic reminded her of Los Angeles gridlock, and crime was at an all-time high. Murders, home invasion robberies, and physical assaults were all up and continuing to rise. And she knew it all was slowly encroaching upon Smythe's tiny enclave.

"I take it then that rent has climbed for current tenants as well, even if their units have not been renovated, perhaps forcing some of them out."

The property manager's blue eyes narrowed slightly. "Well, it's what the market can bear."

"Perhaps, it is what the market can bear, but we aren't talking about the market. It may not be what people can bear, hence the number of units now available." Artie's last statement was a cool indictment.

She understood the need for a business to make a profit, but she also remembered Smythe's explanation of why she moved into the complex to begin with. The complex was centrally located and reasonably priced. Yet, the most persuasive selling point for Smythe was the number of elderly people who resided there. The elderly, she thought, were not well-known for partying. They were mostly quiet and more considerate of their neighbors. They were also in the habit of following the rules, which Smythe appreciated.

Yet, in recent months, Smythe and Artie had watched a mass exodus of neighbors from the complex. The reason was always the same. The current owners hiked the rental prices up a couple hundred dollars, added additional maintenance fees, and changed some of the amenities, including pool hours, with no explanation. Many decided the complex was just not worth the price anymore, while others on fixed incomes were now priced out of their home.

Artie noted the silence between them, shook her head, and smiled. "So, when will renovations in this area begin?"

"We start next week," the manager said coolly.

"Well, I would love to live close to my friend. She's in building five, across the way. Will you have units in that building available?"

Sensing a sale, the managers' face lit up. "That building has some of the best sun exposure. Unfortunately, there aren't any units available at the moment. The building is full and has been for quite some time. However, we will have a tenant that is scheduled to vacate in the next two months. She is moving overseas. It will be taken off of the market for tenancy for roughly two months while renovations are completed and then become available."

"What's the unit number?" Artie asked.

"Unit 554. It's a two-bedroom. Once the tenant has vacated, we will schedule it for renovation. I would suspect that it would be ready by October at the earliest." The manager paused, thinking about the construction team hired to complete the renovations. "I'm thinking that, given our contractors are a bit behind, probably November. In time for the holidays, if you can wait that long."

"That time frame may just work out for me. May I place that unit on hold?"

"Of course."

After returning to the office, the manager walked Artie through the application process and the deposit that would be required. She agreed to the terms, including the nonrefundable fees, completed the necessary paperwork, and paid the deposit. *Another tax write-off,* she thought. She typed a note into her phone, reminding herself to call the office manager in a couple of months to cancel her tentative tenant agreement, losing the nonrefundable fees.

Her team sat in a parking spot out front, surprising Artie as she left the office. Curious, she hopped in her vehicle. Her driver pulled up to the closed gate and used the remote to open it. It was only then that she remembered the remote control to the gate which would have allowed her access past the office was not in her possession.

"Thanks, guys. Wasn't in the mood to hop the gate."

"We figured, boss. You weren't at the client's residence. Thought we would assist," her driver said with a smile.

She later met with Dennis to discuss her conversation with the rental manager and outlined next steps during the renovation of the soon-to-be-vacated unit.

"That's a wrinkle, boss."

"We have some time. Run down the list of contracted companies and get me a complete list of employees."

"It's going to take a while."

"So, we better get started, then. Contractors in and out of the unit that sits right next door to Smythe. The renovations will become too much of a perfect storm, and soon that storm is going to be sitting right next door."

Artie stood at the front door to Smythe's unit. She changed the expression on her face, sensing concern written all over it. She entered, expecting to find Smythe hard at work in the dining room. Surprised she was not there, she quietly closed the front door and listened. She could hear faint tapping coming from Smythe's bedroom.

She removed her jacket, hung it up in the dining room closet, and ambled to the refrigerator to grab a bottled water. She could see Smythe against the far wall, sitting in her recliner with her tablet on her lap. She moved hesitantly toward Smythe's bedroom, softly tapping the bedroom door before leaning against the door frame. Smythe was deep in thought, typing quickly. She glanced up slowly as though she were coming back down from another world.

"Hmmm."

"Earth to Smythe."

"Oh, hey. Give me a minute, I need to finish this thought."

Artie remained standing at the door. Smythe took another minute, lightly tapping her fingers onto her keyboard. She paused every few seconds, as if allowing her thoughts to complete their work before entering them onto the screen. When she finally looked up, Artie was reviewing a text message.

"I'm sorry. I was just in the middle of a storyline and needed to write it down before I forgot it. What time is it?"

She looked toward the onyx wall clock hanging on her wall. "Oh, wow, 4:30. Late. How are you?"

"I'd be better if you weren't sitting there. There are security measures in place, but still, it's a bit of risk, Smythe."

"That would require that I reconfigure the entire room if I wanted to sit in the recliner. I like the feel of it just the way it is. Besides, the curtains are always closed."

Artie sighed loudly.

"Plus, I've been increasing my mileage and speed, and my legs are wiped out. Keeping them elevated helps in the recovery."

"When was the last time you drank water? That helps recovery as well."

"True. Thanks for the reminder."

"Can you come out here? We need to chat for a bit."

Smythe nodded and rose from her seat, standing slightly hunched over. Her legs and lower back felt stiff and achy. She slowly bent over further and stretched her hamstrings and calf muscles before stiffly walking into the living room. Artie took a seat at the far end of the sofa. Smythe regarded Artie momentarily before taking a seat next to her, sensing an energy from her that she had not felt before.

"I met with the FBI agent in charge of your case today. They're still trying to move the case up. She expressed concern about the amount of traveling you are scheduling over the next few months. I need to ask again, is there any chance you can curtail some of it until after the trial?"

"No, there really isn't, Artie. I've already canceled a lot of traveling as it is. I wanted to make some weekend trips, but I'm remaining here. I'm not giving up my best friend's daughter's wedding, nor am I cancelling the ten days for the second conference. It's the last conference for this year-long class, and my presence is required if I want to be certified."

"So, you've decided against the weekend trips?" Artie asked, a bit surprised at Smythe's sudden change of heart.

"Yeah, I have. I thought about it and decided that after this case is over, I'm taking myself on a very, very long vacation. At least three to four weeks along the upper coast. I want to just get lost for a while, maybe even go to Hawaii if I can swing it."

Observing her client, it was then that Artie began to understand the change in behavior—the reason she sat in her bedroom to work. She leaned toward Smythe.

"Smythe, we're working hard to end this case quickly. The justice system is slow when it comes to cases like this. They really want to make sure that their case is tight. You're the main witness, baby."

"Yeah, I know. It's just not what I expected. I thought not going into witness protection would give me more freedom. I had hoped that all I had to do was keep a fairly low profile; I would testify, and that would be the end of it. It hit me last night that this case seems to hinge completely on my testimony. I mean, I've known it, but I'm becoming more aware of it. I can barely drive my own new car, I don't go out, I barely see a movie without having you guys all but stealthily surround my mom and me!"

"You have very few friends, Smythe," Artie said gently.

"That's not the point. I can't even cultivate any new relationships, and what few friends that I do have, I have to lie to, feigning illness or work. I'm just restless, I guess."

"Is that why you're working in your bedroom today?"

Smythe reflected on the question. She knew her energy was low. It had been a struggle to get through a paltry three-mile run, reducing her speed steadily until she walked the last half mile. Earlier in the day, she attempted to sit in the dining room to study but could not bring herself to remain in the open space. Eventually, she found her way to her bedroom and, for most of the day, sat and wrote.

"I've been feeling a bit depressed, that's all, and I've just felt more secure in there. I think I just needed to nest a bit, if that makes sense. Plus, I was hoping that your team could come in and get out of the heat."

Artie nodded her head in understanding. "They have to maintain perimeter surveillance, but it's a sweet offer. Is there anything you need from me or my team?"

"No, not unless you can finish this seminar I am writing, complete my mentor's course, pass the written exam and essays with flying colors, conduct my presentations at his conference, and testify on my behalf."

Smythe glanced toward the door. She wondered what it would feel like once the case was over. She had become increasingly honest with herself over the last 24 hours and admitted that her "crush" on Artie was deeper than she thought. The idea of her leaving at some point was more than she thought she could bear. That was the *real* truth, but one she was unwilling to share with Artie.

"You really like the Pacific Northwest and Oahu, don't you?"

"I really do. I visualize moving to one of those locations in the next few years. My mentor teaches that we can be, do, and have most anything—the trick is to focus on it every day, make it a goal, and create a vision board.

"What is that?"

"It's just a tool that can be used to concentrate, help with clarity, and maintain focus on a specific goal in life. If you do visualizations every day, a vision board helps with that. For example, let's say I have a goal to live along the Northern California coast. I might use any kind of board and pin up pictures of what I want my house to look like, the furnishings I want within the house, the scenery I want to see, and any other pertinent details as a representation of living along the Northern California coast. That board serves as a representation of the future I want. Then, I would place that board in a place that I would see every day."

Smythe pointed to the board hanging on a wall next to her printer. "When we see that board every day and visualize the feeling of having attained that goal, our brains will work nonstop to achieve the images or statements by activating our subconscious mind."

Artie nodded her head. She thought about her own company. In many ways, she had done exactly what Smythe described. She decided how many clients she wanted, what types of cases she would take, and the type of team she wanted to assemble. Law enforcement background would be a must for everyone on her team, and their record had to be exemplary. Over a couple of years, as she gained clarity, the company she now runs was the company she envisioned.

Smythe broke into Artie's thoughts. "What about you? Have you always wanted to stay in the valley?"

"No. I was assigned here when I worked with the FBI. My fantasy is Switzerland. But that will have to wait until after Davey goes to college. I don't want to leave the country until he is an adult."

Smythe made no response.

"Listen, I've got an idea," Artie said, breaking Smythe's long silence.

"I've been at this all day, and I know you have, too. If you are at a stopping point, let me spring for an on-demand movie. I can send the guys out for popcorn and candy, we can darken the living room, and we'll hang out in this makeshift movie theater. Use the sofa as movie seats."

"I'd like that a lot, Artie. I can be at a stopping point."

"Perfect, I'll radio it in so that when their food is delivered, the movie junk food can be delivered as well. Any preferences for a movie?"

"I'm partial to anything that does not involve gratuitous violence, gore, or horror."

"So, if I recall correctly, you like sci-fi, comedy, and love stories."

"You make me sound like such a girl. I also like adventure and disaster films," Smythe teased.

"Ha! You're on."

Smythe smiled. She left the living room to put her work away and fold down her bed. As she headed out of her bedroom, tears began to fill her eyes. Tears of joy that she could spend an enjoyable evening doing something other than reading in bed before lights out a few hours later. She wiped away her tears and headed into the kitchen, opening up her refrigerator. There was a bottle of white wine, two bottles of beer, and a half bottle of Sangria.

"What do you want for dinner?" Smythe asked.

"My favorite, pizza. Canadian bacon on one side for me and mushrooms on the other side for you."

"Hmmm. Just thinking about the type of wine."

"There's a bottle of red in the cabinet, no?"

"Is there? Let me check." Smythe took a few steps to the dining room cabinet. She scanned the top shelf. "Indeed. Red it is."

"Pizza will be here in about an hour. Popcorn and candy, too."

"An hour? Let me guess, The Joint."

"Yep."

"That's a thirty-minute drive without traffic. He'll deliver?"

"Good to know the owner. I know I'm picky about where I get food, but in my line of work, I have to be. There are certain places I trust, others, not so much."

"I'm not complaining, trust me. I love his pizza, especially the crust. It's so light with just a hint of sweetness to it. Let's figure out what to watch together."

They decided on a mega-disaster film before tending to minor tasks around the apartment. Artie made a couple of phone calls while Smythe decided to tidy up her already spotless apartment.

Chapter 26

Retrograde

—

T HE NEXT MORNING, SMYTHE WOKE UP IN A SOMBER MOOD. Contemplating the day ahead, she could barely hold back the tears as she lay in her bed. Her heart ached as memories of an old wound she called the nemesis emerged into her consciousness. The thought of moving through the business tasks she set up for the day seemed insurmountable. After rummaging around in her thoughts, she finally coaxed herself up and into the kitchen to start coffee. To her consternation, Artie was already moving around the kitchen and had prepared hot water for the French press.

"Good morning."

"Morning," Smythe replied softly.

"How did you sleep?"

"Not well." Smythe wandered into the living room, choosing a book as she walked by the book cabinet and settled into a corner on her sofa.

Artie lowered her head slightly, concealing a slight furrow of concern. She moved about the kitchen with deliberate ease, removing the whistling tea kettle from the stovetop and poured the hot water into the French press. She casually stirred the coffee grounds and hot water together before placing the lid over the press, covering it with a tea cozy. With the coffee steeping, she quietly entered the living room where Smythe sat reading. Artie turned up the light to the torchiere lamp which stood across from the sofa and sat next to Smythe.

"Hey. What's going on, baby?"

Laying her book gently on her lap, Smythe looked down at her hands, which rested atop her book. "Today is my father's birthday. Just remembering his death and life, I guess."

"I'm sorry."

With a tone of forced indifference, Smythe replied, "Not sure there is anything to be sorry for. It was, in many ways, a complicated relationship. His death was quick in some respects and slow in others. There's just so much emotion to process through. I'm a bit surprised at my reaction."

"I'll listen if you want to share."

With an abandoned gaze, Smythe shifted her eyes from her hands to the front door and took in a breath. In almost hushed silence, she recalled the events to Artie in minute detail. As if they happened yesterday, her body relived every painful moment, tensing and contracting with each recollection.

She recounted the sexual abuse as a child, at the hands of her father, and a mother who would not believe her, who years later asked her to seek "professional help." She remembered stuffing her emotions into the deepest parts of herself and convincing herself that the abuse didn't happen. It took years of stuffing until it had created a monster inside of her; a monster she kept at bay with cigarettes by the pack and an occasional drink.

She endured years of separation from her family as the outcast member until a series of events brought her back into her family. However, she would never again bring up the abuse again to her mother.

She recounted to Artie that years later, she would move to the valley. By that time, her father would have been diagnosed with a degenerative brain disorder. She was bone-weary during the slow dying of her father at the beginning of the year, her mind mostly on autopilot. His physical and psychological health deteriorated at a rapid pace over just a few months. Hallucinations, severe mood swings, and an inability to walk without assistance had become the norm. He had fallen nine times over a five-week period, and the stress of the next emergency had brought her mother to the brink of despair. She had also grown very resentful of her father.

Smythe began visiting the baker's shop during that period and was just getting to know him. One day, she locked eyes with him as she entered the shop.

"How does one survive this? When will it end?" she recounted to Artie. "My anger was palpable. My protector part wanted so desperately to protect my mother, while my warrior part was at the ready to do battle against both my father and the medical establishment.

"Joao approached my table, placed a cup of coffee and two pastries down in front of me, and then asked to join me.

"I am afraid I won't be very much company, but yes. I don't know what to do.

"'Let go. Do only that which you can, and leave the rest alone,' the baker replied.

"That's not what I want to hear right now. This—this is too much. I know what's happening with him right now is not his fault, but damn it, enough is enough. He. Tried. To. Kill. Her. Fifty some years of marriage, and on two separate occasions of whatever this is, he tried to strangle her. Is this what her life has come down to? He has got to go into a nursing home, but it could be months before a suitable placement is found. Damn it!

"The baker just looked at me.

"I know this is a first-world problem. I get it, but it's *my* first-world problem. It's in my lap, and I don't know how to protect either one of them—as if I should. He could be mistreated in a nursing home, and my mother? My mother has to lock her bedroom door at night because she is afraid he will shuffle up the stairs and kill her while she sleeps.

"'Let go,' the baker said again."

As though examining her hands, Smythe said, "I looked down at my coffee cup and realized I had been gripping it so tightly."

"What happened next with your dad?" Artie asked.

"A short time later, he had fallen again. Only this time, it did significant damage. Unfortunately, neither my mom nor I knew the extent until a few days later. Mom didn't call paramedics during the last fall. She said he seemed ok. I was out of town, so I couldn't assess him. But, within 24 hours, his health had deteriorated. My mom called and asked me to return to the valley because something changed in his color. I asked her to call the paramedics, but she was hesitant. I was a flight away and couldn't catch one out until late that evening.

"It wasn't until after I got there and started to ask him questions that I knew something was really wrong. His speech was slurred, he couldn't stand up without excruciating pain, even to go to the bathroom; he just looked like he was dying. So, I called paramedics, and he was rushed to the hospital. We were told he had broken his hip, sustained a hairline fracture to his leg, and had two brain bleeds. He survived the hip surgery, but he continued to hallucinate. I was told it was the result of the brain bleeds. After a week in the hospital, he was transferred to a rehabilitation center. From there, he was allowed to come home. He seemed to recover enough physically. But at home, he suffered a massive stroke. There was no hope. We had him transferred to a hospice center in the city where he died a few days later."

Smythe took in a long slow breath and released it. The sun was rising into the morning sky, and she stared out her picture window, squinting to see through the partially opened blinds which offered her a modicum of privacy.

"That's a lot."

"It was," replied Smythe.

Artie clenched her jaw and paused for a moment.

"Let me clarify. You, the daughter—the outcast from your family because you told your truth—were ultimately the one who became the caregiver for both of your parents."

"Yeah, kind of. My furniture took forever to arrive, so I stayed with them for a hot minute, quite literally. There was just so much drama every day with my dad's behavior."

"How did you feel when you left? I bet it had to be a relief."

"It was, but I also felt guilty. Really guilty. It was weird. I felt as if I were abandoning my mom to a life of misery, but I was also miserable."

"*You* felt *guilty?*" Artie said incredulously. "She abandoned you when you told her the truth about your dad. You were considered the outcast in the family. If you ask me, it's what she deserved."

Smythe smiled slightly.

"That's not really fair, Artie. I felt sorry for her. She was living with a husband she was hoping to grow old with, hoping to travel around the world with. For her, that all went up in smoke. I remember her saying to me one day, 'Some retirement this turned out to be.'"

"Baby, I'm talking about the abuse. She abandoned you. She chose him over the knowledge that her daughter was telling the truth."

Beginning to choke back tears, Smythe replied.

"She didn't see it that way. I don't know if she has changed her mind or not. Back then, she told me I was making it up. She said that I was 'sick.'"

"What kid makes that kind of shit up?! No. I've done a thorough background check on you, Smythe; FBI even has a psychological profile on you. You're not sick. What the hell!"

Artie paused, catching her own breath.

"You do know it's not uncommon for mothers to take the side of their husbands and boyfriends. And it's not uncommon that they accuse the kid of being mentally unstable. It's the oldest trick in the book."

Wiping away a tear, Smythe explained, "So long ago, I had to stuff it all away and find my own way back to normalcy, and I think I have. There are still shadows that emerge every now and again, but I've bounced back. I had to sit for a very long time with the question if I was making up the abuse. The answer was no. I remember. I remember flashes of detail, but then I'd stuff the memory down again. I just didn't—and still don't want to—remember."

Smythe closed her eyes.

"Can... can we change the subject?"

"If that's what you want."

Smythe let out her breath.

"What I want is to finally feel safe and protected. Right now, this conversation is not making that happen. Given that you're here under the circumstances—"

"Baby, you are safe. I got your back. You gotta know that, deep inside. I got you."

Pursing her lips together, Smythe frowned. *I hear you say that, but there is a piece of me that doesn't believe it.*

"I appreciate the sentiment."

Artie sat both motionless and expressionless.

"Look, I've never shared this with anyone. No one! I'd really appreciate it if you wouldn't add this little detail to the FBI profile of me. I'd rather not have this conversation end up in court. I can see the headlines now: 'FBI loses case because wacko eyewitness tells lies.'"

"Stop it!" Artie reprimanded.

"Just kidding."

Artie's facial expression ran the gamut of disbelief to one of concern.

"No, you weren't, Smythe. From where I'm sitting, you still haven't worked out the lie your mother told you about the abuse. You still want to believe her rather than believe your own truth."

"I'm not sure that's accurate, Artie."

"What part isn't?"

Blood started to rush to Smythe's head. Her heart began to race, and she clenched her teeth.

"I just want her to believe me. That's the accurate part. Read between the lines!"

"There are no lines to read between," Artie replied gently. "She tried to reframe childhood sexual abuse perpetrated upon you by your father by telling you that you were the lie. Baby, I believe you. I believe you. I've heard a lot of stories where the mother takes the side of the husband or boyfriend rather than the kid. But their disbelief doesn't negate the abuse that happened. That's on them. I believe you, Smythe. Yet, all the belief I have in you isn't going to amount to a hill of beans if *you* don't believe you. You stuffed this down so long—"

Tears filled Smythe's eyes, and her throat began to close as she quietly began to weep. Artie moved over and pulled Smythe into her arms.

"Let it out. That's it. Let it all out," Artie softly whispered into Smythe's ear.

"Damn it! God damn it! I thought I had processed through all of this!"

"Abuse has many layers, baby, even when parents believe their kids. You have the added layer of a parent who did not believe you."

"She-she has her reasons. I can't fault her for that," sobbed Smythe, her body tensing with each tear that fell.

"You mean you can't, or you won't?"

Sitting up slowly from Artie's arms, Smythe stuttered, "What-what do you mean? Shit, they're the same."

"No. No, they're not the same."

Artie looked deeply into Smythe's eyes with bottomless concern stretching across her face. She almost whispered her response.

"Can't is a contraction of cannot. It is a disempowering word, baby. Won't is a contraction of will not. Will or will not has the power of choice. You can choose to do a thing or choose not to, but you have a choice, nonetheless."

Smirking a little, Artie added, "I was an English major in college."

Smythe broke eye contact with Artie. She sat, absorbing both the grammar lesson and the implications of it in her own life. Did she feel helpless in her choice to not fault her mother for not believing her? Or did she simply choose not to find fault in her behavior? Did she feel helpless to understand her mother's position, or did she choose to understand her mother's position? And if she chose to understand her mother's position, was it out of compassion and empathy, or out of fear of being an outcast member from her family yet again? Did she even understand "the position" her mother had taken?

"I'm not sure, Artie," Smythe finally answered.

"Start with this: start believing in *you*. Start with believing that you are a tough yet kind, compassionate, smart as a whip, thoughtful human being with a lot to offer. Start with liking the little kid who was abused—"

"I do like her. I love her, in fact."

"Then believe her and stand up for her. Just like I'm standing up for you, you stand up for that little girl. Just like I'm putting my life on the line for you, you put your life on the line for her. Start there."

"How?" came the million-dollar question from Smythe.

"Don't let anyone, and I mean *anyone*, tell you a different narrative other than your own truth."

Smythe nodded, her eyes peering a hole into the bit of sofa that separated Artie from her. Artie gently reached for Smythe's hand and tugged at it. Smythe took the hint and moved closer to Artie, allowing herself to sink into Artie's arms. Artie moved to the edge of the sofa and placed her back against the pillows, pulling Smythe into her and gently holding her there.

After several minutes, Smythe spoke.

"I'm not broken, but I know there are walls that I've put up. I allow people to only get so close. I live in this made-up world in my head where I am safe and loved and cared for. Yet, when I look around, there isn't anyone I trust. I don't trust my friends. I don't trust my family. There's no one I trust," Smythe mumbled into Artie's chest.

"Yeah, I know. I see it. You've got this tough exterior thing going on. Buzzcut, muscular build, Malcolm X glasses. But you and I know it's just a facade. Beyond the look—which, by the way, I dig—you can choose to be vulnerable anytime you want."

"I'm unsure if I know how to do that anymore, and by the time I've decided to let my wall down, people have this expectation that I am somehow this put-together person. But I'm really not. I'm a mess, just like everyone else."

"We're all a mess. I'm a mess. My family's a mess. If your friends expect you to be something that you're not, perhaps they aren't really your friends. Perhaps you may, at some point, need to find a new tribe. Or perhaps, simply show them the real you. Those who like the more vulnerable Smythe will stay. Those who don't, won't. Besides, you let me in, right?"

"Did I have a choice?"

"Yes, kind of. But the kind of part is that I can be very persuasive."

Smythe smiled.

"Is there more?"

"Yes."

Artie held Smythe against her body, feeling the tension in Smythe's shoulders. Artie intentionally relaxed her body, signaling Smythe to speak when she was ready.

"When my dad was in hospice, it was me who went there every day. I remember waking up really early on the day after he was transferred by the hospital to hospice. All I could think about was that he was alone."

"Your mom wasn't there?" Artie asked.

"No. Not the first day. The second day, she was. But it was hard for her. She later said she didn't want to see him like that. His face was somewhat contorted, and his breathing had become laborious. It was only a matter of days. And my sisters couldn't come, at least that's what they said."

"So, you went."

"Yeah I did. I went. And I sat next to his bed and held his hand and talked to him. I never told him that I forgave him. It wasn't that I didn't forgive him, because I had. It just seemed useless to hold that against him or bring up a past that he denied. In light of his current physical condition, it wasn't important anymore.

"It's been said that the forgiveness we extend to others isn't for the other person. It's for us. I wanted my behavior to demonstrate that I had forgiven him. I made peace with his behavior toward me, so I laid it aside. I just sat there and made one-sided small talk and told him I loved him and was there to protect him. He never moved or showed any sign that he knew I was there. Everything in me wanted to leave, but I had this picture in my head of being the better person—the better daughter who did the right thing, even though there were moments when I didn't want to. I ended up staying half the day. And then I did it all again the next day, but that time I brought my mom with me. He died before I could get there on the last morning."

"Why did you go?" asked Artie.

"Because I didn't want him to die alone. He—he was still a human being. And I didn't want to leave him alone. I really did love him. I was just afraid of him."

Tears trickled down Smythe's cheeks and onto Artie's sweatshirt as she held Smythe tightly in her arms. Smythe could feel the musculature of her strength and felt herself releasing her body weight into the arms of Artie as she finally relaxed.

"Smythe. This thing happened to you, and it was traumatic. No one should have to endure what you did, but many have. One of the things I have learned is that an event or a thing is only that thing or event. Nothing more. In other words, it isn't *who* we are. Yet, baby, so many people attach meaning to the thing. Please don't define yourself by any event. It's just that; an event. It's just one thing."

Smythe began to bury herself into Artie's torso. She could feel Artie's breast move with each breath she took. Smythe began to match her own breathing to hers as she listened to Artie's heartbeat. After a few minutes, Smythe spoke.

"English major?"

"Yeah."

"Far cry from FBI to attorney to security firm CEO."

"Nah, it was part of the plan. I had to learn to write well if I wanted to go to grad school or, in my case, study law."

"That makes sense."

"I was a kid from the Bronx. My parents barely had a high school education, and they were bound and determined that my two sisters and I would not only have diplomas but go on to obtain college degrees. A certificate, at the very least!"

Artie chuckled at her last comment.

"Seriously, though. I like English. I find the English language as a whole, rather interesting. Slowly, I became a stickler about what people were saying. Words have impact. I'm not concerned about the pronunciation of the word, but I *am* concerned about the impact of the word itself. What words people use casually tell me a lot about what they're thinking. In my line of work, it's critical."

"What do my choice of words tell you?"

"That you are casual, intelligent, thoughtful, traumatized, emerging, and caring—a bit too caring for my liking."

"Why?"

"Because you end up with the short end of the stick, that's why. Caring is good, but you need to exercise more self-care for Smythe, in my opinion."

Smythe began to sit up, but Artie gently held her in place.

"I'd rather end up with the short end of the stick and less than optimal self-care, as you stated, than to have the opposite and not care at all for fear of self-absorption."

"Why does it have to be caring or not caring? Can you hold both the caring and self-care?"

"I think I do both."

"Do you?"

"You know, you're startin' to dance on my last nerve."

"Oh my god. I haven't heard that term since I left New York," laughed Artie.

"It's a black thing."

"No, it's a Bronx thing."

"Well, I learned it from my auntie."

"Well, my mother and father are straight-up Italian, and they used that phrase all the time."

"They probably learned it from a person of color. My grandfather and grandmother are Navajo, and I heard him say it every once in a while."

"So, you're black and Navajo?"

"Yep. My auntie would always say I was part of everything. I never quite understood what that meant, and honestly, I just left it alone."

"So that accounts for your skin tone."

"What's that supposed to mean?" This time she sat up and away from Artie.

"Hey, I meant no disrespect. As I said, I read your file, and listed under race is African American. However, when I started surveilling you, I thought there was more to the story than a checked box. America has this horrible habit of placing people into tidy little boxes when it comes to race. It's just not that simple."

"No disrespect taken. I'm not sensitive about my mixed race or my skin tone. I'm proud of it. Proud as an African American and proud as a Navajo. By the way, I didn't check the box under African American."

"That figures."

"So, answer the question. Is there enough room for both care of another and self-care?"

"I've been working on that," Smythe softly replied. "Once my dad died, I thought for a minute about moving back in with my mom. I mean, she has this huge house—you've seen it. But it didn't land well in my spirit. Living alone was a far better self-care option for me."

"That's a great start. What else are you doing?"

"Well, as you know, I am working out. Hadn't done it as much as I wanted to. Ever since Dad started to go downhill, it was work: go to their house, come here, eat, sleep, repeat. Which, by the way, I am late. I gotta hit the treadmill since a certain someone will not allow me the luxury of running outdoors."

Smythe bounced off the sofa into the direction of her bedroom. It struck her as she stood up that her energy was different. It wasn't only relief she felt, but also validation. To have someone who cared about her and believe her felt freeing. In that moment, Smythe experienced another truth: the infusion of soulful truth-telling is impactful and releases the soul from its prison.

"Do you want coffee before we go?" Artie called after Smythe.

"Yes, please. I'll be out in a minute."

Artie quickly changed into workout attire and running shoes. She then poured two cups of coffee into two small thermoses. As Smythe came out from the bedroom, Artie handed her a thermos.

"Coconut milk and sugar for you."

"Thank you. Is the team ready?"

"Yep. Let's go." Artie opened her com set and informed her teams she and Smythe were on the move.

"Team 1, we're exiting the apartment."

Once Smythe, Artie, and her team arrived at the fitness center, the team swept the area. As usual, the gym was empty. Given permission to enter, Smythe walked in and climbed onto her favorite treadmill. She pulled up her favorite running playlist on her phone, a mix of contemporary gospel music with a smattering of Indie Arie, Pharrell Williams and Israel Kamakawiwo'ole thrown in.

"How many miles today?"

"Seven," replied Smythe. "Easy tempo."

Artie nodded and spoke into her com. She had devised a numbering system to signal to her team the number of miles Smythe was running and her pace. It allowed them to gauge the time she would be exposed. In this case, "the lucky number times 10."

"Copy that."

As Smythe settled into the rhythm of her pace, she allowed her mind to wander between her conversation with Artie and people in general. She thought about how her mother had toed the line, not pursued her career interests; how people in general tended to simply toe the line of societal norms, allowing their dreams to die in order to fit in.

Was that it? Was that what Mom was trying to do when she disowned me because I spoke the truth? Was she afraid that if people found out, she would be ostracized? What had the baker once said?

"When people get to know us, there are some who want us to change in order to be more like them. If we resist, they become belligerent. It is as if they know what is best for us. So many nosies seems to know what is best for us and refuse to give us credit for knowing what is best for ourselves. You cannot allow that to happen along your journey."

Or maybe she knew the truth and felt guilty herself because she didn't/couldn't protect me. If she chose to leave Dad, one could only assume she may have had to struggle economically to build the life she wanted for herself and her kids. Why wasn't she willing to do that?

Smythe continued to patter through her miles while Artie worked through a weight training routine. She glanced at Artie as she conducted bicep curls.

How could she lift that much weight?

Smythe completed her run, and the team returned to her apartment. Once she was out of the bathroom, it was Artie's turn. She ran a bath and settled into it to soak away the conversation she held with Smythe.

So much abuse, so much heartache for this woman.

She slid deep into the bathwater. *When will we have our fill of it all?*

Tears filled Artie's eyes, and a deep heartache settled into her soul. It was then that her heart burst open and sang. Its melody was one of love for Smythe. It was not a love borne out of pity. Nope. Not out of pity. That would not serve either of them. This love was steady, strong, and enduring. It was a love that had developed over time. It was a love she did not actively seek, but sought after her. She soaked and wondered about the God Smythe loved. Artie did not necessarily believe in God, but she did not believe in coincidences either.

"And the intricacy of the garden that this God she calls her Beloved is tilling," she said aloud. "If you are real, what are you doing? And why?" She took a gulp of air before submerging herself in the warm water.

Willing herself to remain objective, she continued to remain submerged. Yet, as she slowly rose from the water's depths, something shifted within her. She could feel a gentle presence around and through her. It was if an outstretched hand reached into her body and pulled out all of the hesitation she held to pursuing a relationship with Smythe. With the outstretched palm holding her hesitation, she sensed the hesitation had dissolved into mist and floated gently away from her. The only feeling that remained... was love.

Smythe sat in the dining room and opened her tablet to study. Time was slipping away from her as the second conference was fast approaching. As she opened up a video module, flashes of her favorite aunt occupied her thoughts.

Why in the world are you in my thoughts, Auntie?

After several minutes of distraction, she closed her laptop, allowing whatever thoughts that wanted to surface to do so.

Artie emerged from the bathroom wearing a white T-shirt and khaki slacks. With much love and admiration, she observed Smythe for just a moment. Yet, as much as she wanted to wrap Smythe in her arms for the rest of the day, she knew now was not the time.

"Having trouble studying?"

"What? Oh, no. I mean, yes. I guess. I was thinking about my aunt. I guess it was all the abuse stuff that brought it up."

"Was this your dad's sister?" Artie asked as she walked into the kitchen. "You hungry?"

"Yes, and yes. She was well into her adult years when she discovered that she had dyslexia. Growing up, she had always had trouble learning. Her father used to spank and yell at her because she wasn't learning at the same pace as her sisters and brother. It was almost as if Grandpa was trying to yell and punish the 'stupid out of her,' as my mom recounted to me. It was a phrase my aunt had used.

"Yet Auntie was so smart. She could have been a mechanical engineer. She understood the way things worked so easily, but she never had the opportunity to pursue higher education. By the time she was an adult, she had such low self-esteem. So, instead of college, she married out of high school. It didn't last, though. She divorced my uncle and found work as a janitor and then a housekeeper to support herself. She remained a housekeeper until her death, about 20 years ago."

"Wow, she died young."

"Yeah, she had cancer and didn't seek medical help until it was too late. But, as I reflect on her life, I am astounded at how we as a people don't allow the gift of others to emerge. If 'they' don't act like us, walk like us, dress like us, think like us—*anything* like us, they're ridiculed, deemed unworthy of the very air they breathe and often summarily dumped into the trash heap!" Smythe yelled, her fury taking her by surprise. She paused for a moment.

"I just don't understand. We're all different, Artie. There is not a person on the planet that doesn't have a gift to offer the world. But so many don't have the opportunity.

"They're often traumatized out of living out their full potential. And let's not even bring race, privilege, or religion into the mix. Some people make it, but so many do not. She didn't. Today, people would have called it emotional abuse. Just like spanking. It's now called child abuse, even. I agree, mind you. There is no reason to hit anyone, nor is there a reason to belittle someone every day. Don't let me keep going on about this. Thinking about her and others like her—I just become so enraged." Smythe looked down at her hands. She had unconsciously balled them into fists.

"See what I mean?!" she said, raising a fist in front of her.

"You're preaching to the choir, Smythe. A great deal of my clients are underprivileged, and they're up against the advantaged; those of us, and I include myself, as granted benefits and entitlement simply because of the color our skin. Yet, this I also know, that while it's infuriating—heart-wrenching even—the steps that people like you and I make, those little steps toward loving humanity, those steps over time... they make a difference. I won't stay mad, but I will stay focused."

Smythe nodded her head in agreement.

Chapter 27

The Expression of God

—

A FEW GOOD WEEKS TICKED THROUGH THE CALENDAR YEAR FOR Smythe, and she felt more at peace. She continued to write, had secured a couple of corporate clients, and conducted several half-day workshops. After a particularly busy week, Smythe looked forward to Saturday. Like most Saturdays, this was the only day Artie would allow her to drive, albeit with a security detail following her.

After completing their normal workout routine, Artie and Smythe both showered, dressed, and stopped by the baker's shop where they picked up their usual malasadas and coffee. From the bakery, the caravan traveled the 25 minutes it would take to get to Smythe's parents' home. The caravan stopped a block away, allowing Smythe to trade places with the driver of her vehicle. She drove the rest of the way to her mother's home while the security detail stationed themselves inconspicuously amongst the homes in the neighborhood, yet still within clear eyesight of Smythe's family residence.

After greeting her mother, Smythe, who was always wired, gave a code word indicating that all was well in the home. She carried on a pleasant conversation with her mom before the two went off for their weekly breakfast outing. From there, she ran errands with her mother before returning to her parent's home. For the remainder of the afternoon, they sat chatting and watching a movie or two. This was how the normal routine played out, week after week since her father's death.

However, this Saturday, the day before the six-month anniversary of her father's death, Smythe's mother delivered an emotional blow she didn't see coming.

With their first movie playing, Smythe was peacefully lounging on the family room sofa when her mother walked up behind her.

"Here, I want to give this to you. It is an old letter your father wrote after you accused him of—well, you should read it. I found it when I was cleaning out his armoire. I told you that he had a year's worth of stuff just piled into it. You just need to know you were the apple of his eye, and he loved you very much."

Smythe turned around and took the letter from her mother's outstretched hand. As she held the letter, her vision became tunneled. She could feel her heart pounding through the walls of her chest, cold settling in the pit of her stomach as her hand began to shake. She glanced at the letter and quickly shoved it into her pants pocket before turning around to continue watching the movie they had started. Neither of them spoke.

Smythe's hands were balled into a fist inside her pants pocket. She could not help but wonder what the letter contained, but the tone of her mother's voice seemed to hint at an accusation. They both remained silent until the end of the movie.

After the movie ended, Smythe gathered her messenger bag and groceries, hugging her mother goodbye before quickly heading out the door. She met Artie a few houses down and asked if she could simply drive home alone. Artie, although wary of such a request, consented. On the way home, Smythe stopped at a gas station, followed by two of her security detail. She hadn't smoked in months, yet she purchased a pack of cigarettes and a lighter.

Once the security detail was back in their car, they spoke to Artie on her com link.

"Boss. I think there's trouble. She purchased a pack of cigarettes."

"What!?"

With bone-chilling fear coursing through her slender frame, Smythe returned to her car and drove to the nearest strip mall and parked. There she opened up the pack, took a cigarette out, and with her hands trembling, lit it before shoving her hand into her pants pocket to retrieve the letter.

Artie, seated in the front passenger seat of Team 2's vehicle, watched Smythe intently. She sensed something was very wrong, and it was clear that the paper Smythe held in her hand was emotional dynamite.

After several minutes and another cigarette, Smythe signaled the team that she was driving and headed home. Once home, she feigned a headache and made a beeline for her bedroom. In her bedroom closet, she opened the second drawer of her clothing chest and reached toward the back of it. Tears in her eyes, her hand—the same hand that held her fathers' letter—now found what she was looking for.

She held the bottle in one hand and unscrewed the lid with her other, shaking out three pills as she laid the bottle on her bedside table. She walked into the kitchen and grabbed an open bottle of wine. Smythe popped the pills into her mouth and nearly downed the other half the bottle before Artie walked in and gently pulled it from her.

"What's wrong, baby?"

With tears in her eyes, Smythe said, "Nothing that this bottle won't solve in the moment."

"I don't believe that. C'mon—"

"I don't want to talk about it, Artie, not now. If you don't mind, I just need time to process a bit."

In reality, Smythe was well on her way down an emotional rabbit hole. Her inward dialogue started to consume her.

Why would she hand me this letter? Did she need to make a statement?

And why all of this talk about God. He was no saint. Who is he to talk about whether I believe in God or not?! I've never even talked to that asshole about that. Maybe—maybe, God's punishing me. Maybe I'm just as bad as they've always said I was. Maybe I am evil. Why would she do this?

Smythe was unreachable; her mind completely cluttered with self-doubt and loathing. It was now late afternoon, and evening was fast approaching. Her heart shattered, she spoke very little, barely mustering up enough energy to keep busy with chores to complete around her apartment. Artie made several attempts toward small talk, but Smythe remained closed-lipped whenever Artie attempted to coax her into talking about the letter.

For Artie, timing could not be worse. She received an unexpected call from her FBI contact Carole, requesting an emergency meeting. The trial was being moved up, and a credible threat had been made against Smythe's life.

"Can it wait? Something is up with the client here."

"No, Artie. I need to see you. Now."

"What's going on?"

"Artie, just get here as soon as you can. I need to share something with you."

"Where?"

"My office."

"I'll leave now."

Artie prepared to leave, yet an uneasiness began to settle into her body. She couldn't pinpoint whether it was Smythe's unusually solemn disposition or her upcoming conversation with Carole. All she knew for certain was that she felt overwhelming danger and fear—two emotions she wouldn't have normally allowed herself to entertain. All of the reasoning she offered to herself would not abate a heightened sense of both emotions; therefore, out of an abundance of caution, she chose a security detail to accompany her to the meeting.

This case is too volatile for second-guessing.

Artie notified Dennis of her meeting as well as her concern. He posted teams outside Smythe's apartment and assigned a third team to escort Artie to the FBI building.

* * *

I don't just need to think. I'm sick and tired of thinking. Sick and tired of it all.

With Artie out of the apartment, Smythe downed another four pills and finished the last of the bottle of wine sitting on the kitchen countertop.

Time seemed to pass slowly. Smythe stood motionless in the doorway of her bedroom as her feelings rose like the waves of an angry ocean tossed about, going under and under and under again.

Smythe's inner voice began to speak. *I understand now why people don't cry out for help. People all around me—friends, colleagues, acquaintances—all of them. They only see a façade. How could they think of me as strong, confident, brave even? It's the furthest thing from the truth. It's just time to end this, I think.*

I wonder. I wonder about people who take their lives. Those left behind have often said, "If only they could have reached out for help."

Don't they know? Don't they understand the shame we feel? We're supposed to have it all together. Certainly, I'm not supposed to contemplate taking my own life. I'm supposed to be highly functional. I've got everything going for me. Survival of the fittest, right? Top of the evolutionary chain, at least in wisdom. I'm the "why would she take her life" kind of person.

Smythe sneered a chuckle and burst into tears as panic began to overwhelm her.

I really am mentally ill. She was right all along.

I need to leave. I need to leave. Just pack up now. Artie's not here. I could say to the team I'm going to the store. They would follow, and I could lose them. I could just walk away. Walk away. Walk away, walk away, walk away—

Yet another inner voice spoke. Smythe's voice of reason. The voice that connected to her Beloved. *Please don't, please. Call Artie. Call anyone—they're just outside. Tell them what's happened. Tell them what you've done. Artie doesn't deserve this. You don't deserve this.*

Unable to quell her first inner voice, it quietly berated her. *I'm not that strong. I'm not that strong. I can't do this anymore. I'm tired of fighting. I'm so tired. I'm so very tired.*

Her voice of reason spoke again, begging for help. *Please, God, help me. Please help me, please dear God help me. I can't hold on any longer. I can't do this anymore. I don't know what end is up. Please help me.*

Read, just read.

Smythe stumbled into the dining room and picked up a book off her dining room table, knocking one of her notebooks onto the floor. As she reached down to pick it up, the notebook opened onto a page with a note from someone's handwriting she did not recognize. It read:

"The seed of God which lives in everyone merits recognition. For in a specified way, we express the creation of our God. You, my daughter, embody the creative expression of our God."

She began to sob.

Ok, this is a sign. Take a shower, get into bed, and just read. Don't think. Just read. Don't think about tomorrow. Just read. Can you do that much? Please, Smythe. Your life depends on it. Please.

Artie will be back soon. Do you really want her to find you like this? C'mon, pull it together. Go throw up. Before it's too late, just throw up.

"—the expression of God," was Smythe's last conscious thought as she stood rocking to and fro at the entrance to her bedroom.

Chapter 28

Grief Comes in Many Forms

—

Aˢ Aʀᴛɪᴇ ᴀɴᴅ ʜᴇʀ ᴛᴇᴀᴍ ʜᴇᴀᴅᴇᴅ ᴛᴏ ᴛʜᴇ FBI ʙᴜɪʟᴅɪɴɢ, Cᴀʀᴏʟᴇ called.

"Hey, it's me. I've just pulled into the parking lot," she said.

"I'm 10 minutes out. Can you say anything now?" Artie replied.

"No, not on the phone. I'll see you in a bit." Carole ended her call and drove a few feet forward and parked her vehicle. The parking level was dimly lit by flickering overhead fluorescent lights. Earlier in the month, she had inquired about the replacement of them, yet she was met with a polite bureaucratic response—'We are aware of the issue and are working to resolve it.'

Peering up at the light, she made a mental note to inquire again, before turning on the interior light to her car. She thought about her upcoming conversation with Artie as she rummaged around her purse. She pulled out a small notepad and scribbled a note to herself as a reminder to discuss some information with Artie when they met. As she began to roll up her driver's window, a sudden screeching of tires caught her attention, and she squinted into her rearview mirror at an oncoming vehicle driving through the structure. The vehicle abruptly stopped at the parking elevator a few feet away, letting a passenger out before moving forward, parking directly next to her.

Ten minutes later, Artie and her team arrived at the FBI building and made their way up to Carole's department. They surveyed the area, noting the lights were on, but Carole was not present to greet them. *Odd*, Artie thought as she listened to the silence.

"She's probably in her office. I'm going to head back there. Stay here—coms open. I want no surprises."

Her team members nodded and remained at the entrance to the department. Artie weaved her way through a maze of cubicles, her senses heightened once again. Something seemed off. She honed in on her intuition, listening to the only sound in the office—her own footsteps, each boot landing firmly on the tile floor. She neared Carole's office and slowed her pace. With no one in the department, Carole had a habit of sitting in her office with soft jazz music keeping her company—and Artie knew this. She listened to the silence, unsnapped her holster at the small of her back, and placed her hand on her weapon as she rounded the corner.

She stopped short of entering Carole's office, quickly scanning the area. A large janitor's cart sat against the wall outside the office. Within the office, Artie could hear the sound of paper being shuffled and a file drawer slam. After a few moments, a cleaning man, holding a small trash can full of crumpled documents, emerged from the entrance to the door. Standing at least six feet five inches tall, he was a human wall. His black goatee offset his dark brown eyes and light skin tone, and his broad, muscular build accentuated his height. *His blue one-piece jumpsuit is incredibly ill-fitting*, Artie thought as she observed him. It fit too tightly around his midsection, and the length was too short, causing the cuff of his black pants to show underneath. Surprised at her arrival, he eyed Artie with suspicion.

"Hello," the cleaning man said flatly.

"Hello. I didn't know anyone else was here. I'm supposed to meet a friend for dinner," Artie said.

"No one's here, lady. It's just me."

"Really? That's odd. She just called me and said she would be in her office."

"No one's here except for me, and I've been here all afternoon."

Artie nodded and scanned his appearance. She noted the name Jack imprinted on the right chest pocket. Artie slowed her breathing and held a casual yet sharpened tone.

"Jack. That's my father's name."

The man made no reply.

Forcing a smile, a chill ran the length of her spine, causing the hair on the back of her neck to rise. A feeling of electricity coursed through every muscle of her arms and shoulders. Her eyes laser focused on his every move, she spoke again.

"Well, Jack, it's perplexing. She called me just five minutes ago and said she was pulling into the building."

"Don't know what to tell you. I haven't seen anyone here all afternoon."

"Well, unfortunately, I can't wait for her, but here's my card." Artie reached into her pants pocket and tapped her com device before pulling her card out and laying it on a desk that sat just outside Carole's office.

"If she does return, would you give it to her and ask her to call me?"

The man looked down at the card.

"Sure thing, lady."

When he raised his eyes, they were pierced with cold contempt.

His size betrayed how fast he could move. He lunged for Artie, throwing the trash can at her as he approached. Knocking her back onto her heels, Artie had no time to draw her weapon as he pulled a knife from his pocket and jabbed it toward her. She evaded his swing and grabbed his wrist tightly. While moving her body to gain an advantage, he punched with his other fist, delivering a crushing blow to her rib cage. She absorbed the blow, released his wrist, and backed away from the swing of the knife. He lunged for her yet again.

She drew her weapon, unable to get a shot off before he rammed her body, shoving her hard against the desk behind her, bashing her weapon from her hand. She tumbled, hitting her head hard against the tile floor. Her vision began to blur, and the assailant moved menacingly toward her. As he raised the knife to deal a blow to Artie, he caught sight of Artie's detail as they rapidly closed in on her position. The momentary distraction allowed her to roll away from the assailant.

Artie's detail drew their weapons and demanded the assailant drop the knife, giving Artie time to scamper onto her feet. She was pretty sure a couple of ribs were bruised, if not broken. The suspect held his ground with the knife in his hand.

"Put it down—now!" Artie screamed, adrenaline numbing the pain of her fight.

The assailant tightened his grip on the knife and remained still. He glowered at Artie, his jaw stiffening.

"This is my last command. Drop that knife, or my men will fire. Down, *now!*"

The assailant's eyes met the fury contained within the eyes of Artie's. He released his grip on the handle and allowed the knife to drop from his hand, the blade tinging as it hit the tile floor. Artie's team members ordered him onto his stomach, then cuffed him. Taking in a halted breath, Artie hit an emergency wall alarm.

"You ok, boss?" her team member asked.

"Yeah, just peachy."

Within a few minutes, security arrived. Artie identified herself and her team members, showed her credentials to the security officers, and explained her presence.

"I received a call from Special Agent Roberts, who wanted to meet for an early dinner. She asked me to meet her in her office. Upon my arrival, no Roberts, only the suspect rifling through her office."

Amidst her questioning, the FBI agent on call arrived and shook hands with Artie.

"Good to see you, Artemis. It's been a while. Must say, I wouldn't have expected that you would have caught a bad guy in our building."

"Your security is lax, Warren. Good to see you too."

Artie explained her presence in the building once again, divulging she was protecting an eyewitness to a case Carole spearheaded.

Warren scanned Artie's appearance. "Looks like you could use some medical attention."

"Yeah, I know, but not now, Warren. Look, I'm worried. Carole and I were meeting to discuss the eyewitness," Artie said as she glanced at her watch. "Carole isn't in her office, and the last time I spoke to her, she said she had just parked. That was at least forty-five minutes ago."

"I'll send a security team down to check to see if her car is in the parking lot."

"Can we go together? That is, if we're through here."

Warren peered around the office. The assailant, now in custody, sat in a conference room under armed guard. Carole's office had been cordoned off, and Artie's team had been released to return to their vehicle. He agreed and escorted Artie and two additional security officers to the elevator of an underground parking lot.

"She typically parks on L1," Artie said.

"Things have changed a bit since you were here. Her department is assigned to L2," Warren replied.

The elevator door opened. Artie noticed the garage lights were much dimmer than she remembered.

"Are these lights always so dim?" she asked, squinting her eyes to adjust to the darkness.

"Yeah, they're installing a new lighting system for that very reason, but you know the bureaucracy. It's all about timing and endless paperwork."

With very few cars around, Artie spotted Carole's car parked in front of a cinderblock wall at the far end of the garage. She and Warren drew their weapons and quickly approached with caution. Artie tightened her jaw and surveyed the area, her eyes landing on a figure seated in the driver's seat. The FBI agent stopped just shy of the car.

In the driver's seat sat Carole—unmoving, her head slumped to one side. Artie approached the driver's side and found Carole dead with a gunshot wound to the temple. She reached in and checked for a pulse, finding none. Artie could only stare in disbelief at her friend. She stood motionless, feeling sick to her stomach.

This was her childhood playmate, college roommate, and best friend. It was Carole who had persuaded Artie to start her own business. It was Carole who stood by Artie when she discovered she was pregnant after a drunken one-night stand with an old childhood friend, and Carole who celebrated every success and grieved every loss with Artie.

Warren observed Artie's demeanor. He knew of the friendship she shared with Carole, but the area was now a crime scene.

"Artemis. Hey. Back away," Warren said in hushed tones.

As Artie complied, she noticed a torn piece of notebook paper sitting on the passenger seat next to Carole's right hand. Given the recent attack on her own life, she wondered if that paper was connected to the case. She quickly glanced to her left and to her right. *Too risky to grab.*

She hunched her shoulders and slowly moved away. Tears began to fill her eyes, and she allowed them to flow down her cheeks unfiltered. While security officers began to cordon off the scene, she moved with deliberate ease around to the passenger side of the car. Feigning an attempt to assist in the investigation, she quickly grabbed a pair of gloves an officer was holding and opened the passenger door. As she reached in, Warren quickly reprimanded her, reminding her in no uncertain terms of crime scene protocol, which included contamination of the scene.

"What the hell are you doing?! Friend of this agent or not, former FBI agent or not, I'll have you arrested!" Warren barked.

"This is my friend. I know all about protocol, Warren! Let me help."

"You don't belong here, Artie. It's an FBI crime scene now. Period."

"Warren, she's—"

"Leone! I said no. You're not FBI any longer. She's my responsibility!" Warren jutted his jaw out, daring Artie to argue with him. Without a word, Artie stood her ground, staring down her former colleague.

"Do we have your contact information?" he asked.

"Yes," Artie said as she reached into her back pocket and pulled out a business card. "But here it is again."

"Good. We'll contact you if we need to."

"But War—"

"Now, Artemis! Or I *will* arrest you!"

Artie flicked away her tears. Frustrated and grieved, she glared at the FBI agent, shoving her hands into her pockets.

With a broken heart, Artie solemnly walked away from her friend. She reopened her com set and met up with her team in the visitor parking lot in front of the building. At the sight of her, her team rushed to her aide. Her jacket had been ripped by the knife the assailant had used, her right cheek had begun to swell after hitting her head on the tile floor, and she was holding her ribcage.

"Boss!" her team member gasped.

"Yeah, I know. I know. Adrenaline has worn off. It feels much worse than it probably is. Help me in."

Cautiously, they helped Artie into the backseat of their SUV. Once in her team's vehicle, they drove her to a nearby Urgent Care center to tend to her ribs. After tests were run, medical personnel determined her ribs were bruised, but not broken, and she had sustained a slight concussion.

"I'll write a prescription for pain, and my nurse will be in shortly to bandage your ribs," the doctor said. "Ms. Leone, your body has sustained significant damage and needs time to heal. Bed rest. No physical activity for at least six weeks."

Artie nodded and watched as the physician walked away. The room was quiet, something she did not appreciate, for there was nothing to occupy her thoughts. Against her will, her body began to tremble. Her eyes filled with tears as grief began to overwhelm her. Alone in the room, she attempted to sob, but the pain in her ribs did not allow her diaphragm to move freely. She grit her teeth to quell her emotions, and, while only a few minutes had passed since the doctor left her, for Artie, time seemed to grossly crawl to a halt.

"Knock, knock," a nurse said, smiling as he walked in.

Artie lifted her eyes to the nurse. "Where the hell have you been? I chose this location because it's quick."

"We've been a little busy, Ms. Leone, but I—"

"Don't lie to me! There wasn't a soul in the waiting room when my team and I arrived!" she snapped.

Stunned at the foul temperament of his patient, the nurse momentarily paused before moving hesitantly toward Artie.

"Well?"

The nurse composed himself. "It's alright, Ms. Leone. The doctor just left you a little bit ago. A concussion can disorient you to time. But don't worry, I'll have you out of here in a jiffy. I just need to bandage your ribs and give you the prescription the doctor wrote for you. I'll go over that in just a moment and then get your discharge papers for you to sign. You'll be out of here in no time."

Feeling very much like a wounded animal, Artie snapped again. "I don't need you to go over that—I know how to take medication! And I am not disoriented! What I need you to do is *efficiently* get me the hell out of here! Which means turn around and get those discharge orders!"

The nurse turned on his heels and quickly disappeared from her sight. When he returned, he held everything she would need to make a quick exit out of the facility. Artie looked toward the door. She noted another, more senior nurse—one who had tended to injuries she sustained over a year ago—now hovered at the entrance to her room.

After a few minutes, the nurse wrapped Artie's ribcage, handed her an additional wrap, gave her a written prescription, and had her sign the necessary discharge paperwork. In no mood to make nice with the nurse, without a word, Artie gingerly stepped down from the examination table and made her way out of the lobby with a member of her team by her side.

As she slowly walked toward her SUV, she watched as a piece of paper skidded against the rough edges of the parking lot, nudged along by the gentle breeze of the late summer's evening. To her, it seemed the paper was resisting the flow of the breeze, catching every now and again on a single corner of asphalt. When the breeze paused, the paper fell flat onto the ground. A few seconds later, the breeze again gently nudged the paper along. The paper still seemed to resist the movement, tapping against the asphalt as it passed her by. She paused for a moment, watching as the paper continued along its unknown journey. She took in a breath and continued silently to her vehicle.

"Where to, boss?" her driver asked.

"The client," she responded, holding her ribs as she climbed into the back of her vehicle "I'll fill the prescription tomorrow."

Sitting in the back of her SUV, Artie replayed several conversations she held with Carole, including her last one

"Carole, my experience tells me this ring will leave nothing to chance. What you're now investigating isn't just a murder, but it's also a global chem company, judicial officers, and local government officials. Intimidation is their go-to strategy, and then comes the harm."

"Why didn't you listen, Carole?"

Sitting in the back of her team's SUV with a pain prescription in hand, her thoughts turned to Smythe. It brought her a considerable measure of solace. She was falling deeply in love with this woman, and as stubborn and emotionally elusive as Smythe could be, Artie was persistent. Her only thought was to double down on Smythe's protection from here on out.

Chapter 29

It's Going to Get Messy

—

A RTIE YELLED INTO HER COM UNIT FOR TEAM 2.

"Get in here and bring the med kit! Now!"

Artie's hands trembled as she attempted to shake Smythe back to consciousness. A few feet away, she could see a bottle of pills sitting on her bedside table. She quickly dropped to her knees next to Smythe and checked for a pulse.

Smythe lay crumpled and frighteningly still on her bedroom floor, her breathing extremely slow and shallow. Artie struggled to stand up, grabbed a washcloth from the bathroom, and soaked it with cold water. Returning to the bedroom, Artie yelled.

"Damn it, Smythe, wake up!"

Her ribs throbbing with her every movement, she turned Smythe over. Straddling her, she squeezed water from the soaked washcloth onto Smythe's face.

"Smythe, c'mon, wake up! Damn it, don't you die on me! WAKE UP! Please, baby. Please!"

Without warning, Smythe took in a deep halted breath. She could hear Artie barking orders to her team.

"Ar... ee—" Smythe mumbled, unable to fully speak.

"Smythe, baby, come back to me. C'mon baby, it's going to be alright. Come back to me."

Tears filled Artie's eyes.

How could I have not seen this coming—

Smythe's eyes slowly slit open. In a moment, the sweet hope of endless darkness gave way to agonizing light.

"Why, why..." Smythe mumbled before the darkness returned.

Team 2 entered the bedroom with a medical kit, and Dennis surveyed the scene.

"Boss?"

"I think she took a bunch of pills, Dennis."

Dennis scanned the bedroom. He spotted the remnants of a bottle on Smythe's bedside table. He quickly walked over and picked up the bottle.

"Muscle relaxers. Do you know how many?"

"No, I don't. I've never even seen that bottle! She's breathing, but—"

"Let's get her into the bathroom under a cold shower. We've got some ipecac in the kit," Dennis said.

He walked over to the Smythe and bent low to one side of her, gently moving Artie out of the way. Dennis knelt beside Smythe, pulled out a bottle from the medical kit and opened the top. He raised her head and shoulders so that her torso rested on his chest and arm.

"Open up, Smythe."

Smythe's eyes slit open again. Dennis poured some of the ipecac syrup into her mouth. He watched for just a few moments as Smythe resisted swallowing the liquid. Once he was assured she had ingested most of it, her poured again, forcing her to swallow it.

"You're gonna be alright, Daniels. Hang in there." He looked at Artie. "We need to get her into the bathroom. It's going to get messy."

Dennis gently picked her up and carried her out of the bedroom and into the bathroom. As he lifted her from the floor, Smythe began to vomit violently, thick yellow foam spewing onto Dennis' crisp white shirt and her own pants. Artie came in from behind him and gingerly climbed into the tub, sitting on the back edge. Dennis carefully set Smythe into the tub, resting her torso against Artie before turning on the shower. The water was freezing cold. He slowly directed the shower nozzle onto Smythe's body and watched her carefully.

"Oh god," Artie gasped in pain, her body tensing to the cold water.

Smythe opened her glazed eyes, dazed and confused.

"Turn off," Smythe mumbled. "P-please turn off."

"No, baby, not until you come back to me fully. C'mon. Stay with me. That's it."

Dennis took off of his vomit-splattered shirt. He balled it up and walked into the kitchen, opened the door to the laundry room, and placed the shirt into the washer. When he returned to the bathroom, Smythe, although groggy, continued to vomit but slowly became more alert.

"Grab some towels, will you?" Artie asked. "For yourself, and for her."

Dennis opened the bathroom closet door and found a couple of towels and placed them on the floor next to the bathtub. He continued to observe Smythe, looking for any additional signs of medical distress.

As Smythe started to come to, grief was the only thing she could feel, and she began to sob. She sobbed so hard, she vomited again.

"Why would she do that? Why?" Smythe slurred.

Dennis noticed Smythe began to shiver and turned the water from cold to lukewarm. Both he and Artie tended to her for several minutes, working to bring her to full consciousness. Once awake enough, Smythe slowly began to follow Artie's commands. She leaned forward as Artie instructed. She could wiggle her feet, raise her floppy arms, her eyes lost a little of their glassy look, and she could cry. Dennis sighed and nodded his head before he turned off the shower head.

"We got her back, boss."

"C'mon, baby, let's get you out of these clothes."

"She may need to vomit some more, Artie."

"I know, but I need to get her out of these clothes. Give us the room. I'll call you if I need help."

Artie's ribs resisted her every movement. Wrenching pain seared through her rib cage as she struggled to remove Smythe's wet clothes. Her eyes moist with tears, she turned the shower back on, and, ignoring her own agony, slowly, painstakingly washed Smythe's head and body. Smythe continued to vomit, and each time, Artie soothed her.

"That's it, baby. Get it all out. That's it."

Her body shivering from the ordeal, Smythe remained quiet, her eyes staring straight ahead of her. Once she was bathed, Artie assisted Smythe out of the shower. Numb to all else except the tender touch of Artie, Smythe leaned weakly against her and allowed Artie to gently dry her body.

While Artie continued to attend to Smythe in the bathroom, Dennis started the washer to clean his shirt, cleaned the hallway of vomit, found two sets of sweatpants and T-shirts in Smythe's dresser and left them outside the bathroom door.

After she was dressed, Team 2 helped Smythe into her bed. Dennis stared at the bottle of muscle relaxers, before removing the them and placing the bottle in Artie's duffle bag for safe keeping. The team remained quiet and kept a silent vigil over Smythe until Artie had taken her own shower, changed her medical dressing, and put on the clothes Dennis had left for her. Standing in the kitchen, Artie looked down at her phone she now held in her swollen hand.

"I'm going to order take out for all us. How does Thai sound?"

"Yeah, boss, sounds great."

Artie let out a jagged sigh. "I'm hoping that whatever residual medication remaining in her system will be counteracted by the absorption of some food."

A team member looked back toward Smythe's bedroom. "It was close."

"Yeah. It was." Lost in thought, Artie stared past her team member toward Smythe.

Sensing her team looking in her direction, Artie spoke again, her voice commanding. "Thanks for your quick response this evening. Set up a perimeter outside of the complex until Team 3 returns and then rotate every two hours until your relief arrives." She surveyed Dennis, who stood standing in the hallway.

"Go home, Dennis. And tell your wife it wasn't me who stripped you from your shirt," Artie said, smiling at him.

"Copy that, boss," Dennis said with a smirk. "It's in the wash. I'll pick it up in the morning."

Artie accompanied her team to the door and secured it behind them. She walked wearily back into Smythe's bedroom and stood in the doorway, observing her before walking in the room. Expressionless, Smythe lay face up in bed. Artie gingerly sat next to her.

"What happened, baby?" Artie quietly asked.

"I'm sorry."

"Shhh. What happened?" Artie whispered.

"A letter. She gave me a letter... that my dad wrote... a poison pen letter from him, accusing me of being mentally ill. He denied everything, Artie. He only accused."

Smythe could only stare past Artie, lost in her own pain.

"Baby, talk to me."

"Why do you call me baby?" Smythe whispered.

"It's my term for you; a term of love."

Smythe looked away from Artie.

"Don't love me, Artie. Not after this."

Artie attempted to reach for her hand, but Smythe felt the gentle touch and withdrew it from Artie's reach.

"Baby, you're what my heart wants and needs. And you are totally worth loving. You've got to know, this is only a moment, and I really want to understand the tipping point."

"How could you love someone that is mentally ill?"

"What? Who told you—is that... who told you that?"

Artie's jaw began to ache, her eyes laser focused upon Smythe.

"Both of my parents... it's all finally come to a head." Smythe sighed. "My mom gave me a letter from my dad. He wrote it, I guess, once I told my mom about what happened when I was a kid. She had some sort of conversation with him, and he basically accused me of being sick."

Smythe snickered. "Of course, she believed him—but my body knows the truth. My memories don't lie—yet here I sit, doubting my sanity," she mumbled.

"My great-grandma would say they placed a curse on you. Is that what drove this—being called mentally ill?"

Her speech still slurred, Smythe responded. "Yeah. I am, aren't I? I've heard it all my life, off and on. It's like they used it as a weapon. I didn't know any better." Smythe tilted her head to the side and closed her eyes. Her only desire was to crawl back into the silence of darkness rather than endure the cacophony of her thoughts and the rollercoaster of the accompanying emotions.

In an instant moment of clarity, Artie now understood the thing which had infested Smythe for so long—the one that had driven Smythe into emotional seclusion.

"It's been the thing she's held over you," Artie said, almost as though thinking out loud.

"It has, and she just had to get the last word in, I guess. She's been cleaning out all of Dad's stuff, and old stuff of hers. She's been saying she doesn't want my sisters and I to have this big house to empty out."

"I'm not following."

"So, she finds this letter in his armoire. She evidently read it and held onto it. On the six-month anniversary of his death, she gives it to me. Why?"

Artie remained quiet.

"My mom is aging. She had my younger sisters and me later than a lot of women from her generation. Today, I listened as she gave her opinions about every manner of events happening in the world. She seems so set in her ways, and even said she doesn't want to change. She just doesn't. There was anger in her voice. Then she gave me the letter. Even though we didn't talk about the letter, I suppose she made up a story about what the letter means, and that's that. Just like all of us, I guess—we all make up stories about others. But then again, it doesn't matter, does it?"

"What I think doesn't matter. You know I believe you."

"What child grows up afraid of her father? Not every man, just her father. What child grows up trying to tell the truth, but keeps getting shut down and told she is crazy? What child becomes physically ill and shakes inside whenever childhood sexual abuse is brought up? I couldn't watch movies about it or hear someone else's story without being physically afraid. I remember I would just shut down. I felt such intense panic. I still can't watch those kinds of movies.

"It's why I didn't go into social work. I just couldn't emotionally handle all of the abuse stories I knew I would come into contact with. I was just a kid who was searching for a way out—who felt so alone. So afraid of her own shadow and afraid of others."

Smythe slowly began to sob. Artie crawled onto the other side of the bed and pulled Smythe to her chest. Smythe cried long enough that her stomach began to ache.

"I just want this pain in my soul to die, Artie. I can't take the pain anymore. AM I MENTALLY ILL??!" Smythe screamed. "AM ?!"

Artie's eyes filled with tears.

"Maybe I should just say I am a liar and a cheat. Will say anything, do anything..." seethed Smythe.

"You know that's not true," Artie whispered into Smythe's ear.

"Why?"

"Who did your mother know him to be?"

"What do you mean? How did she describe him?" Smythe asked.

"Yes."

"She said he was a liar. That he made a habit of telling untruths all of their adult life. She said she wanted to divorce him but never got up enough courage to do it. At least, that's what she told me before he died."

"So, at some point, she chose to live in a world full of his lies," Artie summarized.

"Yes, I guess. Artie, I feel like God is angry with me. I feel like I've come back to this brick wall. That everything I am trying to manifest in my life just won't happen. Success, abundance, love. It feels like it's slipping away—and at my own hands. It's as though I'm being punished somehow."

Artie again remained quiet for a time. She held Smythe in her arms, feeling each tear that fell onto her T-shirt. Finally, she spoke quietly, holding back her own tears for the woman who had stolen her heart.

"You've come to a crossroads, baby. I know it well. You either have to believe in you, or you will die, right along with your dreams and all the talent you hold within you. I can't make you believe in yourself. No one can; not even God.

"I don't know why your mother would be so cruel as to deliver that letter to you on the anniversary of his death, if at all. She could have, should have, just thrown it out. What mother would do that to her child? To a grown daughter who sacrificed so much for both of them these last few years; what would fuel such a need to hurt you like that?" Artie questioned.

"I don't know—but again, these are the stories we tell ourselves, I guess. Maybe she wasn't thinking. Maybe it was her way of clearing the air—at least for her. I just didn't bite. I didn't read it in front of her. And she didn't ask that I did."

"My sense is that there is a trauma within her that she has not yet named."

"I dunno. There was more to the letter, but Mom held it back, I think. He had started the letter stating it was in three parts. I don't know what part of the letter it was that I read, but the letter wasn't complete."

"Where's the letter now?" Artie asked.

"In my car. Please, please don't read it."

"I don't want to read it, baby. It's not for me to read, nor was it for you to read either. Listen to me. There are thousands of men who seem innocent. They appear as kind, caring men and fathers. Yet, they have done despicable things to their daughters and even their sons; and some of those same kids have taken their lives. They never recovered.

"Their mothers—seemingly kind, strong, even stoic women—feign hurt and choose to believe their men over their own flesh and blood. I don't pretend to understand why. But I do know that if you choose to, you can recover from this. But it will require that you believe in you."

"I don't feel strong right now, Artie. I don't seem to have the will to fight against this. I feel this horrific heartache, and I don't know how to recover from this."

"One moment at a time."

"I'm tired of being in pain. I'm just so tired."

"You've been in pain for a long time now, baby. And you have carried this weight with you for decades," Artie said, kissing Smythe's forehead.

"What do I do?"

"Stay alive, take a breath, and stay right here."

"I just need for my head to shut up. That's all I want—I want my head to shut up. I want to be healthy, and I don't feel like it right now. I want to love you, because I do, but I don't—"

"Start there, baby. Love me right where you are. Give us another day together." Artie gently kissed the top of Smythe's forehead again, pressing her cheek against her head.

"I don't know if I can ever go back and visit. I don't want to talk to her anymore. I don't want to visit her anymore, but in my heart of hearts, I know I will."

"You have that right."

"But her health wanes in and out. All of the rest of my siblings are scattered across the country. She has no one else."

"But she really doesn't have you, either. You know, we've had a lot of 'where would we each love to live' conversations. We even talked about moving out of the country once the trial is over, me to Switzerland and you to the Pacific Northwest or to Canada. There was always a hesitation when you thought about leaving here. How do you feel about that now?"

"Like it's the thing I need to do. Up until now, whenever I have fantasized about leaving the US, I've felt really guilty. How could

I leave her behind? But then I would think, well, she's choosing to stay here. She doesn't have to. Now I think, yeah, I could leave without feeling guilty in the slightest. I'm not sure if it's just because I'm angry or not. I love her deeply, Artie, I really do. And I know, on some deep level she loves me too, but I can't do this with her anymore."

"May I make a suggestion?"

"Yeah, sure."

"I know you will continue to call her every night to check in on her and hide your feelings about giving you that letter, although I wish you wouldn't. You'll go by every weekend and spend one if not two almost full days with her, though I wish you wouldn't. How about you skip this coming weekend? Do something for *you*. We have a week before we head to your friends' wedding. Let her spend a couple of weekends alone."

"Right now, that sounds like heaven," Smythe said with a sigh.

"Good, you need some quality time away from her. Choose in favor of you."

Smythe nuzzled her head into Artie's shoulder. Artie held her tenderly and began to hum. It was the last thing Smythe remembered hearing before drifting off to sleep.

Chapter 30

The Shift

—

Smythe awoke early—even the sun had yet to begin to rise from its slumber. Rolling over gently, she realized she had laid in Artie's arms the entire night. She took in the scent of Artie. Lavender. She breathed deeply and smiled to herself. She could feel her heart burst open as though wrapped in a warm afghan of deep, abiding love.

Remaining wrapped in the smooth, muscular arms of this woman she was falling in love with, she was aware that something in her spirit had shifted. While grief sat somberly within her heart at the action she had taken the night before, during the course of the night, she became aware her perspective shifted. She no longer held within her spirit a sense of unworthiness. She no longer thought herself as a weakened gender. She no longer held the belief she was mentally ill, and she no longer held the reframed truth she had been fed as a child.

As Smythe shifted in Artie's arms, wondering how they laid in that position for most of the night, she became aware of a growing strength that only wavered if she gazed backward in time. Smythe knew she could no longer live in the past. She knew she could only control her present, and she knew she could only imagine and work toward a different future. Quite unexpectedly, a vision with a pail of water with a plastic cup bobbing in the water danced across her mind.

Smythe sat up slowly, untangling herself from Artie's embrace. She thought about Eckhart Tolle and his definition of God as *the Power of Life itself.* You see, life itself played out in all things. It played out in the messy things, the beautiful things, the hurtful things. He had written that, "As soon as you turn away from it, God ceases to be a reality in your life, and all we are left with is a mental construct of God." A belief in God. Of all that he had written, what held in her spirit this morning was the one sentence that sang to her heart: "A belief in God is a poor substitute for the living reality of God."

She sat in silence, pondering her understanding of her relationship with her Beloved. She remembered keeping God on the edges of her life and recalled her ego expressing to her all of its pain that had separated her from her one true love—the Power of Life itself—her Beloved. She realized she had become paralyzed by a fear of her Beloved, remembering all of the untruths about hell, damnation, and retribution.

Yet, brick by brick, step by step, her Beloved showed Itself to her. It was the Power of Life itself that loved her enough to allow her to choose to discard what she had been taught and more deeply develop a meaningful relationship with that Power.

Her Beloved broke into her thoughts and spoke. "My child, you have followed the breadcrumbs and stepped away from what others told you Who I Am and have become fearless as you dared to enter into a relationship of Who I AM. Fear-less is key."

With deliberate intention, she inhaled a cleansing breath and exhaled the grime of yesterday. She knew that the Power of Life itself was contained within her, always expressing itself through her and holding a deep love for her. Her compassion, kindness, intelligence, curiosity, love—even the love of the woman who lay next to her—all of it was the expression of Life itself. Smythe slowly propped herself upright against her headboard, but her movement stirred a wakefulness within Artie.

For the first time since coming onto the case, Artie slept deeply through the night, and the more she became conscious, the more she remembered. She remembered she held her heart's desire in her arms throughout the night. She remembered the fight in the FBI's office. And she remembered the death of her best friend. Knowing it was still very early, she thought of the rising of the day and all that it held. A renewed fiery determination was lit within her bruised body to be by the side of this woman to the end and erode the tyranny of the crime ring.

Artie attempted to shift her body position, but all of the previous day's events came flooding into her body, and she was met with excruciating pain from her ribcage.

"Where are you going, baby?" Artie groaned. "I seem to be asking that a lot, huh?"

Without saying a word, Smythe stretched her arms toward the ceiling. She turned her torso toward Artie and leaned down to kiss her. Artie's lips were soft and wanting. Smythe allowed herself the pleasure of the lingering kiss, her heart singing with every soft touch of their lips.

Their first kiss. As Artie reached to pull Smythe on top of her, Smythe resisted and moved slowly away, sitting up next to Artie. She looked down at her protector.

"Not yet. I need to talk with you." Smythe reached toward her side table and turned on her lamp.

"Umph, ok." Artie's body ached as she gingerly pushed herself up against the headboard. Smythe watched the way Artie moved and saw, for the first time, her physical condition. Artie had a red and blue-black bruise on the side of her left jaw, and her right arm had hints of black and blue bruises. Artie's T-shirt was lifted slightly, revealing the elastic wrap around her ribcage.

"What happened, Artie?" Smythe asked as she scanned her up and down.

"Nothing important for now. Tell me what you were going to say."

"In a minute. Did I do that? I don't remember doing that," Smythe said, as though trying to remember an altercation.

"No, baby, you didn't do this," Artie chuckled. She wondered how much she should tell Smythe, yet she also knew keeping the truth from her may diminish Smythe's trust in her. She looked toward the far wall and then back to Smythe.

"Last evening, after I left you, I was supposed to meet with the FBI agent in charge of your case. When I arrived at her office, she was not there. Who *was* there, however, was someone who tried to kill me. I'm guessing it was a representative from the crime ring the agent had been investigating. He and I got into a fight and he lost, thanks to my team. Police and the response team for the FBI took him into custody."

Smythe listened intently. Her heart raced, and her stomach began to feel queasy. She then asked the questions she sensed she already knew the answers to. "Where was Carole in all of this? That is who you're talking about, right? Is she alright?"

"No, baby, she's not alright," Artie said softly. Looking into Smythe's eyes, she continued. "She was shot at point-blank range. We found her body in her car in the employee parking garage. I can only assume that the guy I tussled with is responsible, or perhaps he had help. The ensuing investigation will uncover the facts."

Artie thought about the timeline of events. She had been exactly ten minutes away from the FBI building when Carole called. It took her and her team roughly three minutes to walk from the visitor parking lot, check in at the lobby, grab a visitor's badge, and take the elevator up to Carole's floor. Her office had been tossed, and Carole sat murdered in her car. It seemed obvious to Artie—the suspect in custody did not have time to murder Carole and then toss her office. Not in ten minutes. *There were two assailants*, she thought.

Smythe shifted in bed to face Artie.

Artie's expression betrayed her emotions. A single tear trickled down the right side of her bruised face. Smythe reached over, and with a single touch of her index finger, gently wiped away the tear. She slowly pulled back the sheet that covered Artie's body and surveyed the damage. Artie's right hand was slightly swollen, and her knuckles had begun to take on a blue-black hue. She had a small cut to her right forearm, and her Ace bandage-wrapped ribcage belied a much deeper injury. Smythe gently rose from her bed and padded into the kitchen. When she returned, she held a large ice pack in her hand.

"This is going to feel really cold, especially at this hour of the morning."

She gently placed the ice pack on Artie's side, taking her hand as if to signal to her to hold it in place. As she returned to her bed, a single word floated to the surface of Smythe's consciousness.

Power.

Power, outside-external power. That was what this syndicate wanted. A power to control the external world. It was using our own fears to gain control of our internal world and maintain that power. It sought, like so many who are steeped into the story of the world, to amplify our own fears of loss. Whether jobs, cars, homes, health, or safety… My safety. The safety of Artie, of Carole. The power of the external world was a thing to be fought over.

Smythe brought her knees up to her chest.

What if this crime ring was there to show us our own vulnerability? We tend to believe the lies that teach us that vulnerability is weakness, especially if we display it. We hide it and hide from it because we fear we will lose our advantage or be taken advantage of. We participate in the survival of the fittest story, so steeped in the language of the world. Yet, our vulnerability is our strongest asset. It can bind us to one another, expand our understanding of one another, and connect us in courage, kindness, compassion, and love.

She turned her head to survey Artie. "I'm so sorry, Artie."

"This was not your fault. To kill an FBI agent—it's a reminder of the extreme lengths this group and those they work for will go to maintain control over the city. We're simply in the way. Carole was in the way."

Smythe and Artie spoke about Carole at length, allowing Smythe to learn just how connected Artie and Carole had been. In Artie's darkest moments, Smythe learned Carole never wavered in her support of her friend. Carole and Artie grew up together in the same neighborhood, attended the same elementary and high schools, were college roommates, and attended the FBI training academy at the same time.

As she listened to Artie's stories of Carole, Smythe began to consider the importance of Carole's role in the city's local FBI office. She began to understand what a badass Carole had been throughout her career in law enforcement, and it was this mighty stalwart who had been in charge of her case.

"I remember we were going after this guy. I thought *I* worked nonstop, but Carole was relentless. She worked this case until she had so much on him, all we had to do was arrest him, put a bow tie on his head, and hand him to the prosecutors. She was meticulous in ensuring there was enough evidence to not just warrant an arrest, but a conviction. The day we arrested him, Carole was up front, leading the charge. He tried to run out the back door, but she was on him so fast! This was her community, and she would do anything to protect it."

Smythe saw the work of the Universe—which had always been watching over her, placing the perfect person in charge of the case—with new eyes and appreciation. She surmised that it was Carole who had referred Artie to her case with an unknown benefactor who financed her protection. With rapt interest, she listened with both sadness and gratitude as Artie revealed more and more of her life. She realized she hadn't taken the time to get to know Artie. She hadn't asked about who her friends were, what her likes and dislikes were, or what kept her up at night. Her relationship with Artie, she reflected, had been only one-sided.

Perhaps the way it was supposed to be, until now.

"Artie, I can't bring Carole back, but I can tell you that I am more determined than ever to testify. All this time, I thought of this case as just a simple annoyance in my way. I've been so self-absorbed that I didn't put all of the pieces together. I didn't consider that people like Carole were in danger as well. It's more than just a case that I stumbled into, and I can see that now."

"It is, baby, and to be honest, it's become more complicated than I could have imagined. I can't tell you the specifics of the case as Carole shared them with me, but it's big. I also know there are some pieces to this case that I am unaware of at this time. We all have our blind spots. I say that because I've come to know you, Smythe. Do not take responsibility for things beyond your control. Carole's death was not your fault, nor was it mine," Artie whispered. Clearing her throat a bit, she continued. "What were you going to tell me? I would really like to know."

Smythe thought for a moment. This wasn't the time to talk to her about her revelations. She wanted to be supportive of Artie. Sensing her hesitation, Artie gently nudged Smythe's hand. "We can't change the past, Smythe. But we *can* look toward the future by discussing the present."

Smythe offered a half-smile and positioned herself so she could look into Artie's eyes.

"Well," Smythe started, "first, I need to offer you an apology. Instead of telling you what was in the letter, I allowed myself to wander down a rabbit hole of sorts. Once I was there, I lost my way back to the surface. The stories that I told myself... they just collapsed inward on me. To be honest, at some point, I just didn't want to scream for help, even though I knew I needed to. This morning's hangover is a terrible reminder of last night."

"Baby—"

"No, Artie, please, let me finish," Smythe quietly interrupted. Artie nodded.

"But I'm different. I'm just unsure of what's different. Looking at what happened on my side of the events which took place yesterday and reflecting on the past 24 hours, circumstances haven't really changed. My life is still at risk. My relationship with my mother feels fractured. I'm still writing endlessly, the business is just puttering along, and, of course, I didn't click my heels, so we're still living in the valley. Yet, somehow, I've shifted, and even more so now. I woke up different, which is just plain weird.

"Before the news about Carole, a new perspective emerged. It was if I saw myself as a child, then as an adolescent, and finally, as an adult, carrying around this incredible weight. And that weight seemed to absorb any light that would come into my life." Smythe paused to take in a breath.

"It wasn't the assault that was the weight. I mean, there's that; but the true weight was the belief in my parents, who said I had simply made up the story all to get attention and that I was mentally ill. Now, I find myself asking, 'How did they make that leap?' How did she make the leap from abuse, to mental illness?

"As a kid, I didn't realize how naïve my thinking was. I didn't know that other kids had gone through any type of abuse, but more importantly, I didn't understand using the weapon of ill mental health was a way of keeping me quiet. I realize now that I grew up somehow connecting that limiting belief and stigma of mental illness with another limiting belief—that my Beloved didn't care about me, didn't really love me. I had convinced myself that somehow, I was defective—and that hurt the most, Artie. Because I really love God. We've talked about it. I'm crazy in love," Smythe whispered.

Artie smiled and nodded, remembering their earlier conversation.

"I believed that childhood lie and walked through the world with a deep sense of shame. Shame of being 'found out.'" Smythe closed her eyes momentarily, shaking her head.

"I wonder if those with mental illness feel that way. Shame, I mean. As though mental illness is something to be ashamed of, when it really isn't. But for me, it was shame, Artie. I couldn't believe in myself, couldn't stand up for myself because I seemed to be carrying around so much shame. All because I believed their lie and the stereotypes around mental illness."

Smythe took a breath and thought about stereotypes in general. As a diversity instructor, she could recite the definition. *Considered social, stereotypes represent an agreement or notion about a group of people. Those stereotypes then become highly efficient because people often quickly generate impressions and expectations of people who belong to a particular group.*

She remembered the most glaring stereotypes were that people with mental health issues are violent and dangerous and completely out of touch with reality, often making up outlandish stories about themselves or others. She noted that media often exacerbates the stereotypes of mental illness by linking it with violence—portraying people as dangerous, criminal, evil, or somehow disabled, with an inability to live a fulfilled life.

Smythe unconsciously turned around and sat up next to Artie, her head resting against the headboard. She couldn't bear the pain of looking into her eyes any longer. After all that Artie went through outside her presence, only to return "home" and find Smythe crumpled on the floor of her own apartment? She could only stare across the room to the opposite wall.

"Artie, with what you went through, it's just not important anymore."

"No, baby, it's just as important. Everything seems to be coalescing at this moment. Please tell me more."

"You were right when you said it was up to me. I replayed all of the people in my life, and I questioned why it was they saw me as this giant of a person, so strong and independent. I kept thinking, *No, you've got it wrong. You don't know me. If you knew me, you'd see that I really am mentally ill, make up stories, and I'm just trying to act normal. I just act a good game.* But something shifted. I woke up knowing and believing in my own truth.

"There have been some extraordinary circumstances that seemed to have brought us together, and I worked hard to keep you at bay with my behavior. I really like you, Artie. In fact, I'm falling in love with you. I didn't want you to see the real me. Yet, I needed you to. The fear I held was, if you really saw me, you would withdraw and eventually just leave. I feared that I would be just another case to be solved, and then you would move on. And in the past few months, with my dad's death, the new business, and all of the angst around it, I was embarrassed, too. In some ways, perhaps my Beloved conspired my feelings for you to surface all this yucky stuff. I dunno, it's just a theory. A theory that I may not know the answer to until the end of my life."

Artie quietly sighed, taking Smythe's hand into her own. "I've always seen the real you, Smythe. You have far more courage, far more compassion, far more love than you think you have. You are what people have said about you, and I'm not going anywhere."

"Thank—" Smythe began.

"My turn. Remember our conversation about moving out of the country, the endless evenings of daydreaming about where we would go and why? I just needed to know where you were going so I could follow. I'm not going anywhere. I want to spend a lifetime getting to know you outside of this mess."

Smythe wiped away tears of joy from her eyes. "I'm happy to hear that."

"I'm still just slightly confused. How did you come to this revelation? I mean, did you just wake up with it?"

With Smythe's assistance, Artie shifted into a more upright position, leaning her head, shoulders, and torso upright against the slatted headboard.

Holding tears in her eyes and a smile on her face, Smythe continued.

"The only way I can explain it is that I just let it all go. I had this 'everything be damned' moment as I woke. I thought, *If God didn't love me, tough. If I never see my mom again, too bad.* It was this kind of strength that seemed to emerge out of nowhere. For so long, I held not so much a reverence, but a fear of God and my parents. I saw myself as less important, less valuable than either of those two. Yet, somehow, I now know that all along, God was trying to show me that I was God's most valuable and beloved soul. Not so much in a competitive way, for all of God's creation is just as valuable and beloved. Yet, in my own uniqueness, as a thought of God, I was valuable.

"I had this image where I watched myself take off all of this protective armor and walked away only in my boxers and a T-shirt. It was as if I made a choice and gave myself permission to live my life the way I was intended to, because in so doing, it was being lived for the good of everyone. Just living a normal life in whatever I did was good enough. And something just burst wide open in me."

"In your boxers?" Artie smirked.

"In. My. Boxers!" Smythe said, as she burst out in laughter.

As if she were pondering Smythe's personal revelation, Artie said, "All kidding aside, I've waited a long time to hear you say that. You have been shouldering this burden rather than facing your unimaginable grief. I'm relieved you've removed it."

"Me too. I think I'll still need to continue to remind myself of this conversation until it firmly takes hold." Smythe turned her body to face Artie again.

"Artie, I know that I know that the power of the Universe, the power of life, is on our side. I know that power was with me when I downed the pills and alcohol and was still there when you found me. It was even there with Carole until she took her last breath, and was there through every tear you shed last night. I can see that power in everything. I don't pretend to understand it all, and I am uncertain I have the language for it, but this seems to ultimately be about love and care. I couldn't cross the divide between the story that I was told and the true story of love with that line tied around my waist. The rope had to be cut, and I was the only one with a knife."

Stretching long and coming up short with a deep ache, Artie gazed at Smythe. Her heart pounded at the thought of how close she was to losing both her and Carole. It was unimaginable. Given Carole's death, it was a thought she shoved from her consciousness. Smythe glanced over at Artie and caught her gaze.

"Is there something in my teeth?" Smythe asked teasingly.

"Let me see, come closer," Artie said, reaching out her hand toward her. Smythe took her hand, knowing that Artie would pull her towards her. She leaned in and kissed Artie tenderly before moving slowly up and away.

Again, a pang of remorse washed over her. While she had deep feelings for Artie, she wondered if she had fractured a deeper connection with her by attempting to take her own life. She sat perfectly still.

Guilt.

She remembered the writing of Neale Donald Walsh. He wrote that it was guilt that kept people stuck. That as humans, we do not grow through guilt, but through awareness. She could not change what she had done, but she also believed that her journey down the rabbit hole allowed for an expansion of her soul. Still, she knew she had to name the accompanying feeling.

Choking back tears, she said, "Artie, can you forgive me? I'm feeling both guilt and shame about my behavior."

"Baby, there's nothing to forgive. We all do things which seem in the moment as though it was our only option, but sometimes we are given the opportunity to later figure out that it wasn't the best choice for us. You once told me there are no mistakes, nor failures, only learning opportunities. You spoke about learning to pause between an event and one's response. One of your long-distance friends, Katie, taught you that if I recall correctly. Sometimes, we need to practice that pause in order to get it right. As she suggested, stop and question the story you tell yourself. It's nothing more than an awareness. You've now become aware and have the opportunity to make a different choice.

"Smythe, I'm just grateful I didn't lose you last night—that it turned out to be a learning opportunity for you and a personal revelation that can set the course for your future. With that said, I am going to need something from you."

"What?"

"I'm going to need a promise. I've watched how you interact with people, especially your cohort people. You've demonstrated that you are a woman of your word, so I need a promise."

"Ok."

"Don't agree until you hear it. I need you to promise to go deep with me, just like you're doing now. I may not understand all of this God/Universe stuff. To be honest, it scares me. If I can't explain it, I'm out of my element, but I am open to it. You understand what I don't, and it has given you a strength that I can almost physically feel. I need you to go as deep with me in expressing what's going on with you as you do with God. I'm not asking you to share your most intimate conversations with God, but at some point, you need to let me in enough to love you deeply, because I want to. I really—"

Smythe leaned in and kissed Artie hard, interrupting Artie's request.

"I promise," Smythe said as she parted from Artie's mouth. Artie smiled and nodded.

"I'm also going to need time to process Carole's death. Not only did I lose my best friend, but the implications of her death are far more grave than I think even she knew. There are some questions that I've got to find answers for, beyond just the normal protection of a client. And, to be honest, I'm really angry. Carole's dead, I was forced to defend myself, and your life was threatened—and will be threatened again, of this I am sure."

"I know," Smythe said, equally concerned.

"Are you strong enough to fight with me to get you to trial?"

"Yeah, I am. If you had asked me a month ago, or even a week ago, I'm not sure I would have been. But today, it's as if there is nothing more important to me right now—other than the truth," Smythe said with a slight smile.

Artie sighed. They sat in silence, allowing the heaviness of their conversation to alight upon their shoulders and determine their next steps. Finally, Smythe's stomach began to growl loudly. She chuckled.

"I don't know about you, but I need to eat," Smythe said.

"I'll order in. What do you wa— Crap!" Artie exclaimed as she suddenly remembered ordering food last night. She could only hope her team had intercepted it.

"Can I have a moment alone to talk to them?"

"Of course," Smythe said, turning around to head toward the bathroom. When she returned, Artie was sitting on the edge of the bed.

"Are you up for malasadas?" Smythe asked.

"Sure, but I'm not showering. Can we go as is and shower later?"

"I guess I can forgo a shower," Smythe smirked. "But when we get back, I'm going to need to jump in."

"You and your shower fetish."

"It's not a fetish. I am just a bit of a germ-a-phobe. I like being clean at all times."

"Then I won't tell you what you did to yourself last night."

Smythe's eyes widened.

Artie smiled, shaking her head while attempting to stand. Smythe helped her as she gently rose from the bed. While dressing, Artie noticed her slacks from yesterday lay crumpled on Smythe's bedroom chair. She picked them up, placed her hand into one of the front pockets and pulled out a blood-stained piece of torn notebook paper. She held the paper in her hands, her fingertips hovering over the stain of Carole's blood. Her eyes scanned the words and a bolt of lightning traveled the length of her body, sending a cold shiver down her spine. She clenched her jaw, narrowing her eyes as she stared at the only two words on the paper.

Chapter 31

A Cup in a Pail of Water

—

ARTIE SAT IN THE PASSENGER SEAT OF TEAM 2'S VEHICLE. SHE stared out the window at Smythe, who stood standing just outside the baker's shop. Filled with grief for her friend Carole, and for Smythe, Artie thought about the conversation Smythe held with her just a little while ago. She thought about the leap Smythe's mother had made from hearing about the abuse to concluding that her daughter was mentally ill.

She did not pretend to understand how a parent would deny a child's truth. *After all*, she thought, *had Davey come to me with an unimaginable truth, as hard as it might be to accept my son's story, I would get to the bottom of it.* And then it hit her.

"It is an unimaginable truth. Too awful to put into words," Artie mumbled to herself.

Perhaps, her mother used the accusation of mental illness not as a weapon but as a defense. A defense to deflect an awful, unimaginable truth that she could not bear to hear, much less deal with. Maybe it was much easier to make the leap into mental illness—chalk it up to a child's vivid imagination.

Not one to let anyone off the hook so easily, Artie grit her teeth, determining the accusation of mental illness wreaked havoc on the life of the woman she loved. Not only did Smythe live with the abuse and the denial of it, but she also held the added burden of being labeled mentally ill.

Several customers were mingling in the baker's shop when Smythe and her caravan arrived. Surprised at the number of people, she looked behind her to find the sun had only recently crested the mountain range. She checked her watch. 6:30 a.m. She wondered if it had always been busy in the shop at that time of morning, or perhaps she had never noticed. She looked toward Artie, who sat resting in one of her team vehicles, bent over slightly. Smythe surmised Artie's ribs were voicing their injury.

Stubborn, Smythe thought. *We should have gone to the twenty-four-hour pharmacy, but nooo. She said she would "deal with it later."*

Smythe watched as Artie scanned the area, fully understanding of her concern. She was standing in the doorway waiting to enter, because Dennis had held her back until the last of the customers left.

The baker smiled broadly as Dennis and Smythe entered and welcomed them into the shop.

"Welcome, welcome, my friends. What may I offer you?"

Smythe approached the counter and ordered her usual malasadas and coffee. Dennis ordered the same.

"I've come to appreciate the pastry," he said as he side-eyed Smythe. "If you ever meet my wife, don't tell her. She's on me enough about what I eat." Lost in thought, Smythe smiled politely.

The baker watched them both closely, his own heart suddenly heavy. He sensed something was grieving them. He separated their orders, offering them each their own plate as an additional customer walked in. Smythe took her usual seat at the back of the shop, and Dennis walked to a table in front of Smythe's and took a seat. He was closely watching the customer with his hand on the weapon concealed under his windbreaker. Only when the baker bid the customer a good day before making his way to Smythe's table did he remove his hand.

"Hello, my friend. You look tired. Are you alright?" the baker asked with an abundance of concern in his voice. "Where is your other friend? Is she treating you well?"

Smythe smiled warmly. "Quite literally, Joao, she's been a saving grace."

She sighed and recounted the prior 24 hours to him, tears trickling down her cheeks. At one point, the baker held up his hand, grieved by what she shared. With tears in his eyes, he walked to the front of the shop. Artie watched in alarm as the baker placed a closed sign into his shop door and a time he would reopen. Knowing Artie as he did, Dennis quietly spoke to Artie over his com set.

"All is well, boss. It's just us in the shop."

Wiping his eyes with a handkerchief and shoving it into his pants pocket, the baker returned to his seat across from Smythe and asked her to continue.

"I'm trying to find my footing with the release of that old belief— that I was mentally ill. I can only now recognize how it had been a ribbon throughout my life. It reminds me of computer programming, silently running in the background in almost everything I've ever done."

"How do you mean, my daughter?"

"Well, rarely are there positive descriptors about mental illness. Growing up, I remember hearing about all of the *stereotypes* around mental illness, and I believed them. It bore out my own thinking. Then, if someone offered me a positive description about me, I would discount it. It's a kind of an imposter syndrome."

"What is this 'imposter syndrome?'" the baker asked, his eyebrow furrowed.

"Well, it's feeling like an imposter in your own life. Being a fake. For example, if people saw Artie as strong, confident, intelligent, powerful, and kind, but she didn't believe that about herself. Instead, let's say she secretly thought the opposite was true. *That*, in a nutshell, is imposter syndrome."

"You forgot compassion. She has compassion in her heart, just like you."

"See what I mean? And what happens is that a lot of people only align themselves with whatever negative programming they have in their heads. For example, someone says you are emotionally strong—"

"But I am," interjected the baker.

"As I said, someone might *say* you are strong. You, however, qualify that statement and think, *If you knew me, you would know I am really weak. I'm only pretending to be strong.*"

"It's not uncommon for people who yield to the imposter syndrome to feel as though they are not participating fully in deep, meaningful relationships. I wasn't until recently..." Smythe trailed off, caught in her own thoughts. "That's what imposter syndrome means."

"That is very sad," the baker quietly said. "To say that I am weak lessens the power of the great I AM. My daughter, listen carefully. You have gone through a great ache of the soul. No one should have to endure such things as you have all of your life. Yet, many do. It breaks my heart wide open. And now, with Artie's FBI friend losing her life..." the baker trailed off. He stopped to wipe his eyes with a napkin from the napkin holder sitting at the far edge of the table.

"As I listened, I heard everything that was spoken in your mind which poisoned your soul. Your mind wandered to great depths of despair and gave you only a brief respite. It caused you such agony. Yet, even though I am a mere baker, I know about the mind. It is also capable of many good thoughts as well.

"We have a mind," the baker continued, pointing at this head, "and it has many thoughts. It chatters at us all day and night, my daughter, even in our dreams. This mind of ours, it is capable of thinking many things, both good and bad. It tries to make us feel things; happiness, sorrow, worry, fear, anger—many feelings attached to our thoughts. But we have power, my daughter. Great power over ourselves. We can choose to push away an unhappy thought and think a better thought."

"I'm beginning to understand that now, Joao."

"Yes, that is good. Also, if you cannot quiet your mind by thinking a better thought, which can be quite difficult at times, focus your mind on feeling the energy in your foot or your hand. It will help quiet the mind."

"I actually do that, because honestly, my mind is a chatterbox," Smythe said with a slight smile.

"Yes, yes. Everyone. It pains me to know that I would lose you, my daughter. You have such a kind spirit. But you must understand," the baker said as he gently gathered Smythe's hands into his own.

"You must know *who* you are and why you are here. We have spoken of this many times. You must now, right now, have a *new* understanding of who you are. The Christian Bible says to be renewed of the mind," the baker exclaimed with a wide grin. "Take on the new truths of a higher you, my daughter. Plop those old ways in the toilet."

"That was a great visual," Smythe said as she giggled.

"Haha! Such poison should be flushed away. Reject bad thoughts. This may take you some time and practice, but it can be done. It *must* be done," the baker said with voracity.

"If a bad thought comes in, catch it and replace it immediately with a good thought. Even the thought of the energy of your body. Do you understand this, my daughter?" the baker said earnestly.

"Yes, Joao, I understand."

"Let this mind be in you which was also in Christ, who being in the form of God, did not consider it robbery to be equal with God."

"Bible verse?"

"Yes."

"Joao, you should know that I am not Christian. There is just too much baggage around that faith."

"Nor am I, my daughter. But you must even read the Bible with a renewed mind. Now that you understand the lies of the many that would preach from it, read it again, for it contains many universal truths, the greatest of which is love. I might also suggest, only a suggestion, that you read from the original work. The Bible has many interpretations based upon selfish power."

Smythe nodded. "Do you read works from other forms of faith?"

"Yes, of course. I only recite the Bible because many of your people were raised Christian. Am I mistaken?"

"No, not entirely. I just so reject the venom of the Christian faith—it's an unconscious knee-jerk response."

"See with a new understanding, my daughter. See what your parents did not see," the baker implored.

"You and I and all of creation come from God the Source." The baker then stood up and hurried to the kitchen. When he returned, he held a small bucket with water in it.

"Think of a pail of water. You take this cup and fill the cup from the pail and then allow it to float in the pail like this." He scooped water from the pail into a plastic cup. He then placed the plastic cup into the pail and allowed it to precariously bob in the water.

"The bucket and the pail of water are the Source. If the cup, which has the water from the Source, could think, it might consider itself as a lone entity. It thinks this because it is confined by the cup. It is only through contemplation and awareness that eventually it comes to understand that there is something beyond what it can see. It senses this new truth as it bobs within the *Source* of its water. And it must consider itself as from this unknown Source. Yet, also notice, the Source surrounds the cup. Do you see it?" The baker asked as he gazed at Smythe, who was looking into the pail.

"That is what we all are. Yet so many do not know this."

"It's funny that you said all of that. I was laying in Artie's arms this morning, and I had a sudden image of a pail with water in it, and I was dipping my hand into it."

"Yes, yes! God the Source is speaking to you, and I am confirmation!"

"Thank you, my friend. You should open your shop again, and I should order food for Artie. I'm sure she is famished."

"I will give a dozen malasadas. Some for now, and some for another time. I will also place a new creation in her bag. It has healing properties."

The baker rose from the booth and shuffled to the back of one of his display cases. Smythe followed him, her eyes observing the sluggish gait to his steps.

"Joao, are you alright? You're moving a bit... tired."

"My daughter, I am only weary. My shop keeps me busy, and today, several events are taking place around our city. I have been hard at work to prepare for them, for many have called to place special orders."

Smythe nodded as she stood before the case, eyeing the various pastries. Her stomach was growling and mouth salivating even though she had eaten her own malasadas while listening to the baker. The baker boxed Artie's order and handed it to Smythe. She reached into her messenger bag and pulled out her wallet to pay for the for order, but the baker waved off the attempt.

"You two have been faithful guests. Extraordinary, actually. She looks after you. It is the least I can do."

"How did you know she looks after me?" Smythe asked. It occurred to her that their interaction before him should not have given him a clue of Artie's original assignment to Smythe, and it was only today that she revealed her personal relationship with Artie to him.

"It is in her eyes, Smythe. Love is in her eyes," the baker replied before hurrying to the door to reopen his shop for business.

Smythe, Artie, and the rest of her detail returned from the baker's shop to Smythe's apartment. After distributing the pastries between Artie and her teams, Smythe expressed her need to get back to her studies.

"I feel like I'm falling a bit behind, and I need to change that."

"Before you delve too deeply into that, we need to discuss the next six weeks."

"Ok."

"First, we have the out of state wedding you're attending in a couple of days. We'll drive. All teams will be present. I have hired additional teams to watch your place while we are away. Second, because the trial has been moved up, everything you are scheduling must be planned as a tentative. I doubt I will have the same access to advanced information that I once had with Carole. Along the same lines, I've received a call from the FBI response team. I have a meeting with them later this afternoon. I'm hoping to meet the agent in charge of your case and begin the process of developing a new, cordial relationship."

"I thought the trial wasn't supposed to come up for several months?"

"It wasn't, based on the last information from Carole. But I just received a voicemail. The case is on the docket for seven weeks from today. My hope is that I'll know more this afternoon," Artie replied.

"Of course, I'll keep things as tentative as I can, but it's a busy month for me, Artie. I've scheduled a community training class, along with trying to complete the book and preparing for a presentation. If you can give me as much notice as possible, that would be helpful."

"I will as I find out. I anticipate the prosecutor is going to want to talk with you prior to your testimony. It's protocol, so I'll work to find out what the timeline for that will be."

Smythe sat, quietly absorbing the information, and noticed she was beginning to panic. Her greatest concern was a presentation she would be required to give at her mentor's conference. Acing the presentation was necessary in order for her to obtain her certification. Artie broke into her thoughts, sensing her concern.

"Let's plan this out. I have a paper calendar I can print out. We can plan out every week in order to make sure you take care of your business and education needs."

"Great idea. I have a calendar in the dining room closet. Let me grab it. You can grab yours so that we have duplicate information."

Both women retrieved their calendars. Sitting at the dining room table, they meticulously mapped out the next six weeks leading up to the trial. For Smythe's part, she would have to double her efforts in areas of her business prep in order to make space for late changes around the trial preparation.

As far as Artie was concerned, she would need every resource available to her to prepare for what was ahead. That would require hiring additional team members.

Later that afternoon, while Smythe prepped for an upcoming class, Artie and her security detail left for the FBI field office. Bracing herself as she entered the building, she was escorted into a conference room where she met not only with Warren and his response team, but also with the lead agent who was now in charge of Smythe's case. She anticipated they would not hold her in high regard, former FBI special agent or not. In fact, she expected they would find her presence in the Daniels case a nuisance, and they behaved in ways that confirmed her hunch. They treated her with rancid suspicion.

"So, Carole just up and hired to you to protect our witness, is that what you are telling us?" asked the new special agent in charge of Smythe's case.

"Carole did not hire me. An unknown benefactor reached out to her, suggesting that Daniels' life may be in danger. Since the witness refused witness protection, Carole had a back-up plan—me," Artie responded. Artie sat with her hands on the table and reflexively balled them into tight fists. She was becoming more irritated, but she also knew that this line of questioning was to find a crack in her story.

Over and over again, she confirmed her prior experience as an FBI agent, defense attorney, and her current position as CEO of her own security protection agency.

"Once again, yes. You all know my work history, my attorney background, and yes, for many of you sitting in this room, if you don't know, I now operate a security protection agency. When a special witness needs protection for one of *your* cases, Carole has looped my company in. Period."

Several times, she recounted her relationship to Carole, her reason for being at their office, and the assault from the intruder. The agents were more than just a bit curious about who hired Artie to protect Smythe, and thus pursued that line of questioning.

"No, I don't know, and while I asked, Carole did not offer the name. I trust Carole; therefore, I took her word that the benefactor is legitimate."

Artie confirmed the benefactor provided all of the necessary funds to protect Smythe and had even increased her original budget after the first attempt on Smythe's life. But, beyond that, the funds were deposited into her business account every week, and they were not traceable.

Still, Artie knew a little more than she was letting on. Carole confided in her that she had given her director just enough information to keep him in the loop, including Artie's involvement. She did not reveal the name of the benefactor to the director, nor would she offer it to Artie, unless absolutely necessary.

After roughly three hours, the agents excused themselves to the hallway. Carole's director abruptly barreled into the room.

"Leone," the director said as he stood before her. His eyes piercing, there was no trace of cordialness in his tone.

"Director," Artie responded flatly.

"We have an ongoing investigation into the source of your budget."

Artie remained quiet, staring down at the conference table.

"Don't you find it strange?"

Artie lifted her head. She was in no mood to play games. "Find what strange? That you've turned your investigation toward me, or that I am being handsomely paid to protect one of *your* star witnesses?"

The director eyed Artie coolly.

"Leone, did you know your money from this benefactor is coming through an offshore account?"

"No, I did not," Artie responded a bit annoyed. "But, if it is coming from an offshore account, the identity of the benefactor can't be traced."

"You are correct," the director said, narrowing his glare to Artie.

"Did you ever think it was the syndicate that is funding the protection?" the director asked, using his hands to create quotation marks in the air.

"Impossible. That would make them extremely stupid, given…" Artie came up short as she thought of the attempts on Smythe's life. If she revealed that, the director would remove Smythe from her protection.

"…given that they would be spending a tidy sum if their main objective is to kill her *before* trial."

The director pressed Artie to place Smythe into WitSec. Yet, the idea of placing Smythe into Witness Protection sent cold chills through her heart. Smythe was no longer just a witness who needed protecting, but her love.

While she respected the work agents in the WitSec program provided to their witnesses, Artie had more than enough experience with this particular syndicate to know that Smythe would be killed shortly after they removed her from Artie's care. As a result, she refused her former director's suggestion. Instead, she intimated, in no uncertain terms, that given his position, he should look deep into her business dealings to alleviate any concern he had in protecting "the witness."

"Trust me, I have."

"I'm not going to lie to you, Leone, I don't appreciate your involvement. I dislike the lack of control over this case. I'm not sure how much Carole divulged to you, but this case has national implications. But," the director paused, "I trust Carole. And, believe it or not, I trust you. You were a stellar FBI agent. One of my best, in fact. Carole expressed her confidence in your ability to keep my witness protected. Now that Carole is dead, protocols are going to change. You will make your weekly reports to me. In. My. Office. Do I make myself clear?"

"Yes," Artie replied.

"WitSec is not off the table, and I alone will decide if and when."

They negotiated timelines, reporting structure and the potential for additional assistance. For Artie, it was a good start. Although they regarded each other as adversaries on the same side, she gathered that the director seemed at least willing to assist where he could. Her biggest obstacle was to continue to tactfully sidestep his threat to force Smythe into WitSec until after the trial.

Artie returned to Smythe's apartment and worked with Dennis to review their security plans. By late evening, both women found themselves weary of the day. Smythe's body had yet to fully recover from the pills and alcohol she consumed the night before, and Artie was gritting through the pain of bruised ribs and a variety of other ailments that had begun to surface.

Artie excused herself to the bathroom. She was hoping a bath would soothe the ache in her body. Once she was out of the bathroom, Smythe took her turn to get a shower. After she exited the bathroom and fiddled around in her bedroom, she found Artie in the living room, making up her makeshift bed.

"What are you doing?"

"Getting ready for bed. It's going to be a long day tomorrow."

"No, love. Your place is next to me in my room. I mean, if you want," Smythe said shyly.

Artie stared into Smythe's eyes. "I didn't want to presume anything. You've been through enough."

"I'd prefer you next to me tonight, Artie, if that is ok with you. I'm not suggesting anything physical, but... I just want you next to me."

"I'd like that very much." Smythe nodded and waited for Artie as she attempted to pick up her pillow from the air mattress. Watching her struggle, Smythe walked over.

"Let me get it. Bending has got to be difficult."

Artie smiled and headed in the direction of the bedroom. Smythe had her tablet sitting on the bed and was ready to watch a show.

"What are we watching?"

"'Star Trek: Voyager'. An old favorite."

"Ahh, Captain Janeway."

"You watched Voyager?!"

"Yeah. I found the series on Netflix and watched it from beginning to end. At times I binge-watched if Davey wasn't around."

"Who knew?!"

"I loved Janeway. Her character offered me an opportunity to believe in what was possible for women. Captain of a starship. The flagship for the Federation. That show set my imagination ablaze."

Smythe smiled and signaled Artie to join her in bed. Artie, in turn, smiled to herself, thinking, *This woman is going to be a whole lot of trouble.*

Her ribs throbbing their displeasure as she climbed into bed next to Smythe, Artie voiced, "This has got to be one of the highest beds that I've ever gotten into."

"I know, right? I bought a new mattress and box spring for the bed frame about a year ago. My old ones were high, but it doesn't compare to this one. I have to do a little hop to get into it, and I'm 5'6"!"

"Yeah, I noticed that last night as I climbed in, but it *is* comfortable. I've never slept so well." The couple settled into bed and watched a couple of episodes before drifting off to sleep. As Smythe lay next to Artie, a single thought emerged: "Sufficiency and grace for the day."

Chapter 32

Benef

—

Artie's piercing, cold stare took him by surprise. Her eyes plunged daggers through him, as though facing an enemy.

"Since I'm not sure where to begin, let's just begin," Artie growled. He gave her only a hint of a nod.

Her words sharp and biting, she continued. "I'm sure you know that Carole's dead. You know, the FBI agent in charge of Smythe's case. My best friend, my confidant, our go-between."

He slowly nodded, his eyes barely showing the fear that now gripped him in a vise.

"Of course, you do. You also know that my life was threatened."

He closed his eyes and offered a single nod.

"And, of course, you remember Smythe. Cute, light brown-skinned woman, buzz haircut, Malcolm X looking black glasses, about 5'6", my girlfriend?" Artie grit her teeth. "The woman I've been hired to protect!"

"Of course, I know her, and I know you, Artie. Why are you so angry?" He searched her eyes, wondering what had happened to cause Artie to show such fury toward him.

"It's been almost a year, that's why! We're into early fall, damn it, and you never once revealed that you were my financial benefactor to protect Smythe! Why not?!"

A slight frown formed around the edges of his mouth. He looked down at his hands. He held them together, his right hand over his left in an effort to ease a slight tremor that had begun to surface. The tremors were the result of a slow-moving degenerative disease which would one day take his life.

"Answer me! Why not?"

"It brings me too much pain to discuss the why; suffice it to say, it is as you say," he offered quietly.

"I'm having a hard time trusting you right now. Just so you know, I have my security detail posted just outside. You will tell me," Artie growled.

The baker stood in the middle of his shop. He had just closed up for the day when Artie knocked on his door. He opened the door and welcomed her in, stating he had nothing to offer her. She flatly explained that she wasn't there for food or drink, but for information. As she entered, she locked the door behind her.

"May I sit?" he asked. "It has been a long day."

Artie nodded. The baker moved to a booth toward the front of the shop, and Artie took a seat across from him. The lights were dimmed low. Artie glanced around, noticing the shop was eerily aglow from the street lamps outside.

"It is a story of love, Artie," the baker began, his sorrow cracking his voice at his memory. "But let me preface that my intention has always been to protect Smythe. You must believe me."

"Then why the secrecy, Joao? Smythe trusted you. She thought of you as this kindly older gentleman baker, the kind of which stories are written about. She confided her most precious inner thoughts to you. How could you pretend not to know the details of the case, or of her? How could you pretend to be so wise? Or were you just pretending to befriend her? Damn it, Joao, you betrayed her!"

"You are incorrect, Artie. I did not know the intimate details of the case. I only knew them as Smythe herself told them to me. Once I learned of her experience—what she saw and what she felt—only then could I counsel her."

The veins in Artie's neck were beginning to protrude, and her ribs ached from the long days in preparation for Smythe's second travel excursion outside the valley. She was physically weakened, refusing to acknowledge even to herself the severe extent of her injuries. She needed rest, but she was singularly focused on engaging in this conversation; her heart broken in jagged pieces at what she believed was the baker's betrayal of trust to Smythe.

"Joao, you were her benefactor from the beginning. That's why the FBI didn't place her in WitSec. My company came in at my friend's urging with the necessary monies already in place because of you. You knew, at least from the beginning, that her life was in danger."

"Yes, this is true, but all that she has gone through I was unaware of until she said so herself. As I discovered the ruthlessness of him, the two physical threats against her, that is when I needed to add more money for security. And I am willing to do so again, if need be."

"Why!" Artie demanded, slamming her fist on the table.

"Let me start from the beginning, please," he implored.

His story wound through the decades of his life. He described his entry into the United States, immigrating from Portugal to Hawaii 35 years ago. His father, an outsider to Hawaii, came to the islands employed by sugar plantations. As he grew into adulthood, he came to understand the colonization of the Hawaiian islands and could no longer remain there. He watched as, year after year, those in power stole lands from the Hawaiian people.

He considered himself a simple man who only wished to bake and, unable to contain his grief in Hawaii, he moved to the valley. It was his single wish to open a simple bakery and delight his customers with his mother's old recipes; recipes she was eager to pass onto a willing son. After a several years of working for other bakery shops, he saved enough money to open his own.

Over a very short period of time, his bakery became tremendously popular, outperforming all other bakeries in the city. He was not surprised by the success because the Universe had placed a vision on his heart. All he had to do was execute it. It also helped that word of mouth about his shop traveled near and far by many from Hawaii who had also made their way to the valley. That was enough for him. He met his wife there in that tiny shop. She was a customer, and after first sampling his pastries, she made it a daily habit to visit the shop.

"Much like Smythe does. Only Isabella wasn't only interested in the pastries," he said. "She seemed to have a genuine interest in me, but I worked such long hours and could not court her apart from our encounters in my shop. So, I devised a plan. I would ask her if she would come and work for me. I knew she had a good job and probably made more money there, but I was desperate to see more of her. To my delight, she said yes. We worked long hours together, but we were happy. I married her, and we had a beautiful daughter together.

"As time went on, our tiny shop became too small for its popularity, and we decided on a larger one. We skimped and saved until we purchased this one, and have been here ever since.

"Our next adventure was to save enough money to send our daughter to college. We were so happy, so proud of her. When the time came, she studied business. She was kind and compassionate, just like Smythe. She was determined to franchise our shop so that her mother and I would not have to work the long hours anymore. She had such big ideas. She was accepted into University through a scholarship and graduated with high marks. So proud we were! She then started to work for a local bank in town. She wanted to add enough money so that the money we would have used for her college could be used to help us franchise the shop. It was then that things went horribly wrong.

"Somehow, I do not know where or when, but she started to date the man that Smythe is going to testify against. One day, my daughter called me and said she unexpectedly visited his place of business to bring him a surprise lunch. She said she saw him shoot a man to death. She was so scared, Artie. She did not know what to do. I told her to go to the police, but she was too afraid. When I pressed her on why, she said she did not trust that the police would do anything. She had met a couple of his friends, and they were somehow connected to law enforcement. This frightened me, Artie. I told her to pack her bags and go to the airport, and I would purchase a ticket in her name. I said I would send her to Portugal, my ancestral home. There, my family could watch after her. Artie... she never made it there."

The baker lowered his eyes, his smile turning to a frown.

"What happened, Joao?" Artie flatly asked.

"Once we hung up from each other, we had no more contact that night. I assumed she made her flight and would call me once she arrived in my home country. But she did not call. When I called my family, they said she never arrived. I called her home, but she did not answer. I hoped she had caught a different or later flight. I checked with the airline, but she never claimed her ticket. I knew then that something bad had happened. I called my Ohana on the island of Kauai, believing she may have chosen to go there instead, as I took her there many times as a child. But she was not there.

"I went to her apartment, but she was not there either. I went to her business, and still nothing. So, I went to the police, but they did not seem to understand the gravity of the situation, except for one young detective. He said he would quietly look into the matter, but then I never saw him again. Over a month went by. Finally, a news report came out about some hunters in the mountains. Near a deep crevice, a decomposing female body was found. My heart sank. I knew it was my daughter. The police notified me days later. It tore my heart to pieces, Artie! And it ultimately killed my Isabella. She died of a broken heart a month later." The baker remained perfectly still and quiet, his sorrow palpable.

"He did this to my family, and I had been looking for a way to pay him back," He said through gritted teeth.

The baker sat for just a moment, adjusting his shirt collar and wiping his brow with a napkin. He closed his eyes, feeling the rhythm of his beating heart. A heart that lost its love. He had not felt the heaviness of his anger for so long, and the memory of his family's death was a searing ache that he had never spoken of before now.

He stared at the top of the table that separated him from Artie's wrath. In almost whispered tones, he continued. "The thing is, the Universe does not reward hatred or revenge. This, I knew, but yet I still hated. I hated him for so long. I worked night and day and simmered in my hatred until I almost went insano. Um, insane, I mean.

"It was the Universe, however, that finally saved me. Day by day, I came to understand my hatred could not bring my daughter or my wife back to me. I saw the hatred in my heart had only blackened my spirit. Of what use was that? After my wife died, I sold our home and moved into the apartment above the shop. It was, and still is, all that I need," he said, pausing for a long moment deep in thought.

"So, when you found out Smythe was the key witness in this man's trial, you saw an opening," Artie said.

The baker lifted his head and met Artie's eyes. It was time for him to tell her what she must know.

"I saw an opening to do good, yes. Yes! He was never brought to trial in my daughter's death, but I knew he was the one responsible. I had received a call from an ohana. Akamu is his name. He had given some papers to his son's son to bring to the valley. Akamu had lost touch with him and was worried. He said these papers were very important to the island, and Alika was supposed to have given these documents to *his* people. Artie, Alika was killed by this man. So, yes. I saw my chance to do good.

"You see, the money of my creations never once stopped flooding in. My shop is so busy. All day long, every day, it so busy. When I heard of an eyewitness of Alika's murder at the hands of this man, I closed my shop one day and met with the FBI agent in charge of the case. I said I wanted to help in any way I could, and that I had money. I said the witness will need protection, and I explained what he did to my daughter and that I knew Alika. She seemed very interested in this. I offered money for protection to the one who identified my daughter's killer. But your friend brushed me off, insisting that they would protect her. No more than a few days later, I received a call asking if my offer still stood. She explained your company to me. I just met Smythe this year before she witnessed the murder.

"Artie, I could not spend all of the monies that I had in the short time that I have left. Smythe is such a kind person. She reminds me so much of my daughter—only difference is in their ages. And she has chosen a path that will ultimately be for the good of all. It makes me happy to help. I did not know it was Smythe I was protecting until she came in months ago with you and told me she was the eyewitness. It was then that I figured it out and that you were her protector. The Universe has rewarded my patience."

"You knew this Alika?"

"Not directly, no."

"Do you know where the documents are?"

"No, I do not. I only know he had them."

"Does this Aku—"

"Akamu."

"Does he know where they are?"

"No, he does not know. I asked him if I could help. He said I could not, and asked that I say nothing of this to anyone. I speak Akamu's name in confidence. You must tell no one."

"Joao, I can't go into specifics about the case, but it is important to find out where those documents are."

"As far as I know, they are lost, Artie. Lost. I am an old man, and Akamu is an old man. The documents—if they are still around—are for the young to find and make right what has been made wrong."

"You are not an old man, Joao."

"Artie, we all have a day appointed to us from God our Source. I do not know when my day is; however, doctors tell me that I will meet that day soon. My hand trembles more, and the weakness in my legs is getting more severe. My life is as a simple baker. This shop allows for the creative energy of the Universe, my God, to work through me. The Universe has rewarded my diligence to root out hatred from my heart by allowing my creations to put a smile on many faces throughout the day. My friend, I could not ask for more, except perhaps that I had my wife and daughter beside me."

The baker released his left hand from the grip of his right. He looked through Artie to the distant past, remembering and tracing the facial features of his beloved wife and daughter. He smiled at the thought and said, "They shared my love for baking, for life itself. Do you know why my pastries are so popular?"

"Because they're delicious."

The baker's eyes lit up. "Thank you, my friend, for those kind words. But it is more than that. Each type of pastry has unique healing qualities. My mother taught me about the herbs she uses for each one. There are just enough in each batch of dough to have a unique effect," he explained.

"There are drugs in your pastries, Joao?"

"No no no, my friend. Please, let me show you."

He rose from his seat and walked gingerly toward the kitchen of his shop, gesturing for Artie to follow. As she trailed behind him, it was only then that Artie truly began to see the physical deterioration of her benefactor. His cautious walk was coupled with a limp that dropped his foot with a louder than normal tap to the floor.

I understand the limp now.

In the kitchen, Joao reached above a countertop into an open-air stainless-steel shelf and removed a single small Mason glass jar with what appeared to be crushed seeds held within it. He poured a minute amount of the seeds into the palm of his hand and pushed the seeds around with his index finger.

"I put a much smaller amount into a particular type of pastry dough. This one is said to have physical healing properties. At least, that is what my mother taught me. And it seems to be so. I have watched many of my guests who have had missteps and have bruised themselves or suffered from pain all recover in just a few short days. Your injuries were extensive, too, but you will recover quickly."

"The pastry that Smythe brought to me," Artie mumbled to herself more than anyone.

Artie remembered that in addition to the box of malasadas Smythe returned with, she also held a bag with two pastries of the same type. She offered them to Artie, stating that the baker said they had healing properties. Artie didn't know how much healing was contained in the pastries, but her stomach was grateful, and she consumed both of them before returning to Smythe's apartment.

"Yes."

"I remember feeling slightly more energized. The pain had dulled, and I could move without feeling so encumbered."

"I do not understand how they work; only that they do. They are common herbs which are found in nature. The ingredients are clearly marked on my board but, alas, no one reads them. At any rate, it is better to repeat the herb daily for a few days."

"Will they not help you?"

"Indeed, they have. Trust me; I would have not been able to keep my shop open for as long as I have without them. But, no, they will not stop the progression of the disease. I do not know enough about them to do that."

Artie's eyes narrowed, and she stared with dispassionate interest toward Joao.

"Trust you? An interesting choice of words. You lied to me, and you lied to Smythe. It's a bit hard to trust you right now, although I am trying."

"Artie, I never lied to you or to Smythe," he replied.

"Omission is the same as a lie. We've been coming here for months. Months! You had plenty of opportunities to take me aside and reveal who you are."

The baker slowly shook his head.

"Why? Why not reveal yourself?" Artie asked gently.

"Because of Smythe."

"What do you mean?"

The baker remained silent, and it was in the silence that Artie noticed his expression took on a graying sorrow. A soft melody that Smythe would hum while writing began to quietly play in Artie's mind. The baker simply bowed his head and withdrew into himself. After a few moments, he peered into Artie's eyes. Artie closed hers, and, in a moment of clarity, she suddenly understood the answers to her question.

"It would have been that much harder to protect her. She would have wanted all of the resources that you provided for her to be used for your own protection and health," she quietly said.

"You understand."

"You still could have told me."

"And then *you* would have had a lie of omission to maintain in your relationship with her. I have watched with great joy as you two have drawn closer together. I could only hope that you would find each other in love through all of this. No, Artie, you could not know."

"I won't be able to keep this from her," Artie said gently.

"I know, and I am prepared for whatever disagreement she will put up."

"What of the suspect's understanding of you? Does he know you are the father of the woman he killed? That you knew the grandfather of Akamu?"

"Not that I am aware. No one knew except for your friend, the FBI agent. She asked for Akamu's information, which I provided, but only after speaking with Akamu. Smythe is incredibly kind and compassionate, and she is only beginning to understand who she is. She will do good by removing him from the valley, but beyond that, she has much good to offer the world. You must leave no detail unexamined on your part. If you need additional security, hire them and let me know. Do not bother the FBI."

"The cost so far has been astronomical, Joao. It has even surpassed my financial resources. I would not have been able to offer the level of protection that we've provided without your backing. How much longer can you afford to do this?"

"I have more monies than you," the baker said with a twinkle in his eyes. "All is well."

"I will trouble you no further."

Pausing for a moment, Artie added, "Joao, I am going to further restrict Smythe's movements. In particular, her ability to see you. It is as much for her protection as it is now yours. Do you understand?"

"Yes, I do, my friend. I only hope she does. Tell my daughter all is well, and one day we will see each other again. And thank you, Artie, for my protection. I have noticed them in and out of my shop."

Artie rose from her seat and slowly made her way to the door, the baker following behind her.

"I'm not saying we won't order our malasadas, but she won't be here to see you personally; after all, your malasadas are life," she said, walking out the door.

Joao watched as she entered her waiting SUV, closing and locking the door behind her. He stood at the door as Artie's vehicle drove away. "I will have your healing pastries waiting for you, my dear Artie," he softly said.

Artie returned to Smythe's apartment and found her in bed reading. She was winding down for the evening, and the lack of Artie's presence allowed her to concentrate more fully on the heady subject she was absorbing from her new book find. Artie bolted the front door behind her, double-checked the indoor security measures she had installed in the apartment, and quietly headed back to the bedroom.

"Hey there."

"Oh my god, you startled me. I didn't hear you coming."

"Part of the trade, baby, I'm sorry. I'm going to take a shower," Artie said, pointing in the direction of the bathroom.

Smythe rose from her bed and approached Artie.

"How about taking a bath? I think you need to soak for a bit."

She lightly kissed Artie's cheek as she passed her and proceeded into the bathroom, where she drew a warm lavender bath. Once Artie undressed, Smythe gently helped her into the bathtub and continued to allow the tub to fill until it covered Artie's body completely. Artie leaned against the back of the tub, playing with the bubbles that conformed to her body's displacement in the water. Turning off the tub water, Smythe turned to gather Artie's clothes.

"Come back?"

"In a moment. Rest in the water for a bit. Let me add your clothes to the washer."

Artie closed her eyes, allowing herself only to think about the baker's condition.

How could I have not noticed the severity of his condition before now?

She continued to sit in the warm water, allowing her muscles to release the tension of the day. She thought of the baker's healing pastry and decided that she would order a half dozen along with malasadas in the morning. She became aware of the hum of the washer, and within a few seconds, watched as Smythe entered the bathroom again. Smythe placed the lid down on the toilet seat and sat upon it.

"How are you feeling?"

"I'm tired, but good."

"Does it matter, or am I being too nosy to ask where you went? You seemed agitated as you left."

Artie offered Smythe a gentle smile.

"You can ask. It concerned you."

"Oh. I expected that you were doing something around Carole, meeting with her family or something."

"The FBI made notifications to her mother. I called her earlier today. I'll have to make arrangements to go out and see her in the next day or so and find out when the funeral is. Smythe," Artie said before pausing. "What I'm going to say next may upset you."

Smythe held her breath for a moment, her face expressionless.

"I met with the baker this evening. I needed to confront him."

"Confront him? Artie, why?" Smythe asked.

"When we found Carole in her car, I found a piece of paper next to her right hand in the car seat. I had just enough time to grab it. Something told me that it was important, so I basically made a fool of myself and finagled my way close enough to take it before the entire area was sealed off. On the paper was Joao's name and the word benef," Artie said.

"What do you mean, Artie? What does benef mean?" Smythe asked, slightly confused. She looked down at the floor.

"Benef, benefec, benefector," she silently mouthed. "Benefactor. Joao is my benefactor."

"Yes. I don't know if Carole knew she was about to die or not, but I think that note was for me, Smythe. When I put it together just like you did, I knew I needed to confront Joao about it."

Smythe rejected even the notion that Joao was the benefactor providing the monies for her protection. *How could he be?* she thought. It seemed too shocking to comprehend. *He wouldn't mask his identity. Not from me. And if he was my benefactor, why would he hide it? None of this makes any sense.*

All of this time, she thought Joao had befriended her, counseled her, loved her.

"What did he say?" Smythe asked, her heartache pained across her face.

"He confirmed it."

Artie went into detail about her conversation with the baker, which included the murder of his daughter, the death of his wife, and his reasons for assisting in the protection of Smythe.

"He says he didn't know that the person he was protecting was you until we came into the shop the day after the first attempt on your life occurred. Do you recall pouring your heart out to him then?"

"I do."

"It was then that he discovered it was you that his money was invested in, and that it was me who was protecting you."

Smythe took in a breath and released it. "I'm not going to pretend like I'm not, Artie. I'm in shock. I'm also saddened by his motivation for bankrolling my protection. I think that hurts the most."

"Baby, there's more."

Smythe looked into Artie's eyes. She suddenly felt weary, her heart grieving for her friend. To experience such tragedy—the thought of it all was more than she thought she could bear. But she wanted to hear it all; she even felt *compelled* to listen to it all. She sat very still and hung on every syllable Artie spoke.

Artie explained Joao's deteriorating health, and that, given her conversation with him, death was imminent but not immediate, and he was insistent no amount of money would save him. Now unable to contain her grief, Smythe's' eyes filled with tears as she looked around the bathroom, searching for the strength to respond.

"I'm so sorry, baby."

"I knew something was wrong, but I thought it was just his age. I always wondered who would take over his business, wrongly believing he had children to take it over," Smythe said, choking back tears. "Can we go see him tomorrow? I'd like to hug him."

Artie slowly shook her head.

"Baby, we can't. They just killed Carole. My gut tells me they're coming for you. For all intents and purposes, consider yourself in a modified version of WitSec. After the trial, yes, of course, we can go see him, but until then, we just can't."

Smythe remembered her promise to Artie. She reminded herself she would double down on her efforts to follow Artie's lead when it came to her protection. Faced with a deep need to see her friend, she found it difficult to keep that promise now.

She expressed her need to disobey Artie; that Joao was the closest thing to a real father that she had. She feared he would die before she had the opportunity to reconnect with him and asked Artie to reconsider. Artie, however, remained steadfast. She said she could not force Smythe to refrain from visiting the baker, but she hoped Smythe would remain in the apartment.

As the bath water cooled, Artie sat up and let the water begin to drain from the tub. The air around her felt heavy, and Artie found it difficult to hold up her own body weight. Smythe steadied her as she stood up and turned on the shower so she could wash her body. Once Artie was finished bathing, Smythe helped her out of the shower, dried her off, and got her dressed into a pair of sleeping boxers and a T-shirt. They got into bed and held each other.

"What if he dies before I can see him again?" Smythe asked again desperately.

"He won't. He has quite a bit of time. I promised Joao we would still order our food from him. My team will pick it up and keep us informed of his appearance. How about instead of an in-person conversation, you send him notes with my team? He can answer them at his leisure. That's the best I can offer."

"Can I call him instead? Or I could buy him a cellphone with texting capabilities so we could text one another."

"Baby, it's too unsecured. Written, sealed notes delivered by my team only."

"It hurts, Artie, but I made a promise to you."

Smythe moved from Artie's arms and rose from her bed. She padded into the dining room, where she turned on the overhead light. Finding a pad of paper and a pencil, she sat at the dining room table. Staring at the pad, she began to write. An hour later, she returned to a sleeping Artie. As she entered into bed, Artie took her into her arms and returned to sleep.

Chapter 33

The Gray SUV

—

THE NEXT FEW DAYS WERE BUSY. SMYTHE SPENT LONG HOURS writing and studying while Artie spent several hours a day in meetings with her teams and members of the FBI, poring over security plans in preparation for a wedding Smythe would attend.

The wedding was for the daughter of Smythe's best friend, Sue McPherson. A single parent, Sue raised her two children, Bernard and Kelly, alone after the death of her husband. She was the finance manager for a government agency and was welcoming of Smythe, who was later hired in as the Training and Education Manager for the same agency. Over a few years, Sue and Smythe became friends, much to the surprise of everyone around them.

They were an unlikely pair. Sue was an older, hazel-eyed woman with straight, blonde hair, jocular in nature with an infectious laugh and witty sense of humor. As Smythe would say, Sue was the only one who could ever get her to relax. Smythe was all work and no play, serious in her demeanor, and polite, yet cautious in dealings with anyone in the workplace.

It was heartbreaking for the best friends when the organization furloughed Smythe, but it deepened their friendship. They confirmed their fondness for one another, calling each other a grade school girlish name—"bestie best." Although a bit quirky, the name was an accurate description of the deep bond they had developed. That bestie best relationship even caused the delay of Smythe's start date with her new employer in the valley, as she wanted to wait until after they had completed a road trip they had planned. The best friends spent two glorious weeks on the road that would take them up through Portland, Oregon, to Seattle, Washington, and finally into British Columbia.

After returning from their trip, they kept in contact with one another through text messages or phone calls. It was Sue who matched every tear of frustration and sorrow as Smythe described her father's latest escapades with his degenerative disease. It was Sue who never missed a birthday or holiday without sending a card, a gift, or unexpectedly showing up to spend a weekend with her friend. Above all, it was Sue who made Smythe feel loved unconditionally. There was nothing they would not share with the other, knowing they were accepted by the other for who they are.

Sue's daughter understood the relationship her mother built with Smythe and graciously invited Smythe to her wedding. It was this wedding that Smythe was now determined to attend.

At first reluctant to make the necessary accommodations, Smythe held her ground, insisting that she go.

"Artie, this wedding is much too important for me not to attend. It is a momentous occasion for my bestie! This case has taken too much from both of us. I won't have it take one more moment of life from you or me! Not one. Stay if you want, but I'm going."

"Smythe, I get it. I do. It's just—"

"It's risky, I know. But, Artie, I haven't seen her in a year. I already have to feign some stupid reason why she can't come to visit. This case cannot be the demise of our friendship. I've got to go."

"Actually, I was going to say that there are just some variables to consider, but I'm working on it."

Smythe smiled. "Thank you. Thank you from me, and thank you from Sue. If she knew—"

"She would tell me I am being foolhardy for planning this." Artie searched Smythe's eyes before turning on her heels and leaving the apartment.

Artie was meticulous in every detail in preparation for travel. She obtained detailed images of the neighborhood and residence where Smythe was scheduled to stay and planned a daily egress rotation into and out of the neighborhood. Earlier in the month, she dispatched a team to conduct reconnaissance of the church and wedding reception hall, gathering a list of all of the employees scheduled to work at both venues and replaced several of them with her own security detail. Several travel routes were created, and cybersecurity protocols were put into place.

On the day of departure, Smythe asserted her independence from her mother and chose to bypass a visit to her to say goodbye, instead deciding to give her a call. Something in her mother's voice sounded different to her, but she shrugged off the odd tenor, refusing to "story tell."

Smythe, Artie, and Dennis traveled in Artie's team vehicle while another team drove in Smythe's SUV. Two additional teams caravanned with the SUV. Without incident, the caravan arrived at their destination. They met up with an additional team that had been dispatched to surveil the residence days before Smythe's arrival. One block before arriving, Smythe was allowed to get into her own vehicle and pull into the driveway of her friend Loretta's home.

Smythe smiled as she pulled up. Loretta was her former director of human resources at the organization where she had met Sue. The two had rarely spoken since the day Smythe left the organization. It wasn't that Smythe was angry at Loretta. In fact, the friendship between them was rather strong. What Smythe really felt was a sense of embarrassment. Smythe often wondered what she could have done differently that perhaps would have changed the executive team's decision to eliminate her position.

"But those were bygones," she told herself. More than anything, Smythe remained grateful Loretta was the one who broke the news of a furlough to her, especially since Loretta was on leave, battling an aggressive form of breast cancer. With a wide grin on her face, Smythe walked up to the door of Loretta's home and knocked.

"Oh Smythe! You're here! You're here!" Loretta exclaimed. She held out her arms and held Smythe in a long, tight hug, refusing to loosen her embrace even though Smythe had begun to loosen her wrap around Loretta.

"It's so good to see you Loretta. It's been a long time," Smythe said, her words muffled into Loretta's shoulder.

"Too long. Come in, come in. Moi isn't here, but will be here shortly. We have so much catching up to do. I want to hear everything!"

Over the next couple of days, Smythe was in constant motion. She spent the first evening catching up with Loretta. As she reflected on her stay much later, she felt it was worth the discomfort of staying at her friend's home rather than the independence of a hotel room—away from the arms of Artie. As she and Loretta engaged in heartfelt conversations about each other's lives, she felt a deep sense of gratitude to her Beloved for allowing a bonding connection to emerge between her friend and her family.

The next morning, Smythe had a quick breakfast with Sue before changing and heading to the church. The church only held 100 or so people, and it was packed. At Sue's insistence, Smythe sat squeezed at the end of the second pew from the front while her best friend sat just in front of her at the opposite end. Smythe glanced around her. She recognized a number of her best friend's family. Uncle Thomas, a tall, slender man with a head which displayed a horseshoe bald patch, sat to her left, alongside his wife Margie, a short Hispanic woman whose head barely reached to her husband's stomach. They were Sue's favorite family. An assortment of cousins sat next to them, and her sister sat at the opposite end of the pew. Smythe smiled at the honor she was offered to sit amongst them.

Artie stood at the back of the church, making sure to still have a clear vantage point of Smythe. She couldn't help but grin. Smythe radiated joy witnessing her best friend dab her eyes, beaming with pride as her daughter and new son-in-law repeated their vows to one another.

After the ceremony, Smythe, Artie, and the teams made their way to the reception. Artie's secondary teams were also in place, blending into the crowd. Yet, Artie also knew a potential threat would blend in as well. She flanked the wedding reception with her teams, who posed as waiters, busboys, and bartenders. Smythe was instructed where to sit, and Artie served as the waiter for her table. Throughout the rest of the evening, Smythe remained at her table, for the most part, enjoying easy conversations with old acquaintances and friends alike.

The following day, a small, intimate party was thrown at Loretta's home—a last-minute gathering which left Artie scrambling to ensure Smythe's safety. A plan was quickly put into place, which included wiring Smythe with a hidden com unit in addition to a tracking device that Artie equipped Smythe with before they arrived.

"So, Smythe, I forgot to ask you—are you seeing someone?" Loretta inquired.

"Me, Loretta? When would I have time?"

"That's your answer every time I ask about your love life. I don't know if you noticed, but there was a beautifully handsome woman who waited on your table yesterday during the reception. She seemed interested."

Seated in the front passenger seat of her SUV, listening to the conversation unfold, Artie raised her head and looked toward Loretta's house.

"Oh, stop it," Smythe replied

"I'm serious. I know you have great intuition, but you're horrible when it comes to noticing when someone's interested. She was definitely eyeing."

"Relent already, Lor. I'm far too busy."

"You're going to have to stop hiding sometime, Smythe."

"I'm going to have to work on my stealthiness," Artie mumbled under her breath as she smirked to herself.

On their final morning, Smythe said her heartfelt goodbyes to her friend and family before driving a block away to pick up Artie and Dennis. As she entered Artie's vehicle, Smythe asked for time to visit the beach before returning to the valley. Artie and Dennis toyed with her for a minute at first, denying her request.

"Nah, Daniels, we've got to get back before traffic gets heavy. Next time," Dennis replied as he eyed Artie.

"I understand. I just thought 10 minutes on the beach wouldn't put us behind in terms of traffic. But I get it."

"We got you covered, Smythe. Which beach?" Artie said as they drove away, watching Smythe's eyes light up.

Smythe chose a beach she had often returned to when in town. It was off the beaten tourist path, an almost deserted stretch of land which held no homes or apartments alongside the shoreline, save a short row of tourist shops a quarter mile from the shoreline with a small parking lot alongside the road.

Once the caravan arrived at the ocean, Smythe asked Artie to join her for a walk along the beach. The couple walked slowly through the sand, allowing the waves to wash over their feet. It was a feeling Smythe had longed for so many months ago. For Smythe, it seemed like a perfect morning. The fog had yet to lift, the crisp ocean air nibbled her cheeks, and she held a hope for a future.

Artie, however, was on high alert. For her, something felt off, yet she knew she should stop long enough to satisfy Smythe's need for this scenery. She peered around, noting her security detail's position on the beach.

"It's been a good couple of days. I'm glad I came," Smythe said as she stared out to the water. Her hands jammed into her navy-blue linen pants, the air felt colder than she remembered for that time of year, and she wished she had worn a windbreaker. She smiled to herself and wondered if her body had become too accustomed to the constant heat of the valley.

"I'm glad you came, too. It was good to see you laugh again."

"Even though you initially objected?"

"Yes. Even though I initially objected. Your friends are delightful."

"I only wish you could have been by my side the entire time. My friends would *love* you."

"Play your cards right, and maybe one day we can come back, and you can introduce me."

"Play my cards right?!" Smythe exclaimed. In a display of playfulness, she kicked up the ocean water onto Artie's legs.

"Oh, you want to start something!" Artie said with a laugh and kicked the ocean water back toward Smythe.

Smythe stopped and turned toward the Pacific Ocean. She remained quiet for some time. Taking in the foggy morning and the smell of the saltwater, she breathed deeply. "I want to live in a small bungalow home."

Artie surveyed her love and nodded as Smythe continued to look out onto the sea. For Smythe, this felt like home, and she was the most relaxed she had been in a long time. They continued to stroll along the sand, watching the endless waves rumble onto the shore. They listened to the echo of the seagulls' cry as the sun only began to glint through the gray sky above.

"Baby, we should get going before traffic gets too heavy."

"Yes, of course. Thank you for giving me the time to do this. I know you're concerned. I can feel your tension," Smythe offered. "Let's go."

They began to turn around when Artie became aware of a greater inner disturbance. Something wasn't right. Artie scanned the road and parking lot before peering out toward the ocean. There, she spotted him. A middle-aged man with his hands in his pocket, gray hoodie and matching pants, walking toward them in the ocean water, blending into the backdrop of the ocean. To anyone casually observing him, he looked just like any other tourist taking in the sights and sound of the ocean. Only he wasn't looking at the ocean; he was looking at Smythe.

"Walk faster, Smythe. Head directly to the SUV," Artie quietly said. Smythe heard the undertone of urgency in Artie's voice and did not question her. She stepped up her pace, ready to run at a moment's notice.

The stranger was too far behind her for facial recognition, but Artie was confident she had seen him before. He had probably blended into the events over the past couple of days. What were the odds that he would end up at this particular stretch of the beach at the same time Smythe was there?

Then, in an instant, she remembered the wedding. A man, same height and build, strode quietly into the wedding hall just as the service had begun. He whispered something to an usher—a family member of the groom. The usher nodded and directed the stranger to a seat at the back of the hall. Artie thought nothing of someone arriving late to a wedding. She had watched enough weddings to know someone was always late. But she also remembered the stranger piqued a heightened sense of interest within her as the evening wore on.

She watched as he interacted with wedding guests at the reception, staring in Smythe's direction from time to time. On a couple of occasions, he began to make his way to her table, but Artie's teams posing as waiters provided a distraction, causing the stranger to lose Smythe in a sea of people. Artie was unsure if he were interested in Smythe romantically or posed a threat. But now she knew the latter was true.

"All teams move in. Potential suspect to my 4 o'clock." Artie described the man and asked for a specific protection pattern. "Dennis, start the car!"

All teams quickly took their assigned positions. Seven members in all, four of them began to close in on the suspect. Another two members flanked Artie and Smythe from behind. Artie grabbed Smythe's hand and took off in a trot to her team's vehicle. She directed Smythe to get into the backseat and moved in next to her. Dennis sat in the driver's seat, speeding out of the parking lot and barely giving Artie enough time to close her door. The stranger did not follow. Instead, coming out from behind a gray SUV, a woman headed directly for Artie's vehicle.

"Boss?" Dennis queried.

"I think I remember him at the wedding. It's not a coincidence he is here right now. And that female! Her, I definitely remember. Dennis, we've been herded directly to her."

"Teams 2 and 3, hold that suspect. Team 4, we've got a female suspect now on our six," Dennis said into his com unit. Immediately, the teams ran for both the suspect on the beach and the female in the parking lot.

"Smythe, get on the floor! Now!" Artie yelled.

Smythe crouched onto the floor. Artie lay almost on top of her, her back resting on Smythe's and her weapon drawn, pointing toward the backseat window.

The teams were now in a full sprint for the suspect on the beach. In the parking lot, the female suspect drew her weapon but did not have a clear shot and chose to run down an alleyway of shops that flanked the parking lot next to the beach. As directed, Team 4 went in pursuit of her.

The female stranger eluded the trailing team, which only infuriated Artie.

"Damn it!" Artie yelled. "Find her. We can't have her trail us. Find her vehicle! And question the first suspect."

"Boss," Dennis started, "she's gone, and there is nothing we can hold the male on. Team 2 is remaining behind to question him—long enough to let us put in some distance. They'll give us another five minutes, but I've got to get them back on the road headed toward us."

Artie poked her head up and looked around.

"Keep down, baby," she said quietly.

"I'm sorry."

Dennis made his way onto the highway. The valley was roughly four hours away. Artie sat up, directing Smythe to remain crouched. As she craned her neck, looking in all directions, she spotted her nemesis.

"There she is. Gray SUV on our seven," Artie alerted. "She seems to be gaining, Dennis. All teams in pursuit. We're southbound and about to hit the grade. There's nowhere to run."

The grade was a steep incline to the highway, completely barren of trees or buildings. At that time of morning, very little traffic traversed the grade, leaving Smythe's security vehicle vulnerable. Artie continued to eye the suspect.

Smythe, trying to remain calm, sat with her head still covered and bent low in her seat. *We're sitting ducks,* she thought. *Keep it together. Just follow Artie's instructions. No need to panic.*

The suspect barreled down the highway but patiently held her distance. Artie watched as the SUV continued its slow approach. *Either the pursuer seems unaware that my teams are closing in on her vehicle, or she does not care,* Artie thought.

"Boss, she is no longer closing," Dennis said.

"Yeah, I see that, Dennis."

Dennis spotted an exit sign. Both he and Artie said in unison, "Take the next exit!"

Dennis immediately veered off, and the suspect watched in fury as Artie's vehicle suddenly took the exit from the highway, giving her little chance to follow. With no other choice, she continued up the grade. One team continued the chase up the grade while all remaining security teams pursued Dennis off the exit. Dennis followed the road and took a quiet street that held the cover of trees. He stopped and got out, quickly opening the door for Artie and Smythe. Artie got out first, followed by Smythe. She quickly walked Smythe to another of Artie's team vehicles.

"All teams, I need an inspection of your vehicles. Now!" Artie said. She was furious. She did not have time to dwell on her growing feelings of inadequacy, nor second guess her protection strategy. Dennis pulled Smythe's vehicle far enough away from the other team's vehicles that the cluster of SUVs hid her vehicle parked at the edge of a grove of trees. He got out and began to inspect the car, quickly finding what he was looking for—a tracking device cleverly mounted on the undercarriage of the car. He continued to search the vehicle until he found another tracking device mounted under the front bumper.

Another team found a tracking device located under their vehicle. Artie was in a cold sweat. Each car had been methodically swept each time they moved locations, including Smythe's, and each team member had been with their cars. Had someone infiltrated her team, or had a team member been turned? She looked over at Smythe. Had she allowed her personal feelings for Smythe to override her judgement? She swept the thought away, focusing on the next course of action. She signaled Dennis and he gave the all clear, driving Smythe's vehicle toward Artie.

Smythe sat in the team vehicle in dead silence. For months, no attempt on her life had been made. It was a risk, she surmised, for her to attend the wedding, but she had been insistent.

My insistence on coming could have cost Artie her life again. It could have cost Sue or members of her family their lives. This is no longer about me, or Artie. This about everyone. Dear God, what have I done?

Artie got into the front passenger side of the team vehicle, where she had secured Smythe. Dennis entered the car from the driver's side.

"Um, who's driving my car if it's not you, Dennis?" Smythe questioned. Although Dennis had not driven Smythe's car since her first encounter with him at her apartment several months ago, over time, she developed a deep sense of trust for Dennis and his driving ability. They were four hours away from home, and she not only wanted everyone to return home in one piece, but she also wanted her new baby SUV to arrive home undamaged.

"Another team member," Artie replied. "I don't trust anyone but Dennis to drive us back to the valley. If you recall, Dennis didn't drive your car to the wedding either."

"I know. But a couple of the guys I don't know. Do you trust whoever to drive my car back to the valley?" Smythe asked.

"Yeah, I do. Believe it or not, if you are not in your car, there is little chance that it would be damaged. They're after you, baby, not your car," Artie explained.

"But they know my license plate by now. Why not just blow it up from a distance?"

"Because the suspect we just lost knows you were not in your car. That's why she was tailing this vehicle. Your car is safe."

"So, then this vehicle is targeted," Smythe replied.

"In a way. But all of the cars look alike—dark with tinted windows, and they're each specially equipped. Remember, we only brought your car so that you would not draw attention to you or the teams by chauffeuring you from place to place. Our vehicle and two others will leave together. Your car and an additional team vehicle will leave ten minutes behind us and take a separate route to the valley. But our pit stops are going to have to change. If you need to go to the bathroom, you might want to do that now because we won't have much time in between stops."

"Yeah, I gotta go, especially after this," Smythe replied. Artie got out and walked behind Smythe. Smythe led them to the grove of trees and began to relieve herself. "Damn it, no TP!" she said to Artie. Artie was behind her doing the same. "You wouldn't do well camping or hiking, would you?" Artie asked.

"Nope. I prefer the comforts of running water and toilet paper," Smythe replied with a smirk on her face. They returned to the team vehicle. Dennis had been reviewing the route and suggested an alternate to Artie. They knew that all routes back to the valley had the potential to be monitored; however, given the time of morning, the major highway would be more densely populated. They chose a longer but more secluded highway to make their way back to valley.

Six hours later, and without incident, Smythe's caravan arrived back to her apartment. Shortly after that, Smythe smiled as her vehicle was pulled into its parking stall—undamaged. Artie and Dennis met in private and reviewed their protection strategy. In the end, without confiding in Dennis, Artie surmised there was a mole. Only she was unsure what agency held it—hers, the FBI, or both.

Chapter 34

Removing the Mask

—

O VER THE NEXT COUPLE WEEKS, ARTIE MORE HEAVILY RESTRICTED Smythe's movements. Only Dennis was allowed to do the grocery shopping for Smythe and pick up her medication refills, and what errands Smythe was allowed to run were done in haste. Smythe's usual dawdling marathon pace through the aisles in whatever merchandise store she entered now became a sprint. Artie even went so far as to personally pick up food from the baker, delivering Smythe's loving notes to him and returning notes from the baker to Smythe.

Overall, Smythe took it all in stride. If this was the price to pay to keep her promise to Artie and remain out of WitSec, so be it. She stayed in her lane and rarely veered off course. It also helped that Smythe's second conference was fast approaching, and her performance would determine if she would be certified in the tenets her mentor taught.

Each day, she coupled action with visualization. She reviewed the necessary material to prepare for her twenty-minute presentation. She wrote her script, memorized and practiced her group activities to drive home learning objectives, and then she visualized. She visualized delivering her presentation—what it would feel like and look like to have done so well. She visualized the clothes she would wear, the breakout room where she would deliver her presentation, and who the other participants were in her small group. She watched herself move confidently throughout the room as she delivered her presentation. Those actions she found contributed to her growth in confidence.

Yet, one morning, during her visualization, she felt the gentle touch of her Beloved.

"Do not *seek* to be," her Beloved whispered. "Simply be."

Smythe understood. She had just recently recognized that she was striving, and in her striving was becoming weary. *Why does this have to be so hard,* she remembered thinking. Here-now, in the midst of her visualization, her Beloved answered the query of her heart.

"It is unnecessary to demonstrate who you already are. Simply grow into the awareness and know."

Smythe took in a breath. She was stunned at the revelation. Immediately, she understood that her striving to be something only ensured she would not be the thing she wanted to be. She realized in that moment of clarity that striving comes from a place of lack, whereas knowing comes from a place of abundance. And, in that knowing is a greater awareness of what she must do to grow into who she already is. She could only smile to herself and nod, making a conscious effort to practice listening to her internal GPS from there on out.

While Smythe prepared for her conference, Artie continued to deliver her weekly reports to the FBI director, but, over time, out of an abundance of caution, she began to withhold information from him—including Smythe's daily movements or future plans for travel. She was deeply concerned that her security vehicles had been so easily tracked during the wedding excursion. She believed her security protocols were sound, and her teams were thoroughly vetted; therefore, she held a deep suspicion that a potential informant to the crime ring was coming from within the FBI. If her suspicion proved correct, she wanted no surprises during Smythe's upcoming conference.

From Artie's perspective, not only had Smythe been resolute in completing all of the requirements for her certification, but she had lived into the tenets that her mentor taught her. Smythe seemed different somehow; grounded in her movements. She slept longer into the morning, spoke with confidence, and made choices in favor of herself. Smythe, Artie believed, earned the right to revel in the company of her peers unencumbered.

Much like her plans for Smythe's attendance at the wedding, Artie meticulously planned for the multi-day conference. She obtained hotel and conference center schematics and blocked specific rooms for Smythe and her teams, inserting members of her team into the hotel employee roster. Artie would be present as well, lying in wait on the opposite side of the curtain that would separate the larger conference room from the smaller conference area.

Smythe would be equipped with a tracking device in order for her to have greater movement, but, similar to her conference earlier in the year, she would be required to remain in the hotel. Finally, instead of driving eight hours to the new hotel venue, Artie arranged for a private flight to their destination. Her previous connections and agency's reputation garnered her favor with a pilot who flew privately. Artie had provided security for a friend of the pilot a few years ago. After the security job, the pilot told her he knew how to mask the identity of a passenger into and out of airports, and would fly her to any destination she requested without asking questions. It was his way of thanking Artie for the protection of his friend. For Artie, it was an offer she rarely used, but her annoyance with the crime ring's hunt for her client made the offer a reasonable one to employ.

On the day of departure, Smythe, Artie, and four teams boarded their flight at dawn and headed north. As Smythe entered the aircraft, she was astonished by the interior space, which looked more like a luxurious living room. Elegant in its presentation, the seats were upholstered in pearl gray hand-stitched leather with finely woven navy-blue fabrics splashed within the space of the cabin. Composite wood veneers were used throughout, providing a less grainy look often seen in luxury cars.

"Who do you know?!" Smythe exclaimed.

Artie grinned as she followed Smythe into the cabin. "It's good to know the pilot."

As Smythe sat down, she immediately noticed how acoustically insulated the cabin was. The external noise of the airport was dulled to barely a whisper. Once was seated, she was treated to imported coffee from the Netherlands and pastries.

"All we need are some malasadas from Joao's," Smythe mused.

"No time. Had I thought about it, it would have been arranged." Smythe shook her head and stared out the cabin window.

After less than an hour and a half of travel time, Smythe and Artie arrived at the hotel without incident. Once she checked into her room, Smythe roamed the hotel "looking for trouble," as she would say.

On her first day, she met up with members of her cohort and sat at the bar whiling away her time reacquainting herself with various people. She laughed easily and hugged often. She hadn't realized just how much she missed the presence of these beautiful souls until their company lit a spark within her dimly lit heart.

Whisky had become Smythe's go-to drink as she mingled with her group. Artie, who sat inconspicuously at the bar, stared Smythe down as she requested a second double. With an earwig in her ear, Artie reminded Smythe she had to remain alert.

"Joy killer. I barely drink, and after tomorrow night, there is no drinking until the final night!"

"Just need you to be on toes. Besides, I see a couple of women who seem to have more of an interest in you than before. Should I be worried?"

"No need to worry. Are you jealous?"

"Nope, just cautious," Artie replied.

"No need to be cautious, love." Smythe glanced into the wide mirror which spanned the length of the wall behind the bar and smiled. The mirror reflected Artie's face, and she smiled back, raising a glass of ginger ale in Smythe's direction.

The pre-conference reunion celebration lasted well into the evening. Returning to their room, Artie swept it before allowing

Smythe to enter. It would be a daily ritual that would grind on Smythe's nerves at times, especially on days where she would have to make a quick trip up and back during conference breaks.

"Seriously, Artie? It's only been an hour since we were up here. Look, housekeeping hasn't even entered the room," Smythe said as she pointed to the unmade bed. Artie didn't offer a comeback, understanding the pressure Smythe felt to perform well during the conference. As far as Artie was concerned, Smythe's vocal annoyance at Artie's insistence to sweep the room was an acceptable way to blow off a little steam.

Smythe's investment in preparation served her incredibly well throughout the conference. While her mentor was pleased with her performance, the true payoff for Smythe was her internal sense of confidence while giving her presentation. She later reflected that she did not need to demonstrate anything to anyone. She simply needed to grow into the awareness of what she already knew. For the sake of her mentor—and her certification—she simply demonstrated her knowledge.

As the conference week began to wind down, Smythe had an opportunity to talk about her own life's journey.

"We've had a wonderful week together," her mentor began. "I've had the opportunity to watch many of your presentations. It was evident that you put in a lot of time and effort, not only to deliver the material here, but it was obvious that you are living into the tenants it—especially given your examples. As we wind down the conference, I would like to offer you an opportunity to come on stage and talk about whatever is on your mind? Who would like to start?"

Several of her classmate raised their hands, and, one by one, they went forward and shared. Eventually, Smythe hesitantly raised her hand. Her mentor made eye contact with her and called her to the stage. As Smythe stood up from her chair, she could feel her body begin to chill, and her palms began to sweat.

Why did I raise my hand? What will I say?

She slowed her breathing as she made her way toward the stage, walking up to a staff assistant who handed her a microphone.

Holding the microphone, she suddenly felt breathless. This would be the first time she shared such a heart-wrenching part of her story in public. She watched as each foot landed on the steps leading up to the stage.

Don't trip. Whatever you do, don't trip.

Once on stage, she looked toward her mentor, who sat on a stool next to her, and then out to her classmates. She paused for a moment, taking in a long breath before beginning. Through tears, she recounted her experience of sexual abuse and her recent attempted suicide, as well as the reasons that drove her there. Her classmates sat in rapt attention, remaining quiet and occasionally reaching for tissues to dry their eyes. At the back of the room, every single staff member stopped what they were doing and listened in stunned silence. She understood the energy of the silence. After all, during this conference, she had portrayed an air of confidence, and during her presentations, she demonstrated her ability to teach. She appeared to have it all together. But then again, you never know the story behind the veil.

As she finished up her story, she handed off her microphone and allowed her hands to fall to her side. Her classmates rose to their feet and began to chant in unison with the help of her mentor, "We believe you, we believe you, we believe you, we believe you!"

Their thunderous voices reverberated in Smythe's chest as each syllable shook the very air of the room. The walls of Jericho indeed came tumbling down, and something within Smythe broke loose at that precise moment. She could not describe the physical sensation, but something… something unhinged from her body and fell to the floor. Her tears continued to flow as she hugged her mentor and left the stage.

Behind the curtain stood Artie. And, with every clap of thunderous applause, tears rolled down Artie's cheeks.

You've come so far, baby. So far. God, I don't know if you are real or not. But if you are… thank you for her.

Artie wiped away her tears and quietly cleared her throat. After an hour, the session ended. It was time to prepare for graduation.

Smythe rose from her table and left for the restroom, but was intercepted by many of her peers who voiced similar stories.

"Me too, Smythe. Thank you for sharing."

"So powerful, Smythe. Me, too. Thank you for bravery."

"I love you, Smythe. Thank you for your courage."

Finally making it to the bathroom, Smythe took in a long breath as she sat in silence in the stall. It was a lot of emotion to take in, but she realized she could not dawdle for too long. A graduation celebration was next up, and she had to make her way to her room to change.

Artie met Smythe outside the bathroom, their eyes locking. Together they quickly but silently walked toward the elevator. Artie walked into their room. Slowly, she meticulously searched the room for any signs of intrusion. After a few minutes, Artie called Smythe in, and as Smythe stepped over the threshold, Artie reached for her and held her tightly in her arms.

"I know you have to get ready, baby. But I just want you to know how moved I was by your courage. As I hold you, I'm just in awe. It took a massive amount of courage to be that vulnerable. You are so much stronger than you could ever possibly know, and I love you. I love all of you."

Smythe leaned back from Artie's embrace, looking deeply into her eyes before kissing her tenderly. "I love you too, Artie. You are right. You've always said it—that I was stronger than I knew. Today, in some way, I finally understood that about myself. I wasn't sure if I wanted to share, but I felt this urging to raise my hand. To be honest, I fought it for at least forty-five minutes before I just gave in—I just wasn't sure I had anything to share."

"You had your story."

Smythe nodded. "Yeah. I did. I just wish I didn't—have my story, I mean."

"I know." Artie slowly released Smythe from her embrace. "You should get ready." She took a step back and searched Smythe's eyes. The frightened woman she had come to know was not staring back at her. Instead, someone new had emerged. Someone she was looking forward to knowing.

After a quick shower and change of clothes, Smythe returned to the conference room and participated in the rest of the evening's festivities. The next morning, Smythe, Artie, and her teams returned to the airport. It was bustling with activity and seemed a bit more congested than usual.

Yet, Smythe experienced a spiritual event sitting in the middle of the airport. She realized her demeanor was different since sharing her story. As she sat in the airport lounge, watching the myriad of people rushing to and from gates, she felt relaxed and at peace. She no longer held fear in her body, nor did she surround herself with an invisible shield.

She watched the throng of people move past her and began to think about them all with great concern and compassion. She recognized, or perhaps understood for the first time that everyone had a story to tell. She now experientially understood that the mask of a well-put-together life was only that—a mask. It was suddenly clear that those masks only hid fear, vulnerability, and the ache for genuine connection.

As she sat reflecting on her week, she recognized that telling her story on stage in front of people, many of whom she only slightly knew, shifted her perspective. Connecting the dots, she surmised that the telling of one's story is the opportunity to become free from the chains of the limiting beliefs that would keep her hidden from the world. It seemed to her that as she continued to let go and speak up, her fear abated, and her sense of connection with others increased. The shackles of shame had been broken, and she felt not only connected to her cohort group, but to all of humanity—including her own biological family. She began to see through to a place of compassion for all of humanity. At once, the grime of her mirror was a little bit clearer, and she sat in peace for what felt like the first time in her life.

Chapter 35

Forgiveness

—

O VER THE NEXT FEW WEEKS, SMYTHE RETURNED TO HER WRITING. The trial loomed ahead, and she felt an urgency to complete as much of her writing as she could so she could devote whatever energy was required for her participation in court. What seemed to surprise Smythe the most since her return from the conference was a shift in her emotional relationship with her mother. She found she wanted to spend more time with her than usual. When she needed a break from the monotony of her everyday tasks, she would ask to visit her. She reflected on this new behavior and recognized she no longer held the energy that had emotionally separated her from her mother.

But, for Artie, the increased visits to Smythe's mother alarmed her. She secretly feared her mother would erode the emerging self-confidence that Smythe now demonstrated, but Artie granted her requests without ever voicing the concern.

One morning, while lying in bed with Artie, Smythe decided to broach the subject of her visitations, sensing the negative vibes from the other side of the mattress.

"Honey, can we talk?"

"Yeah, of course. What's up?"

"First, I need you to know that I fear what I am about to say may change our relationship, yet I love you enough to want to discuss this."

"Ok."

"You've watched and been very accommodating in allowing me to visit my mom more than usual over the past couple of weeks. To be honest, those visits were, in many ways, an unconscious decision that I made. It felt as if somehow, something deep down inside of me needed to see her. I wasn't thinking about it; I just did it. What was weird was I always walked away from our visits feeling better. At first, I surmised that I was just doing my daughterly duty. But yesterday, I had an epiphany of sorts. So much shifted for me once I told my story to you, and then when I shared with my cohort training group, another layer unraveled. I don't know a whole lot about what has been happening, but what I do know is that I no longer hold fear in my body anymore. No more angst. It's rather shocking, really."

"How so?" Artie asked.

"Well, for one, I didn't know I held that much negative energy inside of me until it went away. Once I told my story out loud in front of all those people… something just… shifted. It happened almost immediately. I felt a release of pent-up emotion, and something similar to dark energy simply dissipated."

Smythe took in a breath and let it out slowly, feeling the freedom that came from the deep work she had been doing, including the acceptance of her abuse.

"There has to be a certain level of trust with this group. Actually, *a lot* of trust has to be fostered within the group to be that kind of vulnerable. That said, I experienced what it was like to tell my story and be truly heard. Now I understand how stories connect us to one another. The ability to be vulnerable to others has a healing effect not only for the person telling the story, but for those who hear them.

"I remember when I first told you. I felt better, but it was only you that I told. I felt like we shared this secret that was great. And you held it so beautifully. I didn't feel alone anymore. I felt as if you had given me this gift of not only acceptance but a different perspective. It didn't ever occur to me that I wasn't mentally ill. Artie, that was such a gift of revelation.

"Then, I had the chance to sit in that conference room. We all had an opportunity to share whatever was on our heart, and to share deeply. There was such a jagged calm that washed over me. Eventually, I settled into a deepening sea of peace. Afterward, as you witnessed, so many people came up and shared their stories with me. It was both heartbreaking and life-affirming. I didn't feel alone anymore, and I don't think they did either. And honestly, I think it drew us closer to one another, Artie.

"I say all of that because, in releasing that negative energy, I found myself living from a place of compassion for others, which includes both my mother and my father. I could suddenly imagine their own lives, childhood trauma, limiting beliefs, and the challenges they faced, especially living in a racist society. Out of that compassion, I could finally forgive. I mean, I thought I already had, but this was a deeper level of forgiveness.

"I can only surmise I have unconsciously been drawn to want to spend more time with my mom. There have been times I've needed to feel a sense of protection from her. I guess what I really needed was the *emotional* protection of a parent. Being in her presence gave me that. I realized that as a kid, emotional protection was what I had always wanted and needed but didn't get. It has been comforting that I can now allow myself to feel that from her. She has been so worried about how well my new business is progressing. I can now accept her words of concern as love without all of the chattering negative thoughts that were buzzing about in my head. I just thought you should hear why I've spent just a tad more time with her. It was mostly unconscious until yesterday."

"That's pretty powerful, baby. I must confess, I was annoyed when you asked to spend an unscheduled afternoon with her. In part, I was worried she would somehow snuff the life out of you. I now realize I hadn't given you enough credit to work out your own emotional wellbeing." She slowly sat up, still nursing an ache from her bruised ribs.

"I'm sorry for doubting you, and I'm grateful that you shared your epiphany with me. It makes perfect sense. I'll stand down from my own angst about your visits."

Smythe looked into Artie's eyes.

"I could tell there was an energy that you were holding about the visits. I could have told myself all kinds of stories about it. I could have just brushed it off, but then along with the epiphany came the realization that I was brushing aside your feelings, and that wasn't fair. Even if I didn't know why I felt a 'want' to go and visit instead of an obligation, you deserve for me to at least acknowledge that I felt your energy. After all, why wouldn't you have feelings around visitations with her? In some ways, you have a stake in the outcome."

"Thank you for the conversation, baby. My only stake in the visitations is your wellbeing, and that, my love, is really in your hands. I'm... let's just say I'm an interested bystander."

Chapter 36

You Have What You Need

—

*I*T'S *TIME.*

Those two words replayed over and over in the minds of both Smythe and Artie.

Smythe lay awake from a fitful sleep. A chill filled the early morning air in the apartment, and in her bedroom, a low-level tension was palpable. It was the first time since inviting Artie into her bed that she rolled in and out of wakefulness. With her back to Artie, she knew she would not be able to remain in bed much longer before growing increasingly restless and waking her up.

Lying beside Smythe, Artie remained perfectly still but awake, her senses heightened. Her neck was tight, a slight headache beginning to surface and her body stiff. *What have I overlooked?* she wondered to herself.

She thought about her FBI training. Her training had been a year-long mental and physical challenge. But, in the end, combined with her attorney background, she developed into one of the best FBI agents, bar none. She was doggedly methodical, with a knack for consolidating large quantities of information to identify threats and vulnerabilities.

Not knowing what the day would bring, she mentally reviewed her security plans over and over again, considering every possible threat to Smythe and her team. She questioned what she had yet to consider in her security plans, but more importantly, she wondered if she would be able to successfully shift them once she discovered the gap.

Unable to return to sleep, Smythe gently rose from her bed.

Without saying a word, Artie watched as Smythe changed into sweatpants and a long-sleeved T-shirt. Artie smiled, watching her tiptoe into the kitchen, turning on the light before moving to the pantry door. Smythe reached up for the coffee maker and placed it on the countertop and proceeded to take down all of the coffee cups she had in the house, including all of her to-go thermoses.

Consideration for my teams, Artie thought.

Artie rolled over toward the bedside steamer trunk to find her phone and check for messages. Finding nothing of interest, she climbed out of bed and wandered into the dining room to check the thermostat. It wasn't quite cold enough to turn on the heat, but the temperature in the apartment did require warmer clothes than the boxers and T-shirt she was wearing. She returned to the bedroom to find her own sweatshirt and pants. After dressing, she headed to the kitchen to assist Smythe with the coffee.

"Good morning, baby," Artie said softly.

"Hey, love. You sleep ok?"

"I slept fair. Well enough to feel rested. You, however, did not."

Moving about the kitchen, Smythe stopped and faced Artie.

"It's going to be a big couple of days. I'm a bit apprehensive," Smythe confessed.

Artie poured grounds into the coffee machine and turned it on before placing her hand on the countertop.

"Just tell the court what you witnessed. Keep calm and remain grounded in your truth. A couple of days of testimony can be really draining."

Smythe gently nibbled the inside of her cheek and furrowed her brow.

"It's not so much about what I witnessed, or the amount of time on the witness stand that concerns me, it's the chance of a character assassination in the process."

"This may or may not help, but the defense wouldn't be doing their job if they didn't try to besmirch your character. They have to create doubt, even if what they do feels like character assassination."

"But there's security footage, Artie! Security footage." Smythe thought about that cold February morning. She remembered looking at the victim under the street lamp. She remembered his pleas. She also remembered the growl of the murderer as he spit at the victim before—

"I know, baby, but if I were the defense, I would place doubt on that footage. I haven't seen it, but I might surmise that it could have been anyone on the tape, especially given the hour of the morning and the amount of light beaming across the suspect's face. It comes down to you corroborating what the footage will show. From there, I would work to discredit you. You heard his voice, Smythe. You identified him not only by sight but by his voice pattern. The defense has to try."

Smythe glanced at Artie. Her eyes pained as she recalled her life mistakes—silly hurtful things she said about people, not so stellar job performances as she grew into her positions. Even though anyone could chalk up her life as one of growth—something that happens for everyone—from a myopic view, she wandered into feelings of regret.

"I feel like there are things I should tell you that perhaps, might come out—"

"Baby, let me stop you right there. The FBI and the DA's office already have a file on you. I've seen the FBI's version. I've read every word. I had to. I had to know who I was dealing with—who it was I was protecting. Remember, I don't take every assignment that comes across my path. I then conducted preliminary surveillance on you and your family, which created an overall profile of who you are and what you care about. Before I ever met you face to face, I gave that profile to Carole. It pretty much sums up what I know about you now. I don't need to know any more than I already do, and I certainly don't need the defense attorney for the accused to tell me who you are. I already know."

Smythe sighed. She busied herself by putting out heavy cream, non-dairy creamer, raw sugar, and honey for the team, storing washed dishes from the night before into her cupboards and re-washing her countertops.

"Coffee is almost ready. Why don't you start calling the teams in."

"I will in a minute. I don't think we're done here, Smythe. This is really about who you are, isn't it? Who *you* say you are."

"Yes."

"Tell me, have you murdered, raped, or otherwise pillaged in your past?"

"Of course not."

"Then what is there to tell?"

"The girl who makes up stories," Smythe said, bowing her head.

Artie lifted her head slightly, her chin protruding out and lips pursed. She narrowed her eyes and took in a breath, allowing the silence between them to speak.

"Baby," Artie began. "I know the remnants of your mother and father's lies still rattle around inside that head of yours. Yet, at some point, you will have to dismiss those ghosts as lies, which always work to derail you. I know the person who is standing in front of me. I know the person I want my own son to come to know. That person is emotionally messy. She is complicated. She is compassionate, kind-hearted, and loving, and how you became all of those things required a past. We all have them. See your past for what it is, Smythe. It helped make you who you are today."

"I'm such a private person, Artie. I don't want people mucking around in my life. I resent that complete strangers who don't know me feel as though they have the right to judge my life. I doubt they would approve of someone looking into their past; I doubt they are without blemish!"

Artie dropped her chin toward her chest and looked up toward Smythe, her gray-brown eyes softening. "A lot of famous people have said the exact same thing. Yet, somehow, they've come to believe that kind of scrutiny comes with the territory."

Smythe attempted to counter, but was quickly cut off again.

"Wait—I know you didn't ask for this territory, but it's what you've walked into." She took a few steps toward Smythe, reached for her hand and placed it over her own heart.

"The only thing you can be accused of, my dear Smythe, is stealing my heart."

"Oh, dear God in heaven! That is probably the corniest line I have ever heard come out of your mouth," Smythe snorted.

"Hey, a girl's gotta try!"

"I appreciate the truth of it, Artie. I'll hold you accountable at the end of all of this… if there is an end."

"You got this," Artie said, squeezing Smythe's hand.

"Oh, *now* I got this. All year long, you were the only one allowed to 'got this.' Now I got this?" Smythe laughed.

"Well, yeah, but only this once. Now we can call in the teams. I need to brief them, and I want you in the room to hear it all."

"In a minute. I need some bathroom time."

"Ok?" Artie said hesitantly.

"I think right now I need to think a better thought rather than the ones rolling around in my head. I'll be out shortly."

Smythe turned and walked toward her bathroom and closed the door. She felt nauseous, and panic threatened to upend her. She also did not really want to hear about the security plans. They frightened her, but she knew she was the reason for them and therefore had to muster the courage to face her fear.

I just need a moment. Just a moment to breathe.

She stood before her bathroom mirror. Staring into the brown eyes of her own reflection, Smythe whispered lovingkindness to herself.

"I love you, Smythe. I really do. Yesterday was a great day, and, believe it or not, today will be, too. You have always done the best job you could do with the limited knowledge, skills, and awareness that you have in the given moment. I need you to be the light in this darkness, and remember: I've got your back. I love you."

Smythe continued to offer a loving smile to herself in the mirror. She repeated a couple of her affirmations, which began to cement her confidence. Gazing at herself in the mirror, a quiet thought drifted gently into her thoughts.

You have sufficiency for the day.

In slight shock, she stood perfectly still. In that beautiful, revealing thought, she heard her response to her Beloved's statement.

But I've always just wanted to be self-sufficient.

She paused to replay what she had just thought.

There it is.

She caught her subconscious, and the storage of all things offered her a key.

That's it. Your belief that YOU provide your sufficiency.

She smiled knowingly and spoke aloud.

"Smythe, the reality is your Beloved provides it. That which lives in you, moves through you, that which you have your be-ing, provides it. You are simply the beautiful vessel to move into inspired action. *That* is your sufficiency."

Chapter 37

It's All Come Down to This

—

W HILE SMYTHE STOOD IN THE BATHROOM, ARTIE BEGAN TO CALL in her teams one at a time, reminding each of them what was at stake.

"The FBI never found the weapon that killed the vic. They did, however, conduct ballistics testing on the bullets from the body and determined that the same weapon had been used in several unsolved murders over the past five years. Their link to this specific murder was a credible eyewitness account—Smythe's account. The store security footage corroborates her story. In securing this conviction, the DA feels confident that they will have cut off the head to the crime ring. Our job is to make sure she is able to testify fully and completely and to bring her *safely* home."

Artie reviewed transportation plans to the courthouse. Based on the team's assignment, she described in detail the specific security pattern she wanted enforced. Barring any overt threat, of utmost concern to her was getting Smythe into the courthouse and to the secured waiting room before the trial commenced.

Smythe appeared from the bathroom and walked into the kitchen in time to hear the last of the teams briefed.

"We don't know who they've turned; therefore, we will have to assume everyone—and I do mean *everyone*—is suspect. Pay attention to reporters, security officers, court personnel, police officers, even

FBI agents. Leave nothing to chance. The FBI has arranged for an escort into the courthouse through a secured entrance. Both Dennis and I have walked the route. If your gut tells you there's a problem, assume there is one and report in. All com links will be wide open, and Smythe will have a tracking device placed on her. We will use a two four two pattern once inside the courthouse. Understood?"

"What armor will she have on?" a security member asked.

"Leave that to me," Artie replied.

That was a vague answer, Smythe thought as she looked out toward Artie.

"Any other questions? Ok then, grab your coffee and get set up. Let's bring her home."

Once the security detail left the apartment, Smythe faced Artie.

"Leave that to me? What was that?"

"I'm leaving nothing to chance Smythe, not even my own teams. I trust them, but this is a big case. I've received word that reporters are already beginning to set up at the courthouse, specifically for your arrival. Families of former victims are scheduled to be there as well. I need to bring you back in one piece, and if that means leaving some of the details only to me, so be it."

Artie's voice held an edge to it. The last time Smythe heard that sharpness was on their way back from the wedding a few months ago.

"You think you're missing something, don't you?"

"I know I am. And because I don't know what it is yet, I need to keep some of the security details to my vest only."

"Not even to Dennis?"

Artie did not reply.

"Just tell me you are going to be wearing armor as well."

"Yes, I will be."

Smythe's jaw tightened. She could only begin to see the enormity of the security plan and the impact it was having on her love.

"How can I help?"

"Follow only my commands, and if I say something out of character, trust your gut. You know me. You've watched how I operate. Trust your gut and get yourself to safety."

"Ok, I can do that, but to be honest, I'm a little frightened right now."

"I know, but frightened is good. It will give you an edge if your life depends on it. Besides, you strike me as a woman of action when you're afraid." She glanced at Smythe, sensing the hesitancy.

"Baby, don't worry. I'll be by your side. Let me tell you what will happen, ok?"

"Ok, yeah, I think that will help."

"Once we're to the courthouse, even though you will be wearing your hat, I'll be holding your head down as we move through the doors. You will be held in a secured room until called to testify. I'll outfit you with additional body armor undetectable under your clothes, so I would suggest you wear something loose-fitting. Once you're called, you will be brought into the courtroom by sheriff's deputies. They'll take you directly to the witness stand. Once on the stand, simply answer their questions. During breaks, you will then exit the witness stand and be met by sheriff's deputies to return to the conference room. At the end of the day, I will follow them out with you. They'll walk you to the secured hallway, and once in the hallway, my team and I will resume control over your security."

"Umm. Ok. That's a lot to digest. I think we should eat. It might be a long day."

"You should eat. I do better on an empty stomach. Let's get some protein in you to soak up your coffee."

Together they made a light breakfast of granola and buckwheat toast with almond butter. While Smythe ate, Artie excused herself to take a shower and dress. When she re-appeared, she was dressed in a formidable black suit and gray pinstripe shirt. Smythe nodded at Artie's appearance, admiring how the gray pinstripe accentuated the gray in Artie's eyes. She smiled, thinking about how Artie protected and loved her. She watched in admiration as Artie holstered her weapon and placed the holster to the small of her back. It was now time for Smythe to ready herself.

"My turn. Ten minutes."

Smythe entered the bathroom and closed the door. Artie quietly stood at the door of the bathroom. Once she was satisfied Smythe would not exit anytime soon, she quickly walked into the dining room closet and removed a large duffle bag she had hidden in the furthest corner. She placed the duffle bag on the floor in front of her and unzipped it. She double-checked her list: passport, cash, and enough clothing for at least two weeks.

It'll have to do.

She moved over to Smythe's small office alcove. She took a piece of paper from one of Smythe's notebooks and quickly jotted a note and shoved it into her pants pocket.

Sorry babe it has to be this way.

She zipped the duffle bag, grabbed Smythe's car key, carried the duffle bag out of the apartment, and placed it into the back-storage compartment of Smythe's SUV. She looked around, noting that her SUVs were just beginning to make their way into the complex.

No one should suspect it here.

Dennis walked over to her and held a brief but stern and clipped conversation with her.

"Be careful; you've got too much at stake for this to fail," Dennis said before walking away.

Artie took in a breath, staring a hole into the head of her second in command. She murmured under her breath, nodding before returning to the apartment. She entered to find Smythe dressed and about to pour herself another cup of coffee.

"Unwise, babe. You might find yourself needing to go to the bathroom more often than you'd like."

Smythe nodded and put the coffee pot back on the burner. Artie surveyed Smythe's attire—a navy blue loose-fitting blazer and matching slacks offset by a bright white button-down shirt. She nodded her approval, solemnly approaching Smythe.

"Do you have the vest on?"

"Yeah, I do."

Artie nodded. She outfitted her with three separate tracking devices. One in her messenger bag, one inside her bra, and a third under her pants on the outside of her thigh.

Smythe smiled at Artie. "Um, I think this is a bit overkill, don't you think?"

"No, actually, it's not. If you are separated from your bag, I can still track you. If someone finds the one in your bra, which is where they would look, you still have the one on your thigh."

"And what makes you think they won't pull my pants off?"

"I have a feeling you would be fighting before you let that happen. I've seen you lift. Those pants aren't coming off easy."

"Yes, but—"

"Smythe! I got this. It's not my first rodeo."

"Hey—heyyy! Honey, I was just trying to keep it light."

She stopped Artie from fiddling with her clothing and wrapped her arms around her, kissing her lightly on the neck.

"It's going to be ok. Really. I got this," Smythe said with a mischievous look.

"No, you don't got this. I got this."

Smythe leaned back from her embrace and smiled. Artie searched Smythe's eyes and smiled back.

"I see what you did there. Clever, Smythe. Clever."

"You've had this from the beginning. Never forget that."

Artie smirked and nodded. *God, I love this woman.*

A knock came at their door and Dennis entered as Artie approached him.

"It's time."

Smythe took in a breath.

It seems like only yesterday. Yet, it was a lifetime ago when my world changed the minute I stepped across the threshold of my home out to have a cigarette. I don't even smoke any more.

She turned off the coffee pot and the lights to the kitchen and walked to Artie, who motioned her toward the front door. She took a step over the threshold and let out an audible gasp, stopping mid-step. Eyes widened, she moved her head slowly from side to side to take everything in. Before her, bathed in morning sunlight, sat eight large black SUVs in the parking lot.

Artie took her hand, gently tugging at it to move Smythe forward. Smythe stepped out on to her patio, closed the door to her apartment, and locked it. Her fingers lightly touched the lock. Her here-now was a seminal moment, and she stood wondering—wondering whether she was up for the task set before her. Could she be brave enough to handle whatever the day would bring? Would she live into her dreams, or would she die?

A stillness settled in and around her amidst the energy that everyone around exuded, and her answer rose from the depth of core—a place she had yet to fully explore or understand. She glimpsed a cup of water bobbing in a pail of water, and she knew her answer.

Yes.

She turned toward Artie and followed her to the waiting SUV. Artie escorted Smythe into the backseat of one of the vehicles before joining her on the other side. To Smythe's surprise, Dennis was not riding with them, but instead would drive an SUV positioned in front of them.

The SUVs rolled out of the complex one after another. The scene reminded her of an important government official's funeral procession. Forgetting her recent vision, she silently hoped her internal description would not prove accurate. As her SUV exited the complex, she saw an additional four SUVs idling along the roadside. Artie created four separate caravans containing three SUVs each. Once out onto the main road, each caravan positioned themselves at different locations on the street.

This would have been an impressive sight to watch if it weren't so damn scary.

The courthouse sat at the far end of the historic district of the city—a densely populated portion of downtown. Government buildings flanked the courthouse with attorneys' offices and restaurants dotting the opposite side of the street. Given the time of morning, Artie timed the drive in all directions and determined it would take 20 minutes with all but one caravan converging at the courthouse simultaneously.

Just as Artie had instructed, at the first intersection, the SUVs started their security pattern. Peeling off either left, right or forward, it was impossible to distinguish which caravan held Smythe and Artie. Artie continued to orchestrate the pattern, keeping in constant communication with her teams. Based on time, at the designated halfway point for each caravan, all reported in that no unusual activity had developed.

Hurdle one down.

A lone caravan which had arrived well before all others exited their vehicles and created a human corridor along with sheriff's deputies into a back entrance to the courthouse waiting for Smythe's arrival.

"Five minutes out," Artie said into her com unit. "Lone Star, prepare for arrival."

"Lone Star is set."

One minute later, Smythe's caravan approached the rear of the courthouse. With another caravan meeting up with hers, Smythe peeked over at Artie, who concentrated on the laptop set up before her.

What kind of woman have I fallen in love with? No wonder she's been on edge.

Smythe's SUV pulled up first, next to the entrance. Artie exited the vehicle with Smythe scooting over and exiting behind her. Just as she had been briefed, Artie asked Smythe to bend her knees, torso, and head. Artie walked on one side of Smythe, gently holding her head down with Dennis on the other side. Artie's teams conducted a two four two pattern, taking point behind three deputies. As they flanked Artie, Smythe, and Dennis, additional teams took up positions beside the trio and at the rear of the procession.

The fourth caravan arrived at the front of the courthouse, acting as a diversion for reporters to swarm and allowing Smythe and court personnel to arrive unburdened by the media frenzy.

Artie and Smythe were ushered into a conference room just off of the courtroom. The room was brightly lit but smelled musty, causing Smythe to cough and turn up her nose as she entered in. The floor was covered in a dingy, low pile brown carpet with walls painted beige and lined with floor to ceiling dark brown bookshelves holding case law books. In the center of the room sat a large oak table surrounded by half a dozen brown office chairs. To Smythe's taste, there were far too many chairs around the table, giving the overall energy of the room a claustrophobic feeling. At the back of the room, a small door led to a one-person restroom. Once inside, the door was locked. Dennis took command of the teams and stationed two of them outside the conference room door along with a court deputy.

That leaves only the interior of the courtroom unsecured by my people, Artie thought.

Smythe began to slowly pace. Her nerves were starting to fray. She focused on each step she took and breathed in to the count of eight before breathing out to another count of eight. She looked toward Artie, who stood before the conference table.

"So, what now?"

Artie approached her carrying a backpack Dennis had given her, placing it at Smythe's feet. As she unzipped the bag, she asked Smythe to disrobe from the waist up, leaving on only her bra.

"Even my vest?" Smythe asked.

"Yes, because we are going to replace it with this," Artie said as she pulled out a different bulletproof vest from the backpack.

"Try this on."

"What's the difference?"

"It's better," Artie said dryly as she checked the fit.

Once satisfied, she instructed Smythe to re-dress.

"Now, we wait. Deputies will come for you and escort you into the courtroom in a bit. I can't follow you, but I will circle around and enter the courtroom from the front entrance. Once you have testified, I'll meet you back here."

"Wait, I thought I would be leaving the courtroom from the normal public entrance and leaving with you at the end of the day?"

"Mmm, no."

"Then it's through the back corridor?"

"Perhaps," Artie said, averting her eyes away from Smythe.

Smythe peered at Artie and her shoulders tightened. Her heart began to race.

Remember, Smythe, listen only to Artie. She told you to trust your gut; so, what does your gut tell you?

It tells me Artie hasn't told me everything, but... I trust her.

Then trust her.

She slowly tightened her hands into a fist. "Ok."

Time seemed to come to a standstill, and Smythe found herself using the restroom several times, more out of nerves than anything else. Besides, the last thing she wanted was to have to "go" just as she was called to the courtroom. In between her bathroom runs, she paced, played games on her phone, and forced herself to sit down again.

Artie, on the other hand, sat at the conference table unmoved. To Smythe, Artie seemed unusually quiet, but given the preparation to get her to this point, Smythe chose not to press her for conversation. Smythe eventually settled down and entered into a semi-meditative state, concentrating only on her breath.

Without warning, Artie stood up and walked over to Smythe. "It's time."

Smythe opened her eyes. The room seemed to become very still. She could hear the whirl of air as it passed through the vents. She could hear herself swallow, and a small bead of sweat trickled down the base of her neck. Artie extended her hand to Smythe, which she accepted. As Smythe rose to her feet, Artie pulled her into her arms and kissed her.

"Be the truth," were the only other words Artie spoke before the door opened.

Two deputies escorted Smythe out of the conference room. She walked behind them, matching her pace to theirs. She walked through the frame of a door. All eyes turned to her as she appeared into the courtroom and walked toward the witness stand. The packed room hushed to a whisper. Smythe could hear her own nervous breathing, her footsteps loud and heavy with each step onto the tile flooring.

Through the throng of reporters, families, and an assortment of law enforcement officials, Smythe searched for Artie's face. She found her as she took a seat at the back of the courtroom. A sense of warmth washed over her as she noticed Artie had taken a seat next to the baker. At once, all of the months of a very long year came flooding back to her. From the moment she witnessed the murder, to her first encounter with Artie; their ongoing battle of wills to allow Smythe more freedom than she should have had and her attempted suicide, to the baker and the stake he had in all of it—it all came tumbling into her consciousness.

It's all come down to this.

Smythe had been told by her hairdresser once that sometimes when in the greatest need of divine guidance, the only prayer necessary was one of "help me and thank you." She took note that there was no better time than this to seek out her Beloved's assistance. She quickly glanced up and silently uttered the words, "I need your help, please. Thank you."

In a matter of moments, she was sworn in and took her seat in the witness box.

Chapter 38

Trust My Words

—

SMYTHE'S TESTIMONY LASTED A DAY AND A HALF. ON HER FIRST DAY, she was on the witness stand until the end of the day. While nervous, she offered a timeline of events leading to the murder. She then described her actions directly after that. The prosecution drilled her time and again to offer in meticulous detail what she heard and saw.

After a long, arduous day, she felt grateful to be done with the first bit of the trial. Her temples throbbed and her jaw ached, and she quickly realized it was from clenching. The clenching was an unconscious reaction as she focused on answering each question, and her shoulders felt as though she had been slammed against a wall from the tension she carried. She was released for the evening with an admonishment to speak with no one about the case. Her exit out of the courtroom went without incident, and once in the SUV, she fell asleep. Later that evening, Artie had pizza and salad delivered and ensured Smythe was occupied with a couple of movies.

"The movies, especially comedies, will help release any pent-up anxiety. It'll help—I promise," Artie said as she turned the first one on. And indeed, the movies did help—Smythe laughed often. A little over halfway through the first movie, Smythe rested her head upon Artie's shoulder and fell asleep. Artie smiled and listened to the quiet purr of Smythe's breathing, allowing her to continue to sleep until the movie was over, putting her to bed after a peaceful rest on the couch.

Artie's preparation for the second day varied only in that each team was given a different driving and station assignments. Artie again outfitted Smythe with several tracking devices and the latest in bulletproof vest technology.

Bolstered by the prosecution's questions the previous day, Smythe seemed more confident in herself to continue her testimony. However, at the start of cross-examination by the defense team, it was apparent her second day would become more challenging.

Constant objections from both the prosecution and the defense made her testimony tedious, and she began to wonder if she might have nightmares that evening. Forced to recount the murder in minute detail for a second day, she offered the same answers she gave the day before. At one point, it seemed to Smythe that her memory was being called into question with reference to her father's diagnosis of a degenerative brain disease. That brief line of questioning was followed by recounting her recollection of her statements to police dispatch and first responders at the crime scene. Yet, instead of buckling as anxiety began to mount within her, she focused in on every word of questioning. Her memory intact, she did not waver.

When it was clear Smythe's testimony was solid and consistent, the defense mounted a half-hearted attack against her character. Smythe remembered her conversation with Artie.

Bring it.

He attempted to besmirch her recent employment decisions, her LGBT status, and her decision not to enter WitSec or any other federal protective custody program. The prosecution quelled each attempt, with several sustained objections ending the defense's meager nipping of her character. With a final redirect of questioning from the district attorney, Smythe's testimony ended. She received a final admonishment from the judge to discuss the case with no one and was excused. As she rose from the witness box, she heard the judge excuse the jury for the day and to prepare for final arguments in the morning.

I was the last witness? Maybe just for the prosecution? I don't understand.

Hurried along by two deputies, she looked around for Artie, but could not locate her in the crowd nor find her as she approached the conference room. She watched as the deputies opened the door, allowing her to move past them into the room.

"Here she is," the deputy said to the person in the room. Smythe walked in, smiling brightly at the thought of seeing Artie's face again. She certainly had a few questions for Artie, including what appeared to be the end of the trial. She abruptly stopped short as she crossed the threshold. Her pulse began to race, her breathing quickened, and her vision tunneled, for it was not Artie standing before her but two of Artie's security detail.

"Where's Artie?!" she snapped, her anger and shock evident by the frown upon her face. She looked toward the back of the room to the bathroom door, hoping perhaps Artie was in there. The door, however, was open.

A member of Artie's team Smythe had not met before stepped toward her. "Ms. Daniels, there's been a breach in security within the courthouse. Please come with us. Time is of the essence."

"No, something's wrong. I will not go with you—this is not part of the plan! Artie would want me to stay here. I'm not going!"

"Ms. Daniels, Artemis said you might refuse. She asked us to give you this note," said another team member.

He stepped forward, holding a small piece of notebook paper in his hand. She took the note and read it.

**"Sweetheart, I ask that you follow my team out.
They will protect you and get you back to the apartment
safely. I'll meet you there. Walk closely behind them,
and they will lead you away. Trust my words."
—Artemis.**

Smythe re-read the note several times. She did not move, save her eyes as she canvassed the room. There was no way out except through the door they now stood in front of.

Walk closely behind them... trust my words.

Her faced relaxed, and she nodded. The team turned toward the door, double-checked the area to ensure it was safe to proceed and cautiously but quickly escorted her out of the conference room, leading the way through a back corridor toward a stairwell.

Sweetheart... Walk closely behind them. She's never talked about walking closely behind a team, they always—

Smythe furrowed her brow and gradually began to slow her pace as they approached the stairwell. She darted her eyes from side to side. There was no one around. No hidden door to run through, only the long corridor walls. Her hands began to tremble, and she grit her teeth. To quell her mounting fear, she clenched her hands into fists.

Trust. My. Words... Oh God, no—I'm going to have to either turn and run or stand and fight my way out of here—

Without warning, she heard the sound of quick-moving footsteps from behind her and the sound of Artie's voice.

"Smythe, drop!" Artie screamed.

In one terrifying movement, Smythe fell to the floor and covered her head. The security detail turned and drew their weapons. With her weapon drawn, Artie took a defensive stance without cover and shot several times at her own security detail. Smythe squeezed her body tightly into a ball, her ears ringing at the sound of the exchange of rapid gunfire.

And then silence.

Just as quickly as the gunfire began, it ceased. Smythe lifted her head slightly, peering in front of her, terrified that she would see only the barrel of a gun. Instead, what she could see through blurred vision were both men, a mere few feet to the side of her, unmoving, face down on the tile floor.

She looked behind her toward the previous sound of Artie's voice. Artie was splayed on the floor, barely moving, along with another man. Additional members of Artie's teams and sheriff's deputies were running in her direction. As though propelled forward by some unknown speed she did not know she possessed, Smythe jumped up and ran toward Artie.

"No, no, no, please God, no."

She slowed her pace and slid to the floor next to Artie, who lay face down.

"Artie, honey, it's ok. Baby, please—"

"Smythe, let us through," a team member directed as he approached.

"No! Stay away from her!" In an instant, Smythe grabbed Artie's weapon, which lay at her side.

"Back away, I mean it! None of you can be trusted. None of you!"

The team members halted their advancement. Smythe held the gun in between both hands, her index finger on the trigger.

"Back away, I said!"

"Smythe, we didn't do this. Let us tend to them," another team member said.

Holding back tears, Smythe refused.

"Two of you did this! Two of you! You're *not* going near her!" Smythe screamed.

It was in this here-now moment Smythe paused to wonder at it all. Here she sat on the floor, the weapon in the palm of her hand cold to the touch. It was a weapon that had just splayed two armed security agents assigned to protect her on the floor. To Smythe, it was symbolic. It was a weapon that so many in the United States owned. Touted as a recreational outlet, the right to bear arms had done so much damage. The daily gun violence ravaged her nation— the almost monthly mass shootings, with no real action to stem the violence. The inaction of elected national officials charged to serve and protect the citizens of the land—here she sat, with a weapon, focused on protecting only her part of the world.

"Baby," Artie muttered.

Smythe did not respond. Her eyes darted from one team member to another, glaring at the them, gripping the weapon so tightly her hands began to shake. Two deputies pulled their weapons from their holster and aimed them toward Smythe.

"Don't shoot her. I repeat, *don't* shoot her. She's friendly. Lower your weapons!" yelled one of the team members. He walked cautiously before the deputies, placing his body between their weapons and Smythe.

Smythe swept Artie's weapon from side to side in an effort to keep everyone at bay. She neither heard the others around her or Artie's voice.

Artie, still face down, opened her eyes and looked at Smythe and tried again.

"Baby, give me the weapon. I'm ok. Give me the weapon."

Artie slowly rolled over onto her back. Smythe noticed Artie's movement and momentarily glanced down at her. Smythe growled, willing the cold terror she felt to release its grip upon her.

"Can you sit up, honey? We've got to get out of here. I have to get you to safety."

Safety? How safe was she really with a weapon?

"You need medical assistance."

"No, baby. We're already safe." Artie craned her neck and looked behind her to her teams, who had slowly gathered around. "They're the good guys. Trust me. Lower the weapon," Artie said, in between gasps.

Artie forced her eyes to remain fixed onto Smythe. She nodded toward her slowly, mouthing "please."

"It's ok, baby," Artie said. "It's ok."

With no fight within her frame, Smythe lowered the muzzle of Artie's weapon and then burst into tears, tenderly laying her head on Artie's chest.

Artie's team moved in.

Smythe bolted upright. She screamed so loud all activity ceased momentarily.

"NOOOOOO!! NO!" Smythe cried out. In the here-now moment, the choice was hers to make. Lash out in fear, and perhaps hatred, or choose love. Fury coursed through her veins. Artie reached her hand to Smythe's chest and pulled her down to her own. Smythe began to sob, her hand releasing her grip upon the weapon before lightly touching Artie's cheek.

Step by step, a team member slowly approached Smythe. He bent low and held out his hand.

"Smythe," the agent started.

Her body tightly cocooned around Artie, Smythe looked out to his outstretched hand. She could feel the ache in her back as she raised her torso. The agent's fingers reached toward the weapon and gently placed his hand over it.

"Let me have it, Smythe. You don't have to hold onto it any longer."

Smythe watched as the agent removed the weapon from her hand, slowly standing up and offering Smythe his other hand. She grasped it as if she were grabbing onto a lifeline, allowing him to help her to her feet. He placed one arm around her shoulders, bearing her weight in his quiet strength and walked her to the wall across from Artie.

"I'm going to stay with you, Smythe. You're safe now. Let us help Artie."

Smythe sat back against the wall. Refusing to have another tear fall from her eyes, she watched intently as the agents began assessing Artie.

"Damn, God, this hurts... it hurts," Artie groaned.

"You caught them in the vest," a team member said as he examined Artie's torso.

"Yeah, I know, but now I think my ribs are broken this time. The rounds didn't feel like issued caliber," she gasped.

"We're taking a look at their weapons. They don't look issued."

With help from one of her team members, Artie slowly sat up. She looked over to find two of her detail working on Dennis.

"He caught some bullets, boss—we're trying to get the bleeding under control," one of the team members said. Artie pulled herself next to Dennis. He bled profusely from his upper body, a pool of red seeping out around him.

"We've called for paramedics. They're on their way," a sheriff's deputy offered.

In the ensuing minutes, paramedics and additional sheriff's deputies and police officers arrived at the hallway. Paramedics worked quickly to stabilize Dennis, while deputies and police began questioning Artie's teams. With the help of another team member, Artie moved next to Smythe against the corridor wall and watched the activity unfold.

To Smythe, the scene felt surreal. The cacophony of voices ricocheted off the corridor walls. She stared down at her hands, noticing they didn't quiver. She then scanned her body. She expected to feel fear, but her energy was not fear. It was rage, and she consciously chose to hold that rage, not allowing it to dissipate from her body.

Paramedics transported Dennis to the hospital with a team of agents following behind them. However, it would be over two hours before Smythe and Artie would be released from the courthouse. Both were questioned endlessly about their roles in the events leading up to the weapons fire in a courthouse. Once the necessary reports were taken, Artie and Smythe were escorted to the hospital by Artie's security team.

Along the route, Smythe argued with Artie, finally convincing her to tend to her injuries with a promise she and the teams would check in on Dennis. With Artie placed on a gurney and wheeled into the emergency room, Smythe and two teams made their way to the surgery ward to await word of Dennis's condition.

Artie lay propped up, alone on a gurney in an ER room. She was in excruciating pain and found it difficult to take in a full breath. Her attending nurse hoped the bed position would offer her some relief until tests were taken to determine the extent of her injuries. A member of her security detail remained posted outside her room, allowing Artie to relax enough to drift in and out of consciousness.

"Artemis Leone?" a radiology technician asked as she entered Artie's room. Artie stared blankly at her but nodded. "Hi. I've come to take you for tests." Unfortunately, Artie misunderstood the tech and attempted to rise from the gurney, causing her gasp in pain.

"No, Ms. Leone," the tech said as she placed a hand on Artie's shoulder. "Stay put. I'll wheel you on the gurney." Artie nodded and collapsed back onto the gurney.

"Good," Artie panted. "Don't tell anyone, but I'm feeling a bit banged up."

After several hours, Artie's tests were completed, and a diagnosis made. Her injuries were not life-threatening, and she would be released.

"Your doctor will be in to discuss the findings and prepare your discharge paperwork," her ER nurse said.

"Knock knock," came the sound of a man's voice on the other side of the curtain.

"Enter," Artie replied.

Standing before her was the recent FBI special agent assigned to Smythe's case. She eyed him with suspicion as he approached her gurney.

"We need to talk," he said. With an air of command in his voice, the agent voiced his concern additional threats still existed for anyone connected to the case and cautioned her to tighten security, not only for Smythe but for herself as well. Artie regarded the agent with contempt, but she also understood his posturing. She was no longer an FBI agent and considered an outsider.

She also knew that since the case was now over, he was under no obligation to continue to watch over Smythe, especially since she had refused WitSec. In his own way, she figured he was offering a professional courtesy by voicing his concern. She briefed him on the plan she had set into motion to flush out the team members she suspected had been compromised. She then outlined her security plan for Smythe for the coming weeks.

"Why didn't you notify me of your concerns about your team earlier? This could have been avoided," the agent accused.

"Because I didn't *trust* you. It became evident that someone connected to this case placed a hit out on Carole. I still believe it's someone from your department, but I also knew someone from my team had been tracking Smythe's movements," Artie shot back.

The agent glared at her. "And you thought it was me. Whether you like it or not, we're going to have to work together to keep your client—"

"It's handled. From your end, this portion of the case is over, and you know it. And let's be clear, I contacted your director about my suspicions. Your director also has the outline of my ongoing protection of the client. If you need me, call my office. They'll know how to reach me. Or better yet, contact your director." Artie glared at the FBI agent as he flared his nostrils. Her security detail quietly stepped into the room. The FBI agent understood the gesture.

"I'll be in touch," he said before leaving her room.

"Thanks for the backup, guys," Artie said as they retreated to the entrance to her room.

Smythe wearily arrived at Artie's bedside a few minutes later, after spending the last few hours holding vigil in the surgery ward waiting for word of Dennis's condition. She was followed in by Artie's ER doctor shortly afterward. Smythe immediately recognized the doctor as the same one who tended to her father before he died.

"I remember you—you spoke to my mother and me when my father suffered a massive stroke."

"Oh. I'm sorry," the doctor said, concern etched across her face. "I see so many patients and families. How long ago was that?"

"Don't be sorry. I completely get it. It was earlier this year— around February. You said he would not recover. He died about three days later."

"I'm sorry for your loss."

Smythe nodded.

The doctor turned her attention to Artie, confirming she had hairline fractures on two ribs.

"You'll need to reduce physical activity, ice the rib cage, and use pain medication as necessary."

"How long before the ribs heal completely?" Artie asked.

"Given that you have had recent trauma to the ribs already this year, it will take you roughly 6-8 weeks before you can begin work again. My recommendation is that you sit behind a desk."

"Given my line of work, Dr. Goben, sitting behind a desk is not usually an option. My work requires hands-on involvement. There are times, like today, that my presence requires a more physical presence. But I'll do my best," Artie said, nodding her head in all seriousness.

Smythe scrunched her face at Artie.

"You just lied to the doctor by agreeing with her. I'll do my best—what is that?" Smythe said as she turned to face the doctor. "Don't trust a word she says, doc. But I'll see to it. Thank you."

The doctor smiled and nodded. Once the doctor left, Artie gingerly stood up from the ER gurney and smiled at Smythe.

"Baby! I knew you were a badass. I just didn't know to what extent. You followed my directions and then you held off my team with my weapon. I think I have a slot for you on my team, if you're interested."

"When it comes to you, I'm not playin'. What now?"

"We go see Dennis."

"Just so you know, I have questions."

"I have answers, but not here."

Chapter 39

Trust Your Gut

—

AFTER ARTIE WAS DISCHARGED FROM THE EMERGENCY ROOM, SHE and Smythe made their way to the intensive care unit to look in on Dennis. The main corridor leading to ICU had as much personality as a freeway. It was much like a long thoroughfare, winding its way through the hospital's first floor with several smaller exit hallways shooting off from the main walkway.

Artie peered at the gray walls and then at Smythe. *How did Smythe know how to navigate the corridor?* she wondered. Everything seemed so gray. The walls were gray, the tile was gray—even the ceiling was bathed in pale hues of gray, all of it leading family and friends onward through identical doorways edged in darker hues of gray. Making their way through yet another hallway, Artie stopped to rest, pain etched across her face.

Smythe whispered into Artie's ear. "Would you stop acting like such a badass already? Why don't I find a wheelchair. We can push you."

Artie smiled and attempted to stretch out her torso, but she came up short. "It's ok," she grunted. "Honestly, I'm alright. I won't be so sore tomorrow if I just keep moving."

Smythe nodded but watched Artie closely. It was obvious to her Artie was struggling. All anyone had to do was watch her gait. She had shortened her stride, and her walk had been slow enough that a toddler could out-pace her. She also took in halted breaths, which restricted her forward movement.

After her brief pause, Artie pushed on until they arrived a few minutes later to the entrance into ICU. Leaning on Smythe, Artie stood in the doorway to Dennis's room, observing the nurse as she checked his vital signs.

"I've been told that none of his injuries are life-threatening, and his doctor expects he will make a full recovery," Smythe began. "He took three bullets to his body; one to his shoulder, another nicked his side, and the third lodged into his thigh. His wife was here, but she had calls to make to family. She may or may not be back before we leave."

Artie nodded before walking in. She stood next to his bed and slowly scanned his body as his muscular chest rose and fell to the rhythm of his breath.

Dennis had been the first person she hired into her agency. A former Navy officer, community service was a family career. His father, brothers, and wife were all in various forms of law enforcement. After his discharge from the Navy, Dennis took up the family trade, working for the local sheriff's department. However, after a few years, he felt he could better serve the public by protecting the innocent from those who openly threatened others instead of waiting for crime to occur. He had heard enough about gang and syndicate members and their propensity to intimidate a witness into silence.

As far as Dennis was concerned, he could "prevent the bad guy from ever doing harm" by taking on the job as protector, allowing victims and witnesses to come forward and "do the right thing, which included testifying." A rumor within local law enforcement circles suggested Artie had started her own personal security agency and, more importantly, was hiring. Dennis knew her work as a special agent for the FBI and all but jumped at the chance to work with this giant of a human. She hired him, taught him the ropes, and he eventually became her number two in charge—the designation modified from one of her favorite science fiction television series. That was six years ago.

Artie raised an eyebrow and stared down at Dennis. She thought about her rogue agents. From the moment they met, Artie held an unfavorable hunch about them. After she completed a thorough background investigation, even going so far as to dig into the deep, dark web and finding nothing to confirm her hunch, she allowed Dennis to hire them. Yet, she rarely allowed them to enter into high-profile cases, keeping them at a distance—still digging for information to confirm her suspicion, still untrusting. Dennis, however, had every confidence in them both. He had grown up with one and heard "nothing but good things" about the second.

"It was my fault, Dennis," she whispered." I let you talk me into these two, and look at what it cost us."

Artie sighed as she continued to stare at Dennis. She could give herself any number of excuses why she allowed herself to become swayed by Dennis's argument to hire them in the first place. After they were hired and given the resources Smythe's case was using up, she could have told herself she needed additional protection teams and that, despite her reservations, the pair checked out. She also could have told herself that she trusted Dennis implicitly, which she did, and it was just poor judgement on his part. But, in the end, she told herself none of those things. And the poor judgement, she believed, squared on her shoulders alone.

Her body felt heavy, and it ached. She looked up at Dennis's vital monitors and then again at him before leaning toward him to speak softly into his ear.

"This is the last time, Dennis. This is the last time I allow you to influence me about things I know. Rarely have I not followed my intuition, and I'm at a loss as to why I didn't listen to it. You may not understand it, believe in it or even agree—"

She abruptly ended her one-sided conversation with him and brushed her fingers through his hair. Artie realized the conversation was pointless—he could not respond. This conversation needed to wait until he had fully recovered. She turned her head toward the door and looked out to the nurses' station. Two additional teams had arrived to check in on him. Before leaving the floor, she gave instructions to the teams that watched over him.

"I need to know what you know the moment you know. Everything is suspect."

As Smythe studied Artie, she could see she wore the garment of exhaustion. Her face was drawn, and her color had yet to return. She stole away from Artie momentarily and asked a nurse to provide a wheelchair. Artie eyed Smythe as she rolled the wheelchair before her.

"Get in," Smythe said dryly.

"I'm ok, baby. I don't need that."

Smythe eyes pierced Artie's. "No, you're not ok, and honestly, you don't want to mess with me right now. I'm not in the mood. Get in the wheelchair now, or I'll have the doctor re-admit you. As far as I'm concerned, you can have a room right next to Dennis. It'll make visiting you both that much easier."

Artie stared blankly at Smythe before grinning widely. "Ok, ok. God, you've become such a badass. Where's my kind, tender-hearted, and *compassionate* Smythe?"

"She took a nap. Badass moth—"

"Smythe!"

"I'm in no mood, Artie. Get in. Now!"

Artie looked down at the wheelchair before easing herself into the seat. Escorted by two members of her security detail, Smythe wheeled Artie through the emergency room exit and into an awaiting SUV. Artie shivered, causing her to groan in pain—her body contracting to an unexpected cold front that moved into the valley. They sat in wearied silence until they reached Smythe's apartment.

Once they were safely secured in the apartment, Smythe helped Artie out of her clothes.

"Why don't I sponge bathe you."

"No, baby. I need to feel the warmth of the water on my body. I'm alright, really. A little sleep, and I'll be right as rain on a summer's eve."

"You've become a poet?" Smythe asked as she smirked.

"Hmmph. Hardly."

Smythe gathered Artie's clothes and took them to the laundry room, examining each item one by one. As she held Artie's shirt in her hands, she scanned the blood splattered across the shirt's chest and sleeve, tracing her index finger over the outline of the bloodstains. She was unsure whose blood it was, and her thoughts drifted to Artie's condition. The impact of the weapon's fire against Artie's vest caused her torso to turn black and blue, and she had a small cut under the left breast. Yet, given the amount of blood on the shirt, Smythe surmised it was Dennis' blood.

God, all of this feels like a nightmare. Who would have ever thought I would have played any part in it. When will it all...

Smythe wiped away a tear, took in a breath, and let it out slowly. She started the washer, placing the blood-stained clothing into it and closed the lid. She double checked the locks on her front door and eyed the metal rod butted up against the door, trying to fend off the anxiety. She moved to her bedroom and turned down the bed before returning to the bathroom. Artie stood there, standing in the shower and peering at the floor, the water turned off only moments ago.

"Need some help?"

"Yeah, I do. Feeling a bit unsteady."

Smythe gave a smirk in Artie's direction. "Should have let me sponge bathe you like I asked."

She walked to the edge of the tub, grabbed a towel, and gently patted Artie dry. She then offered her a shoulder to lean on as Artie slowly placed each foot onto the bamboo floor mat.

"Glad this mat is high. Makes getting out of the tub that much easier."

"Didn't plan it that way when I ordered it, but it does come in handy."

Smythe assisted Artie as she dressed into a loose-fitting T-shirt and sweatpants before walking her into the bedroom.

"I'll need only a couple hours of sleep, then we have things to take care of. We'll go after that," Artie said as she climbed into bed.

"Go where?"

"It's a surprise, baby."

"Well, you're not going anywhere until you tell me what happened. I'm really angry, Artie. Those weren't our guys, yet they got into the conference room. And then they tried to kill you and Dennis! All because of me." Smythe could feel the energy of rage coursing through her body. Her hearing was dulled by the ringing in her ears—the result of the gunfire. The remnant sound of the reverberating gunshots remained as an echo in her body.

"Not because of you. Because of your testimony."

Artie took in a jagged breath, wincing in pain as she leaned back against the headboard.

"They were our guys, baby—*my* guys. Both of them."

Smythe stared at Artie in disbelief.

"They were fairly new to my agency; both came highly recommended and had stellar credentials. They had just come off of another security assignment—small in comparison to your assignment, but given the enormity of your days in court, I brought them on board as additional security. The thing is, when I met with them to fill them in on the assignment, I don't know, something felt off."

"That sixth sense energy thing you've got going."

"Yes, exactly. I can't explain it, but it has never failed me as long as I've paid attention to it. Honestly, I should have never hired them. First time I didn't listen to my intuition."

Artie sighed.

"All I knew when I met with them was that they felt dirty. I don't know how I knew, but I just knew they were somehow tracking your movements. So, I decided I had to flush them out. The only one I let in on the plan was Dennis. Needless to say, he was wary. Angry, even." Artie shifted in the bed.

"So, Dennis was in on it. Why was he wary?"

"Well, number one, he believed in them. With my approval, he was the one who hired them. He knew one of them really well. And because both were not involved in your protection *until* yesterday,

Dennis felt confident that they had not leaked your whereabouts when we went to the wedding.

"So, you knew something was wrong with them during the wedding?"

"On our return trip home, I had a hunch. We were followed at will; meaning that the woman following us up the grade knew exactly where we were. And I remembered her from an earlier attempt on your life. When I had my vehicles inspected off the grade that day, they had been tracked. I knew then that someone had either infiltrated my agency or someone in the FBI had leaked information to the syndicate… or perhaps both."

Smythe continued to listen in shock. It occurred to her as she thought about all of the players involved in her case that Artie had been playing a game of chess. Artie's opponent was not just the syndicate. That opponent was bad enough. But members of her own team and the FBI were also suspect. She had to strategically get to the truth while keeping Smythe alive. Smythe slowly shook her head. The scope of betrayal by people Artie worked with seemed incomprehensible to her. Out of compassion, she unconsciously placed her hand over her heart and continued to listen.

"Dennis was also wary because there were a few minutes where you were going to be extremely exposed. I put your life at risk," Artie said, bowing her head for a moment.

"That's why I had you put on the different vest. It could take several direct hits. It's state of the art and expensive as hell. Even my teams knew nothing about it. But it was worth the investment."

Smythe nodded. "You thought they might simply shoot me dead center if they had the chance."

"God. There was just so much at stake. To be completely honest, for the first time ever, I even had my doubts about Dennis. He seemed to be too enthusiastic about these guys coming on board. Why not, I guess. He did recommend them to my agency. So—"

"So, you held back—even from him."

"Yes. I was becoming paranoid. I didn't know who I could trust. Carole was dead, and a new agent was in charge of your case. So, yeah, I held back." Artie winced as she adjusted her back against the headboard.

"Why don't I get some water so you can take a pain pill."

"Not yet. You deserve to hear it all," Artie said, waving off any attempt by Smythe.

"The plan was to create a security breach that the team would believe. I would voice concern about leaving you in the conference room alone, albeit under lock and key. My hunch was that the two newbies would step up and offer to take you back to the SUV and head home. Dennis, to my surprise and relief, played along. I must admit, I had a secondary plan if he had not played along. But I didn't have to worry.

"I made the request to the teams over the com unit. I wanted a team to come to my position just outside of the courtroom and grab a note. Sure enough, they stepped up. I convinced them that you would not go with them and to hand you the note."

"Yeah, I thought that was the oddest thing. I mean, you called me sweetheart! You've never called me that. And then that whole thing about walking close to them threw me for a loop."

"Trust your gut."

In an instant, Smythe understood. She remembered their conversation at the apartment and immediately realized why Artie asked her to trust her gut, and why she used the term sweetheart instead of baby.

"Even at the apartment, you had already put your plan in motion. But I still don't understand why you asked me to walk close to them."

"I knew they wouldn't fire on you inside of the conference room or the courthouse. They wouldn't have made it out alive. Instead, I surmised they would wait to get you into one of my SUVs. So, that meant they would have to walk you through secured portions of the courthouse. I was banking on you being reticent and not doing what I wrote. I knew fear would cause you to filter out everything you knew about me and the way I operate, and whatever remained would be a lie. From where I stood as I caught up to the three of you, I was right."

"Well, yeah. Everything about that note felt off. I even tried to find a side door to run through."

Smythe looked directly into Artie's eyes. "Ya know, I hate to think you know me so well."

"I do. Remember, I was trained as a profiler."

"Yeah, there's that. And a sharpshooter. That skill came in handy."

"Yeah, it did. And... while I was waiting for you to return with news about Dennis, the special investigator in charge of this case paid me a visit. They did some quick digging into my two guys. It appears they were turned by the ring. Both had been former law enforcement. They got caught with their hands in a honey pot a few years back by the syndicate. So, they did some side jobs for them in exchange for the syndicate's silence." Artie let out a low audible breath. "Damn it, I knew bett—"

"Stop it, Artie. You're not perfect."

Artie looked up at Smythe, locking eyes.

"Remember when you asked me about the firm I worked for?"

"Yeah. I knew something had happened."

"A witness was killed after the guy beat an extortion conviction. The extortion trial was fairly high-profile. I was not the attorney on record, but I knew about the case. I also suspected the defendant had associations with another group that laundered money in Europe. After the witness was killed, I left the firm. Working for them was now morally indefensible for me. I say all that because while the FBI couldn't pin the murder on any one person in the ring, the FBI agent I spoke to at the hospital told me my two guys *might* have been involved in that previous case."

"You mean that they could have been the ones who killed the extortion witness?"

"Yeah. God, I didn't know that when I hired them, nor did I know when I brought them on board yesterday and today, but Smythe, my instinct told me something was wrong. I didn't follow it, and I'm sorry."

"Honey. How could you have known? Did you have a magic eight ball that showed you the past events of your teams? No. Did you just decide to roll the dice to see how things would turn out? No. That's not you. Darlin', you are obsessive about planning. As far as I'm concerned, I'm ok with the result. Not ok with Dennis and you getting hurt, but we're alive."

"Smythe, I have always paid attention to my instincts because they have never led me astray. And paying attention to those instincts requires only one thing—one thing. The courage to act on what I know. Even if it doesn't make sense to anyone else, I find that when I move fearlessly, the more my intuition proves to be spot on."

Artie huffed and sat in silence. She was unsure what held her back from trusting herself—from trusting her intuition. Like a whisper in the silence of a room, she learned to discern the whisper of her intuition. She never asked questions of it. If her intuition whispered for her to move in a particular direction, she simply moved in that direction. She learned to take reason out of her decision to act because it was not reason that whispered to her. Reason, she learned, would talk her out of following her intuition. No, it was not reason that whispered to her—it was her soul. An intangible part of herself that she did not understand but trusted.

"I've asked the FBI to conduct a secondary investigation into all of my guys. I just need to be sure."

"Ok, then leave it with them. Will this hurt your chances of getting additional assignments from them?"

"I wasn't supposed to get this one. It was off book by Carole. But no, it will not hurt my chances. The Director seemed satisfied with my role in this case. I have a call with him tomorrow morning."

Artie glanced at the clock on the steamer trunk.

"Look, It's after 8 p.m. We missed our flight. I need to call and rebook for the morning."

Smythe's heart sank, and a pained frown creased her brow.

"Where are you going?"

"Not me, we. You've been through a lot, baby. You've been cooped up in your apartment with me for months. Over the past several weeks, we've barely even gone out for malasadas. I thought we could go to Leonard's and pick up a dozen," Artie said, nodding— her voice conveying a sense of seriousness. She searched Smythe's eyes, waiting for her to digest the information. Smythe sat on the edge of the bed, her eyes darting from side to side, her frown beginning to lessen.

"I don't understand. Leonard's is on Oahu."

"It is."

"It's a long way for just a dozen malasadas, don't you think?"

Artie remained quiet. Finally, after a few moments, Smythe's brow completely relaxed, and a smile lit across her eyes.

"We're going to Oahu?!"

Artie's voice softened. "Yeah, baby, we're going to Oahu. I need to rest, and you need a vacation."

"But what about Dennis? What about the team? Don't I need to be here if they want more testimony?"

"We'll check in on Dennis before we leave. He'll be in good hands with the remainder of my team. Before all of this went down, he was aware we were leaving. He doesn't know where, but only that we will not be in the valley. Second, closing arguments begin tomorrow, and then it goes to the jury. With that said, the trial is over as far as you're concerned. Third, I've already cleared travel with the FBI and the DA's office. While they're unaware of our destination, they know how to reach me."

"You still don't trust Dennis, do you?"

Artie raised an eyebrow and let out a slow breath. "He's my number two. I trust him implicitly. Yet, there's still an uneasiness. I don't know where it's coming from, so I'm keeping things pretty close to my vest until I sort it out."

Smythe nodded. "And the FBI and DA's office? Are they on your no trust list?"

Artie remained quiet.

"Ok. So, we won't know how the trial ends?"

"We'll know. I asked my team to reach out to me. There is a secondary FBI investigation connected to this case. The expected conviction of the suspect will play a factor in opening up a much larger investigation. At least, that is the hope."

"Can you say more about that?"

"No. Not if I want to keep you safe. The less you know, the better." Artie thought about one of her last conversations with Carole. Carole was beginning to connect the dots between open-air GM crops on the island of Kauai and the chemical companies that planted and sprayed those crops with harmful chemicals. Of particular interest to Artie was her own research after her initial conversation with Carole.

The west side of the island, where the open-air crops were located, impacted mostly native Hawaiians and working-class people of color. A lot of the lands the companies operated on were state land—lands stolen from the kingdom of Hawaii. That land was to be held in trust for the betterment of native Hawaiians. And it was those lands that were still contested. Artie would not yet tell Smythe that, in addition to vacationing on the island of Oahu, Artie would take a day trip to Kauai and hopefully meet with local activists and learn more about the information the missing documents contained.

"But, won't they try to hurt us, even if we're on the plane?"

"So many questions, baby. Trust me, I got this."

"You got this. Yes, yes you do. I gotta pack!" Smythe said, suddenly realizing she was not ready. She sprang off the edge of the bed and opened her closet door. Rustling through her dresser, Smythe began to open each drawer.

"You just need shorts, a couple of pairs of long pants, a shirt or two, a swimsuit, T-shirts, and sandals, and they're already packed. Even your running gear. Everything is packed and in the back of your SUV."

Smythe turned toward Artie. "You thought of everything."

"Not everything."

"Toiletries. You haven't packed them because I used them this morning. And my running shoes. They're here in the closet," Smythe said as she looked down at the shoes.

"That's true. But toiletries and running shoes aside, you still haven't said yes."

Chapter 40

All Things Are in Motion

—

THE COUPLE SLEPT UNTIL WELL INTO THE EARLY MORNING. AFTER A
brief visit with the baker, a call to the Director at the FBI, and
a conversation with a now-conscious Dennis and his wife, Artie
returned to the apartment to gather Smythe and their luggage before
heading to the airport.

Smythe was still a bit skittish and easily startled, but once
seated on the plane, she finally began to relax. Of course, the first-
class seat didn't hurt either. She stared out the window with a glass
of whisky in one hand and Artie's hand in her other. She scanned
her body. She realized a new emotion had emerged. Something she
had not felt before.

But it was not happiness she felt. After everything she went
through all those hours, days, and months ago, the people harmed to
either protect her or seek justice—happiness in light of it all was not
the emotion her body evoked. It was not contentment, either. That
would suggest she was at peace and fulfilled, and she knew she was
not either of those states of being—in time perhaps, but not just yet.

Smythe remained quiet for a time, listening for the elusive word
which matched the feeling in her body. And then it revealed itself.
Grounded. She felt grounded in all that had occurred in her life. It
seemed to her that *everything* that happened had unfolded the way

it was supposed to. Equally as important, she felt fully present in her here-now moment knowing that her Beloved was in the midst of everything, and within her Beloved lay perfection.

She sat watching the clouds drift below the blue sky and realized she had been waiting for all of this to make sense. A feather floated above her and landed on her chest. She picked it up and held it gently in her hand.

I have yet to piece it all together, my Beloved, but I am similar to this feather. Moving along a path from beginning to end, emptying parts of myself which no longer serve me. At times I was resistant. Ok, a lot of the time, I was resistant, but now I understand. I am willing to go where you lead me.

Artie took the feather from the palm of Smythe's hand, quickly examining its intricacies.

"The stewardess just walked past us with a pillow. Probably came from there."

"Hmm. You know, I've never flown first-class. What's interesting is that while there's real glass, real silverware and china, and feathered pillows, the view out the window is the same view from anywhere on the plane. You could have saved yourself some money and flown business or coach, you know."

"It's the service one receives here. And, it's safer," Artie remarked. "A private entrance into this section allows me to see who's coming and going."

"Is there a possibility that someone is on board with us?"

"Unlikely, baby. You've already testified."

"Well, all of the movies I've watched make these kinds of people seem vengeful. Why wouldn't they want to kill me? It sends a clear message that they're still in control."

"True, yet not true. For now, from what I am told, the group is in chaos. They're probably starting an internal power struggle, and they'll be too busy infighting to keep you on their radar."

Smythe returned to gazing out her seat window.

"To ask you not to worry is pointless, but I am going to suggest it anyway. Don't look over your shoulder. Don't think about the 'what ifs.' I have daily reports coming in, and it's my job to think about your safety."

"But you need to relax, too. I'm concerned for you as well. They must know who you are, right?"

"They do."

Artie's response was a bit of a gut punch to Smythe. While she appreciated the truth of it, what she really wanted was assurance that Artie would be safe.

Artie searched Smythe's face and then whispered. "Remember, I was an FBI agent, and I worked with a firm that had members of the syndicate as clients. And then, there were my two guys. I assume they've always known."

"But you weren't a threat back then. Now that you're protecting me, aren't you more of a threat?"

"Stop. You'll make yourself sick."

"It's hard not to."

"Choose."

Smythe sighed. She knew Artie was right. She remembered her teachings. All thought is energy. All thoughts create things. All things are in motion.

"While we're away, let's make plans," Artie suggested.

"For what?"

"To leave the valley. You can work from anywhere, and so can I. Let's make our dreams come true. Wadda ya say? You up for a new adventure?"

"Sounds like music to my heart, love."

Epilogue

It Was You All Along

—

SHE LISTENED TO THE MELODIC WAVES WASHING ASHORE, LAPPING onto the grainy beach while she reverently breathed in the scent of her beloved Monterey cypress pine trees mingled with the salty ocean air. The mixture of the trees and the ocean coursed through her body, sending a chill down the length of her spine. With her laptop set up before her, she found herself wandering into an understanding that there are many spiritual paths to awakening, and now understood she needed to be wooed by love and courage.

The air was crisp at that early hour, the sun only hinting of a new dawn. Smythe gently pulled the shawl wrapped around her shoulders closer to her body. She thought of love and her Beloved. God, Universe, the Divine, Source, All, Energy. So many different words to describe the indescribable—the mystery.

She once heard there is a difference in the belief of God from the one who experiences God. She sensed she was in the midst of a growing experience with her Beloved, and the All of Everything continued to beckon her closer, deeper. Her Beloved was everything to her—had always been everything to her, but for so long, she did not know how to access or expand all that the Source of Everything had become to her.

Artie watched Smythe from the kitchen window and grinned. She hesitated to interrupt her contemplation, but it was coffee time. She walked to the kitchen door and opened it, calling out through the screen door.

"Hey, baby, do you want coffee?"

"Yes, please. Could we have it out here?"

"Of course. Let me bring out a couple of sweatshirts. The Pacific air is cold this morning."

Artie padded away and gathered two sweatshirts from the couple's bedroom closet. She returned, handing Smythe her coffee and the sweatshirts and a wool beanie for Smythe's head. Smythe watched as Artie appeared in the kitchen to pour herself a cup before joining her on the deck.

"What a lovely, foggy day," Artie said as she sat down.

Smythe regarded Artie for a moment and smiled before taking a sip of her coffee. "I do love your coffee."

Artie smiled. "You seemed deep in thought before I came out. Care to share your thoughts?"

Smythe took another sip of her coffee and breathed in the scent of pine as she watched the waves lap onto the shoreline. "It seems I was at this threshold. I was standing in this in-between place. I could feel my hand reaching out for a life I so desperately wanted, yet it rarely occurred to me that I was in the midst of living that life—living within this threshold—and actively creating the life I wanted as I went along. I had to wait. The aspects of it needed to be brought together, only I didn't understand it then.

It's that space, the threshold, where I was in so much needless angst. That space between the here and the not yet is where the life we are always creating lives... even now. We're creating life in this moment, Artie. Creating for a future we have yet to see."

Smythe took in a long breath. She explained to Artie that it was here, in this wooded ocean community she so long-ago visualized residing. It was here she envisioned where she would spend her life with a yet-unknown partner. Only she simply saw it as a dream, a mere fantasy. There was nothing that would indicate it would ever be a tangible reality. And, because there were no outside tangibles to suggest her dream would become a reality, she simply folded the desire into her heart, hoping against hope to make it a reality.

"Darkness seemed to envelop me every day. I remember thinking those months were one long, dark night of the soul. But then I remembered meditating on the fabric of darkness, and as I look back, I recognize there was always an illumination—much like the story I told you about when I died. Even though it was dark, there was an illumination. My Beloved was there then. Was there during those awful months; was always there, and so were you. While I don't ever, and I mean ever, want to experience that darkness again, I wouldn't trade it for anything. My soul expanded, and the love for others expanded as well.

"I remember hanging out with our ohana one morning on Oahu, and one of them asked me a question. Do you remember?" Smythe asked.

"I remember. 'How did you distinguish between your own voice and the voice of the sacred?' I found your response interesting."

"Yeah. God's voice has always been one of hope and possibility. One of wonder and joy, even when things got hard. It was a voice of deep, abiding peace. But the other voice, the voice that shook me to my core, was one of condemnation, accusation, guilt, and shame. And that voice roared loud with all of its accompanying emotions."

Smythe paused. She could feel a tingle down her spine.

"I just grasped the difference in the two voices in a deeper way."

"How so?" Artie asked.

"Well, in almost all faiths, it is said that the Beloved's voice is quiet. I remember the voice I was fighting against to stay alive. It was so loud that I couldn't hear my Beloved. I couldn't seem to get quiet enough. It was only when sleep finally came that I was aware of a low-pitched melody playing in my head. An old gospel song that I play when I'm running. It was a song of hope, a song where I didn't need to struggle; it was a song that said my Beloved would help me through. I just needed to hang on and do the next thing I knew I was supposed to do. Even if it seemed outrageous to others, it wasn't for my life. It's what Joao had been talking about. My Beloved was singing the melody of my life, and only I could offer the response song."

"I think I'm still singing the response song," she said, smiling at Artie.

"Yeah, you are." Artie paused with a mischievous look pulling at the corners of her mouth. "So, ummm... about that unknown person in this dream..."

"Oh, for Pete's sake! I married you, didn't I?"

"Just checking, baby. Just checking," Artie replied, smiling widely. She gazed out onto the shoreline, breathing in deep. "Want to go kayaking later today?"

"What time do we pick up Davey?"

"His flight comes in at 7:00 this evening."

"Then, yes, let's kayak. But I also need time to finish a model plane I've made for him."

"He's gonna go crazy over it."

"I hope so."

"Artie?"

"Hmm?"

"I love you."

"I know. I love you too, Smythe."

Smythe looked out onto the shore and reflected on Artie and the qualities she was attracted to. Here sat this woman, full of courage, grit, intelligence, infinite compassion, kindness, and action, making a living as a protector of others. In an instant flash of clarity, she recognized that all of those qualities were actually qualities within herself. Artie was simply a human mirror of Smythe—a mirror of us all, really. Not of what she hoped to be, but of who she currently was.

For a time, she did not recognize those same qualities, for they were wrapped differently and spoke differently than Artie. The only difference between them was that Smythe had not tapped into her potential. She thought about the past year. She had attracted not only what she wanted, but what she *needed*. She marveled at the intricate weave of thought, hope, prayer, meditation, and energy which provided the circumstances for her to recognize all that she was *be-ing*.

Smythe had come home to herself and sat next to a partner; a wife who continued to mirror back to her the questions of her deepest longing. She wondered at the infinite God of the Universe— her Beloved, and she knew her Beloved conspired on her behalf.

* * *

Along the seashore, along the western shores of Kauai, Joao sat with Akamu.

"It is done?" asked Akamu.

"The debt is paid, yes," replied Joao. Joao looked up to the sky. It was a clear day, and he could see far out to sea. He imagined that across the ocean, sat Smythe, gazing out to the sea. He thought about the islands. About Akamu. He knew the islands faced an uncertain future.

"Does she yet understand, Joao?"

"I am unsure. But the one she loves senses it and will protect her. Of this I am sure. I understand she has met with some here on the island."

Akamu remained silent, breathing in deeply as he watched the waves gently rolling onto the sandy residue of a thousand lifetimes.

...what if there is no problem?

About Opa Hysea Wise

—

OPA HYSEA WISE IS AN AMERICAN author, born to mixed race parents. She grew up across the fabric of the United States and currently resides out West.

At 57, with nothing more than a knowing, Opa felt she was called away from her normal, relatively safe corporate life. She resigned her position, pulled her life savings out of the market and step by step followed the wisdom of her Beloved. Her footsteps led her first to Jack Canfield, considered America's number one success coach. Certified as a Success Principles trainer and speaker, Opa now offers half-day and full-day workshops focused on shifting people from where they are to where they want to be, in any area of their life.

CPSIA information can be obtained
at www.ICGtesting.com
Printed in the USA
JSHW010605090920
7721JS00003B/6

9 781641 464772